James Laughlin, New Directions, and the Remaking of Ezra Pound

GREGORY BARNHISEL

UNIVERSITY OF
MASSACHUSETTS PRESS
Amherst and Boston

LC 2004026482
ISBN 1-55849-478-2

Designed by Dean Bornstein
Set in New Caledonia

Printed and bound by The Maple-Vail Book Manufacturing Group

Library of Congress Cataloging-in-Publication Data
Barnhisel, Greg, 1969–
  James Laughlin, New Directions, and the remaking of Ezra Pound /
Gregory Barnhisel.
    p. cm. — (Studies in print culture and the history of the book)
  Includes bibliographical references and index.
  ISBN 1-55849-478-2 (alk. paper)
  1. Pound, Ezra, 1885–1974—Relations with publishers.   2. Literature
publishing—United States—History—20th century.   3. Publishers and
publishing—United States—Biography.   4. Pound, Ezra, 1885–1972—
Friends and associates.   5. Americans—Italy—History—20th century.   6.
Poets, American—20th century—Biography.   7. Laughlin, James, 1914–
I. Title.   II. Series.
  PS3531.O82Z5454   2005
  811'.52—dc22

                                                            2004026482

British Library Cataloguing in Publication data are available.

For Alison and Jonathan Henry

Contents

❖ ❖ ❖ ❖

Acknowledgments
❖ ❖ ❖ ❖

This book—my first—is the product of almost ten years of work. For their help at early stages I am grateful to Brian Bremen, Thomas Staley, Wayne Lesser, Joseph Slate, and the late Robert Crunden. I especially thank Michael Winship for his careful reading, his willingness to push me, and his continuing moral support.

One of the great benefits of writing about people who are still alive, I learned, is that they are more often than not very willing to help. James Laughlin was of immense assistance in my work. I visited him twice at Meadow House near Norfolk, Connecticut, and he was a generous, gracious, and remarkably helpful host. Although he was quite suspicious of the thrust of my project—largely because he felt that it overplayed his role and took attention away from Pound's poetic accomplishment—Laughlin never hesitated to give me his time, information, and assistance, and even to lend me his office. I hope that this book will play some small part in ensuring that his contribution to twentieth-century American literature is not forgotten.

Princess Mary de Rachewiltz, Ezra Pound's daughter, hosted me for an afternoon at her castle in Italy and provided me with valuable information. Although they almost certainly will not remember that they did this, Lawrence Rainey, Ira B. Nadel, Janice Radway, and Ellen Stauder all helped me conceptualize my argument in its very early stages. In addition to having produced *Ezra Pound: A Bibliography,* which has been my most valuable and frequently consulted resource, the Yale bibliographer Donald Gallup suggested that I contact Archie Henderson. Archie, who revised and expanded Gallup's bibliography, was a great help with many of the specifics and also steered me to several references that proved quite important.

The College of Liberal Arts at the University of Texas generously supported my work with a fellowship in 1997–98 which enabled me to finish the bulk of the writing. The final preparation of this book would not have been possible without the opportunity to consult the New Directions and James Laughlin Archives housed at Harvard's Houghton Library—an opportunity made possible when I was awarded the 2002–3 Stanley J. Kahrl Fellowship in Literary Manuscripts. I am extremely grateful to the Harvard Libraries, Leslie Morris, Dennis Marnon, and the staff of the Houghton Library reading room for their patience and assistance. I would also like to extend my appreciation to the staff of the Harry Ransom Humanities Research Center at the University of Texas, especially Lisa Jones, who taught me a great deal about the work of archivists. A special thanks goes to the staff at Yale's Beinecke Library Reading Room, who were unfailingly courteous and solicitous, and to Greg Harold.

Finally, this book is for my wife, Alison, and my son, Jonathan Henry.

Grateful acknowledgment is given to the following copyright holders. Previously unpublished letters of Ezra Pound: copyright © 2005 by Omar S. Pound and Mary de Rachewiltz. Previously unpublished letters of Dorothy Pound: copyright © 2005 by Omar S. Pound. All quotations from previously unpublished letters of James Laughlin, copyright © 2005 by The New Directions Ownership Trust; used by permission of New Directions Publishing Corp. Quotations from the letters of T. S. Eliot are the copyright of the Eliot Estate and Faber & Faber Ltd. Reprinted by permission of Faber & Faber Ltd. Most of these letters, as well as many others that I used, reside in two depositories: the Yale Collection of American Literature, Beinecke Rare Book and Manuscript Library of Yale University, and the Houghton Library of Harvard University. I gratefully acknowledge their permission to quote from the manuscripts in their possession. Permission to quote from the letters of Hugh Kenner was granted by the late Professor Kenner. They and many others that I used are in the collection of the Harry Ransom Humanities Research Center, University of Texas at Austin, and I gratefully acknowledge the center's permission to quote from these manuscripts. Permission to reproduce advertisements was generously granted by New Directions Publishing Corp., by International Publishers Co., and by Regnery Publishing.

James Laughlin, New Directions,
and the Remaking of Ezra Pound

Introduction
❖ ❖ ❖ ❖

Since the appearance of the printing press, relations between authors and publishers have been stormy. Even though they are always quarrelling, neither of the two can live without the other. Now, the logic that determines the publishing of books is the logic of the marketplace. For me it is a logic that cannot be applied mechanically to that complex and delicate operation that consists in writing books, publishing them, distributing them, and reading them. Literature is, and cannot be otherwise, indifferent to the laws of the marketplace. That indifference has become, time and again, rebellion, and that rebellion is part of the history of twentieth-century literature.

— Octavio Paz,
"A Discourse on Literature and Publishing Today" (1996)

THE Mexican writer Octavio Paz expressed what has become the common understanding, especially since the twentieth century, of the relation between literature and the commercial publishing industry: literature and the publishers who bring it to its audiences are at cross-purposes. Whereas publishers must follow the "laws of the marketplace," bringing out those books that will result in the greatest profit, writers have an obligation to ignore those laws, to pay no attention to what will sell. Their obligation, Paz implies, is to art, a realm of aesthetic creation "indifferent to the laws of the marketplace."

Nor, in this formulation, is it publishers alone who impede writers. In 1959, the poet Allen Ginsberg complained that "literature . . . has been mocked, misinterpreted and suppressed by a horde of middlemen whose fearful allegiance to the organization of mass stereotype communication prevents them from sympathy . . . with any manifestation of unconditioned individuality. I mean journalists, commercial publishers, book-review fellows, multitudes of professors of literature, etc., etc."[1] Ginsberg here identifies those from whose allegiance to a system literature suffers —is forced into standardization and conformity. But Ginsberg's stance resonates problematically with his own experience. In fact, it is almost entirely owing to such "middlemen" that he became a prominent literary and public figure by the 1970s. His bearded face became a metonym for the Beat movement, and the mass media made him a star; his works, especially *Howl*, were included in commercial publishers' modern poetry anthologies and in university classes; and his resulting commercial success (along with the paid lectures and poet-in-residence positions that resulted from his fame) provided him a comfortable living. The appearance of his *Collected Poems* (1984)—released by Harper and Row, one of the oldest "commercial publishers" in America—was the occasion for dozens of adulatory reviews in mainstream publications by the "book-review fellows." Ginsberg died, in 1996, one of the most famous and respected writers in America.

Like Ginsberg, the American modernist poet Ezra Pound frequently inveighed against the pernicious effects of the system of mass communication—and in much the same language. Also like Ginsberg, Pound started his career as an enfant terrible and a sensation, and ended his career widely recognized and celebrated as a central figure in the American poetry canon. Unlike Ginsberg's, though, Pound's trajectory included years of publicly vented bigotry, a widely known affiliation with a government—the Italian regime of Benito Mussolini—hostile to the United States, wartime propaganda broadcasts on behalf of that enemy government, an indictment for treason, capture and near execution by Italian partisan forces, a mental incompetence defense, and almost thirteen years of enforced residence in a federal mental hospital. Pound eventually arrived at a broadly recognized status as one of America's most important poets and as perhaps the central figure of Anglo-American literary modernism. For a time in the 1960s and 1970s, scholars published more work on Pound than on any other modernist writer, and a spate of poetry anthologies (themselves edited by poets) both implicitly demonstrated and explicitly argued that contemporary poets considered Pound their most important immediate predecessor. How do we explain Pound's transformation from pariah to canonized, celebrated poet? And given his ultimate success in the marketplace, what do we make of Pound's often-expressed hostility to commerce and trade publishing?

In this book, I explore the ways in which one of Ginsberg's "middlemen"—James Laughlin, Pound's disciple, friend, and publisher—managed and directed the transformation of Pound's public image and literary reputation in America from the mid-1930s, when he became known as a profascist, anti-Semitic crank, to the close of the 1960s, when for a brief time he was seen as the most important and accomplished writer of the modernist period. Laughlin was the most important force in the shaping of Pound's reputation in America, and, through the activities of his firm, New Directions Books, he challenged the very notion that the system of "mass stereotype publication" is always harmful to literature. Laughlin orchestrated, or at least strongly influenced, the activities and attitudes of journalists, "book-review fellows," and university professors, all on the behalf of his cantankerous and often resistant author. It would, of course, be simplistic to ascribe Pound's remarkable public rehabilitation to Laughlin's work alone. But it would be unrealistic, even naïve, not to acknowledge that Pound almost certainly would never have been generally acknowledged as the central figure of American modernism and one of high modernism's great triumvirate (with T. S. Eliot and James Joyce) without Laughlin.

The effects of Laughlin's activities on Pound's behalf reached far beyond Pound. In the interest of "remaking" the poet, Laughlin urged readers to ignore his political activities, biography, and beliefs and to read the poetry for its internal qualities alone—an approach known as aesthetic formalism. By doing this, Laughlin facilitated Pound's entry into modern poetry classes and the canon, helped literary critics explain to skeptical readers why they should buy and read the books of an anti-Semitic crank, turned Pound's works into reliable sellers for New Directions Books, and gave Pound's family financial security for the first time. In a larger sense, Laughlin's activities on Pound's behalf played a significant part in helping bind together literary modernism and the aesthetic formalist approach so often used to read and analyze it. Beyond this, Laughlin's influential support of an increasingly important group of literary critics did much to advance the critical practice known as the "New Criticism" to prominence in the 1940s and 1950s.

Important as he was, James Laughlin was not the only person who helped Pound become a figure so central to American literary history. Dozens of others—publishers, critics, poets, journalists, editors, literary agents, professors, biographers, sycophants—affected how Pound was seen by the public, by readers, and by the academy. Figures so diverse as

Robert MacGregor, T. S. Eliot, Peter du Sautoy, Hugh Kenner, Noel Stock, John Kasper, Marcella Spann, and many others play prominent roles in the story of Pound's remaking. Pound himself contributed a great deal to the management of his public image and literary reputation, although it must be said that much of what he did, especially between 1930 and 1960, only hurt him. But in the postwar period, after Pound had disgraced himself by his pro-Mussolini stance, and when many critics had come to the conclusion that he was more a curious, colorful innovator than a great poet, Laughlin re-created the public Pound. Almost all the other figures mentioned above were only carrying out Laughlin's plan, or reacting to developments Laughlin had set into motion.

In the summer of 1933, James Laughlin, a young Harvard student and aspiring poet from a wealthy Pittsburgh family, came to Europe to travel and meet a number of prominent writers, including Pound. Taking time off from college, he returned the next year to attend the "Ezuversity" (Pound's name for the opportunity to follow him through his daily routine and listen to his observations upon any and all topics). For the first six years of their acquaintance, from the time he first met Pound to the time he obtained the rights to publish the *Cantos,* Laughlin was a combination factotum and literary agent for the poet. Before he founded New Directions Press, he put Pound's works in the magazines (the *Harvard Advocate, New Democracy*) for which he worked; he edited one of Pound's articles for submission to an academic journal; he tried to interest established publishers in Pound's works that had not yet appeared in America; he distributed European editions of Pound's books at stores such as New York's Gotham Book Mart; and he contracted with a small craft printer to publish one of Pound's cantos in a fine-press edition. He also worked as a sort of "spin doctor" for Pound. As editor of publications in which the poet's works appeared, he framed them flatteringly with commentary and placed them in particularly important issues. And although Laughlin was particularly interested in boosting Pound's literary stock and reputation, he was also a believer in the Social Credit economic school and consequently worked to place Pound's Social Credit–influenced economic works in magazines and to make them as appealing to conventional taste as possible.[2]

Just a few years later, Laughlin founded his own annual journal (*New Directions in Prose and Poetry*), and then a publishing house of the same name, and took charge of publishing Pound in America. Laughlin's mistrust of commercial activities—that is, involvement in for-profit commerce in goods and services—motivated him to use his family's fortune (he came from Pittsburgh's Jones and Laughlin steel dynasty) to ensure that Pound would always have a sympathetic publisher. Through New Directions, Laughlin insisted first to his Ivy League compatriots and then to the literary marketplace in general that the eccentric bohemian and political crackpot many of them felt Pound to be was in actuality a great thinker and an even greater poet, and of central importance to contemporary literature. Being published by New Directions brought Pound fully into the realm of mid-twentieth-century literary publishing in America; earlier, his works had been published erratically, in editions of widely varying price, availability, and intended audience, and with varying publisher support. By taking over the poet's American publishing, Laughlin gave himself a great deal of control over the maintenance of Pound's—and modernism's—public image.[3] Instead of trying to fit modernist literature to middle-class tastes and attempting to explain away some of its stylistic or conceptual difficulties, as many of the trade literary publishers of the time had, Laughlin argued that Pound's works promoted healthy values—economic justice and cultural renewal. At this time, Laughlin, like Pound, very much believed that literature must be judged, at least partly, by its commitment to building a better society.

Throughout the 1930s, moreover, Laughlin decried the commodification of art. Unlike the trade literary publishers who were his models in many other ways, he did not want to package his product for the middle-class audience. In this, he sided with the European small publishers and the American little magazines of the 1920s. Addressing an audience that at first largely comprised educated, white, upper-middle-class or aristocratic Easterners, Laughlin offered the opportunity to purchase difficult literature, and only rarely highlighted the material qualities of his books. In the words of the company's first slogan, New Directions sold "books of enduring *literary* value."[4]

By the start of World War II, though, increasing controversy surrounding Pound forced Laughlin to dramatically change his ideas about publishing, and the ideas about poetry, politics, and activism that he had expressed in the first *New Directions* annuals. Then, during the war, Pound wrote and performed a number of radio broadcasts for Italian state radio, many of them scurrilously anti-Semitic and most of them harshly critical of Roosevelt and the Allies. Federal authorities monitored these broadcasts, and a grand jury returned a treason indictment against Pound and other "enemy broadcasters" in 1943. He was captured in 1945 and returned to the United States to face trial, only to be found mentally unfit to defend himself. In lieu of trial, he was held in a federal sanatorium for thirteen years.

Faced with a poet whose books had almost completely stopped selling, Laughlin decided to eliminate any mention of the political or social content of Pound's works from New Directions publicity materials, and began to focus solely on the aesthetic quality of these works. This strategy endured until Pound's death. Laughlin aestheticized Pound, and used other authoritative voices such as T. S. Eliot, Ernest Hemingway, and Archibald MacLeish to argue both for the value of Pound's work and for the need to read his poetry aesthetically, without concern for what it was *saying*. This was a strategy that meshed with the critical approaches of the two most prominent critical groups of the time, the largely Southern and conservative New Critics and the largely Jewish, leftist New York Intellectuals. In 1949, when Pound was awarded the Bollingen Prize for Literature for *The Pisan Cantos,* the decision was attacked by the public at large, who opposed giving a government-sponsored award to an indicted traitor, as well as by a few poets and critics who held to the idea that literature should teach socially valuable lessons and that writers should be admirable figures. Both the New Critics and New York Intellectuals disagreed, though, arguing publicly that "objective aesthetic criteria" justified giving the award to Pound.

In the years following the Bollingen Prize, Laughlin reached out to students and the academy and sought to recast Pound as a great poet and an elder statesman of literature. That Pound continued to produce well-regarded volumes of *Cantos* helped with the first aim, but Laughlin took it upon himself to accomplish the second. To this end, during the 1950s and 1960s he published a great deal of reprinted critical work by Pound, some dating from 1912 or even earlier. Until the late 1960s, however, Laughlin refused to publish any of Pound's newer political or economic writing or to reprint any of his older such material, even though Pound consistently cajoled him to do so—he thus effectively refused the poet the opportunity he so deeply desired to be a cultural and social critic, and, in the process, to remind people of his anti-Semitic and profascist ideas.

Laughlin's remaking of Pound was in many ways a rejection of his own earlier ideas about the interdependence of art and politics, literature and economics—ideas he had drawn largely from Pound. Pound's limited adherence to the idea of aesthetic autonomy (that art has a special type of existence separate from practical, political, or social concerns) did not mean that he believed that art stood independent from social concerns; it simply meant that he wanted society to grant artists great latitude to create works of art. The relationship between the artist who sought to "be independent of the values of a commercial civilization," in Robert M. Adams's words, and the publisher who needed to respond to those pressures in order to promote and make available that artist's work, was one of both conflict and collaboration.[5] In Pound and Laughlin's relationship, we can see the complicated interaction of art and commercial culture, the paradoxical nature of the notion of the autonomy of the aesthetic (which itself had its genesis in the antipathy artists began to feel for commerce in the Romantic period), the construction and critical sanctioning of modernism, and the growth of aesthetic formalism.

Laughlin's campaign on behalf of Pound has ramifications beyond the relationship between one author and one publisher. It took place in the context of two broader issues in the relationship between art and culture. First, trade literary publishing houses naturally had, and still have, a dual and often conflicting commitment to sales and to the promotion of art. In his campaign to rehabilitate Pound's reputation and increase his sales, Laughlin often took a rhetorical stance against what he portrayed as an excessively commercial view of literary publishing. Although he was seeking to enhance Pound's market value, he often did so while excoriating publishers who were too concerned with writers' market value. Pound, as we will see, had always used commercial promotion on his own and others' behalf. The relationship between Laughlin and Pound demonstrates that at least some modernist artists were in fact deeply involved with commerce—dependent on it, resentful of it, but also eager to exploit it. Moreover, in the modernist period, the rhetorical opposition between self-defined experimental or avant-garde writers and those who sought commercial success became so explicit that, in its obviousness, there seems little to examine. By the early 1900s, a writer's distance from commercial success had become almost a measure of the respect accorded that artist by others in his or her field. But many modernist artists—including Pound—had always engaged in such characteristically commercial activities as marketing and promotion to influence critics, professors, and even other poets.

One of the fundamental structuring principles of the American literary world in the twentieth century was the opposition between two very different ideas of how to judge the value or excellence of literature; Laughlin's campaign on Pound's behalf was always informed by this conflict. One loosely constructed school held that good literature somehow had to benefit society and produce better individuals. In the nineteenth century, many influential writers, backed by Kantian ideas about disinterestedness and the aesthetic disposition, began to advance the notion that taste and distinction were qualities that not only characterized highly developed individuals and separated them from the larger public, but also greatly benefited society. The socially beneficial effects of good literature were forcefully argued not just in terms of specific authors, but in the form of a general, theoretical argument. John Ruskin wrote that "the art of any country *is the exponent of its social and political virtues*," and in *Culture and Anarchy,* Matthew Arnold emphasized the edifying and self-improving effects of "the best that has been thought and said."[6] In this view, works did not have value conferred upon them by the esteem of generations of readers (as Samuel Johnson had argued in the eighteenth century); rather, they were the bearers of value and conferred this value upon their readers.[7]

The tension between art and money had been eased by this view of literature. But in the twentieth century, the growing connection between literature's edifying qualities and consumerism ("Buy these books and become a better person!") caused a backlash among artists and writers themselves. In the late nineteenth and early twentieth centuries, many literary writers started to feel that their avocation was losing its special status and their work being evaluated simply on the basis of its commercial success, and began to reject the Arnoldian way of evaluation. The spheres of commerce and of literature, whose close interrelationship had never been fully acknowledged, were now seen as diametric opposites, to the extent that novels such as George Gissing's *New Grub Street* centered on the conflict between the "unpractical artist" and the artist who makes concessions to the marketplace. The early-twentieth-century American critic Van Wyck Brooks lamented that of "Thoreau, Emerson, Poe and Hawthorne . . . not one of them, not all of them, have had the power to move the soul of America from the accumulation of dollars."[8] William Carlos Williams wrote in his *Autobiography* that he set his own writing against the "calculated viciousness of a money grubbing society."[9] As Raymond Williams observed, what Coleridge called "cultivation" and what later writers referred to as "culture"—an important element of which is an "appreciation for literature"—became "a court of appeal, by which a society construing its relationships in terms of the cash-nexus might be condemned."[10]

In response to what they saw as the inordinate influence of commerce, artists and writers constructed an oppositional system of literary value. Commercial success and mass popularity—writing a best-seller, for example—became a sign of compromise, or even failure, for serious artists. Conversely, the failure to make money became the identifying mark of a work's artistic value or of a writer's genius. This value system drew on the closely related philosophical concept of aesthetic autonomy. One of the earliest and most important manifestations of the drive for an autonomous artistic sphere, the Romantic cult of the creative artist, is bolstered by a disdain for prevailing popular opinion. The Romantic artist sought to re-mold public taste to make it more friendly to his own works—Wordsworth famously wrote in 1815 that "every author, as far as he is great and at the same time *original*, has had the task of *creating* the taste by which he is to be enjoyed."[11] This positive assessment of the possibility of "creating taste," though, must be seen in light of the Romantics' more pessimistic statements on public sentiment and esteem. Keats had "not the slightest feel of humility towards the Public"; Shelley wrote that "contemporary criticism is no more than the sum of the folly with which genius has to wrestle"; Wordsworth himself claimed that "lamentable is his error who can believe that there is anything of divine infallibility in the clamour of that small though loud portion of the community, ever governed by factitious influence, which, under the name of the PUBLIC, passes itself upon the unthinking, for the PEOPLE."[12] The artist, now separated from his society, "alienated," becomes what Raymond Williams calls "a special kind of person . . . the guiding light for the common life."[13] His job is to be an outsider reminding society of crucial issues that civilization has repressed; he is to explain that art embodies "certain human values, capacities, energies, which the development of society towards an industrial civilization was felt to be threatening or even destroying. . . . [Romantic-era artists] defined, emphatically, their high calling, but they came to define and to emphasize because they were convinced that the principles on which the new society was being organized were actively hostile to the necessary principles of art."[14]

In reaction to the increasingly consumeristic bent of society, art needed to become less of a commodity; to accomplish this, Williams asserts, Romantic artists constructed a theory of artistic production and reception in which the work could not be reduced to a mere commodity, an object. Instead, it became an active, dynamic thing. Wordsworth, for instance, rejected the notion of artistic taste because taste "is a metaphor, taken from a *passive* sense of the human body, and transferred to things which are in their essence *not* passive—to intellectual *acts* and *operations*."[15] For the Romantics, art had a type of value and existence that derived not from a work's social value, but from some entirely separate inherent aesthetic existence. Importantly, though, the literature of that period maintained a connection with society, commenting on the historical and political conditions of its time, as did Wordsworth's early ballads, Southey's political verse, Byron's "Vision of Judgement," any number of Shelley's lyrics, and much of Blake's work.

Where Coleridge and Wordsworth studied and criticized their society, the modernist writers alienated themselves from it, condemning rather than criticizing. As a result of writers' adoption of the autonomy of the aesthetic—a self-defining position that both distinguished art from other human activities and commented negatively on the ostensibly commercial intentions behind those activities—literature detached itself from the social nexus, and the belief that it had a moral or civic function was weakened as the influence of the modernist artists expanded.[16] The nineteenth-century notion that literature should uphold the nation's values gave way to the image of the writer as a *vox clamanti in deserto*, protesting and lamenting. An artist's independence from his society, his autonomy, and the uniqueness (rather than the social value) of his writings become the signal attributes of the literary text; moreover, such middlemen as publishers (who represented commerce), journalists and reviewers (who

represented commerce's influence over culture), and professors (who represented the academy) began to represent an attack on artistic individu-
alism. The feeling that literature "can improve the tone of a culture and
raise the level of its intelligence," in the words of Richard Brodhead,
persisted, but the end result of an education based on the values advanced
by literature seemed changed: rather than an Emerson or a Longfellow, a
twentieth-century literary education would produce a gadfly, a commentator from the sidelines, an alienated subject decrying the failures of society rather than an involved citizen working to better society.[17]

The autonomy of the aesthetic is a category that has embraced everything from the aesthete to the need for governments to fund artists, but
in the sense that I am using it, *aesthetic autonomy* designates two related
but distinct ideas.[18] The first is the philosophical concept that the aesthetic
has a special type of existence and that art expresses a unique kind of
knowledge; this became the foundation of the New Critical view of literature, and it provided Laughlin with a reason for readers to overlook
Pound's repugnant politics. The second is the literary-critical approach of
aesthetic formalism, the practice of ignoring the social or political importance or meanings of a work in favor of elucidating its formal qualities,
and making the excellence of those formal qualities the basis for evaluation. Laughlin's (and others') attempts to improve Pound's reputation
through aesthetic formalism raise a central question of this book: how
does one use the criteria of art's separateness from the world to convince
the world to accept, respect, and purchase that art? How, in other words,
are twin commitments to Pound's reputation and to New Directions'
profit pursued by exploiting, rather than ameliorating or evading, the ten-
sions between art and world, between aesthetic values and social values,
between disinterested contemplation of and participation in social and
political affairs?

Another issue closely related to aesthetic formalism is commercialism.
Hostility toward commercialism and its effects on art was, as outlined
above, one of the catalysts in the development of the concept of aesthetic
autonomy. Among artists, the term *commercial* is almost always used pe-
joratively—it indicates an undue concern for profit and a willingness to
treat works of art as mere commodities. Many of the figures in Pound and
Laughlin's story rhetorically position themselves against commercialism:
John Quinn expresses his distaste at Horace Liveright's vulgarly commer-

cialistic marketing of books; Pound remarks that "art and commerce never savvy one another"; Laughlin reviles the mass-market book publishers who, he says, sell books like soap. But Quinn (a New York lawyer) made his living in the world of commerce, Pound advised his small-press publishers on how to most effectively market his books, and Laughlin postponed publishing any number of Pound's works because they would not sell. *Commercial* is the term *against* which almost all of the actors in the story of Pound's reputation—and by extension, in the story of modernism's evolution and accession to prominence—define themselves. But almost every figure in modernism engaged, often happily, in commercial activities. *Commercial* is, in other words, what nobody wants to be, but almost everyone is.

The closer one looks at this debate about art and commercialism, the more the terms collapse into each other. Although Pound, Laughlin, and any number of critics and professors of literature have explained Pound's reputation and canonical status as a result of his work's objective aesthetic value, his improved standing in the field of American literature was in large part a product of commercial discourse as well as the growing acceptance of aesthetic formalism. The very concept of disinterested judgment of aesthetic worth, however, and the notion that aesthetic values were somehow objective, were themselves products of the interaction between the world of art and the world of commerce. And although the terms in which literary value were defined in the early twentieth century were resolutely anticommercial, Laughlin's efforts on Pound's behalf were all recognizably market based. As Pound's publisher, Laughlin was interested in increasing Pound's market value, but he accomplished this by a campaign that sought to improve the poet's literary value.

This fierce debate about commercialism can seem almost quaint today. Seen against an age of media conglomerates such as Bertlesmann or Viacom—in which even the largest U.S. publishers (Random House and Simon and Schuster) constitute only a small percentage of overall value—these fights about the marketing of books that sell in the hundreds seem of minuscule importance. In Pound's world, annual royalties rarely topped a thousand dollars, magazine articles paid a hundred dollars, and a check for fifty dollars could help Pound's family get through another month. In the light of today, when an unpublished writer may receive an advance of one hundred thousand dollars for a first novel, and where Hillary Rodham

Clinton receives a four-million-dollar advance for her memoir *Living History,* how can we assign any importance to these tiny sums, or argue that these small firms and cult authors played any significant role in the development of American literary publishing?

But all of these questions provide the context for what is in itself a fascinating personal story. Pound felt an irresistible drive to improve the world through his writings, both literary and political; sadly, whether through prejudice, cussedness, or actual mental illness, he held tenaciously to some abhorrent ideas, which infected and vitiated much of what he sought to teach the world. Laughlin was drawn to Pound's force and energy as a young man but, like many of Pound's friends, was repelled later by those same qualities. But both men believed deeply in the value of Pound's art in particular and, more generally, in the importance of art in a century characterized by venality, cruelty, and violence.

CHAPTER ONE

❖ ❖ ❖ ❖

Pound and the Publishing Industry

Most American [publishing] houses will simply put my stuff in the basement. They want best sellers. . . . They'd all rather be buggered than assist in enlightening the nation.

—Ezra Pound to John Quinn, 27 July 1916

ON 26 July 1943, the day after the Italian king Vittorio Emanuele III dismissed Benito Mussolini from office and Mussolini fled into a Nazi-protected internal exile, a federal grand jury in Washington, D.C., handed down treason indictments against eight American citizens in Europe. Seven lived in Germany and had been broadcasting pro-Nazi propaganda on the radio from Berlin; one lived in Rapallo, Italy, a small Ligurian town near Genoa, and had been broadcasting from Rome. This last defendant, stated the indictment, "being a citizen of the United States, and a person owing allegiance to the United States, in violation of his said duty of allegiance, knowingly, intentionally, wilfully, unlawfully, feloniously, traitorously, and treasonably did adhere to the enemies of the United States, to wit, the Kingdom of Italy, its counsellors, armies, navies, secret agents, representatives, and subjects."[1] In 1945, the penalties for treason ranged from five years in prison and a ten-thousand-dollar fine to execution.

On Thursday, the third of May 1945, two Italian *partigiani* (partisans) affiliated with the Zoagli group of anti-Fascist irregulars arrived at a small house in the village of Sant'Ambrogio, on top of the hill behind Rapallo. In the house was an American poet, a vocal and public supporter of Mussolini who was wanted by the U.S. government. The partisans brought him first to their headquarters at Zoagli, a few miles down the coast. He was kept there briefly, and his wife joined him. The poet and his wife were then taken four miles farther to Chiavari, where the partisans had been *giustiziando,* or executing, Fascists. The poet was asked whether he wanted to stay with the partisans or be handed over to the Americans.

On a mid-November night, two young American lieutenants walked into the dispensary of the U.S. Army's Disciplinary Training Center (DTC) near occupied Pisa. In the room were the charge of quarters and an aging man who was reading Joseph E. Davies's *Mission to Moscow.* The young officers informed the aging man that he had one hour to assemble his personal belongings in preparation for transfer to Washington, D.C., and left. The aging man rose and expressed pleasantries and gratitude to the CQ, As he walked out, he turned and "with a half-smile, put both hands around his neck to form a noose and jerked up his chin."[2]

On the afternoon of 27 November 1945, the American poet Ezra Pound was formally arraigned on treason charges (the indictment mentioned nineteen individual acts of treason) before Bolitha J. Laws, chief justice of the United States District Court for the District of Columbia. Pound's lawyer, Julien Cornell, responded that the poet was mentally incapable of making a plea on his own, and requested that a plea of "not guilty" be entered with the court. Pound was sent to Gallinger Hospital for examination, then on 21 December 1945, transferred to St. Elizabeths Hospital for the Insane. He was sixty years old.

On the fourth of September 1945, the thirty-one-year-old publisher James Laughlin had written to Pound in the Pisa DTC:

Dear EP—

You are probably wondering why you haven't heard from me sooner. The reason is that today was the first time I got a line on where you were, through a mutual friend in Washington. . . .

I should hardly say I suppose that I hope to see you soon, because I'm afraid that things are going to be kind of tough for you here, but rest assured that though you have many spiteful enemies, you also have a few friends left who will do their best to help you. No one takes your side, of course, in the political sense, but many feel that the bonds of friendship and the values of literature can transcend a great deal.[3]

Despite Laughlin's relative youth, he had known Pound for almost twelve years. He had been the poet's disciple, correspondent, agent in the United

States, and emissary to undergraduates in Cambridge, New Haven, and Providence. Most importantly, for almost eight years as the founder and head of New Directions Books, he had been Pound's publisher. The futures of the two men, even then closely linked, were to become intimately intertwined, even interdependent.

In a very real sense, Ezra Pound's future in late 1945 depended on Laughlin and on New Directions Books. Certainly, Pound might have continued to avoid trial for the rest of his life without Laughlin's intervention, although it was Laughlin who had hired an eminently competent lawyer, Julien Cornell, and had therefore managed to keep the poet from facing the charges against him. But it is impossible to imagine the remaining trajectory of Pound's life—his retention of his masterful poetic skills, his public rehabilitation, his accession by the late 1950s to a preeminent place in American literary history, his release and return to Italy and a melancholy but lauded old age—without Laughlin and his work on his behalf. It is equally impossible, though, to imagine the enduring success and influence of New Directions Books and Laughlin, its publisher, without Pound, the firm's cornerstone author and Laughlin's great literary and cultural father figure—and without New Directions, it is impossible to imagine what the life of the brilliant, ambitious, athletic, wealthy young man might have looked like.

In 1945, however, Laughlin's task looked insurmountable. If New Directions Books were to sell any of Pound's books in 1945, in 1946, in 1950, or anytime in the future, it would have to convince a hostile public that Pound's writing had value, even though his actions and views were reprehensible. Laughlin and his staff needed to devise a strategy to minimize public attention to Pound's beliefs and to convince the public that he was the kind of great writer whose aesthetic accomplishments outweighed his abhorrent beliefs and actions. In the longer term, Laughlin needed the critical establishment to come to a favorable judgment on Pound; he needed professors and reviewers and intellectuals to appreciate him, to understand what he was doing, and, most importantly, to rank him among the most important and accomplished American authors. Laughlin needed to make Pound a great poet. But he had to do this by using the tools available to a publisher—that is, the tools of commerce, in many artists' and intellectuals' eyes inimical to art.

The most remarkable part of the story of Laughlin and Pound is that they succeeded. Laughlin and his company brought artists and writers, literary critics and criticism, advertising and marketing, professors and the academy, booksellers, and new developments in the trade publishing industry all to bear on one mission: remake Pound. Laughlin organized, choreographed, exhorted, "spun," denied, gladhanded, cajoled, chided, all on Pound's behalf, and by the late 1960s Pound was no longer a pariah or an oddity in American literature. He had become a—and in many minds *the*—dominant figure of twentieth-century English-language poetry. Laughlin and New Directions Books were the single most important force in bringing this transformation.

At the same time, Laughlin himself was changing. He went from being an eager young disciple and student to being a friend, colleague, advocate, agent, editor, and occasional foil of Pound's. His own development parallels that of his publishing house, a remarkable firm that crossed the lines between trade literary publisher and private press, between profit-making company and vanity project, finally becoming (and remaining) one of the most respected literary publishers in the United States. New Directions introduced dozens of foreign and American writers to the U.S. reading public, pioneered the trade paperback, made available numerous out-of-print classics by such writers as Henry James, E. M. Forster, and F. Scott Fitzgerald, and altered the way publishers marketed to students and professors. It is not an overstatement to say that New Directions changed literary publishing in America.

This book is the story of the parallel transformations of Pound, Laughlin, and New Directions. But to understand fully what Laughlin and Pound accomplished, we must look at their entire relationship, including the twelve years before Pound's return to the United States, trial, and incarceration. Indeed, it is necessary to step even further back, to the years when Pound was having his first encounters with the publishing industry and, slightly later, when Laughlin was first reading the avant-garde and classic literature he was to publish, to fully understand the dimensions of these transformations and the motivations of those involved.

When modernism (the loosely affiliated movement was not generally so called at the time) began in the early twentieth century, its books were published primarily by small private presses in London and Paris and by trade literary houses in London and the United States. In the 1910s and

1920s, Pound frequently worked with both kinds of publishers. Later, when he was advising Laughlin on how to run New Directions Books, he drew on his early experiences with trade literary firms, encouraging Laughlin to adopt their tactics for appealing to a wide audience as well as to influential literary and political opinion makers. At the same time, though, he urged Laughlin to behave like a small-press publisher in other ways that would benefit writers—publishing unprofitable but potentially important works, and allowing writers to have a great deal of influence in the construction of a publisher's list.

When Laughlin founded his firm, he experienced, no less than any other literary publisher, the competing demands of art and commerce. He wanted to publish the writers he liked and thought worthy; at the same time, he wanted New Directions Book s to become self-sustaining (the company had been founded on money from Laughlin's family and from his own trust fund). His opinion of the trade publishing industry, like that of many writers, was uniformly negative, and remained so for many years. Laughlin felt that publishing literary books on the basis of any criteria other than their aesthetic value was philistinery, and that marketing books by using the promotional strategies of modern commerce was vulgar and tainted the works themselves. The writers he was publishing echoed these anticommercial sentiments: especially in the early years, Laughlin was publishing modernist works, and modernism took special pains to attack the commerce-oriented sensibilities of the bourgeois class and the profit motive. But even his own and his authors' anticommercial feelings did not immunize his company from the need to make money. He needed to balance his own and his authors' prejudices with the imperative that his firm profit, and survive. In this, he looked to the earlier trade publishers of modernism, who were not only the first to inject commercial tactics into marketing the movement, but who had also, by the time Laughlin started his business, begun to establish a public understanding of modernist literature in general and of Pound in particular. And just as Laughlin looked to these publishers—Alfred A. Knopf, Albert and Charles Boni, Horace Liveright, Elkin Mathews, John Farrar, Stanley Rinehart, and Ben Huebsch, in particular—for models, Pound interpreted and evaluated their practices on the basis of his own experiences with them in the 1910s and 1920s. The bulk of this chapter provides an overview of Pound's dealings with these publishers and the lessons he learned, which he would try to impart to Laughlin—briefly: treat me as a private-press publisher would, but sell my books as a trade publisher would.

The rhetorically constructed dichotomy between the two kinds of publishers neatly mirrors one of the primary intellectual conflicts within the modernist movement: the tension between the modernists' distrust, suspicion, and even hatred of commercial entities, and their powerful desire to take advantage of modern business practices in order to transform culture by reaching a mass audience (as well as to provide themselves a living). The opposition of art and commerce is in play when we talk about modernism and trade publishing, but often in surprising and unexpected ways. Artists and writers often lamented the harmful influence of commerce upon literature, but at the same time doggedly (if under delusion) pursued commercial success and happily employed promotional and marketing techniques familiar in the selling of books and movies today. At the same time, some trade publishers had a genuine love for literature, and all of them were willing—to a degree—to publish a money-losing book now and then, out of this love.

It is nonsensical, moreover, to talk about the "remaking" of Pound without also taking into consideration the critics who would pronounce that remaking complete, partial, successful, failed, or not worthy of note. And in order to understand fully later critics' opinions on Pound, we must also take a look back at how the critics saw him in the years before he and Laughlin began to work together. In the 1910s and 1920s, it was journalists and reviewers, not professors, who were the first to study and evaluate serious contemporary literature. Writers for the *Century, Collier's,* the *Saturday Review,* the *Atlantic,* the *New York Herald Tribune's Books* section, and other publications pronounced the most influential judgments on contemporary poets and novelists. Literary criticism's migration to the academy came later, simultaneous with Pound's rehabilitation; in fact, the migration was tacitly supported by Laughlin and advanced by New Directions as a response to the hostility of many older, magazine-based critics to Pound's work and to Pound. In the final section of this chapter, I briefly sketch out critical opinion on Pound before 1935 in order to set the stage for the fundamental change that took place in the years after the Second World War.

The New Trade Literary Publishers

In the twenty-five years he had been active in the literary world before he met James Laughlin, Ezra Pound had worked with a variety of literary publishers, from tiny operations such as the Cuala Press, to university presses like Yale's, to large trade publishers like Macmillan. But for the most part, the first quarter century of Pound's career was marked by his involvement with two types of publishers: very small private presses such as the Ovid Press, the Black Sun Press, and the Three Mountains Press, and trade literary houses such as Boni and Liveright, Alfred A. Knopf, and Elkin Mathews. American readers came to know him through the trade publishers. This gave him a very different public image than he had in Europe, where the small presses were his primary outlet. When publishing with them, Pound could produce wildly experimental works, knowing that his books would find a small but almost guaranteed market of readers and collectors who sought out avant-garde literature. But increasingly in the 1920s, Pound wanted to expand his audience beyond that coterie, without sacrificing the integrity of his work to commercial pressures.

As reaching a broad audience was the mission of the American trade literary publishing industry, Pound naturally came to favor those publishers as partners in broadening his own audience, especially in the United States. During the 1920s and early 1930s, he continued to issue his works in Europe primarily with the small presses, but his publications in the United States were now handled almost exclusively by trade literary houses. (*Trade publishing* is a catchall term, indicating for-profit publishing of books that are not academic or scholarly and not intended for a specialized professional market, yet not inexpensive mass-market products with large press runs and broad distribution. Unlike mass-market books, which are often distributed through magazine and newsstand distributors, trade books are generally distributed primarily by book distributors and sold primarily in bookstores.) Although he longed for the artistic purity that a system of patronage or of exclusively small-press publication would putatively provide him, and although he feared that commercial pressure could stifle his ability to publish controversial or difficult work, Pound at the onset of World War I began to see the trade publishing industry as a potential, and necessary, outlet for his and other modernists' work. He solicited trade literary publishers for his own books; he brought Eliot to the attention of wide-circulation magazines such as *Vanity Fair* and, later, to book publishers; and finally, with the assistance of the New York lawyer and patron of modernist authors John Quinn, he secured American magazine and book contracts for James Joyce and helped find money to pay the Irish writer's living expenses.

Notwithstanding his consistent cooperation with commercial outlets, Pound rarely expressed anything but hostility toward the effects of commerce upon art. His mistrust of commercial publishing and bookselling can be traced from his earliest letters home to his parents in 1908. In one characteristic statement, Pound attacked "the curious system of trade and traders which has grown up with the purpose or result of interposing itself between literature and the public"; in another, he simply stated that "art and commerce never savvy one another."[4] Even his most accomplished pre-*Cantos* work, *Hugh Selwyn Mauberley,* focuses attention on the way commerce turns art into kitsch or trash. Much of the esteem Pound enjoyed resulted from his perceived independence from the demands of commerce and popular taste. This image was already widespread by the time of his first well-known project, the 1914 *Des Imagistes* anthology, and persisted throughout his career.

Just as enduring, though, was Pound's less familiar complicity with commercial culture. Before 1910, he had already attempted to use book reviewers and the journalists of his hometown of Philadelphia to advance his career. During the 1910s and 1920s, Pound declared his allegiance to the little magazines and small presses of London and Paris while at the same time submitting his works to such firms as Macmillan and Elkin Mathews and to H. L. Mencken's campus humor magazine *Smart Set.* He cultivated journalists, sought mass-circulation outlets for his works, and dreamed up frankly commercial marketing strategies for his and his friends' books.

Before 1914, most of Pound's work, and that of his colleagues, had been published by small publishers, private presses, and literary little magazines—outlets seemingly free from commercial pressures. While many of the authors of the "New Writing" (one name for the movement not yet known as modernism) craved a broader audience, few of them had access to one before 1914—publishers were not willing to publish their poorly selling books. Discussing his authors' dealings with these private presses, Laughlin noted in a 1992 interview that "the only way that [William Carlos Williams] was able to get his first books published . . . was by doing them through Ezra's friends in Paris."[5] This limitation to the small presses and little magazines was not, at first, a problem for these writers; small publishers such as the Poetry Bookshop and journals such as the *Egoist* allowed artists creative freedom—from strictures on subject matter or concerns about whether the books would sell,[6] as well as a guaranteed, albeit small, audience of sympathetic, interested readers. Modernist writers appreciated the freedom that magazines like the *Glebe* or, later, *transition* offered them, but the spate of memoirs about the time (books such as Alfred Kreymborg's *Troubadour*, Robert McAlmon and Kay Boyle's *Being Geniuses Together*, and Paris bartender Jimmie Charters's *This Must Be the Place*), with their now famous stories of editors and writers drinking and living together, has caused critics and readers to associate the writing too closely with the outlets, and consequently to link modernist artists too neatly with these publishers' anticommercial viewpoint. As supportive as these readers and publishers were, there simply were not enough of them to provide a living to any modernist author. Pound, for one, barely supported himself, obtaining five or six pounds wherever he could from gifts, contributions to magazines, lectures, prizes, and even parental assistance.[7] Largely for this reason, he and many of the modernist writers sought to publish their books with trade firms that might be able to increase their sales.[8]

As financially insufficient and limiting as small-press publication could be, Pound never abandoned it, and other modernist writers—Joyce, for instance—also continued to publish occasionally with small presses even after they had worked with the trade firms. While in Paris in the early to mid-1920s, Pound encouraged and supported the small presses and often published his work with them. Later, he continued to look to small-press publication as an effective antidote to what he saw as the harm that large trade publishers did to experimental literature. Writing to Caresse Crosby of the Black Sun Press in 1930 regarding a reissue of his 1917 *Imaginary Letters* (first published in the *Little Review*), Pound exulted that this book would "be useful in breaking the stranglehold that s.o.b. [most likely Bennett Cerf] has on ALL publication."[9] The difficulty and controversial nature of their writings, and often the very physical format in which they wanted their works to appear, ensured that the modernists would continue to rely, at least in part, on small presses and little magazines. In a 1923 manifesto for one of these small presses, the Three Mountains Press, Pound wrote that "the aim of the press is to free prose writers from the necessity of presenting their work in the stock-sized volume of commerce."[10] He wanted the same treatment for his own *Cantos,* as well, writing to Kate Buss in 1924 that his almost-finished *Draft of XVI. Cantos* "is to be one of the real bits of printing; modern book to be jacked up to somewhere near level of medieval mss. . . . Not for the Vulgus."[11]

During the 1920s, though, writers like Pound found it increasingly difficult to earn even the meager livings they had had in the previous years. Pound retained the post he had held since 1912 as foreign editor of *Poetry,* and continued to contribute to magazines such as *Smart Set* and the *Dial,* but from 1918 his work began to appear less frequently in America, and his financial situation became precarious. In response, he and his colleagues adopted some of the techniques of commercial operations in order to promote their (still small press–produced) works and boost the value of their books.[12] Many of the modernists engaged in such marketing ploys as limiting the press runs of their books to increase their value, or issuing a limited-edition run of a few copies that preceded the official first edition. Lawrence Rainey has described in detail how writers such as Pound and Joyce and small publishers such as the Cuala Press and the Olympia Press began to emphasize the limited availability of their works as a selling point in itself, implicitly subordinating artistic value to commodity value.[13] These books, written by writers possessed of a degree of literary reputation and published in a format that had become associated with good literature, had prestige not possessed by ordinary books in the marketplace—the fact that their availability was severely restricted differentiated them, in collectors' minds, from mass-produced literature.

Their value was not only symbolic, though. Publishing in such "limited editions," Pound wrote to William Carlos Williams in 1922, "is a means of getting in 100 dollars extra before one goes to publisher. Yeats's sisters press in Ireland [the Cuala Press] has brought him a good deal this way. I got nearly as much from my little book with them as from the big Macmillan edtn. of *Noh.*"[14] Numbered first editions (like Liveright's first run of Eliot's *The Waste Land* in 1922) and unannounced first printings intended for book collectors and influential critics (such as the first sixty copies of the Knopf edition of Pound's 1917 *Lustra*) emphasized the book's market value as an individual objet d'art over its value as infinitely reproducible literature, and assertions of the book's literary value were of secondary importance. Pound told Margaret Anderson in 1917 that "IF it is any use for adv. purposes, you may state that a single copy of my first book has just fetched £8." Seven years later, when William Bird's Three Mountains Press was about to issue *A Draft of XVI. Cantos,* Pound would make the same point: "Do recall that the title of that book," he told Bird, "is 'A DRAFT of 16 Cantos for a poem of some length.' If you will stick to that you will produce something of gtr. val. to collectors. . . . Yr. best ad," he continued, "is the quiet statement that at auction recently a copy of Mr. P's 'A Lume Spento' published in 1908 at $1.00 (one dollar) was sold for $52.50."[15] "These remarks," Rainey points out, "far from advancing assertions of intrinsic artistic value based on the presupposition of Art, offer straightforward claims about the performance record of investments within a commodity economy."[16] In effect, Pound used the promotion of private-press editions as a way to reap the benefits of the marketplace while being protected from its uncertainties: by using the increase in his books' value to collectors as a way to "sell" himself to publishers, he was boosting his own market value without making arguments about how his works would sell in great quantities.[17]

This cultural moment that Rainey identifies, though, was short-lived, and Pound himself helped bring it to a quick end. Rainey, in fact, probably overemphasizes the dependence of modernism on new incarnations of patronage based on limited editions, private-press publication, stipends for authors, and subscription. Although Pound and many of the other modernist writers and publishers (one should note here especially the Paris private-press publishers such as John Rodker, Robert McAlmon, and the Crosbys) did make important use of limited editions and this kind of updated "patronage" to nurse modernism through its early years, this was largely an avenue born of necessity. Most modernists did not shun the opportunities provided them by larger-scale publishing, when those op-portunities arose. Pound is perhaps the emblematic figure here again, for he avidly pursued the larger markets available through the trade publish-ers when those publishers (Liveright, Knopf, Huebsch) began to show interest in modernist writing. It is also important to remember that almost none of these authors actually ended up making their livings through this system of patronage; most—William Carlos Williams's medical career comes immediately to mind, but Joyce worked as a Berlitz language teacher to pay the bills, Wallace Stevens was employed by Hartford Accident and Indemnity, and Eliot worked at a bank and then for years in a management position at Faber and Faber—had to work at professions often completely unrelated to their careers as writers.

Pound, like the other modernists, also tried to persuade the small-press publishers to use the commercial strategies of the trade publishing industry to promote their books. As early as 1908, he was attempting to use such ploys to get his self-published first book, *A Lume Spento,* into print in America: "The American reprint has got to be worked by kicking up such a hell of a row with genuine and faked reviews that Scribner or somebody can be brought to see the sense of making a reprint. I shall write a few myself and get some one to sign 'em."[18] Pound also used such tactics to promote the careers of other writers. He and T. S. Eliot orchestrated a campaign to promote each other's work: while Pound encouraged magazines such as *Poetry* and publishers such as Elkin Mathews and Horace Liveright to publish Eliot's work, Eliot wrote the short book *Ezra Pound His Metric and Poetry,* which Knopf published in 1917. Worried that this ploy would seem too crass, Pound insisted that Eliot's essay be anonymous: "I want to boom Eliot," he said in a letter to John Quinn, "and one can't have too obvious a ping-pong match at that sort of thing."[19] He also told H. L. Mencken, who had inquired as to the pamphlet's authorship, that "Eliot wrote it, but it would be extremely unwise of him, at this stage of his career, with the hope of sometime getting paid by Elder reviews, and published by the godly, and in general of not utterly bitching his chances in various quarters, for him to have signed it."[20] Pound was so well known for being a promoter of himself and others, in fact, that D. H. Lawrence confided to Amy Lowell that he suspected Imagism—the poetic movement started and promoted by Pound in 1914, and later headed by Lowell—was "just an advertising scheme."[21]

Although he had used commercial promotion strategies from the earliest days of his career, Pound in the 1910s and 1920s still mistrusted the motives of the American trade publishing industry. Once he began publishing with the larger American houses during World War I, his profound drive to transform American taste suddenly seemed realistic, but he still feared the cheapening of his ideas that wide distribution could cause. "You cant get a book printed in America unless it conforms to the commercial requirements," he wrote to Quinn in 1915, and the next year he complained that "most American houses will simply put my stuff in the basement. They want best sellers. . . . They'd all rather be buggered than assist in enlightening the nation."[22] Pound also had no faith in Americans' degraded tastes, referring to "that many-eared monster with no sense, the reading public."[23] The uncertainties of commercial publishing, the baseness of the profit motive (when he was not profiting), and the crudeness of public taste clearly made him distrust trade publishers. Pound's contradictory and compromised position on the interaction of art and commerce illustrates the complexity of the modernists' plight: On the one hand, they felt strongly that commerce was the enemy of sincere creation, and many, including Pound, were convinced that only a form of patronage could support truly experimental art. Yet, forced by economic necessity and the desire for wide recognition, almost all worked with the very commercial entities they felt were doing such harm to serious writing.

In the 1920s, a new group of American trade literary publishers, all of whom had important dealings with Pound, helped to collapse further the distinction between art and commerce. Including such firms as B. W. Huebsch, Alfred A. Knopf, and Boni and Liveright they differed from earlier literary publishers in that each adopted, to varying degrees, a sales approach that drew upon the idea of aesthetic autonomy—that great art exists on its own plane, must be judged solely on aesthetic grounds, and has no moral responsibility to society. Each of these publishers assumed the special existence of literature in its advertising; their blurbs and marketing copy rarely, if ever, stressed the social usefulness, morality, or uplifting quality of their books. But aesthetic worth was not valuable in itself; the possession of works of recognized aesthetic value would help consumers obtain and maintain a degree of cultural status, for the owning and displaying of literature conferred distinction, sophistication, and prestige.

Knopf and the other new trade literary publishers also brought Pound and his group of modernist writers before a broad section of the middle-class American public, a goal that the literary magazines and small presses not only never could have accomplished, but (with the exception of *Poetry*) never wanted to accomplish. As the modernists continued to struggle to obtain patronage, they found the greater economic promise of these new trade literary publishers very attractive. The literary movement that at the start of World War I proudly proclaimed its aloofness (as with Imagism) or its opposition to everything conventional (as with Vorticism) entered the 1920s seeking to take advantage of the very consumer culture it so vocally abhorred.

The relationship of publishers and authors was symbiotic. Giving difficult and often frankly antibourgeois works the comforting appearance of a consumer product, as these literary publishers did with the work of Pound, Eliot, and Joyce, encouraged the public to accept this new type of writing, or to at least grant it entry into the realm of the edifyingly literary (as opposed to the realm of the bohemian and avant-garde).[24] The publishers, moreover, recognizing consumers' reluctance to buy experimental works by avant-garde writers, were careful to publish and promote those writers' most accessible books before issuing the more difficult works— Gertrude Stein's readable *Autobiography of Alice B. Toklas,* for instance, was published by Harcourt before the firm published *The Making of Americans;* Knopf published Thomas Mann's *Buddenbrooks* before *The Magic Mountain.* At the same time, these experimental authors gave their publishers important cultural prestige.

Although most of this symbiosis developed in the United States, Pound's relationship with early-twentieth-century literary publishers had begun in England. In 1909, seeing the need for the resources of a commercial publisher in order to get his heretofore self-published books noticed, the newly expatriated poet looked to Elkin Mathews, one of the most prominent names in London's late-Victorian literary scene, who combined established respectability with an interest in the avant-garde. With John Lane, Charles Elkin Mathews had founded the Bodley Head publishing company in 1887, using Mathews's Exeter-based antiquarian bookshop as a starting point. The two men set up business in London in September, 1887, and quickly established a particular character for their books: printed on fine, often handmade paper, using a title page whose design distinguished it from the spidery title pages characteristic of the Victorian book, and employing larger-than-usual type, leading, and margins. By virtue of creative financing and production techniques, the Bodley Head was able to sell its books at prices significantly below those of most poetry books. Soon, John Lane had signed on many of the most important and innovative authors and artists of the 1890s for the Bodley Head list. Oscar Wilde, Lionel Johnson, Arthur Symons, William Butler

Yeats, and Kenneth Grahame all published with the Bodley Head; the notorious artist Aubrey Beardsley designed and illustrated many of the firm's books as well as its scandalous journal, the *Yellow Book*. In a dispute over the risqué nature of some of the books that Lane brought to the firm, the prudish Mathews dissolved the partnership in 1894. The Bodley Head, however, had left its mark on the publishing world, associating itself with its authors to the degree that each helped establish the other's public image. (Moreover, the firm also inspired at least two important American publishing houses—Boston's Copeland and Day and Chicago's Stone and Kimball—whose literary lists and Harvard origins make them parallel not only with their English predecessor but also with New Directions Books.[25]) Mathews also produced several series of inexpensive paperbacks intended to expose unknown writers to the public: the Shilling Garland series (1896–98) featured young experimental writers such as Robert Bridges, and the Vigo Cabinet series (1900–1918) boasted Yeats, J. M. Synge, John Masefield, and Max Weber among its authors.[26]

Pound had read Bodley Head writers in his college days, and also knew of Lane and Mathews: it was no coincidence that one of his first stops in London had been Vigo Street, where both publishers' offices were located. Mathews responded to the brash young poet, and the two quickly became friends. When Pound gave him a manuscript in 1909, it suited the publisher's tastes perfectly; after all, in this period Pound was still heavily influenced by Swinburne and other Georgian poets Mathews had published. During the 1910s, when he was establishing his early fame in England, Pound worked almost exclusively with Mathews, who not only published his poetry but employed him as an editor for anthologies of contemporary verse (such as the *Catholic Anthology 1914–1915*) and for collections of work by Mathews's older authors (such as the *Poetical Works of Lionel Johnson*).

As Pound's poetic vision became more original and "modern," Mathews found it less to his liking. Pound knew this, and published some of his more daring works with small or private houses—*Certain Noble Plays of Japan* (1916) with the Cuala Press, and *Quia Pauper Amavi* (1919), containing "Homage to Sextus Propertius," with the Egoist Press, for instance. During World War I it became clear to both that their interests were diverging. The publisher was criticized by Christian groups about the "misleading" title for the *Catholic Anthology,* received complaints about the choice of Pound as an editor for the Johnson anthology, and finally objected personally to some of the poems in Pound's 1916 volume *Lustra*. The two wrangled for months over the contents of this last book, but Mathews finally got his way, and a number of poems were omitted. (Many of the poems Mathews deleted were restored in Knopf's 1917 American edition.) After a four-year hiatus, Mathews published Pound's *Umbra, the Early Poems of Ezra Pound, All that he now wishes to keep in circulation from "Personae," "Exultations," "Ripostes," etc.* in 1920, but the work simply served to cap the relationship between publisher and poet.

Both Pound and Mathews benefited from their twelve-year affiliation. For Mathews, publishing Pound was his claim to being avant-garde and still relevant after the decline of the Decadents. For Pound, choosing to throw his lot in with Mathews was a brilliant decision. Through the force of his personality, although penniless and unknown, he obtained a foothold with a respected London publisher, and was assured an instant entry into the London literary world. His books gained notice in the mainstream press, notice he would never have been able to achieve had he published only with the small presses and magazines. Pound also gained an understanding of how a trade publisher could bring his works to a much broader audience than a small press could reach, and learned firsthand the frustrations authors can suffer as a result of the commercial and moral pressures a trade publisher must manage.

As Mathews had grown leerier of Pound's experimentation during the war years, Pound had begun to despair that he would ever gain wider popularity in England. He turned his sights on America, hoping (but doubting) that he could find a publisher who would bring his works out without adulterating them. He had published books in America for a number of years before World War I, but his publishers, disappointed by his low sales, had dropped him from their lists. After publishing a number of works with Boston's Small, Maynard and Company (another firm influenced by the Bodley Head), Pound found that by late 1913 his books were no longer appearing in his home country. His American representative, John Quinn, shopped his manuscripts around, but got little interest from the established Boston and New York houses. Finally, in mid-1917, the fledgling publisher Alfred A. Knopf picked up the contract for an American edition of the controversial *Lustra*.

During Pound's years in London (1909–20), a new group of literary publishers was emerging in New York. This group saw no contradiction in publishing works of serious or experimental literature and employing modern advertising and promotion techniques to market them. Ben Huebsch, who had begun publishing in 1902, was joined by new publishers such as Alfred A. Knopf, the Boni brothers, and Horace Liveright in combining the mass-market outlook of the large publishing houses with typically private-press appeals to the object-value of the book and to the snob appeal of owning experimental literature. Even though the bulk of their lists resembled that of the established trade publishers, these new American houses were associated primarily with modern literature because of the presence of a Joyce or Pound on their lists. In return, the success of the publishers' innovative marketing techniques provided many of the modernist writers with income, and brought these often extremely difficult writers before the type of middle-class consumer who had no interest in searching out and purchasing limited editions.

In the late 1910s and the 1920s, this group of publishers provided modernism with a public image drastically different in America than its European face. In Europe, the modernists' primary outlets were the private presses and the little magazines, both of which expressed their audience's self-selection and insularity: these were not books one could obtain in any bookshop, nor were they advertised heavily in outlets read by a broad public.[27] In the United States, though, the publishers of modernism had a much more inclusive approach, encouraging a wide audience to purchase these works and advertising the books in popular magazines and newspapers.

The idea of the book itself, and of what purpose the book should serve in bourgeois life, was changing. Janice Radway has argued that the physical circumstances of "a book's appearance and availability as well as . . . potential readers' awareness and expectations" of that book, publisher, and author all contribute to a purchaser's understanding of what any particular book is, and consequently to a decision to buy.[28] Certainly, consumers had always based their decisions on more than just the value and usefulness of the text. But Radway locates a shift in the conception of the book in the late nineteenth century, attributing it to the growth of inexpensive mass-market editions. In a "more traditional discourse . . . the book was conceived of as the emanation of an author, as serious, as a classic, and as a permanent and precious possession," she says.[29] The cheap book trade was an affront to this notion, and many commentators worried that this breakdown of the distinction between art and commodity, the diminution of the object-value of the book, would cause a concomitant devaluation of its intellectual value. The *New York Evening Mail*, for one, announced that "the publication which may be bought for a few pence, however worthy its contents, is likely to be regarded like a newspaper, as something to be skimmed over and forgotten."[30] In response, the new trade publishers of the 1900s attempted to reassure middle-class consumers that their books were anything but ephemeral. Their appeals emphasized the permanence of their books—both the physical permanence of the object and the cultural permanence of the literature conveyed by the book.[31] But at the same time, these publishers made their cases to the public using advertising techniques that consumers and critics associated with the cheap book trade—and they priced their books accordingly.

Many figures involved in the publishing industry of the 1910s and 1920s were unenthusiastic about this adoption of modern commercial techniques to sell literature. The notion of art's necessary hostility to commerce had become so commonplace that even Henry Seidel Canby (who, because of his position as editor of the popular and widely circulated *Saturday Review of Literature,* was closely associated with the supposed detrimental influence of commerce on literature) described his career as a struggle "between two views of civilization, between two ideas of living . . . Plato versus John Rockefeller, Shakespeare versus Benjamin Franklin, Milton against the stock exchange and the YMCA."[32] The objections raised to the commercialization of literary publishing are grounded on the notion of publishing as a privileged industry in which self-interested capitalism is tempered by a genuine respect for artistic creation and a collegial atmosphere among the businessmen. In his book on *Henry James and the Profession of Authorship,* Michael Anesko points out that American trade publishers of the late nineteenth century saw themselves as a genteel branch of commercial culture that did not allow the profit motive to get in the way of fair play or of respect for the writer's production. "Even though publishers were not wholly innocent of the more notorious aspects of capitalism of the Gilded Age," Anesko writes, "the larger and more successful firms succumbed least to these practices. Among the leaders in

the industry there existed a code of etiquette that was honored far more
often than it was ignored. Gentility had its uses, of course, as a means of
restraining competition; but the fact remains that the regular trade publishers were among the industry's most scrupulous men rather than its
most grasping."[33] Although Knopf and Liveright, among the new trade
literary publishers, heartily upheld this code of etiquette—and Knopf, in
later years, especially cultivated it in order to bolster his personal prestige—the extent to which they adopted the marketing strategies of modern capitalism served as convenient excuses for such figures as John Quinn
to cast aspersions on their motives.[34]

While these new publishers saw their first successes during the years
of World War I, the American publishing industry was still dominated by
many of the names that had been prominent since the 1800s: Appleton,
Doran, Dutton, Lippincott, Henry Holt, Harper Brothers, Houghton
Mifflin, and Little, Brown. Few of these houses put much effort into what
has become known as "branding," a manufacturer's establishing a particular personality for a brand of product, whether soap or books. The new
trade literary publishers felt differently. By giving their books a distinctive
appearance, by maintaining a consistency of types of books in the frontlist
(even when the list as a whole contained a number of different genres),
and by aiming books of seemingly limited appeal at a heterogeneous national audience, publishers such as Knopf, Huebsch, and Liveright gave
the industry a new preoccupation with the value of a brand name. Knopf
and his colleagues were by no means the first publishers to commercialize
literature; their breakthrough was to emphasize how the presence of
"quality" books should be a requirement for a middle-class home—and
how the publisher's name guaranteed a quality book.[35]

Ben W. Huebsch was the earliest of these publishers, and he was a role
model to the new generation. Pound was aware of Huebsch by World War
I: in a 1916 letter to Joyce, Harriet Shaw Weaver of the *Egoist* explained
that Pound "considers Huebsch the best of the younger American publishers and by best he means the most imaginative honourable and re-
sourceful."[36] Huebsch resisted the more commercial tendencies of the
other publishers of his group, calling the aggressive promotion of books
"a disease we caught from the movies" and arguing that "culture is not a
commodity to be dealt in wholesale."[37] Huebsch's dust jackets, for instance, were "sedate and his advertising modest," while Knopf's early

jackets were printed with promotional copy and his advertisements were exercises in self-promotion and branding.[38]

Although his promotional materials were more understated than those of his colleagues, Huebsch's sales approach exemplifies the philosophy of the new trade literary publishers. Knopf, Liveright, and Huebsch all attempted to convince consumers that experimental modernist literature was a product that conferred status upon its owner. Consumers were told that literature was good for them and that, notwithstanding any anti-bourgeois or anticommercial sentiment expressed therein, modernist literature, simply by virtue of being literature, was fully compatible with bourgeois values and would display its owners' taste and distinction. Prefiguring Knopf's advertising, Huebsch's publicity attempted to mainstream modernism, to sell it to middle-class consumers by touting its permanence, rather than its experimentation, and by convincing them that the possession of good literature was in itself edifying, even if the precise nature of this edification was difficult to identify. One advertisement for seven books of poetry (including Joyce's *Chamber Music* and Lawrence's *Look! We Have Come Through*) begins with the statement that "readers may feel assured that each book has a genuine reason for existence and possesses claims to survival."[39] Huebsch's sales pitches underscore the continuity of the literary tradition and reassure consumers that the firm's literary books, although highbrow, are by no means aimed at a coterie. These advertisements downplay the revolutionary nature of modernist technique, emphasizing more familiar qualities. "The psychological insight, fascinating simplicity of style and the extraordinary gift of vivid expression make it a promise of great things," read an advertisement for Joyce's *A Portrait of the Artist as a Young Man* in the *New Republic* in late 1916.[40] By the next year, Huebsch was using blurbs by such literary celebrities as H. G. Wells and Francis Hackett. Ironically, because of their placement in magazines such as the *New Republic*, these advertisements made their appeals directly to many of the same middle-class consumers much of the advertised literature execrated.

Pound's first publisher from this group employed many of the same techniques as Huebsch. Alfred A. Knopf was the most important of all the new trade literary publishers because he most clearly melded the approaches of the small publisher and the trade publisher. He combined the diverse list of a trade publisher with the attention to craft and the physical appearance of books characteristic of small-press publishing. Through his brief affiliation with the firm, Pound first made inroads into the American mainstream. Knopf, who founded his company in 1915, wanted to be more than a strictly literary publisher such as Elkin Mathews. Before his house's first anniversary, he had already produced a list striking in its diversity. An early *Publishers' Weekly* advertisement featured W. H. Hudson's *Green Mansions,* a "big novel" that sold very well, along with blurbs for a cookbook, a doctor's memoirs, a "popular survey of Russia," a number of translated Eastern European novels, an "adventure tale," a dictionary, and an anthology of avant-garde poetry (in which Pound appeared) edited by Alfred Kreymborg.[41] Knopf, however, was by no means strictly a mass-market publisher. By 1920, his house was already known for its finely made books and its concern for every part of the production process. Knopf himself often wrote colophons that would appear at the end of the books. In addition to making sure that the trade editions of his books used quality paper, fine boards, and attractive typefaces, Knopf also often printed limited runs of the same books, using even better materials. Pound's desire to see his work appear in limited editions that would become rare and valuable met with Knopf's desire to supplement his ordinary offerings with higher-quality printings, and for a short time both parties were satisfied.[42]

Kreymborg's 1916 anthology *Others* included six poems by Pound and was one of a number of avant-garde anthologies published by American trade publishers at this time. It was also Pound's first appearance in a widely circulated anthology in the United States (Albert and Charles Boni had issued few copies of the book version of *Des Imagistes,* the 1914 anthology that first brought Pound some fame in literary circles).[43] Initially, Pound was skeptical about Knopf, writing in a 1916 letter to Quinn that "Kreymborg recommends Knopf. But Kreymborg is not wise in the affairs of this world and I shouldn't much trust to his recommendation. Knopf is probably the only publisher he knows."[44] But Pound's appearance in *Others* signaled the start of Knopf's promotion of his career, and Knopf published four of his books in the eighteen months between January 1917 and June 1918. In September 1917, Knopf published *Lustra,* portentously calling it "the first volume of his poems to appear in America for five years."[45] Knopf distributed sixty advance copies to important newspapers and magazines in an effort to broaden Pound's appeal, and followed this up with a second, much larger printing in October. *Lustra,* however, did not sell well; Pound wrote to Harriet Monroe on New Year's Day 1918 that "Knopf writes that he sold 323 copies *Lustra* in Oct. and 9 in Nov., and that nobody had offered any assistance [promoting or reviewing the book]."[46] Before *Lustra,* Knopf had issued 350 copies of the British printing of Pound's essay on Japanese theatre, *"Noh" or Accomplishment.* The book barely earned back its initial investment, but apparently Knopf was trying to stir up interest in the forthcoming *Lustra.* In January 1918, his firm published, in a hardbound edition, Eliot's *Ezra Pound His Metric And Poetry.* Finally, in June 1918, Knopf published Pound's *Pavannes and Divisions,* a compilation of critical essays.

All of these books positioned Knopf as a publisher of the avant-garde with important commonalities with the small presses. The publicity for *Pavannes,* though, epitomizes all of the most important differences between the small-press publishing philosophy and Knopf's desire to make Pound a writer with a large audience. On the dust jacket are two paragraphs of jacket copy (later lifted verbatim for the magazine advertisements described below), and on the inside flap Knopf gives a number of "blurbs," from the Cleveland *Plain Dealer,* the Philadelphia *Press,* and the *New York Times*—the fruit of his promotional efforts for *Lustra.* Knopf prefaces a 1918 quarter-page advertisement for *Pavannes* and Wyndham Lewis's *Tarr* with the motto *"FOR THE INTELLIGENTSIA,"* but the copy of these advertisements reads much like the publicity for any up-and-coming young writer, calling Pound's book "arresting and provoking, but too important to be overlooked by the lover of poetry." There is none of the self-satisfied, insular, self-congratulatory publicity found in little magazines such as the *Egoist* or *Blast.* Knopf was careful to maintain Pound's avant-garde identity, but at the same time he reassured consumers that the poet's work would not be incomprehensible. By 1918 Pound produced *Instigations,* another group of essays similar to *Pavannes and Divisions.* He submitted it to Knopf, but the publisher backed out of his promise to publish it, most likely because of the disappointing sales of *Pavannes.* Eliot noted this as well, writing to his brother in 1919 that "Knopf . . . wrote to Pound that the success of his book *Pavannes and Divisions* had not been sufficient to warrant his undertaking any new contracts with him or Wyndham Lewis or myself."[47] Pound was furious at what he saw as Knopf's treachery, but when John Quinn, his agent in New York, shopped the manuscript around, it was quickly picked up by Horace Liveright's brand-new firm, Boni and Liveright.

If Knopf allowed commercialism to color his sales appeal, the flamboyant and high-living Horace Liveright made that willingness the cornerstone of Boni and Liveright. While Liveright had no prior publishing experience when the firm was founded, Albert and Charles Boni were already important figures in New York's avant-garde scene because of their Washington Square Bookshop and its "house magazine," the *Glebe* (edited by Alfred Kreymborg, this journal had published the 1914 *Des Imagistes* collection).[48] Where Albert Boni brought to the house knowledge of and acquaintance with the avant-garde writers of the day, Liveright brought enthusiasm for literature and a talent for innovative advertising and publicity campaigns. Liveright published *Instigations* in 1920, and *Poems 1918–1921* the following year. Pound was pleased with Liveright's interest and intrigued by the young publisher's devotion to his authors. During the 1920s, Liveright's office in midtown Manhattan was a center for Jazz Age revelry; many New York literary and entertainment figures of the time casually mention that one could drop in on Horace for smuggled liquor and a good time. It is perhaps not coincidental that Liveright's office was only a few blocks from the Algonquin Hotel and its famous Round Table of wits and writers, for the two locales seem to have reinforced each other's personalities. In terms of public recognition, even notoriety, Liveright's firm far surpassed its fellows among the new literary publishers. Where Knopf published much new European writing, though, Liveright published older European classics and such contemporary American writers as Dreiser and Sherwood Anderson, giving Boni and Liveright less of an avant-garde identity. And although his name lives on because of the literary authors he cultivated, the book that brought Liveright the most success and fame in the 1920s was Anita Loos's eminently of-its-time *Gentlemen Prefer Blondes*.

Boni and Liveright's first undertaking, in 1917, was the highly profitable Modern Library. As initially conceived and marketed by Albert Boni and Horace Liveright, the Modern Library's mission was to put out new and classic works of quality at a low price, concentrating at first on such nineteenth-century Europeans as Nietzsche, Wilde, and Ibsen. To many American consumers, "the Modern Library was a kind of insurance policy guaranteeing that if a book was included in the series it *had* to be good," according to Liveright's biographer Thomas Dardis.[49] The Modern Library was a remarkable example of the success of branding; the identity developed was so powerful that consumers would buy books simply because they were in the series, without knowing anything about the authors or content. The Modern Library emphasized the utility and value of their books in their early advertisements—"each volume is hand bound in limp Croft leather, with stained top, and is stamped and decorated in genuine gold," a list advertisement from 1918 boasts.[50] The advertisement also reminded readers that "People Are Judged by the Books They Read," appealing to the middle-class desire for objects that could indicate status. Eventually, this campaign accomplished its goal, as the possession of a shelf of easily identifiable Modern Library books came to confer upon its owner a modicum of respect as a well-read, cultured person—or so many consumers believed.[51] The Modern Library's effect on the American literary market is hard to determine precisely, but certainly its primary accomplishment was linking literature in the public mind with a physically solid, attractive, affordable, and easily obtained object.[52]

When he signed on with Liveright, one of Pound's responsibilities was to seek out European works the firm should publish. Pound was again fulfilling the role of literary gatekeeper that he had always relished, having performed those duties for *Poetry,* the *Dial,* and the *Egoist.* Again, he would have the power to promote his vision of "our modern experiment." "Pound believed that Horace could become the main publisher of his brand of literary modernism," Liveright's biographer states.[53] Pound—who had, as is well known, first brought Eliot to the world's attention when he got "The Love Song of J. Alfred Prufrock" published in *Poetry*—shepherded Eliot to Liveright when the younger poet was ready to publish *The Waste Land.* Liveright's willingness to publish the poem without reading it, on Pound's recommendation, encouraged Pound even more; his agreement to put the poem out as its own book, although it was far too short to justify independent publication, cemented Pound's faith in him.[54]

Liveright's eagerness to employ modern publicity techniques set him apart from the older American literary publishers. The important patron John Quinn, though, found Liveright's huckstering vile, but Pound simply replied that Liveright was "the best of 'em. He is still young enough to think an author ought to be paid a living wage."[55] "Inclusion in [Liveright's] Modern Library," Quinn wrote James Joyce in 1922, when the

Library had offered to reprint *A Portrait of the Artist as a Young Man,* "is a decadence, a declension into the sunset proclaiming the dark night of literary extinction." Quinn thought Liveright vulgar because he sought publicity for himself as well as for his books, and Quinn generally opposed all of these new publishers for what he saw as their crassness in injecting the basest techniques of the market into the rarefied atmosphere of high art.[56] Even when Liveright wanted simply to contribute funds to help support Eliot after the poet quit his bank job, Quinn was outraged. "[Liveright] is vulgarity personified. He would advertise it all over the place."[57] (For Quinn, advertising was one of the hallmarks of vulgar—and Jewish—commercialism.)[58]

Notwithstanding Quinn's repeated objections to Liveright, Pound never changed his opinion of the publisher. Surprisingly, even when Pound's anti-Semitism was at its worst he never directed vitriol against Liveright: "Liveright was OK a fighting jew if ever was one. Have I ever crabbed Horace?" he asked Laughlin in 1940, when Laughlin was pressuring him to curb his public anti-Semitism (see Chapter 2 for an extended discussion).[59] Liveright, for his part, was generally honest and forthcoming with Pound, telling him that while he respected the poet's intellect and his experimental temperament, he simply would not be able to sell many of his works. In 1928, for instance, when Pound attempted to get Liveright to publish *How To Read,* a precursor of his *ABC of Reading,* Liveright told him plainly that "I don't think we could sell 300 copies of How to Read. What's the use of trying to fool each other? I could write you a long letter explaining why we don't want to publish the book, but you would read between the lines and realize that all of my sweet sounding phrases meant nothing, and that all I was trying to convey was what I started out to say, that the book won't sell."[60] Liveright, hoping to cash in on Pound's fame, had been encouraging him to write a novel instead.[61] Convinced, especially after the Great Depression began, that the only literary books that would sell large numbers (and would thus be worth publishing in inexpensive editions) were novels, Liveright not only refused to issue Pound's literary-critical works but also turned down one of his perpetual desires, an inexpensive anthology of his poems, along the lines of Faber's *Selected Poems* (1928). Where Pound wanted him to issue a lower-priced edition of *Personae,* the collection of his early poetry that the firm had published in 1926 at $3.50, Liveright felt that such a work could never recoup its investment: "We cannot issue a cheap edition of your Collected Poems at this time because there is no prospective market for it. Cheap editions of poetry are not treated the same here as they are in England. This would not be true of a novel or popular biography which inevitably reach cheap editions, but it is true about collected verse."[62]

In addition to convincing Liveright to publish Eliot, Pound also tried (and failed) to cajole him into signing James Joyce for his list. Pound's involvement with Liveright, although it was ultimately disappointing, did give him a glimpse of what it was like to work with a publisher who, unlike Knopf, actually attempted to influence what he wrote for commercial purposes, rather than simply managing his public image through a promotional campaign. Liveright did not, as did Knopf, tout his books' physical attributes as a sales appeal; instead, he intended to make Pound into a writer whose works enjoyed genuine commercial success.

While Pound never had a volume included in the Modern Library series, he was published for a number of years by Boni and Liveright. Beginning in 1920, the firm put out *Instigations* (1920); *Poems 1918–21* (1921); *The Natural Philosophy of Love* (1922), a translation of Remy de Gourmont's *Physique de l'amour; The Call of the Road* (1923), a translation of Edouard Estaunié's *L'Appel de la route; Personae* (1926), Pound's collected poems up to 1921; and *Jefferson and/or Mussolini* (1936), a meditation on political economy and Fascist Italy.[63]

In 1933, after the demise of Boni and Liveright, Pound (on the advice and through the intercession of his agent Anne Watkins) began to issue his books with the new publisher Farrar and Rinehart. John Farrar and Stanley Rinehart had both been with the George Doran firm when it merged with Doubleday in 1927 to make one of the true giants of publishing, but they left Doubleday Doran in 1929.[64] Pound worked with both John Farrar and editor Ogden Nash in publishing his works with Farrar and Rinehart. By the time he began publishing with Farrar, he had begun to concentrate his literary efforts almost exclusively on the *Cantos*. Poetry, though, was not his main concern at this point, and he spent much of his time working on the political and economic topics that informed the artistic creation of the *Cantos*, producing numerous works of political and economic commentary. Farrar, however, was interested only in publishing the *Cantos*, and partly on this impasse their relationship broke apart.[65]

Farrar and Rinehart obtained the contract for the *Cantos* because of the intercession of two very different figures—the eminent modernist poet Archibald MacLeish and the young editor of the North Carolina literary magazine *Contempo*, Milton Abernethy.[66] In 1932, Pound, wanting a genuinely broad sales effort (Liveright was foundering), was unhappy when MacLeish placed his work with Farrar's small firm. MacLeish wrote back to Pound that "You can take some comfort in the fact that you are making the reputation of a publishing house at the same time that you are making whatever small amt of dough a great poet gets while on this ball of whatever."[67] Pound feared that Farrar would not be able to mount the large-scale publicity campaign that he wanted, and soon Farrar, confirming Pound's fears, delayed the publication of *A Draft of XXX Cantos*, and publicized the book minimally when it did appear.

For the ten years of its existence, the Farrar and Rinehart–Pound collaboration produced little to benefit either party. Sales were remarkably low, even considering the conditions of the Great Depression and the poet's own increasingly controversial public persona, and Pound felt that Farrar's almost nonexistent publicity campaigns were at fault. In 1939, for instance, the essentially moribund Liveright Publishing Company sold seventy-nine copies of the thirteen-year-old title *Personae* at $3.50 a copy; by comparison, from July to December 1939 the very much alive Farrar and Rinehart sold eleven copies of *A Draft of XXX Cantos* (1933, at $2.50), no copies of *Eleven New Cantos XXXI–XLI* (1934, at $1.50), and six copies of *The Fifth Decad of Cantos* (1937, at $1.50).[68] What really seems to have frustrated Pound, however, was Farrar's reluctance to publish his economic and political works. In 1932, for instance, after Pound had just signed with Farrar and was eager for them to get on with issuing all his works, Nash asked him to "withhold these miscellaneous items until after the publication of the Cantos. That, after all, is the important book, and I think that with it we have a chance to widen your market far beyond what it has been. Once that is done it will be easier to get a hearing for the other things."[69]

Unfortunately, Farrar and Rinehart's minimal advertising doomed the firm's marketing of an increasingly difficult author. Sharing with Knopf, Liveright, and Huebsch the idea that literature can and should be effectively marketed to the middle class, Farrar and Rinehart never made a genuine effort to do so when it came to Pound's work. They did make some attempts, issuing the short pamphlet *The Cantos Of Ezra Pound:*

Some Testimonials in 1933, but this did not satisfy the poet, who continued to hound them to issue his other works, specifically his *ABC of Economics*.[70] John Farrar—perhaps wisely—equivocated, in one letter complimenting Pound extravagantly on his accomplishments, talents, and wisdom, but finally begging off, citing "the intricacies and madness of American publishing at the moment" and explaining that "one's first effort through these damn fool years is to keep solvent." "At any rate," he wrote in this same letter, "when are you going to write some more Cantos? That would interest me enormously."[71] Pound, apparently, didn't accept these excuses, and wrote back angrily in late 1934 complaining about the firm's continuing refusal to issue his political works, and lavishly insulting Farrar in the process. After becoming yet another one in a long line of publishers and friends subjected to his condescending and abusive invective, Farrar answered Pound as did most of the poet's offended friends—calmly and rationally, calling attention to Pound's "amazing lack of common sense" and telling him that "when you finally at last found publishers who admired your work, were liberal in their thought, and also had a certain measure, if you will allow me, of commercial soundness . . . [i]t would seem to me pretty silly of you to throw away their friendship."[72]

Pound's dealings with Farrar and Rinehart and other trade literary publishers model the complicated interaction of commerce and literature in the early twentieth century. Knopf, for instance, used the status of literature and the physical qualities of his books as selling points, while Liveright embraced commercialism and, instead of using Pound's prestige to sell his works, attempted to make him produce more commercially viable works; Farrar and Rinehart concluded that selling Pound was a lost cause as a commercial endeavor, and kept him on their list in the hopes that their firm would benefit from whatever prestige he might retain. But in each of these arrangements Pound learned more about what he wanted from a publisher and how he could use marketing and promotion to help his sales. His ultimate goal—to see his works read by vast numbers of Americans and Europeans and the ideas in his works put into practice—remained unattained, and perhaps unattainable, but his experiences with these publishers provided him with a model for what New Directions, a publishing house he would essentially call into being, should be. The publishers themselves—especially the Modern Library and Knopf—created a new way of marketing literary books to Americans, arguing that inexpensive literary books, when branded with a reliable and prestigious name, could confer much of the cultural status of small-press works of avant-garde literature. James Laughlin, who had grown up as a consumer of these very books, did not need Pound to teach him what their publishers had done.

Pound in the Critics' Eyes, 1910–1933

If Pound used the trade publishers to reach the American public in the years before he joined New Directions, he relied on critics and writers to introduce him to that public, to shape public understanding of him as man and poet. In the 1920s, the academy was not the primary venue for literary criticism, as it is today. Academic literary study was still largely dominated by the German tradition of philology, in which scholars embarked on biographical and historical studies of texts rather than evaluating them, and it paid little attention to modern literature of any sort. Experimental literature such as Pound produced was not primarily an academic concern; rather, it was frequently reviewed in large-circulation outlets that could broaden its appeal or could simply develop awareness of major figures, and this made for a potentially large market for the modernist writers. As befit a culture in which the dominant form of media entertainment was print, the most influential evaluators of literature were in mainstream publications such as the book review sections of the major newspapers (especially the *New York Herald Tribune*) and magazines from the wide-circulation *Vanity Fair* and *Saturday Review of Literature* to H. L. Mencken's *Smart Set* to the *Nation* and the *New Republic*, with their more intellectual aspirations. Although he never enjoyed large audiences for his books, these outlets did build public knowledge of Pound and the modernist movement through reviews, through feature articles on the poet himself, and even through his occasional role as a staff member.

Because it was explicitly antibourgeois and also frequently explicitly aestheticist, the movement that would become known as modernism was a test case for contending ideas about the role of literature in society, and a new group of book review periodicals became an arena in which bourgeois anxieties about antibourgeois art were played out. Both the *Saturday Review of Literature,* with its editors William Rose Benét and Henry Seidel Canby, and the Sunday *Books* supplement to the *New York Herald Tribune,* under the editorship of Stuart Pratt Sherman, brought modernist literature—particularly novels—into middle-class living rooms. Like the *New York Times Book Review* today, *Books*, founded in 1924, did not use staff members to write reviews, instead paying important or well-known figures in a book's own subject area (Ford Madox Ford, for instance, wrote on Pound in 1927, when *A Draft of XVI. Cantos* was published in Paris) to do so.[73] The power of celebrity was a commercial tool the trade literary publishers also sought to employ. The influence of *Books* was limited, though, by the *Herald Tribune*'s essentially local readership (although the supplement was distributed nationwide by subscription). The *Saturday Review*, by contrast, was a national operation from the beginning; in addition, although it used many well-known guest contributors, most of its editorial content was provided by its board of Canby, the poet Benét, Christopher Morley, and Amy Loveman.

Books was a conscious attempt to package the avant-garde for the middle classes. Royal Cortissoz, arts editor of the *Herald Tribune*, felt that the avant-garde's self-imposed isolation was ending and that large-circulation publications were beginning to include serious literature, telling Sherman in 1923 that "the Greenwich Village dodge is tottering. The Times, with its huge circulation, goes in for seriousness in its literary department. So does the Herald. So does the Evening Post."[74] *Books*, seeing the success of the new trade literary publishers, wanted to step into the gap created by the dissolution of many of the small-press or little-magazine American outlets for the avant-garde, and to become an influential source of reviews. Through the supplement's success, Sherman helped advance the acceptance of modernist literature. He by no means appreciated all of it, and resisted the most radical experimentation, but he did make clear that he felt that the middle class could come to buy, read, and even like some of these experimental books. Sherman felt that literature could raise the moral character of a people, and wanted his publication to advance this in the United States; according to Joan Rubin, Sherman "based his American canon on a national heritage of moral idealism that combined respect for popular democracy with aspirations to an 'aristocracy of talent.' "[75] He provided the middle class with a reason—objective aesthetic value—to accept seemingly amoral modernist literature. "Sherman's 'middleness' on the merits of modern literature was just what was required to ease a conservative reading public toward unfamiliar genres," Rubin explains.

Although *Books* presented modernism to middle-class consumers in the friendliest possible terms, some modernist authors objected to what they saw as the effects of commercial pressure on what was ostensibly a journal of literature. Sherman himself, over the course of his tenure with *Books*, changed his view of how to evaluate literature, adopting a "cheer leader" approach to the promotion of contemporary writing because, he acknowledged, *Books* was a "publishers' organ" for the large firms, intended to "help them move the season's crop of new books."[76] Characteristically, Pound, who was "Visiting Critic" for *Books* in 1929, complained about this, even while eagerly pursuing the benefits of exposure to the American middle class. "You know perfectly well," he wrote to Irita Van Doren, "that I consider BOOKS like any other American advertising medium, IS engaged in retarding the entrance into America of any and every live thought. . . . You are NOT as stupid as the groveling bugs on some of the other papers, and for that reason you are all the more RESPONSIBLE for the impossibility (wherein most americans live) of keeping in touch with what is BEING thought."[77] Pound felt that an outlet such as *Books* should use its commercial and marketing efforts to promote modernism and improve what he saw as the degraded state of publishing in America.

Pound's hostility to *Books* pales in comparison with his loathing for the *Saturday Review of Literature* and its editor, Henry Seidel Canby. Much like his contemporary Van Wyck Brooks, *Saturday Review* editor Canby sought to strengthen the American literary tradition by emphasizing its organic connections to American society. Unlike Brooks, though, Canby subordinated his politics to his literary outlook, which was "deeply sympathetic" to but at the same time "puzzled and skeptical" about modernist experimentation.[78] Canby explained in his autobiography that although he found modernism interesting, he had decided while editor of the *Literary Review*, the Sunday books supplement to the New York *Evening Post*, that "we would let the vigorous Little Magazine of the day conduct the renaissance. . . . Modernist prophecy we in no way suppressed, but set it in the back of the magazine, and published much prose and verse from abroad as well as at home which in our opinion gave samples of the future."[79] In this capacity Canby had his first encounter with Pound, whom he called one of the "wild men." Pound offered to write a piece for the *Review*, but insisted on reviewing an art show, "and was abusive when not paid twice our rates." His fury at Canby only grew over the years, and by the time

Laughlin arrived on the scene, Canby had become the poet's greatest foe. (See the following chapter for a further discussion of this.)

Canby's cautious feelings about modernism persisted as he started work on his next magazine. The *Saturday Review* was founded in 1924 as an independent publication after the demise of the *Literary Review*. During the 1920s and 1930s, the *Saturday Review* promoted contemporary literature to a largely middle-class audience, but it also—at least in its attitude toward Pound—brought a bourgeois political sensibility and a knee-jerk Americanism to its evaluation of literature. By virtue of their friendly, comfortable appearance as mainstream periodicals and their rejection of the little-magazine model for literary journalism, *Books* and the *Saturday Review* deradicalized the avant-garde, stripping the literature of its revolutionary aura but providing its authors with the potential for much wider influence.

Although he appeared sporadically as a contributor to the mainstream review magazines, and although his books were occasionally reviewed by them, Pound had very little presence in American intellectual life in the 1920s and 1930s. He represented little, in the public mind, beyond the spirit of the "new writing" that he helped bring into existence from 1908 to 1920. When he left Paris for Italy in 1924, he also left behind the mainstream of European literary life. Although his work appeared occasionally in his home country, Pound published the great majority of his work abroad, in small English magazines such as the *New Age* and *Athenaeum* (often under the pseudonym "William Atheling"), as well as in the Parisian *Exile* and the Paris edition of the *Chicago Tribune*. But even among the community of American literary critics and booksellers, polls conducted during the 1920s rarely showed him with much of a reputation. A 1922 poll in *Vanity Fair* asked ten critics to rank authors on a scale of +25 to −25; Pound scored a +4.1. In a poll of 1921 in which booksellers were asked to look beyond mere salability and judge authors on greatness, Pound failed even to rank, while only Edith Wharton, of the top five, is still much read. In Amy Lowell's widely circulated works of criticism and anthology—*Tendencies in Modern American Poetry* (1917) and *A Critical Fable* (1922)—she pointedly omitted the names of Pound and Eliot from her lists of the most important American writers, placing them instead under the category of "odds and ends." Of course, Lowell's personal rivalry with Pound could account for this. In other works—or at least in the post-1922 ones, after *The Waste Land* was published—Eliot fared a bit better than Pound, but modernist literature remained marginal until the intellectual and academic communities adopted it in the 1940s.

In the 1910s and 1920s, in order to get his works published in America, Pound was forced to reach beyond the world of the small presses and the little magazines to the world of trade publishing. But he did not reap the benefits of the new literary publishers in the way that many modernist writers did. None of his *Cantos* appeared in book form in America until 1933, and he did not have a lasting, productive association with any of the new trade literary publishers—he broke off relations with Knopf before that publisher truly hit stride, his most important work with Liveright (*Personae*) came out when that publisher was gradually sinking into bankruptcy, and his relationship with Farrar and Rinehart was mutually unsatisfying. During this period, Pound also experienced the negative effects commercial pressure can have on writers; Knopf, Liveright, and Farrar and Rinehart all declined to publish particular works, or refused to publicize his works to his satisfaction, either because they were controversial or simply because they had limited sales prospects. Nor were Pound's works suitable for the mainstream review magazines; they were too experimental, too harsh, too unyielding to public taste.

Pound's experiences, though, made him realize what he wanted from a publisher and taught him important lessons about promotion. Knopf's and Liveright's use of branding, snob appeal, and testimonials in the marketing of their books showed him that these ostensibly vulgar activities could be in the service of literature. As a consequence, he would encourage Laughlin to employ just such techniques after New Directions began publishing his books. Similarly, his involvement with the review magazines taught him the central importance of reviews in promotion, and impressed on him the need for someone who explains the significance of a work to the larger public. (Pound would both resist and embrace such agents throughout his career, resenting it when his publishers encouraged him to use one but eagerly stepping into that role himself for other authors he considered underappreciated.) The publishers and reviewers of this early part of Pound's career, therefore, set the stage upon which Laughlin would soon make his appearance.

CHAPTER TWO

Fighting the "Enemy": The Birth of New Directions

I am merely trying to hit an effective balance—I do as much as I possibly can for your honor's books without getting in a jam by going whole hog for your honor's programs. . . . I think I can do a certain amount of public service by sticking to literchoor and that is my intention.

—James Laughlin to Ezra Pound, 26 November 1939

IF James Laughlin IV would go on to play a central part in the general acceptance of modernism and in the remaking of Ezra Pound, the Jones and Laughlin steel company had already been an important player in America's industrial development. Laughlin's great-grandfather James B. Laughlin, a Scots-Irish immigrant and banker originally from County Down, Ireland, had helped to start an iron business on the right bank of the Monongahela River in Pittsburgh in 1855. Laughlin's Eliza Furnace made pig iron, which was shipped by boat and, eventually, by rail on the "Hot Metal Bridge" across the Monongahela to Benjamin Franklin Jones's mill, where it was refined in the "puddling" process and prepared for shipping. American Iron Works—Jones's company—and Laughlin and Company (loosely unified in the nineteenth century under the former name) produced iron for the rapidly expanding American railroads and then, in 1860, for the Union army.

American Iron Works (later American Iron and Steel Works) remained a family owned company through the nineteenth century, with James B. Laughlin's four sons (including James Jr., the publisher's grandfather) all joining the board of directors. The company was in the midst of many of the violent labor disputes that characterized this period (although it was the Carnegie Steel plant under the leadership of Henry Clay Frick that experienced the Homestead Strike in 1892), and benefited from the weakening of the steelworkers' unions that followed Homestead. Also in the late 1800s, B. F. Jones, following the lead of Andrew Carnegie, had moved into large-scale production of steel using the new Bessemer converter process. The two firms—American Iron and Steel Works and Laughlin and Company—officially merged into one privately held company in 1900 (James Laughlin Jr. served as a financial manager). Responding to the greater demand for steel from the railroad and construction industries, the business was producing a million tons each of pig iron and steel annually by 1905. In response to its need to expand, Jones and Laughlin built a factory town—Woodlawn, now part of Aliquippa, Pennsylvania—twenty miles down the Ohio from Pittsburgh, which was incorporated in 1909. The Aliquippa plant eventually matched the Pittsburgh plant in output, and James Jr.'s son Henry, the publisher's father, supervised electrification there.[1]

While Jones and Laughlin thrived, the company's board of directors increasingly looked to professionally trained managers to run the company, and succeeding generations of Laughlins and Joneses stopped feeling the need to work in the family business. Few of James Laughlin IV's generation joined the company, and Laughlin himself did not stay long in Pittsburgh (he was sent to boarding school). The Laughlins, though, remained part of the Scots-Irish, Presbyterian ruling stratum of Pittsburgh society, and the publisher reminisced that he was related by blood or marriage to twenty-seven families in one small stretch of Woodland Road in Pittsburgh's Squirrel Hill district (now a funky, predominantly Jewish neighborhood, but at the time one of the most *haute-bourgeois* quarters of the city). Laughlin had resolved early on that he did not want to work in steel. His father had preceded him in this sentiment, working only until his own father died in 1922, at which point he took his four-million-dollar inheritance, and in the words of his son "quit and devoted the rest of his life to golf, fishing, and shooting birds of various types."[2] Henry Laughlin, though, had wanted his sons to know where their money and privilege came from, and the publisher spoke about this in a 1986 interview: "Every Thanksgiving my father would take my brother and me down to the mill. . . . It was like the *Inferno*. . . . In those days they hadn't automated the mills, and there was this terrible flame leaping out of the furnaces and hot, molten ingots rolling out of them and then going on to the rollers to be thinned. There were terribly frightening giant cranes moving overhead carrying huge buckets of molten metal. . . . [I]t was terrifying."[3]

Laughlin also bore some guilt about his family's role in the brutal history of the steel industry. In 1992, he reflected on how this determined his future course:

I have a strong family concept of how we have to make up for being in the steel wars. I wanted to show that there was something more left in the family—that something was being carried on in a strong, constructive way. A great-aunt of mine married Henry Clay Frick, who broke up the Homestead Strike. He brought in Pinkerton guards. He was a nasty man. They were all rough customers, and the steel business was the conjury of these successful, rather ruthless men who made up the powerful families of Pittsburgh. They all knew that God wanted them to make money, and that making money was a virtue. . . . I wanted New Directions to go a little way to redeem the family in their dullness and sordidness, in their search for money.[4]

James Laughlin himself was brought up in the world of East Coast money—boarding school in Switzerland and at Choate, college at Harvard—but, he said, always felt out of place there. Harvard was "extremely stuffy," he felt, and in the boarding-school social hierarchy new industrial money was déclassé.[5] He had a sense of humor about his origins, though: in a 1935 letter in which he asked Pound for some free copies of his books, he joked, "Please forgive my tactlessness in going in for these matters when I ought to be writing about the 'ineffable translucency' of your metric, or something like that, but hell, you know, I was born in PITTS-BURGH, Pa.'[6] Although his upbringing had equipped him poorly for a literary career (his childhood house had "nothing but sets and the Bible, and the sets were never read," he said in 1986), Laughlin had been deeply influenced by two literary-minded Choate teachers, Carey Briggs and Dudley Fitts, and in his teenage years he began to think about devoting himself to the literary life.[7] At Harvard, Laughlin was similarly inspired by such teachers as Theodore Spencer F. O. Matthiessen, and Theodore Morrison (later one of the founders of the Bread Loaf writers' conference).

Fitts did not just preach literature, either: he knew many of the important writers of the day, and he was happy to provide introductions to his students. Because of this, Laughlin's European vacation in the summer of 1933 was a dream trip for a fledgling writer. His first stop was with Gertrude Stein. While with Stein, Laughlin wrote press releases for her upcoming U.S. lecture tour, and then changed tires for Stein and Alice B. Toklas as they drove through southern France. Tiring of this, he decided to visit Ezra Pound, whose writing he had always admired. Armed with an introduction from Fitts, Laughlin wrote to Rapallo from Gauting, Germany, on 21 August:

> Dear Ezra Pound—
> Could you and would you care to see me in Rapallo between August 27–31? I am American, now at Harvard, said to be clever. . . . I want 1) Advice about bombarding shits like [Henry Seidel] Canby & Co; 2) sufficient elucidation of certain basic phases of the CANTOS to be able to preach them intelligently; 3) to know why Zukofsky has your support. . . .
> I am in a position (editor Harvard Advocate and Harkness Hoot) to reach the few men in the two universities who are worth bothering about, and could do a better job of it with your help.[8]

"Visibility high," the poet replied, and Laughlin eagerly took the next third-class train to Italy. A visit to the notoriously bohemian and experimental Ezra Pound capped Laughlin's first sojourn in the world of expatriate American writers and artists. Taking temporary leave from Harvard, he returned the next year for an extended stay. In Rapallo Laughlin found

> that it was possible to enroll without any tuition fees whatever, in what was known as the Ezuversity. This meant that you could have lunch with Ezra—you paid for your own lunch, but things were very inexpensive then in Italy. You could spend the afternoon with Ezra, either taking walks, or playing tennis with him, or going rowing with him when it came to be summer. Then you could have tea with Ezra and Mrs. Pound, and you could even have dinner. . . . All the while that this was going on there was this continuous monologue of information on every conceivable subject coming out of Ezra, and this is what constituted the Ezuversity.[9]

Laughlin adored Pound immediately, calling him "this marvelous, dynamic eccentric, a most hospitable man, a born teacher, a person who loved to talk to young people, carrying on fantastic pedagogical monologues."[10] Of course, the poet's polymathic expostulations were not what Laughlin had come for—he had brought a sheaf of poems with him for the master's evaluation. Pound, though, had a low opinion of Laughlin's promise. The young man was too verbose for his taste; he'd "had too much Harvard."[11] Writing after Laughlin had departed, Pound concluded that "it's hopeless. You're never gonna make a writer. . . . do something useful. . . . Go back [to Harvard] and be a publisher."[12]

The offhanded advice Pound offered Laughlin would have a profound effect not only on his own life but on the history of literary modernism in America. Pound, perhaps more than Laughlin, was aware of the good the steel heir's money could do the modernist movement—and of the ultimate good Harvard would do for Laughlin. "I think you better stick in Hawvud a bit longer. I mean, don't leave the country prematurely/ you might have to return later in life. You were ??? 18 ??? last summer. IF there is a U.S. bust up, it might be interesting."[13] And although Pound's evaluation disappointed the young man, he took his advice, and on the strength of a recommendation from the poet signed on with Gorham Munson's Social Credit journal *New Democracy* to write a literary column, which he named "New Directions," and from that post preached Poundian ideas, Social Credit economics, and modernist literature to the magazine's readers.[14]

The initiation of Pound's friendship with Laughlin coincided with the decline of the poet's public reputation and financial fortunes in his home country. From the early 1930s to 1939 Pound wrote numerous political and economic books and articles, mostly aimed at stopping a war that he felt was preventable. By 1933, he was already a crank in the U.S. public eye, and his vitriolic pronouncements on Roosevelt and the New Deal did not endear him to the suffering American public. Although there was certainly an audience for his pro-Mussolini and anti–high finance diatribes, he was simply too intellectual, too European, and too strange to appeal to the mainstream. His explanations of the sorry state of world affairs generally took the form of attacks and conspiracy theorizing, and occasionally of anti-Semitic invective; consequently, few readers saw him as the force for peace he felt himself to be, and gradually they ceased paying any attention to him. Publishers were afraid of him, booksellers shunned his works, and Pound seemed to be disintegrating personally, his writing growing ever more angry, convoluted, and abrasive.

Pound's desires were simple: he wanted to get his political and economic ideas out, and get them out to influential people. But he was not having an easy time doing either. The volatile political situation and the depressed economic conditions of the mid-1930s made publishers leery of backing controversial projects, and Pound's quasi-revolutionary books were very controversial. In England, the small publisher and Social Credit sympathizer Stanley Nott issued Pound's nonliterary works, while Faber and Faber published his poetry, but in America his only outlet was Farrar and Rinehart, who remained utterly uninterested in political and economic writing such as *ABC of Economics*. "The god damn bastards have wasted a year and a half NOT printing ABC////. 10 months NOT printing Jeff/Muss Three years NOT getting an Americ/edtn / How To Read," Pound wrote Laughlin late that same year.[15] Another work that Farrar continued to reject was *Jefferson and/or Mussolini, Fascism as I Have Seen It*. "What I most want is for Houghton . . . to publ the Jefferson and/or Mussolini," he wrote Laughlin on 23 January 1934, when Laughlin had mentioned that his cousin Henry headed Houghton Mifflin's Riverside Press.[16]

Characteristically, Pound insisted that *Jefferson and/or Mussolini* (which was finally published by Liveright in 1936) be circulated among influential readers and opinion makers. In retrospect, Laughlin said that Pound was "quite content if something he had written and given to an obscure magazine reached the eyes and beans of twenty-seven readers, if they were the right readers," but one of these intended readers demonstrates just how far Pound had diverged from the very mainstream of American popular opinion he wished to influence.[17] Hoping for a radio mention of his book to boost sales, Pound demanded that T. R. Smith, his editor at Liveright, send a copy of *Jefferson and/or Mussolini* to the Reverend Charles Coughlin, the anti-Semitic priest and radio broadcaster:

> I want you to GIT a cawpy of my Jeff/Muss to the Rev? Chas. E. Coughlin. . . .
> You can say I greatly admire his January speeches. I dont care WHAT

you do/ you can even charge to copy to me, BUT as purb/ you orter
reCOGnize that IF the Rev/ C/ shd/ MENTION it in a discourse it wd/ be
bigger publicity than any peevish reviewer.
I cant *ask* Coughlin to mention it. But I don't see why you shouldn't.[18]

Pound was convinced that Coughlin would find his work indispensable,
and that his economic theories would be taken up by the broad American
populace (whose innate wisdom he often praised), and told Smith that

> I have always known my stuff wd/ REACH the people IF it cd. ever be
> got past . . . the beastly pseudo/Hig/browz.
> IF the J/M/ cd. really get going you could take on the rest of my econ/
> specially the new Money book. There is no harm in telling Coughlin
> that ONCE you got me going you WOULD go on publishing the "new
> economics."
> There is NO difference between my Jefferson and Coughlin's Jackson.
> And the more of his five million who read me, the more seereeyus his
> pubk/ becomes.[19]

In Pound's eyes, the main obstacle to his ideas' acceptance as respect-
able and to his writing's success was the conservative literary and political
culture in the United States. The American public was possessed of good
sense, he was convinced; the problem was that its cultural leaders conspired to prevent original ideas (such as his) from entering the mainstream. For Pound, *Saturday Review of Literature* editor Henry Seidel
Canby was the head of the American literary establishment. Canby did
indeed wield a great deal of influence over how the American public
viewed literature. Although the *Saturday Review* published a very laudatory retrospective on Pound when *A Draft of XXX Cantos* appeared in
1933, Canby and his audience were suspicious of his attempts to bring
extremist political theories into literature. Pound took frequent potshots
at the *Saturday Review,* as well as at the young *New Republic* and the
established *Nation,* both of which magazines appealed to the same moderately intellectual, middlebrow audience that Pound excoriated yet
craved. In conversation Pound told Laughlin that his "obligation to society" was "assassinating Henry Seidel Canby," and in a 1935 letter he
fantasized about an editorial cartoon depicting "that foetid Canby, fat,

bald bespectacled in pram . . . sucking large bottle of 'Same Old Dope' British Liberal Weeklies."[20] Although this is typical Poundian hyperbole, he did have a genuine gripe against the safe, conservative type of literature the *Saturday Review* promoted. "I think [Eliot] cd do good, by a manifesto against current american fahrting/ as per Canby," he wrote Laughlin on New Year's Day 1934.

For Laughlin, who was immersed in the mainstream literary culture of Harvard and Boston and Kirstein's *Hound and Horn*, prospects for experimental literature were even worse:

> It is utterly hopeless to dream that literature will ever be taught, because the homes from which collegians come are so hopelessly wallowing in library sets, the book clubs, and Palgrave's Golden Arsehole. . . .
>
> The only thing that can be done, is to try to sneak into each college & prep-school one instructor capable of saving the few minds that may have a chance. . . .[21]

Laughlin here identifies both the persistence of outmoded poetry (Palgrave's *Golden Treasury*) and the growing influence of commerce on literature (epitomized by the book clubs) as the culprits. He, too, resented the conservative influence of the *Saturday Review* editors, writing Pound in January 1934 that "I got in a good wallop at Canby & Phelps in the issue [of the *Harvard Advocate*] now on the press. I said, in the conclusion of an article on Little Mags, just exactly what sort of pustular and beshitted criminals they are."[22] The American public, Laughlin felt, simply had no interest in good poetry. "Poetry don't sell over here no matter how good it is," he told Pound in 1934, "unless its that Jeffers Robinson Millay Frost Masefield Sandburg stuff. & MacLeish sells about 1000 copies usually. Cous. Henry [Laughlin, who headed Houghton Mifflin's Riverside Press] says 250 is average sale on poetry book."[23]

Because readers had lost interest in Pound and his writing, Laughlin needed to convince them of his relevance. In the 1930s, Pound was increasingly seen as a spent force, an aging revolutionary of the pre–Great War period, and he was remembered as such by his early compatriots. A typical example of the memorializing of the "old" Pound is Iris Barry's "The Ezra Pound Period," appearing in the *Bookman* in 1931.[24] Reflecting on his importance to an earlier generation of writers, Barry observes wist-

fully that now, "he pontificates rarely, has few disciples, as though with
that immense effort of his from 1912 to 1919 he had done all that (had in
truth done more than) could be expected of anyone and were glad of the
years from thirty-five onwards to till his own plot."[25] Although Pound was
pontificating as much as ever, his exhortative activities were decidedly
nonliterary in the early 1930s, a period in which his fascination with economics and with the Fascist solution to economic problems consumed
him. The lack of public awareness in America of Pound's frenetic activities
is almost certainly the fault of his publishers of the time—Farrar and
Rinehart and Liveright—who declined to issue or publicize his nonliterary works.

Laughlin used his influence to reacquaint young, well-educated readers
with Pound, throwing himself into the project of reminding his peers of
the importance of Pound's poetry and ideas from his posts on the editorial
boards of the *Harvard Advocate* and *Harkness Hoot* (the last of which, he
assured Pound, "reaches a few young men who have a chance to *do* something"[26]). When the *Active Anthology,* Pound's "attempt[. . .] to show by
excerpt what had occurred during the last quarter of a century," was
published by Faber in 1933, Laughlin eagerly wrote that "I plan for the
first number [of the *Harvard Advocate,* to whose editorial board he had
just been elected]:. . . . proper praise of ACTIVE ANTH. when it comes."[27]
Similarly, in 1933 Laughlin imported a number of copies of Pound's *ABC
of Economics,* and wrote that "I am circulating the *ABC of Ec.* privately
among my reasonably intell. confreres. It goes better than I had hoped."[28]
He even volunteered the *Harvard Advocate* as a forum in which to publish Pound's *Jefferson and/or Mussolini,* telling Pound that "if you can't get
it going anywhere, ADVOCATE cld. run it serially to get it out while still
hot. We have, after all, a circulation of nearly 2000 in the most cultured
(they say) community in USHIT . . . Further," he continued, "I have gotten
the new york bookstores to handle HOOT & ADVOCATE which carry stuff
by you."[29]

In addition to working through the student-aimed periodicals, Laughlin also wanted to make headway with the book-publishing industry. In
1933, he had told Pound that "I am going to try to interest Houghton
Mifflin in HOW TO READ. My cousin Henry is boss of their Riverside Press
and sits at the director's board." Pound's response, though, is characteristic: "God DAMN an GODDAMMMMMMM!!!! Houghton Snifflij . . . are the

bastuds that have printed all the safe and tranquil poems of H.D. Get cousin Henry to poison the stinking lot."[30]

This didn't mean that he rejected the suggestion, of course; Houghton Mifflin would be useful in disseminating his economic ideas, as he told Laughlin: "the use of Hottin Pufflin. WOULD BE to have 'em bring out the ABC of econ at once/ AT ONCE."[31] He also considered letting Houghton Mifflin publish the upcoming *Cantos* installments: "the piffling Mifflings or any other damn bastids/ that say outright they will PUBLISH the XXXI/ XLI can have it, if Farrar ain't found his manhood by Jan. 15."[32] (Laughlin continued to try to persuade his cousin to help Pound, and in 1939 pitched a "Founders of Democracy" series for Houghton Mifflin—a volume of which, presumably, would be authored by the poet.[33])

Pound even encouraged Laughlin to act, in a very legal sense, as his agent (Pound's actual agent was the well-established New York literary agency Ann Watkins, Inc., but he often violated the spirit of that agreement by having friends and acquaintances shop his books around), and told Laughlin in 1934 that "If Douglas Howell (also an ass/piring agent) hasn't clicked the Jeff/Muss with mr goldbergerstein/ or somewhere, you can/ I don't care a god damn where/ but the sooner the quicker/ In fak you can do EXACTLY as you deem best. . . . Your judgment ON THE SPOT is damn sight better than mine from here. Macleish is trying that and this, and he DID GET the XXX printed [by Farrar and Rinehart]."[34] Later, Pound proposed that they make the arrangement formal: "Say you try to look after such of my affairs as don't go thru Hann Watkins," he wrote Laughlin in 1936, and confirmed their agreement in 1940, when Watkins severed ties with him.[35]

At the same time, Laughlin was making his first forays into publishing on his own. His efforts date from late 1933, when, while Pound was preparing his 1934 volume *Eleven New Cantos XXXI–XLI* (titled in England *A Draft of Cantos XXXI–XLI*), Laughlin expressed an interest in buying one of those cantos for publication in the *Harvard Advocate* and, later, for a fine-press edition from Boston printer Florence Codman. "I want Canto 38 in print for people like that," Pound urged Laughlin, referring to Laughlin's young Harvard contemporaries, who, he suspected, were voraciously consuming Social Credit theories, and Laughlin eagerly jumped on the opportunity:

I, together with a lady publisher who can be trusted, want to buy one (or some) of the new ones I saw. That is if we can afford it. I haven't much money; she has some. But I doubt, thanks to American publishing stupidities, if your work fetches one fifth of its real value. . . .

. . . The plan would be to run them first in the ADVOCATE and then to publish them in good type and format on her fancy press (Arrow Editions). Of course, one would have to be sure that the rights were quite clear, i.e. that Fabre [*sic*] or Farrar had no claim on them.[36]

Codman's canto would be aimed not at a student market but at collectors, the type of readers and purchasers who had supported the modernist writers in the 1910s and 1920s. Laughlin envisioned the book this way:

An edition of 600 size 6 by 9 or 5 by 7 on fancy paper, handset by a *very* good typographer at the Rydal Press, bound in stiff paper. She would sell at 75 cents, make no profit, giving you $50, or at a dollar and, with good sales, be able to make something. My idea would be this, hoping to make you some money and get myself some experience. To whack out another 400 on very good watermarked paper, different from hers, have a different title page and a "justification" and your signature at end. These to be bound in cloth with a silver stamp of that swell head of you which Gaudier made. I don't know what all of this would cost, but with the type already set, it shldn't be too much. These could be sold around $3.50–5 I should hope, and there might be some decent money for you.[37]

Pound was eager for the money from this project (the *Advocate* paid him $25 for Canto 38) and envisioned it as an ongoing arrangement: "What cd/ the Advocate plus Miss C/ with her fawncy press offer for separate cantos, one atter time?"[38] The canto was never published, though, because Pound, Laughlin, and Codman could not agree on fees to be paid to Pound. Laughlin also pursued, unsuccessfully, publication of a number of other Pound works apart from the *Cantos*. He proposed printing the *Active Anthology* in a student edition and selling it at the money-losing price of fifty cents "for the cause of literary cleanliness," but that project also never came to fruition.[39]

Neither Pound nor Laughlin, though, were interested in moving Pound exclusively backward in this way—returning him to the small-scale, collector-based market that had supported him in his London and Paris years. Both the poet and the young publisher-to-be wanted Pound to be a presence in the trade market; the impediment here, though, was Pound's publisher, John Farrar. The poet's impatience with Farrar's slow pace and lackluster promotion of the *Cantos* made him willing to consider violating the spirit or even the letter of his agreements with the "god damn bastards" Farrar and Rinehart, and he wrote Laughlin in December 1933 that

> If you can bung those [Cantos 30–34 and 38] QUICK without bitching the arrangements IF any with Farrar, I'll accept the lady's 50 bucks, down, and decent cut of the profits if and when any. But this cd/ only be for a few hundred copies de luxe. a cheap edition of more than TWO cantos, wd/ bitch the Farrar edition of TEN.[40]

"Farrar has spent all 1933 NOT printing a second vol. of E.P. while Faber were doing FOUR vols/// so I don't feel particularly obliged to WAIT forever on Johnnie's fair and ambulating pleasure," he wrote Laughlin later that month.[41]

By 1936, Laughlin was beginning to realize that Pound's concentration on political matters and his bombastic, insulting economic commentary were damaging not only his image but the reputation of his poetry. From this time on—not coincidentally, the same year that he began publishing his *New Directions* anthologies—he started to encourage Pound to be more circumspect about his pronouncements, to make a division between the poetry and the politics, and to pay some attention to how the public perceived him. Pound resisted these efforts. When Faber wanted to issue an anthology of his literary essays, he insisted that they instead compile a collection of nonliterary works selected by him: "Faber bumblin about my nexx bk/ ov licherary Essays/I.E. they NOT wanting what I am interested in/ I HAD a real book planned, but it contained Jeff/Muss Chinese Writ/ Character and Ta Hio. . . . Have I ever written anything ELSE worth reprintin' [?]"[42] Realizing that the absence of inflammatory political writing didn't hurt Pound's reputation one bit, though, Laughlin found Faber's final product (entitled *Polite Essay*) was actually quite good: "The olde Eliotic serpent has done a damn clever job in selectin the Perlite. I didn't suspect it until yessrdy when the prooves come. Seems much easier readin than M[ake].I[t].N[ew]."[43]

Laughlin also "translated" some of Pound's ideas for public consumption. When the *North American Review* agreed in 1936 to run his article on the Jefferson-Adams correspondence, Pound accepted Laughlin's argument that it should be edited so as to cut as much bombast as possible while still retaining his personality—the article "would have to be rewritten by Jas or somebody who knows how to squirt hairoil," he agreed.[44] Pound trusted Laughlin, and had granted him permission "to revise and edit article as you like."[45] "What they wanted was a short, polite, coherent essay," Laughlin reported back to Pound after the editors accepted the article, "and that is what I made for 'em out of your manuscript."

> What I did you see, was to cut your ms. about in half, weed out all peripheral reference which would "disturb" their readers, explain who the hell Frobenius was, put in transitions where you "jumped," explain what you meant when you were too deep or poetic, etc. . . . If I were you, I would suggest that you do next a very peaceful article on Van Buren, as the forgotten president.[46]

Laughlin also pestered the *Review* to run the piece quickly and to pay Pound up front: "I think you should send him something right now," he urged them in late 1937. "He always lives from hand to mouth and I understand at this moment it is mostly mouth, I mean, the mouth is pretty empty."[47] (At this, the *Review* sent Pound a $50 advance on the $175 fee for the article.)

With his usual exuberance, Pound had seen the *North American Review*'s interest in his article as an indication that American readers were hungry for his insights.[48] A flurry of letters to Laughlin, in which Pound made plans for himself and Laughlin to embark on a campaign to convince citizens that the New Deal (or "nude eel," as he called it) was criminal, followed their exchange about the article. Laughlin dissuaded him, arguing that Pound should just "hold your peace and try to get some cash out of him [John Pell, the editor]. That's all he's good for." Again,

Laughlin had to reel Pound back into reality: "You see Boss, America is not like what you think it is. There is nobody here who is interested in taking life as seriously as you do. . . . Everybody is having fun with the [1936 presidential] campaign and nobody gives a damn about serious questions."[49] The previous year, when Pound had suggested that "mebbe I ought to do a lexchoor tewer.??? fer noo econ??" Laughlin advised him against such a foray: "About a spring ramble. Boss, nobody over here would pay you to talk on ec, because there are twenty dozen guys six times as crazy as you talking on the same subject." Returning to a theme that would soon become a constant refrain, Laughlin added that "of course, you could always lecture on poetry."[50] In another letter a month later, Laughlin had to stress the same point to Pound: "I don't advise your trying to come here without some definite contract with an institution or lecture outfit, unless you plan a trip purely for pleasure and edification."[51] Laughlin won out; Pound stayed in Italy, at least until 1939.

By 1936, Laughlin was moving closer to becoming a publisher. Coming up with an idea for a name—"New Directions"—from his literary column in *New Democracy,* he started his own annual journal, *New Directions in Prose and Poetry,* because, as he put it, he was fed up with the absolute lack of exposure for the experimental writing he loved. Interviewed in 1980, Laughlin explained that he had the idea for starting his annual because "the publishers, such as Liveright . . . and the Boni brothers, who had been engaged in bringing out avant-garde literature, had nearly gone broke and dropped out of business so there was nothing left. The *Dial* had stopped publication, Margaret Anderson's *Little Review* had stopped publication, Bill Williams' *Contact* and Richard John's *Pagany* had stopped publication. The only important little magazine that was going at that time was Lincoln Kirstein's *Hound & Horn.*"[52] In a later interview, Laughlin also noted how much he had been impressed by Alfred A. Knopf and his firm: "I admired him—the way he kept doing wonderful stuff. . . . He did good books—he didn't do any trash. He was a pro."[53] Laughlin also wanted to use his annual journal to explore the possibility of a trade publishing house, subsidized initially by his family's wealth, that could withstand the pressure to publish only potentially profitable books. He knew the private presses that had initially published so much of the important modernist work—"I was particularly influenced by McAlmon's

Contact Press books and I did also know the books that Sylvia Beach had done," and he was also influenced Harry and Caresse Crosby's Black Sun Press—but, encouraged by Pound, he wanted his books to reach a broader audience than the private presses could reach.[54] But mostly, Laughlin wanted good writing to get out to the widest possible audience because it was, he felt, good for society. "In those days," he reminisced in 1992, "publishing was as much a social contract as a money contract. I came along in the Depression, when publishers were having a hard time. I had a sense of mission—I thought I was saving the world from Bennett Cerf."[55]

In these early years, Laughlin depended heavily on family money. His family, in turn, were torn between wanting him to run his business as a properly profit-oriented capitalist should, and wanting him to give up his hobby and return to Pittsburgh to join the family firm. Even as he immersed himself in the literary world Laughlin was reluctant to leave his upbringing behind entirely; in 1938, for instance, he wrote to *Partisan Review*'s Dwight Macdonald that "I certainly would like to talk to you about steel. That is a great subject. When I finish Harvard I hope to go work in our Allequipa [*sic*] plant and get some lowdown for a book on it."[56] But he also felt his family's influence as a "dead hand" over him, pulling him back to the "terrifying" world of factories and mills. Writing to Delmore Schwartz in 1939, he mourned that his family

> wd. love to stamp [New Directions] out; on the other hand, they have the natural affection for their young. I am just sitting tight, trying to compromise—to keep New Directions going and still not alienate them altogether. They cannot disinherit me because my father left money in trust for me, but the hell of it is I don't get it until my mother dies and she is healthy as a horse. Fortunately I have a little of my own— enough to keep going for six or seven years at the present rate. My hope is that by that time they will have woken up to the fact that what I am doing is not a disgrace to the family but a credit to it and will kick through again. As I told you, both Father and Aunt were very generous when I started the thing because they thought it was going to be harmless and polite, I guess. Aunt froze right up as soon as she smelt sex. . . . It takes money to run a press like New Directions and although the

books might conceivably come to pay their way you cannot count on that. The minute I began to count on making money I would drift into printing crap.[57]

The idea that money-making books were mostly "crap" underpinned the philosophy of publishing that Laughlin set forth in the 1936 first issue of *New Directions in Prose and Poetry*. In the "Preface" to *New Directions 1*, he laid out what he saw as the essential conflict between commerce and art. A literary publisher must take a stand on the great debate of content versus form, of formalism versus contextualism, of the social importance of a work versus its aesthetic excellence. Drawing from his own experience on *New Democracy*, Laughlin explained that his section of that magazine

attempt[ed] to collect in its pages all the most technically-advanced prose and poetry of American writers, all the work which exhibited a desire on the part of its author to set out in a new philological direction, collect it *because* it, and the fact that it existed at all, reflected the change in the state of the world mind whose spearhead was the New Economics of Major Douglas.

The emphasis of leadership was then upon the economist rather than the poet.[58]

Laughlin had, in other words, allowed the content of works and the personal importance of writers to determine his judgment of their value; "the economist" had been a more important figure than "the poet."[59]

But in the intervening time, the 1936 essay continued, Laughlin had revised his opinion. "Nearly a year of hard experience in the propagation of Social Credit has led me to feel that the emphasis should be reversed: it is the poet—the "word-worker"—who must lead," he asserted. He had not changed his mind about the viability of Social Credit; rather, the practical difficulty of trying to convince people of the need for a radically different economic system had led him to the conclusion that an even more fundamental transformation of thought must occur—and that poets, through their command of the ineffable aesthetic affect and the almost mystical power of language (especially of what Pound, for one, considered to be the most important aspect of the use of language: exact terminology), were the only ones who could bring about this transformation. "Language controls thought," Laughlin repeats: "The world is in crisis, and language is at once the cause and the cure. New social concepts could stop the waste and the destruction. But they can only be introduced into minds ready to receive them, minds *able* to think along new lines, minds capable of imagination."

In this preface, Laughlin publicly asserted his commitment to literature as an agent of social change, but added that literary evaluation must not be a crude weighing of the social efficacy of a work. Literature works in more subtle and fundamental ways at changing systems of thought; experimental literature is a catalyst for that change.

> Experimental writing has a real social value, apart from any other. . . .
> However my contributors may see themselves I see them as agents of
> social reform as well as artists. Their propaganda is implicit in their
> style and in probably every case (originally, at least) unconscious. . . .
> Their points of departure and immediate objectives are various, but all
> have a similar ultimate aim—the perfection of a clearer, richer, more
> meaningful verbal expression.

"Social reform" (the exact qualities of which are nowhere detailed) brought about through literature is clearly a political idea, but it also resembles the undefined "taste" or "culture" the new trade literary publishers argue that their books will bestow upon consumers.

The Birth of New Directions

Soon after the first appearance of *New Directions in Prose and Poetry*, Laughlin brought New Directions fully into being by publishing his first book from the firm's Norfolk, Connecticut, office (actually the barn on his property). He wrote Pound that "I am publishing [William Carlos Williams's novel] WHITE MULE in February. It is a swell book as you know, and it does me good to see how happy the Doc is about it."[60] Williams loved the book—"it's a splendid book, excellently presented," he wrote Laughlin.[61] Pound loved it: "White Jackass arruv/ waaaal you ain't lived in vain."[62] The volume also contains a statement of Laughlin's feelings about the proper relationship of commerce to literary publishing. Appended to the end of this first edition of *White Mule* was a postscript entitled "White Mule and New Directions," in which Laughlin wrote that

> *White Mule* has nothing in common with the book business and everything in common with pure books like those of Villon or Flaubert or Radiguet.
>
> It is time I think to damn the book publisher as hard as you can damn them. They're traitors and enemies of the people. They have made literature a business. They have made the writing of books the production of cheap-goods. They have made a book a thing no more valuable than an automobile tire. They have forgotten their social responsibility. They have forgotten that the word is holy. They have made writing, which was an art, a business.
>
> And with that business *White Mule* has nothing in common and neither has New Directions.[63]

The same sentiments dominate the preface to the second issue of *New Directions in Prose and Poetry* (1937). Again here, Laughlin forcefully drew a distinction between literature, which is aimed at changing and bettering the world, and commercial publishing, which robs literature of its special status and turns writing into a commodity. Furthermore, he adopted Pound's apocalyptic tone. "I am angry," he wrote,

> with the big publishers because they are not doing their jobs. . . . In spite of the money which they must be making on their wretched bestsellers they are not doing what they should for the pure writer.
>
> . . . Nothing short of a decent economic order will clean out the editorial pigsties of Fourth and Madison Avenues. What that new order will be is anybody's guess. My own choice is Social Credit. But whatever it finally proves to be, there is no doubt that it is coming—and in the meantime New Directions will do what it can to clean up the mess and keep the ideal of serious artistic writing alive.[64]

As always, Laughlin's greatest disgust was heaped on those who treated literature like just another commodity. "The publishers," he would write two years later in the 1939 *New Directions,* "chucking overboard all sense of their responsibility as arbiters of taste, sprawling flat out for profits, cater to the lowest common denominator. I expect soon they will be binding in cigars and candy with each book."[65]

More of Laughlin's early feelings about the difference between his firm and the commercial publishers, and his hatred for those who handled literature as merchandise, erupted in 1937 when Williams tentatively mentioned that he might want to publish *White Mule*'s sequel with a larger publisher, perhaps Harcourt Brace or Simon and Schuster. (Williams had been very upset when Laughlin left the country on a ski trip just at the time that *White Mule* was enjoying critical success and could have used a publisher's push. For his part, before leaving Laughlin had tried to convince Eliot to import sheets of *White Mule* for publication at Faber, a publisher he clearly did not view in the same light as the "commercial publishers" he reviled.[66]) Responding emotionally to Williams's suggestion, Laughlin poured out all his youthful despair at the idea that Williams could consider such a move:

> You are my symbol of everything that is good in writing, and if you go over to the enemy I just won't know where the hell I'm at.
>
> Because they are the enemy. Look what they've done to our kind. Look what they've done to you yourself. Would they take the *Mule*? . . . You are different from their trade. You are literature and not merchandise.[67]

Laughlin went on to recount the story of Kay Boyle's experiences with Harcourt, pointing out that although her books sold well for the firm, it still would not publish her poetry or her novelette. Signing on with New Directions, Laughlin insisted, was the only way Williams would be able to effect a change in the way American publishers treated writers:

> In New Directions you will be the head man. The thing will build up to you. . . . I know that I need you in order to do anything for the young ones coming on. I can print their books for them. But unless the name New Directions stands for something they'll have a hell of a row to hoe. With you, New Directions does stand for something and the people it prints will get a start and a break. . . . If you stick with me and Ezra perhaps comes in we'll be able to make a machine that can fight the

New York machine. You see it takes more than cash to do it. It takes a *White Mule* and a *Cantos*.

Finally, Laughlin outlined a strategy for publishing Williams in a way that would guarantee long-term success and penetration into American cultural life:

[I will] bring out [*Life Along the Passaic River*] in February, with the two additional stories. Print a thousand more *Mules* now before we chuck the type so that they'll be on hand when needed.

Do the book on your mother next. Then reprint the *American Grain* in a dollar edition. . . . Then have a good book about you, either by one guy or a dozen—a symposium. Then Part II of *White Mule*. Then a volume of essays.

In other words a steady barrage of Williams, that will be backed by articles and reviews and word-of-mouth advertising. Also regular advertising where it is likely to do good. Thus, in the present [*New Directions in Prose and Poetry*] you have a double page spread and we are sending along return cards with it.[68]

Williams was swayed by this, and remained with New Directions for many years, until an acrimonious parting in the 1950s. In their three decades as business associates Laughlin always resisted Williams's desire for more publicity and a more commercial approach to promotion.[69] Daniel Morris explains that "Laughlin could provide the funds to print [Williams's] works but for ideological and personal reasons could not fully accept Williams as an author interested in reaching out to ordinary readers through commercial appeals."[70] Morris also shows how Williams protested Laughlin's efforts to eliminate commercial tactics from his promotional repertoire. "The pressure Williams placed on Laughlin to advertise his work," he continues, "belies the poet's subscription to the public's view that modernism and huckstering were mutually exclusive practices."[71] This was Laughlin's view as well. The next few years, however, would show him that his marquee authors were willing to engage in "huckstering" and eager for him to employ commercial tactics. It was Pound, not Williams, who would finally show Laughlin that in order to give his poets the success he felt that they deserved, and in order to establish a reputation for his own publishing house, he would have to relent on his strongly anticommercial outlook.

Unlike Williams, Pound presented significant political difficulties for New Directions, and after founding the house Laughlin began to see that two of his most important goals—faithfully serving Pound's desires in the United States and establishing a publishing house with a chance for long-term viability—might clash. The 1930s saw numerous conflicts between publisher and poet, prompted by differences of opinion over the degree to which Pound was to be a political figure in America. They clashed over the content of potential New Directions magazines, over Pound's 1939 trip to the United States, and over his desire to be a pundit rather than a poet. Increasingly in the 1930s Laughlin began to realize that in order to ensure Pound's lasting success, he must, when acting as his publisher, emphasize creative work over political writings, but—unlike Farrar and Rinehart—must also continue to promote the poet aggressively.

After starting New Directions' book publications with Williams's *White Mule,* Laughlin decided that the next mission was to get many of Pound's earlier books back into print, to present him as a poet rather than as the political thinker he had frequently portrayed himself to be. Offended, even angered, by the lack of vigor that Liveright and Farrar and Rinehart gave to marketing Pound's books, Laughlin resolved that his own house would sell them far more effectively. John Farrar had been paralyzed by the statements emanating from Pound's Rapallo base, and because of his own house's precarious financial position refused to publish the poet's more inflammatory political and economic works of the 1930s. Pound, although he was producing works of poetry and criticism at a furious rate, had slipped into oblivion as a result both of Farrar's reluctance to call attention to his politics (a reluctance Laughlin came to share) and of a growing critical belief that his works were second-rate in comparison to those of writers like Joyce and Eliot.

Laughlin's solution, as it had been with his proposal for the *Active Anthology,* was to put those works into a series of inexpensive books of modern literature aimed at students. He had the same plans for Williams, whom he told in 1938, "I want to start the 'New Classics Series'—dollar books like the Modern Library, of which you and Ezra will be the backbones."[72] In the 1939 *New Directions,* Laughlin wrote that "it will be the aim of this Series to make available to students and readers the best modern books at a low price. The Modern Library does a marvelous job with fiction and we have no intention of encroaching on its territory, but it does tend to neglect modern poetry, criticism, belles lettres and unconventional fiction."[73] As he envisioned it, this New Classics series would have important similarities with one of the most successful publishing ventures of the 1920s, the Modern Library. The influence of the Modern Library on Laughlin's New Directions is evident in both firms' use of inexpensive hardcover bindings, in their attempts to be brand names that stood for good literature (the Modern Library for fiction, New Directions for the contemporary avant-garde), and in both firms' ardent pursuit of the student market. (Ironically, given Laughlin's dismissive statements about publishers who bundle candy together with books, the Modern Library actually began as the Little Leather Library—books that *were* bundled together with candy.) Laughlin's choice of the word *Classics* for his series title, moreover, indicates his desire to give these modern works— many of which were by no means accorded the kind of cultural authority accompanying the term—the aura of quality, timelessness, and authority. Publishing "classics" differentiated his firm from the small publishers specializing in contemporary literature. Laughlin's was to be a house of "enduring literary value," in the words of its first catalog, a firm that published innovative modern works, not limited to the immediately notable.

The authors included in the New Classics series would concomitantly, Laughlin hoped, gain the status of classic authors, and in the 1930s Pound eagerly desired that kind of prestige. He had always hoped to have his books remain consistently in print in the student-aimed collected editions that can give a poet a place in literary history. Although Liveright's *Personae* had accomplished this to a small extent, Pound wanted more. In a 1950s complaint to the English publisher Peter Russell, he recalled that he had "been yelling for cheap books for? 30 years."[74] After World War II, when the New Classics series finally began to appear regularly, Laughlin promised to provide just this opportunity. (Pound, typically, suggested that Laughlin initiate this series with a collection from the classic Chinese author Mencius.[75])

Becoming a classic author, though, was not Pound's most immediate concern. By the late 1930s, his reputation as a fascist had made his works almost impossible to sell. "In most stores they refuse to stock your books," Laughlin wrote him in 1939. "Either they say they won't have them because you are a Fascist, or they say that the youth has lost interest in you and they can't sell them."[76] As booksellers were reluctant to carry the works of this controversial, slow-selling author, producing a cheap edition of Pound's poetry, preferably to be sold by mail order, was imperative. Laughlin put this plan into action by pricing Pound's books (at one dollar) to be irresistible to young readers; he thus built up a market for Pound's writings—and for the fledging New Directions list.

In another effort in his campaign to focus public attention on Pound's poetry rather than on his politics, Laughlin wrote on *Homage to Sextus Propertius* in the October–December 1938 issue of the *Sewanee Review*. The article, which appeared at a time when Pound was quickly becoming notorious—and when his anti-Semitism was growing more vehement and coming out more frequently in his massive correspondence—was in essence a review of a twenty-year-old work, whose transformations of and commentary on its source text were a model for the *Cantos'* use of historical sources.[77] Pound's *Fifth Decad of Cantos* (1937) had just appeared, and many of the reviews expressed boredom or bafflement with the poet's continuing experimentation.[78] Laughlin's defense of the *Homage* struck back, arguing that these reviewers misunderstood the technique they found so tired and uninteresting. Implicitly, of course, Laughlin was defending Pound's most recent work and asserting his continuing relevance.

Notwithstanding his intention to build his company around the works of Pound and Williams, as late as 1939 Laughlin had not yet been able to secure the rights for the *Cantos* from Farrar and Rinehart. During the period 1936–39, therefore, he was looking for other works of Pound's to publish or distribute. The first volume he wanted was the Faber anthology *Polite Essays* (or, as Pound called it, "Polecat Essays"), which he could import, but when he suggested this the poet grumbled about the small amount of money he would receive for the book.

> There is no mony fer me in having sheets embedded. I mean whazzer USE in Nude Erections importing what won't keep papa? . . . I shd/ think Nude Erek/ cd. do something more active than merely sheeting the Polecats?[79]

Laughlin, eager to have Pound's endorsement for his nascent venture, wrote back that "I had hoped you would think of my suggestion not as an oppocasion for yr enriching yr concededly improperly rewarded self but for setting yr stamp of benedixhum of new directions."[80]

When the effort to publish *Polite Essays* foundered (mostly because Laughlin and Pound agreed that the book would not even make its initial investment back), Laughlin began to look to *Personae*, the compilation of Pound's early verse that Boni and Liveright had first published in 1926. Laughlin especially desired *Personae*, a collection containing the poems that had given Pound his early fame (the Imagist and Vorticist works) as well as the more sophisticated *Homage to Sextus Propertius* of 1917 and the well-known *Hugh Selwyn Mauberley* of 1920. The collection showed Pound as a verse experimenter, an aesthete, a poetic rebel, and a polymath, but not as a figure interested in contemporary politics; consequently, it was the ideal volume with which to begin the task of rebuilding his image. Writing to Pound in 1938, Laughlin complained that "Liveright has finally gotten around to putting *Personae* back into print. . . . But the damn trouble is that they are still charging $3.50 for it, which precludes any student sale. No kids have that much dough. I think your worships works ought to be available in a dollar edition . . . and I think when I get my dollar series going we should try to get you away from those turds."[81] While *Personae* never precisely went out of print, the Liveright Publishing Corporation's financial troubles in the 1930s made the volume difficult to find, primarily because of poor distribution to bookstores. Laughlin felt that a reappearance of this work would serve Pound well, deflecting public attention from such controversial works as *Jefferson and/or Mussolini* and focusing it on Pound's early experiments and successes, and he told him so:

> I told Ann Watkins I was wanting [the *Cantos*], but more immediately interested in the possibility of getting those bastards at Liveright to lease me the copyright on the *Personae* for a period of years so that I could bring them out at a dollar. I think this would be the best move at the moment to save your reputation. Your early work is still held in just esteem (they say they can't understand the CANTOS) and I feel that a dollar edition (like we are doing of Bill's GRAIN) would be a good thing.[82]

Pound agreed with Laughlin's strategy, telling him that he was in favor of "editions at a possible price . . . it would make a bargain at a buck." He was also angry at Liveright, who he felt had not treated him fairly by not allowing the *Personae* copyright to revert to him: "They certainly lapsed on the original agreement (by letter with pore old Horace) but got under the line and reprinted a couple of years ago."[83] Laughlin's desires were thwarted by Liveright's refusal to release the contract for the book— Liveright editor Arthur Pell wrote in 1940 that "we are not interested in disposing of Ezra Pound's *Personae*," and the company released a final printing of the book (the sixth) in 1944.[84]

The failure to obtain *Personae* was a setback for Laughlin's restructuring of Pound's image. Saving his reputation necessitated bringing the poet back to the realm of literature, and with his early Pound publications, Laughlin followed precisely that track. *Personae* contained none of Pound's pronouncements on politics or economics. By reprinting this anthology, Laughlin attempted to ensure that he would not be thought of as merely an acolyte of Pound's social and economic ideas. Moreover, to reprint thirty-year-old poems at a time when Pound was preaching *Mussolinismo* and writing for British fascist publications would blunt the effect, in America, of his rantings. Pricing *Personae* at a dollar would not only have brought Pound back in the public eye as a poet, it would have brought him within reach of the student audience whose taste would determine literary reputation in decades to come. The relationship would be symbiotic: New Directions would reconfigure Pound's image, emphasizing the literary over the political, and Pound's presence (along with Williams's) on the New Directions list would give the new firm an air of seriousness and establishment.

The firm's first Pound book, *Culture* (1938), though, did not accomplish this aim. It was an American issue, using imported sheets, of what had already been published in Britain as *Guide to Kulchur*. Laughlin was eager to publicize his firm's association with such a well-known, if controversial, author, and announced his acquisition of *Culture* in a press release given to *Publishers' Weekly* four months before he published the book.[85] Significantly, though, at this early stage in their relationship Laughlin was already shaping Pound to make him more palatable to American audiences, and changed the book's title to rid it of any possible German or Nazi resonances. "When we first brought out this book," Laughlin wrote later, "we were timid about using the spelling 'Kulchur' and settled for 'Culture.' Emboldened as time went by, and with Ezra now more famous, we reissued it with its present title."[86] New Directions seems to have had difficulty convincing retailers to ignore Pound's ugly public image, but in the end was successful, or so Laughlin wrote to Pound in October 1938: "Everything going fine with KULCH. The book will appear Nov. 10. We have gotten almost all the stores to stock it. . . . A few hate your guts as a Fascist (they say). But most are stocking a copy or more."[87] In January 1939, Laughlin reported to Pound that "320 out of 500" copies of *Culture* had sold: "There was a very heavy demand from outoftheway places for review copies of the KULCH, but recalling your instructions on the subject we sent very few out—perhaps 40 in all. Had the edition been much larger we would have filled all requests. But AS YET there have been no reviews in print at all, so I think we were right. My guess is that all the reviewers are so scared."[88]

Although the book sold a fair number of copies (at least for a Pound title at this time), reviews were "antagonistic," as Laughlin told Eliot.[89] While *Culture* did nothing against the accusation that Pound was an almost incomprehensible crackpot, though, it did divert attention from his politics. It contained some references to Mussolini, but here Pound's bombast, obscurity, and low public standing benefited him—the book sold only 431 copies by mid-1939 (earning him royalties of $95.67), and few readers took enough note of the book to remark on Pound's growing public affiliation with Italian Fascism. William's review in the *New Republic* followed Laughlin's lead and tried to separate politics from cultural accomplishments, but concluded that Pound had taken the gamble of "making a bloody fool of himself" and lost.[90]

Pound, however, wanted something more than just a sympathetic American publisher for his books. With the decline of such Social Credit magazines as *New Democracy*, he was having a difficult time getting his ideas heard in America, and was looking for a periodical similar to *Action*, the weekly magazine of Sir Oswald Mosley's British Union of Fascists, to which he contributed almost weekly articles during 1938. By that year, Pound had begun hinting to Laughlin about allowing him some editorial input on the annual *New Directions in Prose and Poetry* anthologies. Laughlin had always known that Pound felt entitled to a degree of control over New Directions, that he saw it as "a kind of puppet publishing house for him."[91] But Laughlin also knew that he could not allow New Directions to become a political publisher, even though he was (and remained) a Social Credit advocate. Politely and diplomatically, he steered Pound away from the idea that he might be given editorial rein. Instead, he proposed the "Founding Fathers" collection, an inexpensive series of tracts that would bring to a student audience the works of Adams, Jefferson, and others Pound found particularly important. Pound naturally thought that he would write the introductions to the material—in fact, before the books even went into production he contacted the Italian education ministry about New Directions providing these Founding Fathers books ("plus a few Italian statists") to Italian public schools.[92] Clearly, he saw the pamphlets as a vehicle for his interpretations of their contents, felt that the schools of Mussolini's Italy would welcome his ideas, and viewed New Directions as the kind of firm that would welcome such a lucrative opportunity.

Laughlin, however had come to want to keep politics as far away from New Directions as possible. He was willing—even eager—to cultivate authors with well-known political leanings, but was utterly opposed to New Directions being identified as a "political" publisher—especially one aligned with fascists. When Pound requested that Geoffrey Stone, a fascist-leaning American literary critic, be contacted to write a book for New Directions, Laughlin replied unequivocally: "Wouldn't dare be caught with a fascist. It'd sink the ship. Similarly, it would be fatal to the Founding Fathers to let the books be in any way tainted. Have to be very careful or you'll queer 'em. Too good an idea to spoil."[93] Pound accepted this refusal genially, understanding Laughlin's reluctance to jeopardize commercial prospects. Besides, he felt that he still had influence over the proposed Founding Fathers series, and had already volunteered to choose the texts to be included.[94]

Although he did believe in the Social Credit ideas Pound championed, Laughlin was opposed to the way the poet aligned Social Credit with fascism. "I'm all for his monetary principles," he wrote to Delmore Schwartz in 1939, "but when he became a Franco and Hitler man, I found the going thick."[95] Laughlin had sent Schwartz one of his own poems, entitled "A Letter to Hitler," a short work about the futility of book burning. Schwartz liked the poem, and in reply Laughlin wrote that "I would like very much to have that poem appear in PR [*Partisan Review*]. My connection with Pound always lays me open to attacks of being a Fascist and that is not very pleasant. The poem might help to clarify my present position. I don't make political statements in *New Directions* because I want that to be strictly non-political."[96]

Schwartz's influence at *Partisan Review* was great, and Laughlin knew that associating his name with such a leftist magazine would balance the political tilt of the right-wing writing and public persona of Pound. He had made his nonpolitical agenda for New Directions clear from the beginning, in fact. In a 1937 exchange of letters regarding mutual advertising, *Partisan Review* editor Philip Rahv wrote Laughlin that the "New Masses boys" were tarring his magazine as "camouflaged Trotskyists" when "while we don't think that Trotskyism is criminal, we at the same time hold it to be quite extraneous to the literary intentions of the magazine. The campaign against us is nothing else but an attempt to frighten people away from any independent literary program." Laughlin commiserated: "yes, this political criticism is a stinking business. I don't pay any attention to it."[97] New Directions needed to appeal, as a brand, both to the left and the right, to the increasingly important New Critical outlook on literature (represented by such critics as John Crowe Ransom, Cleanth Brooks, and Robert Penn Warren) and to the leftist New York Intellectual approach (represented by the *Partisan Review* group). In fact, the firm published works by members of both groups at this time—John Crowe Ransom's *The New Criticism* (1940) and Delmore Schwartz's *In Dreams Begin Responsibilities* (1938)—and Laughlin had maintained close correspondences with Ransom and with *Partisan Review* editors William Phillips and Philip Rahv.[98]

As Laughlin grew less interested in Pound's politics, Pound grew more vehement and began to feel it urgent that he affect politics in his home country. Urged by friends such as Williams, Ford Madox Ford, and Laughlin, the poet made a trip to America in the spring of 1939—his first visit to his native country since 1910. Friends were all eager to see him yet apprehensive how he would behave when back on home shores. For some time now, Laughlin had been pleading with Pound to stop aggravating other writers. "I urgently counsel your eminence not to sign letters to America with Arriba Espana, as you did to Williams the other day," he wrote in 1939.[99] (Because of Williams's opposition to Franco's regime, this "was a bit more than Bill could keep down," Laughlin informed Schwartz in April, 1939.[100]) Yet Pound continued to bait friends and adversaries alike with his declamations on Franco, Mussolini, and Hitler, and showed no sign of curbing himself while in America. Before his departure, Laugh-lin (with a residual trace of anti-Semitism) cautioned Pound about the impression that he was liable to make if he continued to utter political pronouncements at every opportunity:

> If you want to come you have got to decide whether you want to be
> disliked.
> If you come as a Poet and keep absolutely mum about money
> > > Jews
> > > fascism you will be
> liked.
> If you mention any of them subjects you will have one hell of a time.
> You have no idea of the entrenchment of the Jew in the intellectual life
> of the country.[101]

Pound arrived in New York on 21 April 1939. Although Laughlin had sent a shipboard telegram urging him to "GIVE ECONOMIC BUT NOT PO-LITICAL VIEWS TO THE PRESS WHEN INTERVIEWED," the poet ignored the advice and immediately held a press conference with the reporters who met him at the docks.[102] He stayed with E. E. Cummings in New York, then went to Washington, where he was refused an audience with President Roosevelt but was received by secretary of agriculture Henry Wallace and by the office of Idaho senator William Borah, who told one of his staffers that "I think he's crazy."[103] Later, he toured campuses, ped-dling his "Introductory Text Book," a short tract concentrating on Found-ing Fathers material—perhaps hoping to stir up interest in the forthcom-ing New Directions Founding Fathers series or in his own *Culture,* of which the "Text Book" was a drastically abridged version. Because he felt that American readers and students insufficiently appreciated the "Intro-ductory Text Book," he published it in the first (summer 1939) issue of James Jesus Angleton's short-lived literary magazine *Furioso.*[104] (Perhaps coincidentally—or perhaps with the intention of counteracting the inevi-tably negative publicity Pound's visit would generate for New Directions—Laughlin published three poems in that same issue of *Furioso,* two of which were from a series entitled "America I Love You.") In June, Pound went to Cambridge, Massachusetts, to give a public reading at Harvard's Sever Hall. Pound biographer C. David Heymann relates that "Laughlin, then a student at Harvard, was present at the reading. . . . Four years later, Laughlin . . . related to FBI special agents that Pound, 'after noticing that the preponderance of the audience consisted mainly of Jews, changed the poems he planned to read to definitely anti-Semitic poems.' A second observer, also interviewed by the FBI, noted that he read as if he wanted to pick a fight with the audience."[105] Pound's behavior did not convince anyone that he was not a crank or an anti-Semite. He finished his tour of America by accepting an honorary doctorate at his alma mater, Hamilton College, in Clinton, New York. There, the degree ceremony went smoothly, but at the luncheon following, Pound picked a fight with another of the honored guests, the well-known radio commentator H. V. Kaltenborn, about the relative merits of democracy and fascism. But his behavior did not succeed in offending everyone. On the day of the luncheon, the *New York Times* editorialized about Pound's "doctoring" by Hamilton: "Few professors are as variously learned. He must keep one of the fattest books of quotations in the world. Chinese is baby talk to him. He thinks in Provençal . . . was there ever a more vigorous tracker of culture from Confucius to T. S. Eliot?"[106] That the *Times* would laud Pound for his broad learning and his willingness to be an iconoclast, given the poet's boorish behavior, is strange; even Pound's ugliest side is cute—"the catholicity of his hates," the editorialist comments, "is itself engaging."

Notwithstanding the lighthearted tone of the *Times* editorial, the trip was a public relations disaster, serving primarily to distance Pound from old friends, who saw his defense of fascism as evidence of serious problems, perhaps even mental illness. Williams, for instance, wrote to Laughlin that "the man is sunk, in my opinion, unless he can shake the fog of Fascism out of his brain during the next few years, which I seriously doubt that he can do. The logicality of fascist rationalization is soon going to kill him. You can't argue away wanton slaughter of innocent women and children by the neo-scholasticism of a controlled economy program. Shit with a Hitler who lauds the work of his airmen in Spain and so shit with Pound too if he can't stand up and face his questioners on the point."[107] The trip also had a personal impact on the poet. Many years later, in his reminiscence "Ez as Wuz," Laughlin explained that "Pound's . . . trip back to the United States in 1939 . . . proved to be a depressing experience. He had come over hoping to meet Roosevelt and certain members of Congress. He would tell them what to do about the national economy and international policy. But no one of importance in Washington would see him. This failure to be recognized as a thinker, not just as a poet, broke his spirit."[108] Clearly, Pound craved recognition and respect from important political figures: one of the greatest moments of his life, told and retold to friends and visitors, was his personal audience with Mussolini in 1933, during which he felt that "the Boss" had listened eagerly to his advice on economic policy. But when he was snubbed by the American authorities, he concluded that American was "30 years arseward of the present"—and despaired that war could be averted. And in order to keep New Directions free of the taint of fascism, Laughlin would refuse Pound the bully pulpit he craved.

"Sticking to Literchoor": *Cantos LII–LXXI*

On 1 September 1939, Nazi Germany invaded Poland, and the Second World War began. Italy, though, was not yet a combatant, and Pound, who had just returned there, "carried on as if nothing out of the ordinary were happening," in the words of his biographer Humphrey Carpenter. He worried about the proofs of his new installment of *Cantos,* then in the hands of T. S. Eliot at Faber and Faber, and wrote letters musing on the contemporary literary situation. Eager to obtain a forum for his views in America, he continued to urge Laughlin to found a political magazine that would complement the strictly literary *New Directions in Prose and Poetry,* or in Pound's words "another Little Review/ I mean with EZ as foreign editor/ on about the same terms." Mindful of Laughlin's unwillingness to associate New Directions with politics, though, Pound suggested an "out" for the publisher: "Guess mebbe the magazine better be sep/ from N.D./ on other hand you might publish, with statement, that you have NO bloody influence on editorial policy."[109]

In this same letter, Pound rants extensively about a "Jewocracy" in America, and signs off with a "Heil Hitler." By this time, his letters had grown consistently more belligerent. He had even had Fascist-themed stationery made up: the left side of his letterhead from 1935–37 reads "ANNO [year] XIII" (or XIV or XV), referring to Mussolini's proclamation of the year of his ascension to power, 1922, as Year One.[110] The typeface on the stationery was the sans serif block capitals that Mussolini used on handbills, posters, and public buildings. In every way, Pound was adopting Italian Fascist ideas and modes of self-presentation. It was no surprise, then, that Laughlin was increasingly leery of his participation in New Directions periodicals.

In fact, given Pound's performance on his American tour, Laughlin had come to a painful decision about the Founding Fathers series and about his willingness and ability to carry out the poet's wishes.

> Now reverent sir, I hope that you will softpedal that German propaganda stuff—your present position makes it impossible to contemplate the Founders series with you at the helm. I mean, nobody would touch it because of your association with it. . . . I sorrowfully decline. I can't take on what would be a dead loss, or jeopardize the other lads, especially Bill, by association. I don't think I'll lose any great number of readers because I publish your books, but I've got to be careful just the same.
>
> Now I imagine you will be wrothful with your servant and consider that I am traitorous to you and next thing to a jew. But no. I am merely trying to hit an effective balance—I do as much as I possibly can for your honor's books without getting in a jam by going whole hog for your honor's programs. . . . I think I can do a certain amount of public service by sticking to literchoor and that is my intention.[111]

"Sticking to literchoor," of course, could not be farther from Pound's own approach to culture and his desire that New Directions be publisher for his ideas as for his favorite works. From the beginning, he had wanted Laughlin to publish all of his works, for he saw his oeuvre as a whole, as arguing consistently for cultural and economic renewal. Although he had gently nudged Pound or quietly managed the poet's image in America in the previous years, however, Laughlin during these negotiations expresses for the first time his growing sense that an emphasis on evaluating literature without social criteria was the approach to take in marketing Pound. Moreover, he finally states categorically that for New Directions to be a strictly literary publisher would be a "public service."

Laughlin's next letter (5 December 1939) marks a turning point in their relationship and in his outlook on publishing. First, he refuses in no uncertain terms Pound's continued entreaties for "another Little Review," a magazine that Laughlin understood well would be a forum for Pound and his Italian and British fascist associates. Laughlin tells Pound that New

Directions will not be "a kind of puppet publishing house for him, where he could get his friends, and things that he liked, published," as he recalled in 1985. He offers a compromise, though: a "broadside called NEWS FROM EUROPE."

> But here's the point. It would have to be absolutely anonymous. There could be no connection with New Directions and no hint that you were connected with it. If anybody smelt you in it, or your Italian hand, they would simply discount the whole thing as lies. But if you supplied me with facts—not hints and suspicions, but facts—and I rewrote them in a plain style so there would be no trace of you in it, then we might get somewhere.[112]

Crucially, even though this "broadside" would have no visible association whatsoever with New Directions, and Pound's involvement in it would be hidden, Laughlin refused to let Pound turn it into a forum for anti-Semites. In addition, he condemned anti-Semitism and Pound's involvement with it.

> I will not run an anti-semitic sheet or be in any way connected with one. . . . I think anti-semitism is contemptible and despicable and I will not put my hand to it. I cannot tell you how it grieves me to see you taking up with it. I do not for one minute believe that it is solely the Jews who are responsible for the maintenance of the unjust money systems. They may have their part in it, but it is just as much, and more, the work of Anglo-Saxons and celts and goths and what have you.
>
> Now I dare say that will make you mad with me, but there's how it is.

While not rejecting Social Credit—a doctrine he continued to espouse late into his life—Laughlin here definitively rejected the anti-Semitism Pound had tacked onto it. Moreover, "News from Europe" seems to have been a sham from the beginning. Laughlin knew that Pound would not have been able to produce a political magazine without it becoming an "anti-semitic sheet." Laughlin had himself used anti-Semitic language before, and would again, but here he distances himself from Pound. The offer of a magazine seems to be a way of dismissing one of Pound's ambitions before moving on to a more important topic—how Pound's poetry would appear under the New Directions imprint.

Laughlin's intention to "stick to literchoor" was made immeasurably easier by the fact that, after much negotiation, he finally obtained the American rights for the *Cantos* from Farrar and Rinehart in late 1939. During the 1930s Farrar and Rinehart were cautious in selling Pound, printing up only 1,000, 1,500, and 750 copies, respectively, for the three collections of *Cantos* in the 1930s—none of which had sold out by 1940. Understandably leery of drawing unwanted attention to his firm for one of its authors' controversial views—according to Laughlin, he was "peeved" by Pound's pronouncements—Farrar downplayed Pound's works.[113] The poet had always resented Farrar's halfhearted devotion to the *Cantos,* but wavered about transferring the rights to Laughlin. He was noncommittal about his young admirer's newfound desire to publish the *Cantos*: "[I]f ANN Watkins . . . thinks you can do 41/51 the FIFTH DE-CAD better than Farrar, it is O.K. with me," he wrote Laughlin in 1937, but apparently she did not; Farrar issued the *Fifth Decad of Cantos* in November 1937.[114] Another two years of wrangling among Watkins, Farrar, and Laughlin followed, during which Laughlin grew impatient with Pound's lack of support. As late as July 1939, Laughlin was still frustrated. A postcard arriving in Rapallo about the time of Pound's return from America states, "I see Mr. Farrar has decided to keep them Cantos. Ok. Ok. We'll get on with something else." But in December 1939, Laughlin was finally able to take over the rights, and wrote Pound to inform him and to float an idea for a long-term plan: "Farrar will sell me the plates of the three books of CANTOS and the rights for $150.00, and the copies on hand for $216.30. That seems to me a fair price and if you OK the project I'll go ahead with it. My plan would be to go ahead with the next twenty or so next fall, pushing the earlier ones on the side, and then perhaps in a year or so do a complete volume up to the stage then reached. . . . We'll just tip in a New Directions title page and announce to the trade and the libraries that we have taken over."[115] Pound was pleased, replying that he sent "Ann [Watkins] my benedictions for transfer of Cantos from Farrar. 52/71 are easy to understand."[116] As Farrar let its rights to the *Cantos* go, Pound was pleased to transfer that agreement to Laughlin, writing pseudo-legally that "Copyright is granted to you for as long and YOU PERSONALLY run New Directions/ or at any rate own and RUN the publishing business that publishes the Cantos.terminates automatically if you go bust, and rights then return to me/ they do NOT go to binders; printers or sons of belial. The Cantos are not an asset in liquidation to be sold off at auction to hell."[117] Combining an apology with a plan for the future, Laughlin wrote eagerly of his plans for the *Cantos LII–LXXI* volume (the proofs of which were at that point with Faber in London) and for a *Selected Poems* that would be priced at a dollar—the student-aimed anthology Laughlin had been proposing since 1933.[118]

Pound's admiration of Mussolini was a matter of public record at this time, but his anti-Semitism was not. Many of those who knew him well, though—Laughlin included—were growing wary of the way anti-Semitic themes were beginning to crop up in his writing. The famous outburst against "usura" in Canto XLV and the viciousness of his attacks on the Rothschilds and other Jewish financiers were the most obvious evidence of this in the *Cantos* up to this time, but in his correspondence Pound lapsed more and more into anti-Semitic rantings. In keeping with his continued concern for the image of his publishing house, and with his own growing disgust, Laughlin in the 1939 negotiations for the purchase and American publication of *Cantos LII–LXXI* demanded something that Pound would find difficult to accept: "[I]n regard to the Cantos I will not print anything that can be fairly construed as an outright attack on the Jews and I want that in the contract in the libel clause. You can take all the potshots at them you want, but no outright attack on the Jews as jews. . . ."[119] It is important to remember that at this time Laughlin was only twenty-five and that Pound, whose force of personality and charisma are rarely described as less than impressive, had been his most important intellectual influence for more than six years. Laughlin continued to advocate Social Credit and economic reform. At times during the 1930s, he even held some of Pound's anti-Semitic prejudices and listened attentively to the poet's arguments that Social Credit beliefs necessarily led one to mistrust Jewish financiers (although he was never very sympathetic to Pound's profascist arguments). But here, Laughlin finally decides to "stick to literchoor," to minimize the risk of a backlash against New Directions, to separate his admiration for Pound from his more fundamental desire to make the house viable. This marks the moment when Laughlin moves from being a disciple to being a publisher and an equal.

Knowing full well that this shift would engender the poet's resentment, Laughlin attempted to counteract Pound's objections:

> I dare say you are in a rage with me over my lack of fire in matters of politics and money, but I think I can assure you that you will not suffer by having me as your publisher.
>
> I agree with what you said about commercialization and the ruin of art. I am not trying to commercialize. I am simply working like hell to make my business an efficient mechanism.[120]

Laughlin shares Pound's distaste for the melding of art and commerce, but his own commercialization is of a different sort—it is a packaging or reframing of Pound for an audience that will not accept anti-Semitism. He is not vulgarizing Pound, merely attempting to eliminate those aspects of Pound's work which has caused his books to almost stop selling. Laughlin's frankness about his practical concerns is one of the earliest indications that he will not allow Pound's intransigence to threaten his business; his strategy for improving Pound's literary value will rely partly on a campaign to increase the poet's market value.

More striking even than Laughlin's taking a stand against Pound's anti-Semitism, though, was Pound's defensive backing down: "all right/ d'accord/ not 'solely as jews'. But no immunity SOLELY as jews; solely because jews,"[121] or, in another letter,

> If you want a statement that shd/ satisfy yr/ scruples you can take this over my signature.
>
> I do NOT consider it antisemite to WARN the millions of working jews that THEY and NOT the big usurers and monopolists are endangered by the activities of high finance and monopoly.[122]

Laughlin did not let Pound change the subject: "What about including in the contract, along with the libel section, something like this: 'The author further affirms that the book contains no material that could properly be called "anti-semitic," that is, which treats of the Jews in a propagandistic, as opposed to an artistic, manner.'"[123] Pound was a little more conciliatory about anti-Semitism in his next letter; he hardened a little, however, on the suggestion that his poetic work might be obscure or, worse, "propagandistic":

> I don't mind affirming in contract, so long as I am not expected to alter text. You can putt [*sic*] it this way. The author affirms that in no passage shd/ the text be interpreted to mean that he condemns any innocent man or woman for another's guilt, and that no degree of relationship, familial or racial shall be taken to imply such condemnation.
> But no group national or ethical can expect immunity not accorded to other groups. Damn the word artistic. This poem is HISTORY.
> . . . I shall NOT accept the specific word anti-semitic in the contract.[124]

Laughlin had suggested this formulation, and in doing so, had uncharacteristically used Pound's language: "That's pretty broad, but also gives me protection. I mean I can shove that under the nose of any kike editor who accuses me of being anti-semitic."[125] Finally satisfied with Pound's compromise, Laughlin apologized in a letter two months later for the "boyish idealism" of his proposed anti-Semitism clause.[126]

In this negotiation, however, Laughlin accomplished what he had set out to do: setting the tone of the publisher-author relationship as that of a balance of equals, not the devotion of a disciple for his teacher. Where Pound continually urged Laughlin to make New Directions a mouthpiece for his political opinions, Laughlin judiciously maintained the firm's non-political nature, knowing that this would benefit Pound in the long term. He rejected the poet's desire to direct the New Classics series; he denied Pound's request for a New Directions–funded, Pound-edited political magazine; he refused to publish the *Cantos* if Pound turned them into an anti-Semitic rant. Both Faber and Faber and New Directions substituted thick black lines for a number of Pound's anti-Semitic, anti-Rothschild comments on the first two pages of Canto LII, and the original words were not restored until the 1986 printing of the *Cantos*.[127] Laughlin did, however, fulfill Pound's request to "PRINT 52/71 [*Cantos LII–LXXI*] in time to prevent at least six electors voting for Roosevlt"[128]—if Pound did not have the impact on the Electoral College he had hoped for, it was not because of Laughlin's tardiness.

The debate over the libel clause was not Laughlin's only attempt at using this volume to modify Pound's image—and, he hoped, to make Pound a valuable author for New Directions. He also urged Pound to include a summary or preface to the new installment of the *Cantos* because "the attitude over here [in the United States] is that the CANTOS are incomprehensible, and where comprehensible, propaganda."[129] Notwithstanding his conviction about the backwardness of American readers, though, Pound refused: ". . . Cantos can NOT have a preface IN the book. . . . the new set is NOT incomprehensible. also its sale dont depend on the immediate condition of pubk/ shitterentiality. Nobody can SUMMARIZE what is already condensed to the absolute LIMIT."[130]

This was not good enough for Laughlin, who desperately wanted Pound to regain the favor of a public that had admired him ten years before but that now thought him an obscurantist crank. The *Cantos* themselves were not a risk-free proposition for Laughlin, and he had expressed some anxiety to T. S. Eliot, writing that "I'm a little worried about it as the last batch are pretty hard to grasp and there is much murmuring here against the Sage. . . . At the risk of having him bite my head off I am going to get up a little brochure on the CANTOS to go out with the next lot. Try to explain to people what the devil is going on in all that long trail of winding. I notice your blurb-writer takes the cold-turkey attitude—'here you are and to hell with you.' I'm not sure that is the best for here. I'm all against the snob-appeal line."[131] Eliot did not respond to Laughlin's idea about a brochure, although he did acknowledge that "my line in blurbing poetry has usually been the take it or leave it attitude, with the implication—this is F&F poetry, and that fact ought to be good enough for you. But I can quite see that that is not the best advertising method for your purposes."[132] Laughlin, who although very young had an excellent understanding of the literary audience in America, explained his brochure idea to Pound: "I will just try to explain a few things about the structure and nature of the poem in plain language and remind a few of these here conks that poetry is not a matter exclusively of birds and bees. Further, D[elmore] Schwartz is willing to say a few words about your mastery of metric and idiom."[133] Pound provisionally accepted: "I like the idea of YOUR doing a pamphlet," he told Laughlin in May; in June he agreed: "go to it and print and REMIT."[134]

Of the 1,000 copies of *Cantos LII–LXXI* printed by New Directions, only half contained this pamphlet. Pasted into the inside back cover, a small envelope enclosed sixteen pages with "Notes on the Cantos" by "H. H." and "Notes on the Versification of the Cantos" by "S. D."[135] Laughlin's—"H. H." 's—essay is a remarkable example of the publisher as spin doctor. Pound's opinions on political and economic matters were well known by this time, but Laughlin attempts to put the best face on them: he ignores anti-Semitism, and explains Pound's fascist sympathies as a natural outgrowth of his true, egalitarian, *democratic* sympathies. Pound is a poet whose great moral sense has carried him away and has led him to make some regrettable statements:

> What is the moral structure of the *Cantos*? . . . [H]is bases for moral judgment . . . are these: credit and money, of which gold is only a yard-stick, are public—social—commodities, and their volume and value should be controlled by the state as trustee for the people. Instead, thanks to the way the modern banking system has developed, credit and money are controlled and misused by private forces; whence, de-pressions . . . and war . . . Evil, then, is the force which promotes or condones the anti-social use of money; good, that which opposes it.

This seems to be an entirely humane, democratic politics, not altogether different from those of contemporary leftists—and it is quite possibly to those Left intellectuals the pamphlet is addressed:

> In the past decade—the heyday of Marxism—it has been customary for critics to sneer at Pound's economic ideas. Current events, with a sinister irony, give them the lie—the success of Hitler's national infla-tion has proved that the idea of a socialized credit system is not ridicu-lous. Perceptive observers have pointed out the salient aspect of the present war: it is a struggle between two concepts of money, privately controlled money and state controlled money. . . .
>
> Naturally, Pound never hoped to see the theories he advocated put to such horrible uses . . . [but] if the democracies are not totally stupid . . . they will learn from Hitler's experiment and finance their war with a statal economy; they will suppress the private banker in his role as war profiteer.

An attack on private profiteers, an appeal to peace, the demand for a "socialized credit system" that would not rely on the profit motive of bankers . . . Pound's program includes many of the proposals characteristic of the Social Credit program, and in the late 1920s and the 1930s Social Credit had attracted leftists as well as right-wingers (indicative of its broad appeal to intellectuals is the fact that both Pound and William Carlos Williams were Social Creditors in the early 1930s). But anyone who read Pound or listened to his public statements would have known better— much of his trip to America in 1939 was spent denouncing the too-easy availability of Marxist literature.[136] Pound was no leftist, as much as Laughlin's essay tries to make him sound like one.

In this essay, Laughlin makes the poet into more than a garden-variety political thinker. Rather than an unwitting dupe of charismatic fascism, as some of his other apologists described him, he is the philosopher who must not be held responsible for how his theories have been put into practice. "Often Pound is branded a fascist because he likes to live in Italy and has not hesitated to commend the good points that do exist, among the bad, in the fascist program," the essay continues. "But he is no fascist at heart." The approach is significantly different from what Laughlin's postwar promotional efforts will be, for here he actually attempts to convince readers of the validity of Pound's theories.

Schwartz's ["S. D." 's] essay, on Pound's versification is odd, considering that Schwartz had already declared how repugnant he found Pound. In a 1939 letter, deeply disgusted by the poet's continued anti-Semitic outbursts, he had written Pound that he wanted "to resign as one of your most studious and faithful admirers."[137] Upon reading the Faber edition of *Cantos LII–LXXI* a year later, however, Schwartz apparently changed his mind, and wrote Laughlin that "I've been reading the new cantos with the greatest pleasure. The man may be the biggest jackass in the world and working hard at getting even bigger, but he has the best ear for versification since Milton, and maybe the best ear that anyone ever had who used the English language."[138] The anti-Semitic material that Schwartz had feared would predominate was also muted in this volume: "Your concern about attacks on Jews can be dismissed. Outside of the first page, in which he quotes a passage from Franklin, which is, I am told, a fabricated remark which Franklin never made, there is nothing at all about us poor bastards."[139]

To Schwartz's mind, the brilliance of the formal qualities of Pound's work and the repugnance of much of its content made obvious the separate existence of form and content. The two spheres must be separated for Pound to make any sense as a figure in literary history—or, perhaps more correctly, if he were to ever have a chance to become a important figure in literary history. Schwartz would be an important voice in the New York Intellectuals' 1940s advocacy of the special status of art, and he had always urged fellow leftists to grant art special privileges. He knew, however, that not all readers had come to that conclusion. When Laughlin proposed that Schwartz write a brief essay for this pamphlet, Schwartz was quite willing. His "Notes" have an equivocal tone, but are in the main laudatory; his negative comments are subtle, considering the blunt tone of his earlier letter: "No other poem in English attempts to take hold of so great a variety of subjects. Whether or not the poet's insight is equal to his scope is a different and difficult question. . . . But it should be clear that what we have in the *Cantos* is nothing less than a revolution in English versification, a new basis for the writing of poetry, which, when it has been dissociated from Pound's particular vision, should have an immense influence on the poetry of the next hundred years."

The political ramifications of "Pound's particular vision" obviously troubled Schwartz; his letters of this period to Pound and Laughlin attest to that. In a narrower sense, though, "particular vision" refers specifically to the subject matter of these *Cantos,* which many reviewers dismissed as boring and encyclopedic. While Schwartz did not share that view of these poems, Laughlin did, feeling that it was Pound's worst installment. Although Schwartz's essay was anonymous, many readers deduced from the content of the essay and from Schwartz's close association with Laughlin that Schwartz had written it. The essay was crucial for the aims of the pamphlet, for Laughlin needed a recognized leftist intellectual to endorse this volume. And since Schwartz was also an important, emerging voice in American poetry, Laughlin could show readers that Pound was a fundamental influence on contemporary poetry, content notwithstanding. This idea would become increasingly prominent in New Directions advertising in the 1950s, when the company began reissuing Pound's earlier critical work.

The poems of *Cantos LII–LXXI* deal primarily with Chinese history and John Adams, and many of them consist of long lists of names, of exchanges between ambassadors, counselors, and ministers of state; the voice of "Uncle Ez" heavy-handedly underscores the points he find important. For Pound there could be no more currently relevant subject than the development of the Chinese state and of American foreign and economic policy, but few readers shared this feeling. This volume is the first selection of *Cantos* obviously intended to be as didactic as it was artistic. Laughlin, however, downplays this in his pamphlet, making Pound's affinity for fascism more abstract and less visceral, and reminds us to always think of this book as poetry, albeit poetry that must be read in a social context. Schwartz's notes use this as a jumping-off point, and go back to the one element of Pound's writing that even his harshest critics had always admired: his mastery of the poetic line.

Laughlin's efforts to determine the book's interpretation are seen not solely in the pamphlet but also in magazine advertising. Kafka's *Amerika,* Dylan Thomas's *Portrait of the Artist as a Young Dog,* and Rimbaud's *A Season in Hell* (translated by Schwartz) were on the same fall list as *Cantos LII–LXXI,* and they were the books given separate advertisements in such publications as the *Saturday Review.* Not wanting to call too much attention to Pound at a time when his fascist sympathies were especially inflammatory, New Directions advertisements either ignored the book or couched its politics in the best possible terms: "The newest selection of a great modern epic. John Quincy Adams is the hero of ten cantos," reads the 1940 fall list announcement in *Publishers' Weekly,* and the advertisement in the *Saturday Review of Literature* calls the book "the story of Adams' European embassies in the days when our newborn democracy was fighting for its life."[140] In addition to his apprehensions about Pound's notoriety, Laughlin's desire to push New Directions to profitability forced him to reduce the emphasis on Pound in advertising and promotion. At this time, New Directions was still losing money (it did not make a profit for ten years), and Laughlin was having to economize in every aspect of publishing and marketing.[141]

The fact that Pound's books were not given an independent, publicized release lessened the impact of his politics on the firm's public identity. Releasing his book in the middle of a list heavy with young lions (Dylan Thomas) and Continental classics (Baudelaire, Rimbaud) buried Pound somewhat. Had it been released separately, with fanfare, reviewers would have paid more attention to it—and at this point in his career, a great deal

of public attention would have been extremely harmful. The advertisements and the pamphlet, as well as Laughlin's refusals to allow Pound to
have influence over New Directions policies and projects, combined to
make the New Directions Pound primarily a poet, when he wanted to be
considered a poet *and* a political thinker. Only four years after talking
about the central role literature should take in the transformation of society, Laughlin was now trying to reduce the potential social impact of his
cornerstone author's writing. This treatment of one of the firm's two most
important authors helped build the image of the house as nonpolitical, as
a publisher afraid neither to court controversial authors nor to curb their
output when it would hurt the firm.

Laughlin managed to make one careless error in the production of
Cantos LII–LXXI, but because of the general apathy, it took years for
anyone to point the error out to him publicly. The dust jacket and advertisements for the book misidentified John Adams as John Quincy Adams.
To most readers, this either went unnoticed or was simply taken at face
value. But once Pound finally saw the book's jacket—which was not until
he returned to America and was already in St. Elizabeths—he sent Laughlin a scrawled missive expressing his horror.

> My deah Jas—
> Do you realize that if
> a man weren't already in
> bug house. To read
> J. Quincy Adams on cover
> when it shd be
>   John Adams
>   père
> not fils is enough
> TO PUTT a
> man there
>
> really there is no
> known language TO
> EXPRESSSSSSSSS
> B A L L S
> John not J.Q.

who was N O T
a founding father

. . . Blurb not bad but Harrold Hairbrain
is ignorant as a sow's cunt of
American history. Has
never read the constitution.[142]

Even if they missed the J. Adams/J. Q. Adams mix-up, the critics were snide, for the most part, about Laughlin's attempt to "explain" Pound, and even more hostile toward the book itself. "Ten years ago it was the custom for *avant-garde* critics to call those people who were puzzled by Ezra Pound's Cantos imbeciles," Louise Bogan commented in the *New Yorker*. "Such people then were beneath explanation and contempt. Now it is different." Louis Untermeyer, in the *Yale Review,* wrote that "Pound, like the system which he scorns, is beginning to break down. For the first time, he is offering 'explanations' of his method." The poetry did not fare much better: to the *Nation* these new *Cantos* were "longer-winded than any that have gone before . . . not as imaginative as they once were"; to *Accent,* the second half of the volume was "perfunctory and thoroughly dull"; for Allen Tate in *Partisan Review,* "the less said the better."[143] Laughlin had, however, at least in part, accomplished what he set out to do. Pound was not made into a political issue, even though *Cantos LII–LXXI* was a profoundly political work, intended to educate readers on the proper organization of a state. Hostile as many of them were, the reviews generally mentioned politics only in passing, and dwelt on the poetry.

New Directions issued no more of Pound's work during the next five years, nor did the house reprint any during this time. This is due in part, of course, to the cutoff of communications between Italy and the United States, which made any negotiations, submissions, or editing impossible. But Pound's growing notoriety also led Laughlin to cease advertising the works that were on the New Directions backlist. He significantly declined to pursue Liveright's rights to Pound's mid-1930s political tract, *Jefferson and/or Mussolini,* even though he had sought contracts to works by Pound that were owned by other publishers, and even though Pound urged him to acquire this one. "Yr politics have cooked yr reverend goose to a point you wd. not believe and we cdnt hardly sell 17 copies of such a book now,"

Laughlin explained in early 1941.[144] Six months later, answering Pound's continued requests for an edition of his political and economic essays, Laughlin reiterated these same concerns: "Re that buk of essays you suggest. I think we better not try that now. You are pretty much disliked for your orations. Yr name in general might be said to aspire but not attain to the dignity of mud. I would rather fill this unfortunate interim with fairly uncontroversial things like the cantyers selections and the Cavalcanti."[145] Pound's political position, combined with the sheer difficulty of publishing during the war, forced Laughlin to stop promoting his books after publishing *Cantos LII–LXXI* and issuing *Polite Essays* in 1940. As the United States moved toward war, Laughlin lost contact with his most famous author; he would not hear from him again until 1946.

CHAPTER THREE

❖ ❖ ❖ ❖

"The Objective Perception of Value":
The Bollingen Award

I am one who still thinks Ezra Pound's poetry is good—very good—
notwith-standing his political folly. These people who changed their
minds about the merits of Pound's poetry the day he was indicted for
treason make me sick and angry. A poem is a thing in itself. You judge
it by itself, for itself and of itself—not by the politics of the man who
wrote it.

—James Laughlin,
from the "Editor's Notes" to *New Directions* 9 (1946)

IF Pound's political beliefs and statements before World War II had
already made him a pariah in the United States, his notorious radio
broadcasts during the war—and the resulting treason indictment and institutionalization—only worsened the public's impression. His fame after
the war was not the kind to further Laughlin's aims to sell his books; any
publicity, in Pound's case, was bad publicity. Laughlin could no longer
simply put the best face on the poet's writings and activities. Now he must
wholly reconstruct his image. Responding to this imperative, he increasingly began to employ the category of the aesthetic to explain and market
Pound. Urging readers to ignore Pound's beliefs and to look for an exclusively aesthetic experience and value in his work was not only a shift in
the New Directions approach to marketing the poet, it was for Laughlin a
rejection of one of the publishing house's founding ideas. A cynic might
say that Laughlin abandoned his principles for the benefit of his publishing house. Pound's troubles forced Laughlin, who had always been devoted to the socially transformative power of literature, to accept the
aesthetic formalist approach to literature—at least publicly. In the 1930s
Laughlin had been willing to link Pound's political beliefs to his artistic

achievements; now downplaying the person and his politics was imperative if the poet were ever to attain the combination of literary and market success Laughlin sought for him.

New Directions was both responding to and, later, contributing to driving a larger cultural shift to an aestheticist position about how to judge art. During the 1940s, an uneasy consensus of two influential American intellectual groups—the New Critics and the New York Intellectuals—held that the aesthetic need not be intimately enmeshed with the social, and must not be held to answer to mundane political concerns. Both groups had ties to New Directions. Where the conservative New Critics were primarily concerned with literature, the leftist New York Intellectuals addressed art, politics, and society. Laughlin and New Directions now embarked on a publishing and marketing campaign that drew on both the New Critics' aesthetic formalism and the New York Intellectuals' willingness to overlook an artist's political and social views, and argued that Pound must be judged strictly on aesthetic grounds. What complicated this relationship, at least at first, was that Laughlin could not base his campaign entirely on this consensus. Both groups had explicitly judged Pound to be a second-rate artist. Laughlin and his firm, though, needed to begin by grounding their campaign to reconstruct his public image on these problematic critical philosophies, hoping later to recruit critics friendlier to the poet.

The Radio Broadcasts, the Trial, and the "Counter-Swing"

During the war years, Laughlin had almost lost contact with Pound. "We were totally cut off," he explained; "we didn't know what was happening to Ezra, because there was no mail coming through from Italy."[1] What was known was that Pound had taken a job broadcasting for the Rome outlet of the Italian state radio network EIAR (Ente Italiano Audizione Radiofoniche). Word quickly got out in the United States about his strange, virulent, and often anti-Semitic programs—in 1941, Laughlin wrote that "I have not managed yet to hear any of your orations. . . . However, you seem to have touched Doc Williams under the skin."[2] News of the broadcasts was so widespread that Laughlin found it necessary to print an exculpatory note in the "Notes on Contributors" for *New Directions in Prose and Poetry* 6 (1941): "Certain explanations are in order with regard to EZRA POUND, who is still living in Italy. People who hear him broadcasting for the Italian Government do not realize that possibly he has no choice in the matter. If they knew, for example, that he cannot leave Italy because he has close dependents who are not American citizens, they would perhaps be more charitable in their judgments. Those are the facts in the matter." (Laughlin did not know that Pound did the broadcasts willingly and enthusiastically.) But this explanation fell on deaf ears—the poet's career seemed finished. Even Pound's old employer *Poetry* proclaimed in 1942 that "in the name of American poetry, and of all who practice the art, let us hope that this is the end of Ezra Pound."[3] Naturally, the mainstream magazines Pound had been attacking for years took his disgrace as an opportunity for eulogies; in one example, William Rose Benét of his old nemesis the *Saturday Review of Literature* wrote that Pound had become "a permanent exile and slowly but surely assassinated himself."[4]

On 26 July 1943 a federal grand jury in Washington, D.C., indicted seven pro-Nazi propagandists and Pound for treason. The indictment, which stated that Pound "knowingly, intentionally, willfully, unlawfully, feloniously, traitorously, and treasonably did adhere to the enemies of the United States, to wit, the Kingdom of Italy . . . and the military allies of said Kingdom . . . giving to the said enemies of the United States aid and comfort within the United States and elsewhere," later had to be revised because its terms applied specifically to the activities of pro-Nazi and pro-Japanese broadcasters, and might have let Pound evade conviction. (After his capture a second indictment, handed down on 26 November 1945, specifically accused him "of accepting employment from the Kingdom of Italy in the capacity of a radio propagandist.") Pound heard of the indictment via the BBC and quickly wrote to U.S. attorney general Francis Biddle, protesting that "I do not believe that the simple fact of speaking over the radio, wherever placed, can in itself constitute treason." In a 1960 interview with the *Paris Review*, Pound told Donald Hall that he had been "completely surprised" at the charges, given his agreement with his Italian employers: "You see I had that promise. . . . He will not be asked to say anything contrary to his conscience or contrary to his duty as an American citizen.' I thought that covered it. . . . I thought I was fighting for a constitutional point. I mean to say, I may have been completely nuts, but I certainly *felt* that it wasn't committing treason. . . . I thought I was fighting an internal question of constitutional government."[5] His live broadcasts had ended at the same time as his indictment, for Mussolini's government had fallen the previous day. (Even after Mussolini fell, though, Pound continued to send scripts to his government-in-exile, and these were read on the air.⁶) Pound spent August 1943 in Rapallo, waiting to see what would happen, and returned to Rome in early September. Italy, under the Badoglio government, officially surrendered on 8 September, and two days later German troops occupied Rome, which officially became an "open city." On 10 September, Pound checked out of the Albergo d'Italia and began walking north. After some days of travel (not all on foot), he arrived in the Tirol, 450 miles from Rome, at the house of the Marchers, the farm family who were raising his daughter Mary for him. He later returned to Rapallo, but in May 1944 he and Dorothy were forced out of their apartment there because foreign nationals were not allowed to live near the coast; they went up the hill to live with Olga Rudge, Pound's longtime lover and Mary's mother. For a year, the three lived together, uneasily and in grinding poverty (Pound apparently lost almost fifty-five pounds). Northern Italy experienced chaos during 1944 and 1945, as Allies, partisans, Nazis, and Fascist loyalists fought for control. Eventually, the partisans, with Allied assistance, gained the upper hand and began to search out Fascist officials and sympathizers for capture or execution. Fortunately for Pound, the partisans knew of the U.S. warrant out for his arrest. After his capture on 3 May 1945, they turned him over to U.S. forces, and he was held in the U.S. Army's Disciplinary Training Center north of Pisa, spending part of his time in an outdoor "gorilla cage" (his term). In November, he was returned to the United States to face trial.

When Pound was extradited to America, Laughlin was not optimistic, but quickly resolved to jump to his defense, writing the poet that "I should hardly say I suppose that I hope to see you soon, because I'm afraid that things are going to be kind of tough for you here, but rest assured that although you have many spiteful enemies, you also have a few friends left who will do their best to help you. No one takes your side, of course, in the political sense, but many feel that the bonds of friendship and the values of literature can transcend a great deal."⁷ The case garnered national attention; articles in *Time* and *Newsweek* detailed the proceedings, while Henry Seidel Canby, in the *Saturday Review,* argued that Pound "should not escape penalty for his misdeed."⁸ The left-wing press, which had lost its enthusiasm for him when his attacks on financiers had begun to be directed also at Jews and Marxists, gleefully followed the poet's fall. "Should Ezra Pound Be SHOT?" asked the 25 December 1945 headline of the *New Masses,* and playwright Arthur Miller was one author who responded in the affirmative.[9] After much legal maneuvering, however, Pound in 1946 was instead found incompetent to stand trial, and the charges remained unanswered. In the FBI's own words, "On March 2, 1946, Mr Donald Anderson of the Criminal Division telephonically advised Supervisor [blacked out] that since Pound has been declared incompetent by District Court jury, no further prosecutive action can be taken against him at this time. The indictment will remain outstanding, however, and in the event Pound should be declared sane at some future time, he will then be brought to trial."[10] Pound continued to be held in St. Elizabeths Hospital for the Insane, a federal facility in Washington, D.C., where he had been transferred soon after arrival in America.

While Pound was experiencing great tumult, Laughlin—having escaped military service with a 4-F classification on psychiatric grounds—had spent much of the war running his ski lodge at Alta, Utah, where the Army was training paratroopers. He had also continued to operate New Directions, but wartime restrictions on paper—Laughlin explained that "you could only have as much paper as you had used in the year 1937, a year when we'd done almost nothing"—curtailed the house's output.[11] Even though he could not actually publish much, Laughlin was gradually developing his firm's list and his own ideas about publishing. The passing years had not changed in the slightest his attitude toward commercial publishing. In his introduction to the 1946 tenth anniversary issue of *New Directions* Laughlin restated the same sentiments about commercialism he had been expressing for a decade. Attacking the practice of "applying to books and writing the merchandising methods developed to sell the mass production of ice boxes, hair oil and chewing gum," Laughlin again made it clear that he felt that the use of commercial techniques to sell literature was abhorrent. In a prescient attack, he linked the publishing industry to Broadway and Hollywood. "Every day," he continued,

> some new and more disgusting ulcer forces its way into the skin of the putrefied body—just yesterday I read in a trade journal that Warner

Brothers have established a special department to "inspire ideas" for writers to make into books and later into pictures.

In the course of ten years I have used quite a number of derogatory epithets to denote the gentlemen who operate the most flagrantly commercial of our great publishing houses, our widely read magazines, some of our literary agencies, our theatres, our motion picture industry and sometimes even our libraries, universities and so-called "liberal" journals, but I think I like the term "sinners" about the best of them all. For me, who passed a good part of the Sundays of my youth under the stone pulpits of the Presbyterian churches of Pittsburgh, the word "sinner" is redolent of Hell and its fires, and I sincerely hope that the worst of these pecunious offenders who are polluting our culture will burn there for a considerable length of time.[12]

Referring to the lost promise of those writers who gave up the vocation because of economic hardship, the article continues: "Damn your souls, you fat sinners swilling at the Stork and 21, driving your Cadillacs down Sunset Boulevard, throwing your penthouse parties, you cannot give us a literary culture with your occasional conscience-salving uncoordinated, half-hearted promotion of a book of poems by some man whom you think you can seduce away from his true art into writing one of your slick novels."[13] It is hard to take Laughlin's sermonic rhetoric seriously, but his self-construction as a passionate patron is quite interesting. A product of privilege himself, he had been led by love for literature and a desire to make up for the philistinism of his family to found a money-losing publishing house. The targets of his attack are those publishers who, to put it plainly, ran their operations as businesses. Laughlin here is clearly resisting the incursion of bourgeois capitalism into the privileged sphere of art, and using the term *commercial* to designate any publisher who thinks primarily about profits, not artistic value. Only six years before, however, in his letters to Pound about *Cantos LII–LXXI,* Laughlin had acknowledged that he himself could have been accused of "commercializing" because he wanted to "make [his] business an efficient mechanism."[14] In addition, his rhetoric of sin, rot, and decadence resonates with the idea of the work of art as an organic, whole, sacred body, incursions upon which cause it to putrefy.[15]

While continuing to decry the harm that commerce did to publishing, Laughlin was finally seeing the appearance of his firm's own commercially minded offerings, the New Classics series and the Makers of Modern Literature, both of which were aimed at a student market that had been steadily increasing and would balloon after the war ended. In a promotional pamphlet, New Directions explained its new series.

> The New Directions publishing program is being advanced simultaneously on several fronts. The most recent project is a series of monthly poetry pamphlets—THE POET OF THE MONTH—issued on an annual subscription basis. . . .
>
> The first book in the MAKERS OF MODERN LITERATURE Series will be *Henry James* by R. P. Blackmur. . . . These dollar books, written by creative critics, are designed as baedekers to the work of the great moderns. . . .
>
> Two volumes are now available in our dollar reprint series—THE NEW CLASSICS. . . . Sensing an increased interest in recordings of poets reading their work, we plan to issue two albums of five poets each, the project to be edited by Norman Pearson. . . .[16]

Both series were attempts to improve the literary value and reputation of the authors showcased—Williams, Forster, James—but were also aimed at increasing the market value of these same authors. (In this, they were only moderately successful: Laughlin remitted to Knopf in June 1942 royalties for 2,291 copies of *Three Tales*, 2,843 copies of Forster's *Room with a View*, and 2,172 of his *The Longest Journey* that had been sold in the previous year.) The difference between these projects and the publishing undertakings of the "fat swillers" seems to be not in the swillers' intent to construct market value, but in a by-product of that desire—the diminution of literary value because of the increased potential market value of their products. By turning authors' works into commodities, Laughlin suggests, the large publishers move them from the realm of art to the realm of commerce. He implies, though, that his own low-priced, student-aimed books are somehow not commodities. Perhaps sensitive to this finessing of the distinction, he also emphasizes the corruption inherent in the profit motive.

During the war, reprints of older work dominated the New Directions lists, whereas in later years the house concentrated more on contemporary works. The 1942 fall list contains only one book of new poetry (Delmore Schwartz's *Genesis*), three books of reprinted poetry (two anthologies and the Poet of the Month pamphlets), three critical studies, a reprint of Lautréamont's *Maldoror*, and the 1942 *New Directions in Prose and Poetry* anthology.[17] The complete catalog for 1943 added only one book of new poetry to this (Robert Fitzgerald's *A Wreath for the Sea*), as well as six reprinted works of fiction and a new work of criticism. Looking for new books to include in the New Classics series, Laughlin kept his eye on the Modern Library list to see what that imprint was dropping, and in 1945 he unsuccessfully pursued such volumes as Frank Norris's *McTeague*, Arthur Koestler's *Darkness at Noon*, and a collected edition of Hart Crane's poetry. By 1946, though, new works were heavily represented in the catalog: five new novels, five new books of poetry, and only two critical studies, in addition to a new anthology, *Spearhead*. Laughlin also started to seek out student-aimed books, asking his Choate teacher Dudley Fitts to "put me in line of any textbooks which New Directions might profitably publish . . . the best way to handle the problem [of rising book-production costs] seems to be to build up a line of good sensible textbooks on which there would be a steady sale."[18]

Laughlin also began to call upon the literary establishment he had generally excoriated in order to ensure a wider audience for his books. In fact, he asked poet Stephen Vincent Benét to provide a blurb to be used in a flyer for the Poet of the Month series, and Benét agreed, writing that "Young poets need an audience as much as they need bread—and the young poet today finds great difficulties in the way of getting his work published. . . . Mr. Laughlin's scheme should be a help—not only to individual poets but to poetry itself."[19] Laughlin wanted established poets for the series, too, and offered Eliot a hundred dollars and a ten-cent-per-copy royalty if he would agree to let him use "Little Gidding" for a 1943 selection. Not everyone viewed the series positively, though; the Book-of-the-Month Club sent Laughlin a cease and desist letter in 1942 demanding that he change the name to " 'The Poet for December' or 'This Month's Poet.' " Laughlin balked, countering that he had used the name for two years and insisting that he would only change it on the condition that the club "re-imburse me for the reprinting of two issues which are already printed, and also for the reprinting of our promotional material and our mailing envelopes." (The club sent him $150.[20])

During the war, while Laughlin was broadening the New Directions list and building bridges to American literature's elder statesmen, he still had needed to devise a strategy for selling his cornerstone author. But Pound's indictment for treason, and the later public impression that he got off unfairly in being found insane, could hardly have hurt the market appeal of his books more. Laughlin concluded, then, that including Pound in the sizable list of new books New Directions was publishing just after the war would be a waste: in a 1945 letter to Dorothy Pound, he admitted that "sales [of Pound's books] have stopped almost completely."[21] He therefore resolved to initiate a concerted, wide-reaching, and long-term campaign not just to rehabilitate but to remake Pound—to initiate what he called a "counter-swing" in public opinion. The goal was to bolster market value and literary value simultaneously by convincing readers that the poet was not a fascist, and that even if he was, his politics should not affect appreciation of his poetry, because he was one of the truly great poets of the century.

Laughlin's first action was to recruit Pound's most eminent admirer, T. S. Eliot. He had been acquainted with Eliot at that point for over a decade, for at the same time (1933–34) that he set out to meet Stein, Pound, and Williams, he had also sent Eliot a "prose piece" for consideration by Faber. He admired Eliot as a poet, but from the beginning of their association he had approached him more as an editor than a writer. (In 1934, for example, Laughlin had asked Eliot's advice on where he should send his book-length manuscript on Gertrude Stein, which was "definitely not up to Faber" but still "rather a commercial proposition" intended to introduce Stein's work to the Americans who "saw her opera and read her autobiography."[22]) Throughout the 1930s, Laughlin and Eliot had interacted as business associates. But, more frequently as the war neared, they corresponded as concerned friends of Pound. "I am glad to hear your report [on *The Fifth Decad of Cantos*]," Eliot wrote in 1936, "and to know that Ezra is not altogether abandoning poetry to devote himself to economics and boosting Mussolini." "I rolled out of bed this morning," Laughlin wrote Eliot in 1939, "and there on the editorial page of the BOSTON HERALD was a letter to the editor from Ezra. The Sage was putting up Uncle George Tinkham for president."[23] In a mournful letter of 1942, referring to the radio broadcasts, Laughlin writes "Poor old EP. He seems to have gone the whole hog. He is 100% disgrace over here except for me, who can never forget what a wonderful guy he was."[24] The two transatlantically separated publishers—one jealous of his own place in literary history, one young, devoted, and increasingly ambitious—saw their own relationship mature through the medium of their absent and wayward friend and mentor. More to the point, in Laughlin and Eliot's association we see two central figures in the modernist movement helping each other in a seemingly most unmodernist activity: marketing and promotion.

Pound's incarceration, though, gave their friendship an urgent purpose. A cautious Eliot wrote Laughlin in October 1945 that "[w]hat I think is essential is that he should be persuaded to put himself entirely in the hand of a good lawyer and not attempt to talk much except under his lawyer's instructions."[25] Laughlin agreed and hired the capable Julien Cornell, who probably saved Pound from a treason conviction. Public opinion was very strongly against Pound—the *New Masses* was not the only publication calling for his head. "People like ourselves," Laughlin wrote Eliot, "tend to say 'Oh forget it, he's a good poet and the war's over.' But verminous creatures like [Walter] Winchell keep whipping up indignation and there are many great literary figures like Louis Untermeyer who have been sharpening their knives for a long time and will go after pounds of flesh."[26] Pound was strapped for money, and to pay for his defense Laughlin (on behalf of the new Committee for the Defense of Ezra Pound) had to obtain a $1,000 check from E. E. Cummings and, from Liveright, $300 in royalties accumulated during the war.[27]

Even while he was orchestrating Pound's defense, Laughlin was devising the strategy by which New Directions would handle the editing and marketing of his books. The plan Laughlin created in the dark days of late 1945 would determine the course of Pound's publication and promotion for the next ten years and, in its success, would assure his place in the American literary canon. Laughlin's initial ideas were modest, and centered on a dollar edition, aimed at students, of selected *Cantos:*

> If I can get him to pry himself loose from those morticians who hold his copyrights I hope to put on a revival campaign for the poetry. In

James Laughlin I was one of the founders of Jones and Laughlin, which would become one of the largest steel producers in America by 1900.

James Laughlin IV in the offices of New Directions—the barn at Meadow House, Norfolk, Connecticut—in 1941. (Courtesy of the Laughlin family)

New Directions' first advertisement for a Pound book, in the *Saturday Review of Literature,* 19 November 1938. (Courtesy of New Directions Publishing Corp.)

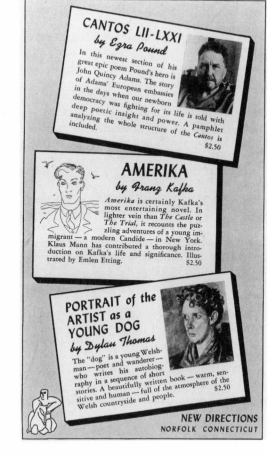

Saturday Review of Literature, 19 October 1940. The photograph of Pound was taken by James Jesus Angleton, who edited the literary magazine *Furioso* at the time and would later become the CIA's chief of counterintelligence during the height of the Cold War. (Courtesy of New Directions Publishing Corp.)

Ezra Pound at the time of his arrival in Washington, 1945. (Wide World Photos)

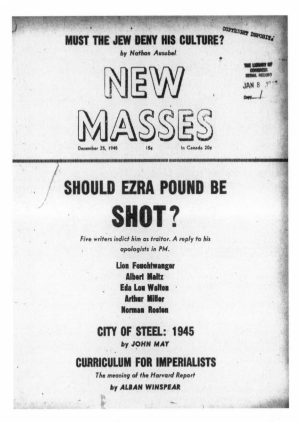

NEW MASSES

December 25, 1945   15¢   In Canada 20¢

SHOULD EZRA POUND BE
SHOT?

*Five writers indict him as traitor. A reply to his
apologists in PM.*

**Lion Feuchtwanger
Albert Maltz
Eda Lou Walton
Arthur Miller
Norman Rosten**

CITY OF STEEL: 1945
by JOHN MAY

CURRICULUM FOR IMPERIALISTS
The meaning of the Harvard Report
by ALBAN WINSPEAR

New Masses cover asking a question on many people's minds in 1945. (Courtesy of International Publishers)

Ezra Pound on his admission to St. Elizabeths Hospital, 26 December 1945. (Wide World Photos)

Inside front cover of the *Quarterly Review of Literature* 4.3 (1948). (Courtesy of New Directions Publishing Corp.)

Partisan Review, April 1949. New Directions did not hesitate to use the Bollingen Prize in its advertising, notwithstanding the ensuing controversy. (Courtesy of New Directions Publishing Corp.)

Hugh Kenner in 1958. Laughlin said that Kenner's *Poetry of Ezra Pound* (1951) "got Pound listed on the academic stock exchange."

Ezra Pound on his 1958 arrival in Naples. (Wide World Photos)

Pound's *Impact* was published by Regnery, a company that has always specialized in conservative books. (Courtesy of Regnery Publishing, Inc.)

Pound and Laughlin in 1965. (Courtesy of the Laughlin family)

James Laughlin in the New Directions offices in New York in 1974.
(Courtesy of New Directions Publishing Corp.)

that connection I would like to urge you some day to mark in the margin with a pencil in the books of the cantos the parts that you think the finest. I'd like to try a selection. . . . I don't think a selection would be unfair to the poem as a whole. I have saved the plates of all four volumes and will do a complete reprint in due time, but the little dollar selection might be a shot in the arm. One or two of my Stalinist authors might quit me in protest but I don't think any of my really good ones would. They incline to be sympathetic.[28]

Laughlin soon realized, though, that simply reprinting Pound's poetry would not be adequate. This republication campaign had to be accompanied by a publicity push—a "propaganda campaign," Laughlin called it— that would need to recruit influential figures to support those few voices (his own and Eliot's) arguing on Pound's behalf.[29] In a late 1945 letter, Laughlin told Eliot that "there has been so much publicity about his being (not being accused of being) a traitor that we must go to work here with a campaign to reestablish his standing. If we can get Hemingway to let us use publicly what he has said privately in letters to Julien [Cornell] we will have something to work with. Hem states that bitter anti-fascist as he was he never hated Ezra because he realized he was not responsible for what he was doing. If we can get that around it will start the counter-swing." The momentum of this counter-swing would be provided by a public relations push, Laughlin continued:

> The next step will be to get the good critics to write about him again, and to get little magazines to devote special issues to his work and pieces about him.
> In this connection, anything you can find in England will be most helpful, either statements by big literary "names," or articles pointing out the great merits of his poetry or other writings.[30]

Less than two weeks later, Laughlin saw an opportunity and urged Eliot to go into action.

> [T]his is to tell you that the editors of POETRY, who three years ago "renounced" EP with some nasty language, are now repentant of their folly and want to devote a special issue to him. . . . Now I am greatly

hoping that you will want to write the cornerstone essay for this issue. . . . It will be the first blow in our battle to reinstate Ezra and a strong one because POETRY has a wide circulation and goes to every college and library. With this lead, many other things will follow. But the first blow has to be a strong one. I think we can get some pretty top people interested on this side, and I hope that you will ask one or two others over there to contribute, in addition to your own piece.[31]

Eliot quickly agreed. On hearing this, Laughlin gratefully wrote him both about the campaign and about his own assessment of Pound's mental state.

I was delighted to have your letter in which you say that you will find the time to write an essay about EP's poetry for the special number of Poetry Magazine. That is wonderful and will help so much in the publicity campaign to clear him of the stigma of the treason charge. . . .

[Pound] realizes that he is not insane but is willing to have the world think so if it will enable him to live to go on with his work. . . .

I must tell you however that I am beginning to feel that the diagnosis of the doctors—"a paranoid state in a psychopathic personality"—may be medically correct. Today as we talked his mind did wander frightfully and he told me the following tale: that he could not understand why the Jews wished to conspire to hang him since he had worked out a complete plan for rebuilding their old temple in Jerusalem.[32]

With Pound's conviction now only remotely possible because of increasing recognition that he was mentally ill, Laughlin quickly began to incorporate the rhetoric of aesthetic formalism into his appeals. In an early manifestation of this publicity campaign, he wrote testily in the "Editor's Notes" for the 1946 issue of *New Directions* that "a poem is a thing in itself. You judge it by itself, for itself and of itself—not by the politics of the man who wrote it." Ten years after the manifestolike activist rhetoric of the first "Preface" to *New Directions,* Laughlin was retreating from that position, having learned from ten years of trying to market Pound that an appeal grounded in the integration of politics, art, and culture, although it was Pound's—and his own—viewpoint, was not the best approach to promoting the poet's books.

Pound's fortunes were harmed by his indictment and New Directions also experienced some disapproval for supporting him. In response, Laughlin sought to reinforce the apolitical image he had built for his firm. Although resolved to publish Pound, he sought advice before taking on other controversial authors—Louis-Ferdinand Céline, for instance. Laughlin asked Malcolm Cowley's advice about the prospects of publishing Céline in America, and received the response that "He is a crazy Jew-baiting French fascist. You can't reprint his work now, at this moment, without, by implication, defending his anti-human politics. Ten years from now, it will probably be a different question. And it is a different question from that of Pound, who was never dangerous, not even when he was speaking over the Rome radio. . . . Pound's work as a whole contributes to life, because it *can* be separated from his crazy politics. Céline's works can't be separated, at present, from his hatefulness. Wait ten years."[33]

Laughlin certainly had made peace with the publisher's imperative to act pragmatically, as a retrospective story in *Publishers' Weekly* on New Directions' tenth anniversary illustrates.[34] Here, he credits his Choate mentor Dudley Fitts with being an early inspiration, but neglects to mention Pound in describing the firm's beginnings—a remarkable omission, for it was Pound who had told Laughlin to go into publishing, who had gotten him his position as the editor of the "New Directions" literary column of *New Democracy* magazine, and whose works were the focus of the house in its early years. Nor is Pound mentioned when Laughlin discusses early experiences with publishing controversies. The only hint of political strife appears late in the article, in a section titled "The Common Denominator: No Political Frontiers": "The only least common denominator among all these widely assorted authors is their contribution to the world of literary thought, divorced from political, racial or geographical boundaries. . . . [T]he authors on the New Directions lists range from fascist to communist in political views."[35] Pound is mentioned only twice (once as an example of the "cosmopolitan" nature of the house, and once noting that his "Unwavering Pivot of Confucius" would be published in the New Directions periodical *Pharos*). Instead, the focus is on the literature, the proven (Melville, Henry James, Baudelaire) and up-and-coming (Djuna Barnes, Kay Boyle, Pablo Neruda) names on the New Directions list, and the exciting variety of imprints and series the house was offering.[36] Given Pound's well-publicized trial only seven months earlier and his role in the founding of New Directions, his absence is conspicuous.

The "New Literary Consensus"

At the end of the war, Laughlin's task seemed almost impossible. Never a critical favorite, Pound had now become a political pariah, and readers who felt that literature had any social responsibility at all had rejected him. Laughlin could no longer rely on finessed explanations such as he had given in the "Notes on the *Cantos*" in 1940; now, the mere mention of Pound's politics was damaging to the poet's fortunes. Even his poetry was tainted by anti-Semitic themes and, at times, language: when Eliot and Laughlin were plotting out their "propaganda campaign," Eliot had pointed out Pound's use of the slur "yidds" in the still-unpublished *Pisan Cantos* and suggested that "we ought to censor this a bit."[37] Laughlin now outwardly rejected his earlier contention that experimental writing had a task to play in transforming the world, and fell back to the position that art should not be evaluated on its social impact. Fortunately for Laughlin and for Pound, these same years saw the rise of two groups of intellectuals—the New Critics and the New York Intellectuals—who both argued for aesthetic autonomy (albeit to differing degrees) and for freeing literature from commercial pressures. After World War II they formed a "new literary consensus," in the words of Lawrence Schwartz.[38] Like Laughlin—and Pound—both groups were profoundly suspicious of corporations, the middle class, and capitalism. "Consequently," Janice Radway points out in *A Feeling for Books*, "they labored industriously to establish their own distance from capital by insisting on the categorical difference between the economic and the cultural, between the market and art."[39]

Both groups had also been active in moving literary criticism toward aesthetic formalism. By the 1940s, the endorsement of aesthetic formalism that especially the New Critics pioneered was already a powerful force. Random House publisher Bennett Cerf provides a characteristic example of how this sentiment was gaining prominence. After his 1944 decree, on the occasion of the publication of Conrad Aiken and William Rose Benét's *Famous English and American Poetry*, that Pound could never appear in a Random House publication, Cerf was taken aback by vehement arguments that political concerns should have no bearing on aesthetic judgment, writing that "I discovered to my intense surprise and horror that almost every important critic sided with him and not with me. They said that it was a poetry anthology and I was acting as a censor."[40] The joint efforts of the New Critics and New York Intellectuals in the 1940s and 1950s to strengthen nonideological aesthetic criticism made formalist criticism almost orthodoxy in America; at the same time, they enabled Laughlin's promotion of Pound into the elite of American artists.

The New York Intellectuals and the New Critics worked together through much of the 1940s and 1950s on panels, symposia, cultural exchange programs, and foundation-sponsored publications. They competed for Rockefeller and Ford Foundation grants and cooperated on such organs of American cultural propaganda as *Encounter* and *Perspectives USA*.[41] Although their political attitudes differed drastically, they shared similar outlooks toward art, especially after the Intellectuals' strong leftism was diluted by their postwar anti-Communism. In addition, as Hugh Wilford points out in *The New York Intellectuals*, "*Partisan Review* [the Intellectuals' journal] maintained a cordial relationship with the *Kenyon* and *Sewanee Reviews* [journals dominated by New Critics]. The three magazines shared a number of contributors; their editors collaborated professionally (Philip Rahv taught at John Crowe Ransom's Kenyon School of Letters) and mixed socially (Rahv and Allen Tate were good friends)."[42] Both groups, interestingly, were published by New Directions (Ransom's *The New Criticism* and Rahv's *Image and Idea*, among others, were important critical statements issued by Laughlin's firm). Both granted wide latitude to the realm of literature and gave a special importance to T. S. Eliot. Both groups believed that art is a "special kind of knowledge" or a particular "mode of perception" that cannot be equated with the knowledge and perception of everyday activity.[43] Most importantly, they converged in their arguments for an essentially (if not strictly) aestheticist view in which the political stance of the artist or the work should not matter in evaluating the work. Neither group, however, took the extreme aestheticist position that denies the work any social role.

The New Critics were a loosely constituted group sharing a fundamental belief in the special and unique existence of works of art, especially literary ones. The early New Critics John Crowe Ransom, Cleanth Brooks, Robert Penn Warren, and Allen Tate began their careers at schools far removed from the centers of academic power on the East Coast, and became known for their anticommercial cultural and pro-

Southern political stances. Their group's genesis coincided with that of the great works of later modernism—*The Fugitive* (their journal, from which they took their initial name), for instance, was founded in 1922, the year of *The Waste Land* and *Ulysses*. As their ideas about poetry began to overshadow their political ideas, the Fugitive movement evolved into a much larger yet more specifically literary movement known as the New Criticism. Recognizing in modernist literature their own disgust with contemporary bourgeois industrial society, the New Critics adopted that literature, but more importantly joined with Eliot in rewriting the canon of English literature, devaluing the Romantics and focusing on what Eliot called "the metaphysical poets" in their search for ideal forms of poetry.[44]

New Criticism's founding principle was the special ontology of the poem and the unique kind of knowledge and experience it contains. In his entry for "New Criticism" in the *Princeton Encyclopedia of Poetry and Poetics*, Brooks put forth one of the salient aspects of the approach: "A crucial premise is that literary art contains a distinct kind of knowledge. Yet that knowledge is not essentially a matter of 'statement': rather, the poem, drama, or fiction renders an experience, and in describing the nature of such an experience, many of the New Critics rejected the old dualism of form and content."[45] Vincent Leitch, in his *American Literary Criticism from the Thirties to the Eighties,* expands on this. For the New Criticism, Leitch explains, a poem "stood alone—timeless . . . separated from its producers and consumers. . . . What was highly esteemed were complex, free-standing poems filled with intricate semantic interrelations."[46] Part of a poem's timelessness was the omission of any type of sociopolitical content in favor of the cultivation of the aesthetic sensation. John Crowe Ransom commented that the truly "modern" poet "has disdained social responsibility in order to secure this pure esthetic effect. He cares nothing, professionally, about morals, or God, or native land. He has performed a work of dissociation and purified his art."[47]

Although they endorsed the idea of aesthetic autonomy, the New Critics also shared some of the Arnoldian sense that works of art have a social function. Good artworks elevated taste, brought about refinement, and conferred distinction on individuals who opened themselves to the aesthetic experience. This, of course, strongly resembles the claims of the new trade literary publishers as to why literature was good for consumers, but "taste" and "distinction" meant drastically different things to the two groups. For the New Critics, these qualities made better citizens who would help construct a more ideal society; for the publishers, these qualities were simply personal attributes that helped consumers position themselves in social fields.[48]

The New Critics' ideal poet was Eliot; in addition, many of his critical pronouncements became foundations for their method. During the heyday of the New Criticism, roughly from 1935 to 1970, Eliot was a leading figure in English poetry, his critical opinions expressive of the dominant attitude toward literary works of the day. John Guillory, in his essay "T. S. Eliot and Cleanth Brooks," argues that since the critical judgments of those two writers were systematically laid down in the late 1930s and early 1940s, "the canon of Eliot and Brooks" has been dominant in academic literary study.[49] Hugh Kenner agrees, though he identifies Eliot's collaborator as the British critic F. R. Leavis.[50]

While the New Criticism offered an approach to Pound's allusive, difficult method, his aims too clearly exhibited what Cleanth Brooks called the "didactic heresy"—the desire for art to serve a sociopolitical purpose. Consequently, most of the New Critics saw Pound as a figure of secondary importance who insisted on diluting the aesthetic effect with such aims.[51] Pound's work (especially the *Cantos*), seen in relation to Eliot's, was judged incomplete and, most important, lacking in unity. For Pound, it had unity—in his overarching vision of what was lacking in society and what needed to be done to remedy this deficiency. His readers, confronted by the seeming jumble of styles, influences, languages, allusions, concepts, and historical personages, were less sure that a unifying principle somehow underpinned this epic-in-progress. Allen Tate, otherwise a defender of Pound's work, felt that the *Cantos* were "formless, eccentric, and personal . . . about nothing at all . . . Mr. Pound is incapable of sustained thought in either prose or verse. His acute verbal sensibility is thus at the mercy of random flights of 'angelic insight,' an Icarian self-indulgence of prejudice which is not checked by a total view to which it could be subordinated."[52] Another New Critic, R. P. Blackmur, had stated in 1934 that

> Ezra Pound is neither a great poet nor a great thinker. . . . Mr. Pound is at his best a maker of great verse rather than a great poet. When you

look into him, deeply as you can, you will not find any extraordinary revelation of life, nor any bottomless fund of feeling; nor will you find any mode of life already formulated, any collection of established feelings, composed or mastered in new form. The content of his work does not submit to analysis; it is not the kind of content that can be analyzed—because, separated, its components retain no being. . . . Mr. Pound is explicit; he is all surface and articulation.[53]

When he read Blackmur in the Harvard-based quarterly *Hound and Horn,* Pound wrote Laughlin that it was "24 depressing pages."[54] Laughlin assured Pound that Blackmur "is unwilling to see that the CANTOS are the one non-defeatist poem of the age that shows what life is like and where it has been and what about it."[55] For the New Critics, however, the formal attributes of a poem mattered tremendously more than its content; where balance, subtlety, tension, and ambiguity were held in the highest regard, Pound's often vehement, formless *Cantos* stood little chance of immortality.

As the most influential American literary scholars, the New Critics became the most important audience for Laughlin's campaign. Their general beliefs about art made them amenable, for the poet's most obvious obstacle to literary respectability was his personal history, and a poet's personal history, according to the New Critics, was of little importance in evaluating a body of work. The New Critics did see Pound as a second-rank poet, but for Laughlin, getting him readmitted to the mainstream of literary history—even if it was, for the time being, only to the second rank—was a great accomplishment. Once the New Critics accepted Pound, Laughlin and Eliot reckoned, their public would also accept him. And although the New Critics never did accept Pound as a great poet, they altered the methodology of literary evaluation in a number of ways that enabled Laughlin to later argue precisely the position on Pound that they had opposed: that he was a great poet. Their emphasis on the importance of reading a poem in isolation, and their insistence that a poem contains a special kind of knowledge, provided Laughlin with grounds for arguing that Pound should not be judged on his political utterances, only on the aesthetic quality of his poetry.

The New Critics' domination of American literary study also led to the migration of literary criticism to the universities—another development exploited by Laughlin. In his book *Who Are the Major American Writers?*, Jay B. Hubbell notes:

> As late as 1920 American literature was just beginning to be a respectable subject for scholarly investigation and only then for writers who had been dead for a quarter of a century. Until after the First World War the professors had only a minor part in determining the status of American writers living or dead. The actual work of revising the American literary canon was done—often in spite of the opposition of academic critics—by young intellectuals led by such critics and propagandists as H. L. Mencken, Louis Untermeyer, Van Wyck Brooks, Amy Lowell, and Conrad Aiken.[56]

The power to define what is "literary," then, moved from the sphere of journalists and professional writers to the more closed, self-selecting world of the academy. "The success of the New Criticism," David Shumway writes in *Creating American Civilization*, "definitively marks the capture of the literary by the university."[57] As Shumway points out, the New Critics transformed the job of academic criticism from historical or philological excavation to hermeneutics, or interpretation. In 1938, Ransom expressed the New Critical desire for a "professional" class of literary critics, practicing a "scientific, precise, and systematic" method; he argued that the college professor is "the very professional we need to take charge of the critical activity." "Rather than occasional criticism by amateurs," he said, "I should think the whole enterprise might seriously be taken in hand by professionals. Perhaps I use a distasteful figure, but I have the idea that what we need is Criticism, Inc."[58]

Ransom's idea epitomizes the compromises and contradictions inherent in maintaining aesthetic autonomy. His goal was to preserve the special sphere for art that the doctrine had been developed to defend. By institutionalizing literary study, he hoped to take evaluation out of the hands of amateurs (who were likely to be influenced by passing trends or other social factors) and put it into the hands of disinterested professionals, who would practice a "scientific" (logically sound) form of evaluation. These disinterested professionals would be unlikely to be influenced by political or social climate shifts, and could reliably evaluate art without regard to controversy or commercial influence. Literary criticism was to be a specialized branch of knowledge with its own training regimen and positions of authority. Ransom's metaphor of a corporation also hints at the intrusion of commerce into the autonomous sphere of art. His call to bracket art, to set art's "special knowledge" apart for interpretation only by a trained few, displays the very mark of the commercial culture it attempts to escape.[59] However fraught with contradictions the call for professionalization was, though, Ransom's project was, by the 1950s, largely successful. Perhaps the most important and widely influential statement of the New Critics, Cleanth Brooks and Robert Penn Warren's 1938 textbook *Understanding Poetry*, codified New Critical reading and teaching practice and became, in American colleges and even high schools, a sort of training manual for future literary professionals.[60]

The professionalization of literary criticism had broad implications for Laughlin, Pound, and New Directions in the coming decades. Mainstream literary journalism—in magazines and other periodicals—had long since deemed Pound unfit for wide popularity, primarily because of the difficulty and allusiveness of his poetry; his post-1941 political troubles only solidified the notion that his work did not belong in any American canon. This judgment, though, sprang from the notion that literature needed to be edifying, to build a better citizen. The New Critics would make it possible, at least theoretically, for Pound to attain the status of a classic author.[61] This, though, would not be accomplished until the 1950s, when they had been joined in the academy by a new generation schooled in the New Critical method but unwilling simply to reproduce New Critical judgments on specific writers.

In postwar America, only the New York Intellectuals rivaled the New Critics in literary influence.[62] Both groups began from explicitly political grounds, and both moved—though to differing degrees—to defending the need to judge art apolitically. Although they did not reach the height of their influence until the late 1940s and early 1950s, the New York Intellectuals had begun to formulate their approach to art and culture in the early 1930s. The group—which, in the beginning, consisted of William Phillips, Philip Rahv, Mary McCarthy, Delmore Schwartz, and Dwight Macdonald, but later numbered among its members Lionel and Diana Trilling, James Farrell, Norman Mailer, Alfred Kazin, Hannah Arendt, Irving Howe, Irving Kristol, Lewis Coser, Daniel Bell, Nathan

Glazer, and many others—followed in the tradition of American cultural critics (from Benjamin Franklin and Ralph Waldo Emerson to Henry Adams and Van Wyck Brooks) who examined culture's relationship to politics and history instead of examining it as solely a product of politics and history or an isolated realm with little relation to politics or history.[63] Their pull on postwar America's cultural thinking was enormous, and they provided a model for left-wing intellectuals who rejected the Soviet stand on cultural and political issues. The Intellectuals' outlet, *Partisan Review,* consistently opposed the Marxist idea that art must serve a political purpose; art had some degree of autonomy from social function, and needed freedom to range over all subjects and to experiment with form.[64]

Like the New Critics, the New York Intellectuals were key in moving American intellectuals to an acceptance of modernist literature, the complexities and ambiguities of which they saw as evidence of its artistic superiority.[65] Perhaps because of their backgrounds as the children of immigrants (or, in Philip Rahv's case, as an immigrant), the Intellectuals had little deep-seated connection to "Americanism" and embraced modernism, cosmopolitanism, and internationalism. "The New York Intellectuals ... played an important role ... [in] the emergence of academic modernism at the center of the elite culture of the intellectual establishment, in the universities and in publishing circles," according to intellectual historian Alan Wald, and Hugh Wilford adds that, conversely, "the Intellectuals owed the success they belatedly enjoyed in the universities to the knowledge of Modernism they had acquired during the 1930s and early 1940s."[66] The acceptance of modernism by the academy and the rise of the New York Intellectuals were symbiotic, and Pound naturally benefited both from the Intellectuals' endorsement of modernism and from modernism's acceptance by the university community.

Perhaps the New York Intellectuals' most enduring idea has been their designations of levels of culture—"lowbrow," "middlebrow," and "highbrow."[67] This stemmed from a very non-Communist horror of the masses, of vulgarization, and of the simple gratification offered by cultural products such as popular music, Hollywood films, and "subliterary" novels. Their hostility toward the lowbrow and the middlebrow was based on the judgment that both levels simply encouraged passive consumption of mass culture. This mass culture, in turn, was an unadulterated expression of the ideology of bourgeois society, and in consuming it lowbrows and middlebrows uncritically ingested the ideological with the cultural.[68] Many of the Intellectuals then compared this passive consumerism with the effects of Stalinism, and in an interesting rhetorical turn equated middle-class capitalism with Stalinism, each seen as attempting ideological coercion in all forms of cultural production. Middlebrow culture was incapable of critique of or resistance to the dominant ideology, for it was entirely infected by it. Only the complexities and difficulties of modernism, the Intellectuals reasoned, resisted the insidious simplicity of middlebrow and lowbrow culture. Just as modernism resisted the easy answers of mass culture, the institutions of middlebrow culture saw the danger to bourgeois ideology posed by modernism and actively opposed it. As the predominant institutions reproducing bourgeois ideology, the American educational system and the business community—the New York Intellectuals felt—were bent on snuffing out modernism. In his 1946 *Partisan Review* essay "Pilgrim to Philistia," William Barrett wrote that the "crusaders in the anti-modernist witch hunt" included "tweedy professors of English, the Book of the Month businessmen, [and] the nostalgic fantasists of Americana." In other words, these antimodernist crusaders were not representatives of the degraded lowbrow masses, but important figures in middlebrow Establishment culture.[69]

The role the New York Intellectuals played in Pound's remaking is central, but perhaps the most direct effect they had was to suggest to American leftist intellectuals that an admiration of modernism in general and of Pound's work in particular did not necessarily contradict a radical political outlook. The Intellectuals did find Pound's politics repellent, of course, and their deep (if often unacknowledged) mistrust of everything that took place outside of the large cities or west of the Hudson River compounded their difficulties with him; Irving Howe felt that Pound had a "streak of the Midwestern crank, the cracker-barrel philosopher" in him, and in another essay he inaccurately referred to the Idaho-born, Philadelphia-raised poet as a "midwestern provincial."[70] Notwithstanding their personal distaste, though, the Intellectuals genuinely respected Pound's achievements as a poet, and were certain that this in no way invalidated their own revulsion at his politics, especially his anti-Semitism.

An important effect of the New York Intellectuals' influence was the cultivation of a general intellectual and academic disdain for mass or popular (for the Intellectuals, the two were almost indistinguishable) culture and a privileging of the "highbrow" or difficult.[71] At a time when poets like Frost and novelists like Hemingway, who had genuine middlebrow appeal, were becoming popular, the Intellectuals forcefully argued that their simplicities were a poor substitute for the rewarding complexities of an Eliot or Kafka—or Pound.

While the New Critics were comfortable in the "ivory tower," and gradually moved from their home bases at Southern universities to the country's elite academic institutions, the New York Intellectuals (with the exception of Lionel Trilling) stayed away from the academy. Delmore Schwartz—a close friend of Pound's and an early New Directions author— even warned *Partisan Review*'s readers in 1952 against the professionalization of literary study: "As the New Criticism naturally tends to attach literature to the university, so only a critical non-conformist intelligentsia, inside and outside the university, can right the balance and keep serious literature from becoming merely a set of courses."[72] Philip Rahv felt that intellectuals' flight to universities actually signaled the *"embourgeoisement* of the American intelligentsia." Where the New Critics felt that academic professionalization enshrined and protected their disinterested, unbiased perspective on literature, the New York Intellectuals felt that such professionals would simply transfer their loyalties to the institutions of bourgeois education and, in turn, to bourgeois society. Rahv proposed, instead, a new avant-garde, motivated by dissent and a refusal to accommodate to mass culture. In addition, Irving Howe's contribution to *Partisan Review*'s 1952 "Our Country and Our Culture" symposium argued that assimilation into the university system had enervated intellectuals' drive to critically analyze society. "The relation of the institutional world to the intellectuals," Howe explained, "is as the relation of middlebrow culture to serious culture, the one battens on the other, absorbs and raids it with increasing frequency and skill, subsidizes it and encourages it enough to make further raids possible."[73] Howe's notion of the "middlebrow" certainly would include the New Critics, for their position within the academic establishment made them complicit with the "institutional world." His "serious culture" encompassed such modernist texts as *Ulysses* and *The Waste Land*, and the development he decries here is the institutional drive to void such works of their transgressive or oppositional character and make them simply formal and aesthetic exercises. The fact that Howe was able to identify a progressive social function in modernism without referring to the reactionary politics of many modernist writers facilitated the New York Intellectuals' endorsement of modernism.

Notwithstanding their disagreements on the question of professionalization, and notwithstanding the New York Intellectuals' desire that literature work social change, the transformation that the New Critics and the Intellectuals brought to literary study prepared the way for Pound's rehabilitation, even if neither group felt his works worthy of serious study. Both groups argued, in essence, that those "ordinary" citizens who were so horrified at Pound's activities and who allowed that horror to keep them from his poetry were incapable of a sufficiently full view of literature. The Intellectuals' denigration of the lowbrow and the middlebrow was grounded in the belief that neither class could make aesthetic judgments, tainted as they were by the bourgeois ideological content of the cultural products they consumed. Only superior commentators such as themselves, they believed, could approach literature in the refined and disinterested manner required to make a truly legitimate evaluation. Similarly, the New Critics' drive toward professionalization was based in the notion that the special nature of literature necessitated critics with specialized training. Lay commentators were not sophisticated enough, not privy to the mysteries of the metaphor, and were thereby unqualified to pass judgment. Both of these attitudes toward literary study entirely devalue the idea of "common sense," of the quotidian or middlebrow approach to literature exemplified by the *Saturday Review*. Furthermore, they reject the desire that literature be socially useful, for it is now to be judged "good" on formal, not social, criteria. Consequently, the conclusions of the commonsense approach—which often found Pound either too obscure or too personally offensive to be ranked with the greats—were simply dismissed as the result of amateurism. If Pound were to be judged deficient, it would have to be on the specialized criteria of formalist evaluation.[74]

Postwar Publication and the Bollingen Prize

The grounds of literary evaluation were clearly changing. But to take advantage of this new (and New) critical climate, Laughlin had to produce new books for critics to evaluate. Immediately after the end of World War II, he led New Directions through a period of rapid growth during which the house finally began to turn a profit. The end of the war meant the end of restrictions on paper, and Laughlin took advantage of the drop in paper prices to increase output significantly. Postponed projects by Christopher Isherwood, Thomas Merton, and Pablo Neruda, all of whom later became important authors for the house, appeared in 1946, and in the catalog for that year Laughlin also added two new series, also aimed at a student audience, to the previously established New Classics and Makers of Modern Literature: the Selected Writings series and the Modern Readers series. In addition, he announced a number of critical studies—of Kafka, Mann, and others—for this year. Although Pound had not yet appeared in any New Directions series and was yet to be the subject of a New Directions critical publication, Laughlin announced in the 1946 catalog the imminent publication of the first "complete edition" of the *Cantos*, as well as the reissue of *Personae*, newly available from New Directions.[75] The "counter-swing" was working up momentum. Dudley Fitts was correcting Pound's Greek in the eagerly anticipated *Pisan Cantos* manuscript, and Laughlin wrote E. E. Cummings jubilantly that "we will soon bring them [the Pisans] out, also re-issue the others, also take over *Personae*, also issue a dollar selection of all the best poems. I dare say a lot of the people who think Cerf is God will throw ND books out the window as a result."[76]

In the immediate postwar period, Pound was primarily interested in his Chinese material, and Laughlin used this shift as an opportunity to distract his readers' attention from the poet's legal troubles. He even cautiously mentioned Pound's beliefs and Pound the person in advertising for the resulting books. Pound had published three separate translations of Confucius in Italy during the war years, and New Directions collected them as "Confucius, The Unwobbling Pivot and The Great Digest" in Winter 1947 issue of the New Directions *Pharos* periodical. (*Pharos* was a New Directions magazine published only from 1945 to 1947, each issue devoted to one text. The magazine series was later renamed *Direction*.) Exercising his customary caution, Laughlin gently urged Pound not to use the literal translation of the original Italian title, *"L'asse che non vacilla"*: "Possum [T. S. Eliot] says for you to call it PIVOT not AXIS on account of the recent You Know What."[77] Although he knew the work had little mainstream appeal, and although he was well aware of Pound's sinking in public opinion, Laughlin even spent some money advertising the book. A seven-book list advertisement in the Summer 1947 issue of *Sewanee Re-*

view places Pound discreetly in the middle and explains the public anger at his politics as a result of circumstances beyond the poet's control:

EZRA POUND

has always been a profound admirer of Confucius, his understanding of the master's teachings deepening with the years. During the intervals of his illness he has had the opportunity to prepare a completely revised version, with expanded interpretive notes, of *Confucius' Great Digest and Unwobbling Pivot* ($1.00). It is Pound's contention that these texts reveal the secret of his own misunderstood political philosophy and provide bases for a stable world order.

This advertisement distances New Directions from the accusations of treason and anti-Semitism by both citing "illness" and placing responsibility for any political statements on poet, not publisher. It also tells us that Pound desires precisely what the reasonable and admirable men behind the United Nations also want: "a stable world order."

In 1947 Laughlin followed up the Chinese translations with several important new editions of Pound's poetic work. The first and most obvious project was to get into print the poems that Pound had written while in the Disciplinary Training Center in Pisa. The volume, entitled appropriately *The Pisan Cantos,* was published on 30 July 1948. Pound here talks frankly about his imprisonment in the "gorilla cage" in Pisa; he continues to suggest anti-Semitism in his economic themes; and he makes no concession to his detractors. The book begins by eulogizing Mussolini: "The enormous tragedy of the dream in the peasant's bent shoulders . . . / Thus Ben and la Clara a Milano/ by the heels at Milano. . . ." The book's subject matter appeared to run directly counter to Laughlin's desire to depoliticize Pound, to separate his work from his personal history, for everywhere in the poetry his beliefs and experiences appear. The almost unanimous praise with which critics greeted the book is thus surprising.

The reviewers' positive tone and their failure to discuss Pound's personal travails is striking. Robert Fitzgerald, in the *New Republic,* praised both New Directions and Pound, saying that "We find ourselves, again, in debt to New Directions, now that the latest cantos of Ezra Pound are available in a volume to themselves. . . . The publication is admirable—

and far from being simply an admirable act of piety. . . . I submit that these Cantos in which light and air—and song—move so freely are more exhilarating poetic sketch books, 'Notes from Upper Air,' than can be found elsewhere in our literature."[78] Louis Martz came "with pleased surprise to the new *Pisan Cantos*," admitting that "perhaps . . . our interest in a great part of the new Cantos lies at the edge of the poetical . . . that *The Pisan Cantos* are really a brilliant note-book held together by the author's personality," but felt that they were the best of the *Cantos*.[79] In *Imagi*, William Carlos Williams expressed a similar positive ambivalence: "I have not (even yet) read every word of the *Pisan Cantos*, nor deciphered half those I have read. But I have seen enough to be indifferent to many of them and to find myself wonderfully enlightened by the art of others."[80] Each of these reviews implicitly employs formalist New Critical criteria, and Martz even implicitly opposes the formal excellence of the work and the less worthy interest in it caused by Pound's notoriety. Not everyone was convinced, though, either by the poems or by Laughlin's marketing. The *Saturday Review*, predictably, was among these. For William Van O'Connor, writing for the magazine, the organization was "chaotic," his statements "multiple and muddled," and Pound himself "mad."[81]

New Directions' publicity for this book was a definitive statement of the change in the house's stance regarding the relation of art to society. "We want to release the new editions," Laughlin informed Eliot just before *The Pisan Cantos* appeared in the United States, "reinforced with a press release designed to intimidate the idiots who would try to be amusing at Ez's expense. We got a marvelous statement from Tate and five or six others have also come through in good style. One from you would be the best possible of all. Just say anything you want. You don't need to commit yourself in any way as to the merits of the Pisans. What is needed is just something that will remind people to look at the poetry as poetry, not at what Winchell is yapping in his column about Ez."[82] Eliot acquiesced, and in a *Quarterly Review of Literature* advertisement, New Directions borrowed the prestige of three of the leading poet-critics of the day—Eliot, Tate, and John Crowe Ransom—and addressed the political question frankly. In this advertisement, Tate says that "Whether Pound was guilty of treason I do not know: he could not be brought to trial. And to be indicted is not to be convicted. . . . Call it, if you will, a political mistake, unless it is a failure to distinguish between the imaginative and historical orders . . . One of the Popes had Dante's works burned because he had supported the cause of the Emperor. Who cares about Dante's politics today?"[83] Smaller advertisements, list ads featuring *The Pisan Cantos* prominently but including other books, also ran in publications aimed at academics and intellectuals, such as the *Western Review* and the *Kenyon Review*. Laughlin's successful publicity strategy for *The Pisan Cantos* did much to reconcile him to Pound. In 1945 and 1946, Pound had been displeased with Laughlin for many of the publisher's decisions—he had even told Charles Olson that he believed Laughlin had "no flair as a publisher."[84] A month later, though, the mercurial poet was again impressed by Laughlin's energy and talent, calling him "the last hope [in America] of publishing surviving the deluge."[85]

Although critics were enthusiastic about *The Pisan Cantos* and the simultaneously released collected (with the exception of numbers 72 and 73) *Cantos,* Pound's poetry did not command public attention until February 1949, when the Library of Congress announced that he had won the inaugural Bollingen Prize in Poetry. Sponsored by the Bollingen Foundation, a group associated with Carl Jung and the Mellon family, the prize awarded $1,000 to the author of "the best book of verse by an American author published during the preceding calendar year." The committee in charge of the award was composed of the thirteen Library of Congress Fellows in American Letters for 1948: Allen Tate, Robert Penn Warren, Louise Bogan, Karl Shapiro, Robert Lowell, Conrad Aiken, W. H. Auden, Katherine Garrison Chapin, T. S. Eliot, Paul Green, Katherine Anne Porter, Theodore Spencer, and Willard Thorp. Meeting on 18 and 19 November 1948, it considered the prize. That the award would go to Pound was, Tate observed, almost a foregone conclusion; the only other contender was Williams's *Paterson* (Book Two). At this meeting, however, the committee could not come to a consensus—two Fellows abstained, three (Shapiro, Aiken, and Chapin) voted for Williams, and the vote of one recently deceased member (Theodore Spencer) went to Pound because the committee deemed that Spencer would have so voted had he been alive.[86] The committee decided to take another vote, by mail, the following February. On that ballot, the proposal to honor Pound carried, and the committee issued a press release on 20 February 1949. Acknowledging the inevitable furor that their decision would spark, the Bollingen committee attempted to defuse any potential controversy by appealing, just at Laughlin was doing, to the autonomy of the aesthetic and to the "objective perception of value":

> The fellows are aware that objections may be made to awarding a prize to a man situated as is Mr. Pound. In their view, however, the possibility of such objection did not alter the responsibility assumed by the Jury of Selection. This was to make a choice for the award among the eligible books, provided any one merited such recognition, according to the stated terms of the Bollingen Prize. To permit other considerations would destroy the significance of the award and would in principle deny the validity of that objective perception of value on which civilized society must rest.[87]

Luther Evans, the Librarian, warned the committee of the consequences of awarding the first prize to Pound, but they refused to change their minds. Evans argued that "The reaction would be, for the most part, emotional rather than intellectual; public conscience would be outraged; the progress of poetry would be arrested for a generation; international relations, particularly with Italy, would be embarrassed; confidence in the Library of Congress would be seriously impaired; their faculties would be suspected, their motives rejected, their principles deplored; Congress, inevitably, would intervene. . . ."[88]

A public uproar was sparked, and commentators quickly took sides. Laughlin read about the immediate response in Switzerland (where he was skiing) and was pleased with an editorial in the *New York Herald Tribune* that "stated the case for the purity of poetry, and its isolation from politics in a very fine and dignified way."[89] Supporters of Pound and the committee included Dwight Macdonald, *Partisan Review*'s William Barrett, and George Orwell. As the de facto leader of the New York Intellectuals (by virtue of his position as editor of *Partisan Review*), Barrett expressed what became essentially the Intellectual stance on the Bollingen controversy in particular and the Pound question generally in the April 1949 issue. He endorsed the underlying claim of the panel that the "objective perception of value" was needed to guide aesthetic judgments, but cautioned that "it would be a pity if in the enthusiasm of affirming an 'objective perception of value' in one direction we ceased to affirm it in another, if in the aesthetic recognition of Pound's poetry as valuable we chose to forget all about the humanly ugly attitudes of which he been a spokesman both in his writing and in his brief but lamentable career as a broadcaster."[90] Referring presumably to the "Stalinoid" attitude toward art that *Partisan Review* so vehemently opposed, Barrett commented that "during the 'thirties literature was subjected uncritically to all kinds of aesthetically distorting or irrelevant political attitudes. These political attitudes have by this time collapsed, leaving behind them a deposit of vague sentimentalities which, while obstructing any current of new political thought, still makes it impossible for many people to separate aesthetic from other considerations."[91]

In the next issue, *Partisan Review* convened a symposium to discuss the award, and although all of the Bollingen judges were asked to submit responses only Tate, Auden, and Shapiro did so. Auden explained that he felt that only immature minds would be influenced by Pound's immature anti-Semitism, and that a poetry prize must not be concerned with how poetry is received by immature minds. Shapiro, on the other hand, stated frankly that he voted against awarding the prize to Pound because "I am a Jew and I cannot honor antisemites."[92] Tate, who had always been Pound's strongest advocate among the New Critics, contributed a short and hostile piece. Feeling that Barrett had accused the Bollingen jury of anti-Semitism, Tate shot back that "I consider it cowardly and dishonorable to insinuate, as Mr. Barrett does, without candor, a charge of antisemitism against the group of writers of which I am a member. . . . I hope that persons who wish to accuse me of cowardice and dishonor will do so henceforth personally, in my presence so that I may dispose of the charge at some other level than that of public discussion. Courage and honor are not subjects of literary controversy, but occasions of action."[93] Many readers, including Irving Howe, considered Tate's retort a challenge to a duel (although this may have stemmed from the New York Intellectuals' distorted or stereotypical view of Southerners). In the July 1949 issue of *Partisan Review,* Tate again explained his rationale for granting the award to Pound. Although he stated that "from the time I first read Pound's verse . . . I have considered him a mixed poet," he justified his vote by stating that "The specific task of the man of letters is to attend to the health of society *not at large* but through literature, that is, through *language.* As a result of observing Pound's use of language in the past thirty years I had become convinced that he had done more than any other living man to regenerate the language, if not the imaginative forms, of English verse. *I had to face the disagreeable fact that he had done this even in passages of verse in which the opinions expressed ranged from the childish to the detestable.*"94

Not everyone was as measured as Barrett or Tate. Among those who opposed the award were Bennett Cerf and *Saturday Review of Literature* contributor and poet Robert Hillyer. In his articles "Treason's Strange Fruit" and "Poetry's New Priesthood," Hillyer expanded his attacks beyond Pound to a purported conspiracy in the literary establishment including Jung, the Mellons, Pantheon Books, Eliot, the New Criticism, and a number of literary journals.95 The Bollingen award demonstrated an "esthetic contempt for mankind," and was the result of the "stranglehold" Pound and Eliot and the "new criticism" held over American letters. Laughlin, alerted before the articles saw print, wrote to Eliot that "the SATURDAY REVIEW is going to come out next week with a rather objectionable stink about the Bollingen Prize. This seems to have been instigated by that awful Robert Hillyer, who apparently can never get over his jealousy of the fact that you are a good poet and he is a bad one."96 The resentments Hillyer expressed, though, had struck a chord with many readers. Two months later, Laughlin reported to Eliot that "One of those societies for the prevention of modern vice in poetry has awarded [Hillyer] a $1000.00 cash prize for his good work. All of the little white slugs have come out from underneath their logs to applaud him, and at least it gives one a written record of who they are."97

In response to Hillyer's pieces, a large group of writers and critics issued a protest letter, rejected by the *Saturday Review* and finally printed in the 17 December 1949 *Nation*. Calling Hillyer's invective a "philistine attack on modern literature," the *Nation*'s literary editor Margaret Marshall set the terms of the debate: philistines who subordinate art to social concerns versus enlightened, reasonable individuals who recognize the special status of art. The poet Archibald MacLeish, who had been Librarian of Congress and assistant director of the United States Office of War Information from 1939 to 1944, followed by a one-year stint as assistant secretary of state for cultural affairs, and who was also a friend of Pound's and had been one of his staunchest defenders since the 1930s, underscored the implicit distinction between the aesthetic and the social, writing to *Saturday Review* editor Harrison Smith that "it is discouraging to

see contemporary literary journalism imitating the worst features of contemporary political journalism."[98] (In 1950 *Poetry* magazine, which eight
years previously had declared "The End of Ezra Pound," issued Mac-
Leish's defense as a pamphlet.) Laughlin also wrote Smith, asserting that
Hillyer had made the well-respected *Saturday Review* look foolish, and
received the following response:

> Our innumerable correspondents agreed that poetry and its criticism
> had fallen into the hands of a clique subservient to Eliot, whose great
> merits as a poet were not, in my opinion, germane to the discussion.
> That this clique was overwhelmingly represented among the Fellows
> in American Letters was as obvious as it was plain that Pound's influ-
> ence and Fascist conceptions were reflected in their work. . . . I do not
> think that Hillyer made a fool of us. If this controversy had been con-
> ducted in the manner, let us say, of the Partisan Review, it would have
> been dismissed in short order as a tempest in a literary teapot. As it
> was, it resulted in a national affair and resulted in putting an end to the
> power of the group we were attacking.[99]

In a small book entitled *Poetry and Opinion*, in which he presented a
dialogue between "Mr. Bollingen" and "Mr. Saturday," MacLeish attempted to elevate this messy political controversy to the philosophical
level. "The case against the jury of award comes down to the allegation
that the jury had given a great and semi-official prize to a poem containing
'bad' opinions and written by a 'bad' man," he suggested. "The savage
indictment of the jury, therefore . . . rested on the proposition that a poem
is necessarily 'bad' if its opinions are 'bad.' To derive it, as the attacker
did, from political and social sanctions is to open the way to . . . censorship
based on dogma."[100] Like Laughlin, the New Critics, and the New York
Intellectuals, MacLeish argued for recognizing the special status of literature. His dual position as a political and cultural insider (as a result both
of his governmental employment and of his friendship with *Time's* powerful publisher Henry Luce) and as a respected poet made his assertion
of an impermeable distinction between the two realms especially
significant.

Although he had not emphasized *The Pisan Cantos* in the 1948 New
Directions catalog, Laughlin certainly used the prestige of the Bollingen

award to sell the book after February 1949. A full-page advertisement that ran in *Partisan Review* and other journals highlights the award in prominent type, then employs blurbs by T. S. Eliot and Louise Bogan to bring home the book's enduring value. Although the advertisement uses most of its space to sell *The Pisan Cantos*, the bottom quarter lists all six Pound titles New Directions has in print, as well as two forthcoming books: *Selected Translations* and *Selected Essays* (edited, the advertisement emphasizes, by Eliot). For the next two years, most New Directions advertisements that featured Pound's books mentioned the Bollingen award, many making it a primary focus.

The Bollingen controversy served, in another sense, to solidify the dominant cultural position of the New York Intellectuals and the New Critics. Acting as a "literary coalition," in the words of Lawrence H. Schwartz, both groups supported Pound—not because either group had any affection for his politics or even for him as a person, but because the controversy involved the social role of literature. Where Hillyer and Harrison Smith endorsed the idea that art must answer to larger social concerns, New York Intellectuals such as Philip Rahv and Clement Greenberg and New Critics such as R. P. Blackmur and Randall Jarrell argued, together, that art must be granted a greater degree of freedom. Of the quick coalescing of support for the Bollingen committee, Schwartz comments that "the new aesthetic direction for the literary elite in the United States, at the end of the decade, is nowhere more fully revealed than in the machinations to defend the award to Pound."[101] Aesthetic formalism became the consensus of these two groups. And although the debate centered on the Bollingen award, Hillyer's attacks—on Eliot and aesthetic formalism more than on the ostensible subject of the controversy, Pound's award—made the issue much broader. Along with Allen Tate and John Berryman, Cleanth Brooks was instrumental in organizing the response to Hillyer, and took Hillyer to task for mentioning certain nameless "traitor-critics" who had defended Pound (and Eliot). For Brooks and the other New Critics, Hillyer's real offense was impugning Eliot and New Criticism. [102]

Vincent B. Leitch, though, argues that the New York Intellectuals actually sided against aesthetic formalism and the "Higher Criticism," and were much more conflicted in their support for the Bollingen committee. Using Irving Howe's *A Margin of Hope* (1982) and the stance of William

Barrett as evidence, Leitch maintains that the Bollingen affair showed that for the New York Intellectuals, "aesthetic . . . claims were secondary to the primary conditions of history, society, and morality. As a category, culture subsumed aesthetics."[103] Leitch's and Lawrence Schwartz's contradictory interpretations of the Intellectuals' position on the Bollingen controversy arise from the fact that the question split the New York writers themselves. A number of these critics certainly sided with the Bollingen committee, but did not do so out of the sense that Pound was blameless or that aesthetic formalism was the proper critical approach. Their motivation, rather, seems to have been a strong opposition to two related tendencies: the reductive—and characteristically 1930s Marxist—idea that art is no more than an expression of sociopolitical conditions and should be judged in that light, and Hillyer's "philistine," bourgeois idea that intentionally difficult art is unsuitable for a democratic society. For the New York Intellectuals, each of these ideas represented a stance on culture that they opposed: the first Stalinoid, the second middlebrow. Consequently, the support of some of these Jewish critics for an anti-Semitic poet was a qualified and thoughtful endorsement not of the poet, but of the necessity to evaluate art by primarily formalist criteria. Barrett's position, stated in the April 1949 *Partisan Review*, exemplifies this ambiguity, for he both attacks the reductionism of the anti-Poundians and expresses a serious disapproval of radical formalism.

Pound's widely recognized accomplishments made his politics irrelevant, according to an ideology that dismissed the personal history of a poet. Even before the Bollingen controversy Laughlin had adopted this attitude as his strategy for marketing this poet. The press release issued with the publication of the collected *Cantos* in July 1948 showed this:

Ezra Pound's complete CANTOS to date are being published in one volume on July 30th. The publisher of New Directions feels that this is an event of major literary significance—not merely because of the extent of Pound's influence on modern poetry, but particularly because the obvious poetic value of the CANTOS has lately been confused with the political issue of Pound's past.

To allow this confusion to continue is to do serious disservice to *Pound's* art, and, if the precedent is established, to *all* art. And in an attempt at clarification and a dispassionate evaluation, the following

statements have been assembled. [The press release included statements from Allen Tate, T. S. Eliot, Conrad Aiken, John Crowe Ransom,
William Carlos Williams, Delmore Schwartz, Richard Eberhart, Robert Lowell, Theodore Spencer, and Horace Gregory.]

Pound, Laughlin argued, was the test case that proved the validity of the
belief that evaluations of art must be separated from any type of real-
world issues. The prize provided an opportunity to begin marketing
Pound as the great American poet of the age, and as Laughlin reissued his
earlier works at a furious pace through the 1950s, he always used this
philosophical principle in publicity materials, jacket copy, and promotional pamphlets.

The fact that Laughlin's implicit New Critical separation of art from
daily concerns was in direct conflict with the ideas of the poet he was
marketing is an irony of their relationship. Beyond Laughlin's control was
the cultural debate among the *Saturday Review*, the New York Intellectuals, and the Bollingen committee, but that debate succeeded in advancing what became Laughlin's fundamental stance regarding Pound. Leaving behind his earlier belief that the purpose of experimental literature
was to transform society, Laughlin now, out of necessity and with the
prevailing cultural climate supporting him, embraced the idea that literary value was disconnected from social utility. Most important, though,
for Pound's future fortunes was the fact that the Bollingen award conferred upon him an undeniable mark of official approval. From now on,
he *had* to be taken seriously.

CHAPTER FOUR

❖ ❖ ❖ ❖

Prying Apart Poetry and Politics

There are more colleges in this country than you could throw rocks at and they are full of earnest young people who dearly want to understand literature and read the right things. 50% of their professors are dead wood and either give them no encouragement or lead them to the wrong things. These books are for those kids.

—James Laughlin to T. S. Eliot, 1 April 1940

THE first two components of Laughlin's "counter-swing" were thus fully in operation by 1948. Laughlin was arguing, in publicity materials, jacket copy, and critical projects, that Pound should be defined by his poetry and not by his person or his activities. The Bollingen committee had conferred its recognition on Pound, implicitly endorsing this mode of reading and evaluating literature. When many of the New Critics and New York Intellectuals came out publicly in favor of the prize, it seemed as if the entire literary establishment—conservative academic critics, leftist intellectuals, even the government's institutions of culture—had given their imprimatur to aesthetic formalism.

In the second prong of this campaign Laughlin looked to republish Pound's early writings, omitting any work that had to be read politically or that called too much attention to Pound the person. The reappearance of *Personae* and the earlier Cantos had initiated this; many of the projects outlined in this chapter continued with this work. But in the period following the Bollingen award, Laughlin also put into motion a third prong of his strategy: reaching out to the student audience, which in 1948 and 1949 was increasing dramatically. By the mid-1950s, Laughlin hoped, he would be able to offer a bookshelf full of Pound titles, complete with a critical method of reading them apolitically, to a growing audience with increasingly fewer memories of Pound's disgrace.

Selected Poems, John Berryman, and the
"Objectionable Paragraph"

In the years following the Bollingen Prize, Laughlin aimed to direct readers' attention to the poetry Pound had produced before *The Pisan Cantos*,
and to urge them to read it according to aesthetic formalist practice. The
collected *Cantos* published in 1948 would, Laughlin felt, bolster Pound's
reputation only among readers already familiar with his work and willing
to spend five dollars for such a book (the second most expensive on the
New Directions list). Pound's Confucian translations from the 1940s could
do little to improve his reputation as a poet; moreover, sales of those books
were slim. Laughlin needed a book that would appeal to the general
reader.

As early as the discussions about *Cantos LII–LXXI* in 1939–40, Laughlin had urged Pound to provide a selection of his poetry that would serve
as an introduction to his work (especially to students), explaining that
"what I am really most interested in at the moment is doing a selected
poems at one dollar. That is one of my big schemes, to see if poetry, good
poetry, cannot be made to sell if the price is lowered."[1] At that time,
however, Laughlin had not yet been able to put together such a collection,
for the copyrights on much of Pound's older poetry were still held by
other publishers. The war had then intervened; Pound was incommuni-
cado in Italy for the duration and could not give his consent to copyright
transfers, and such publishers as Liveright were reluctant to grant New
Directions permission to use individual poems. In 1946, Laughlin found
a temporary solution when New Directions took over the distribution of
Liveright's edition of *Personae*, a pre-1920 collection that presented the
poet apolitically.[2] (After 1920, Pound largely restricted his poetic production to the frequently highly political *Cantos*.)

Despite his reluctance to include any poems that would remind readers
of Pound's politics—or that would even conjure images of Pound the
man—Laughlin felt a personal responsibility, stemming from friendship
and his devotion to Pound, to produce his own selected edition that would
include excerpts from the poet's most important and mature work, the
Cantos. He also wanted to add a brief, nonacademic critical introduction
to show readers why Pound was important, and how to read his difficult
poems. This introduction should be aimed particularly at college stu-

dents.[3] Laughlin had been starting to put the book together in 1946, when—without Pound's knowledge or permission—he asked John Berryman to compile and introduce a selection for inclusion in the "New Classics" series. Berryman agreed to undertake the job in a 30 July 1946 letter, but was leery about providing a preface or commentary: "One by me seems impertinent, after the one by Eliot, but if he really wants it, and you do, I'll write one when I get a chance."[4] Busy with other projects, though, Berryman produced nothing, and after a year Laughlin became impatient. In 1947, he asked Pound—who was still unaware that Laughlin had already started working on the project—to suggest potential editors for the collection. Among Pound's suggestions were poets he respected like Berryman, Theodore Spencer, and Charles Olson.[5] Laughlin and Dorothy (who was still in charge of Pound's business matters) began to correspond seriously about the collection. In a letter in the spring of 1947, Laughlin outlined his thinking:

> It would be best if this book were assembled by a small committee. There is no need to state that it has been selected BY anyone at all. The main thing is to have a selection which will appeal to the not too bright blokes who run poetry courses in the colleges.
>
> There is a very large sales market to be tapped if we can shape the book to that market correctly. It must not be too wild, if you see what I mean, because these critters are afraid of losing their jobs, especially in the state institutions.
>
> I dare say Berryman would be willing to work with me on the selection and we should find perhaps a third person who would assist harmoniously. Ted Spencer—if that's whom EP means by "Ted"—certainly knows the college mentality, and would be useful.
>
> EP seems to be worried about weakening the sales position of *Personae* by taking things out of it for other volumes . . . I think the thing to do in the Selected is to take nothing out complete—just selections from each type or period. In the notes it can be frequently repeated that the whole thing is available in *Personae*. Thus the Selected would be a feeder for *Personae*.[6]

Dorothy wrote back to Laughlin with Ezra's specifications, emphasizing his desire that the preface be minimal:

I saw the boss yesterday & tried to sort out some questions.

There seem to be two points he is determined about!

Not a committee for that Selections vol. to be done by one man's taste—he doesn't seem to mind so much which man. Either Spencer "Ted," or Berryman—

Alternatively possibly Ray West, Robert Duncan . . . or even D. Paige.

. . . Let the new Editor have the pleasure of writing a BRIEF foreword! A minimum of notes-for-students—2 pages, at most.[7]

After a visit to Pound on 3 November 1948, Berryman finally completed his long-delayed selection and his introduction. Pound had wanted *Selected Poems* to be a brief book that would consist primarily of short, pre-1920 poems, apparently not understanding that readers would not buy something that was simply a shorter version of *Personae*.[8] Laughlin knew that such a book would not appeal to potential buyers, and insisted that the *Selected* include selections from the *Cantos,* as well. He assured Pound that the *Cantos* section would not comprise more than a quarter of the book, and Pound agreed to this: "I have given way on letting [Berryman] include dabs (or least not too much) of Cantos. but still DOUBT the necessity."[9] Berryman and Laughlin's selection, though, was almost half *Cantos*. Learning of this, Pound objected. The *Cantos* section was "overloaded," and he told Laughlin that "to make half the book Cantos. is flagrant violation of the agreement . . . I acceded to request to put in a FEW bits of cantos/ and you have made the thing HALF Cantos."[10] Laughlin took responsibility, explaining that Berryman's plan for the anthology "had given no representation at all to certain very important major themes, such as the Italian, the Chinese and the old Yankee. So I felt that suitable chunks from these epochs had to be added to give a rounded picture."[11]

Pound was also leery about the section of *Pisan Cantos* that Berryman had included, objecting both to his choice of excerpts and to the typographical method Laughlin and his printer, Vail-Ballou, had chosen to indicate ellipses. He told Laughlin that it was a "hash. . . . The PISAN chunk is just a mess of snippets/ and CANNOT stand as is. Better omit the whole of it. . . . the ONLY possible alternative to TOTAL and preferable omission is to put in one or two coherent bits."[12] In a number of letters from late 1948 and early 1949, Pound complained about *The Pisan Cantos'* place in the *Selected Poems*. His objection to the inclusion of fragments from the *Cantos* derived from his wariness about being misinterpreted and his insistence that, if readers truly wanted to understand his thought, they needed to read the *Cantos* in full.

More heated, though, was the controversy surrounding the introduction. Confident that Berryman's would be suitable, Laughlin had announced the *Selected Poems*, "with an essay by John Berryman," in his 1948 catalog. After he read it, though, he found the piece unacceptable. Although it "treats of [Pound] from the point of view of a practising poet," to Laughlin it seemed to be aimed at specialists and those already familiar with experimental poetry, not at general readers. Writing Berryman on 2 December 1948, Laughlin asked "whether it is not too difficult and profound for the purpose. My idea of this selected volume was, that it should be for students and for the general public, and not at all for the special high brow audience which reads the little magazines and the essays of the new criticism. I am afraid . . . that it would simply put the students off from reading the poetry."[13] Sending the introduction on to Pound in St. Elizabeths, Laughlin sought his counsel:

> I have got a little bit of a problem on my hands with the introduction which Berryman wrote for the selected edition of your poems in the New Classics series. . . . As you know, my idea about the SELECTED POEMS was to put them out at a cheap price in our popular [New Classics] Series, and try to get literally thousands of young people to read them. Now what is needed to stir up the interest of these young students is a bit of sugar candy. I am afraid that the Berryman essay would simply scare them to death. I think it is quite brilliant, but it is almost impenetrable in its difficulty. . . . I would like to ask your advice about using it in the new edition of PERSONAE, and getting someone more popular to do a short job for the selected writings.[14]

Pound shared Laughlin's doubts: the essay was "NOT good. it is clumsy. unreadable and the facts are not accurate . . . a lot of damn argument mostly with 2nd/ rate critics . . . NOT a preface . . . NOT whetting anyone's appetite for the text."[15] In early 1949, Laughlin rejected the essay, a decision that Berryman initially protested but later accepted.[16] Eliot also agreed with Laughlin's evaluation, adding that "the less said about Ezra's present position the better. Berryman ought to stop and think how anything he says now will look in ten years time."[17]

Soon after seeing Berryman's introduction in early December 1948, Laughlin had commissioned a second. On Pound's advice, he chose Rolfe Humphries, a poet and critic who had favorably reviewed *The Pisan Cantos* in the *Nation*.[18] Humphries eagerly accepted Laughlin's offer, adding that he was "far from feeling that a 'popular' piece of writing is below my dignity. . . . The function of the chairman is to get the Introduction made as briefly as possible so people can listen to the speaker."[19] He quickly finished the essay and sent it to Laughlin, who found it, for the most part, "extremely good. It is simple and enthusiastic and does not raise a lot of false issues."[20]

However, when Pound read Humphries's introduction in March 1949, one section troubled him greatly. In the only negative note in the preface, Humphries had written:

> What all he may have said over the Fascist radio leading to his arrest on charges of treason, I do not know: rather worse than attacks on the United States of America, I think, are those violations of the peace and dignity of the human race which he commits by the anti-Semitic remarks that can be found, if not in this selection, here and there in the Cantos. . . . My own economics, such as they are, deriving from Marx rather than from Major Douglas' theories of Social Credit, I think Pound knows not wing from tail across that field. The black is pretty black, however fair the candor; Pound has, I think, been guilty of mean hates, fostered in vanity, niggard in charity, rathe to destroy.[21]

Pound shot a letter back at Laughlin stating that "if there is one place where a discussion of jews and Marx does not belong it is in an Introduction to E.P.'s early poetry. . . . Even if it were apropos the Cantos E.P. could not accept the statement as it stands."[22] Dorothy echoed this complaint in a letter to Humphries a month later, arguing that Humphries clearly misunderstood Pound's views and that "a Preface to the Early Poems is no place to consolidate a mass of lies hurled at EP." She added, however, "apart from the paragraph to which we take exception, your preface seemed most suitable."[23]

Conscience, though, would not permit Humphries to write an introduction that entirely ignored the activities that had gained Pound such notoriety, and he told Laughlin:

> Please get somebody else, now. I've done the best I can, and gone as far as I can go.
>
> I realize I can't please irrational people, who toss around terms like "kike," and think I am influenced by the smears of Henry Luce. I do have to live with myself, and with people who would despise me as an abject coward if I passed over with complete indifference the fact that E.P. was, however crazy and pro. tem., on the side of Hitler and Buchenwald. . . .
>
> It seems to me wrong for them [the Pounds] to claim irresponsibility on the one hand, and on the other to exercise responsibility to delete every unflattering word. Literature and people can't be divorced as much as all that; probably I've been a fool to try this much.[24]

The following day, he suggested that his "objectionable paragraph" should be "sen[t] out, in mimeographed form, with all review and publicity copies . . . with a statement to the effect that it was taken out of the introduction at the urgent insistence of Mrs. Pound and over the protest of the undersigned. That would meet her objection that politics has nothing to do with literature, and prevent my remarks being kept in permanent form."[25] Pound's own ironic suggestion was for Humphries to append a statement reading "I believe E.P. to be a complete skunk when not writing poetry, I believe all his historico-political and economic-political ideas to be utter hog-wash, but I have not read a line of his writings on these subjects all of which bore me to death, and I have no intention of doing so."[26] Laughlin, not wanting to lose an introduction that would provide readers with a way to read Pound apolitically, proposed a compromise of "an extraneous disclaimer apart from the text."[27] Humphries provisionally agreed, and wrote a disclaimer that read: "No praise here of Pound's contribution to literature is to be construed as an endorsement of his political or economic ideas, particularly of anti-Semitic ideas alleged to have been made by him over the radio, in writing, or anywhere else."[28] Laughlin suggested to Pound that the word "allegedly" be inserted between "of" and "anti-Semitic," and told the poet that he would be afforded space to give his "opinion of these charges of anti-Semitism which people have levelled at you. And for my part, if you don't mind, I would like to add my own two bits' worth after that, which would be a citation of the medical opinion expressed at the hearing that such attitudes are a part and in fact, a symptom, of the diagnosed condition."[29] Pound did not relent: "There will be no allusion to jews or to mental condition or the whole deal is off. There is no need of a preface."[30]

No solution proved satisfactory to all parties. Humphries insisted that he could not submit an introduction without some reference to the politics; Pound rejected any such mention. He still resisted the idea that an outside agent was needed to help rehabilitate his reputation, even after Humphries told him to

> get it into your head that we're trying to help you, and leave us to do it our own way, however damnfool and even unfair you think it. This is not a pleasant spot for us to be in, either, though we're not idiots enough to think you're in a better position. But if in what I write as introduction there's not a single word of disagreement with you on any point, the job is going to look like the most fatuous and hypocritical kind of blurb-writing, not the considered opinion of a guy who tries to be honest, and admires the "Personae" and "Cantos" over and above disagreements that he nevertheless thinks he has a right to and must express.[31]

Letters continued to fly back and forth; the debate grew to be one about "free speech" and complicity. Pound even accused Laughlin of being in "partnership" with Walter Winchell.[32] Laughlin became exasperated: "I am really awfully fed up with his inability to face up to the realities of the situation which he has created for himself," he wrote Humphries, and he confronted Pound in language reminiscent of the *Cantos LII–LXXI* incident:

> permit me to say most respectfully that I think you are throwing away something really priceless as far as public opinion is concerned when you refuse to go along with that line. It will be hundreds of years before history clarifies itself to the point where people will realize there was merit in your position. In the meantime they are going to think you are

an awful bastard unless you let them think you were off your head when you broadcasted. . . .

All of your friends with whom I have discussed the matter, including Possum, have all agreed with me that that line was the best one for bringing about a temporary softening of the heart toward you on the part of the public.[33]

Finally, Laughlin gave in to Pound, and the book was published without an introduction. Telling Humphries that "if I didn't already know Ezra was nuts, I would certainly know it now," he thanked him for his efforts and released him from his contract. (He even offered to pay Humphries for the introduction, but Humphries declined.) The only mention of Pound's politics, besides the comments on "Usura" and such in the *Cantos* excerpts themselves, is in the one-page chronological "Autobiography" that introduces the book, wherein Pound refers to his speaking against U.S. involvement in World War II in 1940.

Even though its production and editing were torturous, the book was successful both financially and as part of Laughlin's ongoing strategy to separate Pound's politics from his poetry. Priced at $1.50 and included as number 22 in the New Classics series, *Selected Poems* sold well at first— the first printing of 3,400 copies sold out in a year, making it Pound's best-selling work to date, and a second impression of 4,500 was ordered in late 1950. Apparently hoping to win over potential buyers who were put off by the *Cantos* and Pound's politics, New Directions advertised the book as "a choice of Pound's best work, highlighting the early lyrics."[34] For the most part, the reviews were favorable and did not even mention the Bollingen Prize controversy. In the *Saturday Review of Literature,* though, which Bennett Cerf co-edited and which had published Robert Hillyer's recent attacks on modern poetry, Gerard Previn Meyer reviewed *Selected Poems* sardonically. Regarding Laughlin's flood of Pound publications in the period 1948–50, Meyer wrote:

New Directions, avant-garde publishing house, counters, or disregards, the Bollingen blow-up with what looks like the program for a veritable Pound jubilee. . . . If Mr. Laughlin and his associates are working to prove (as I suppose they are) that poetry goes on, even though the poet has died or gone into paranoia, the project is worth while. . . . Here, if anywhere, is the ideal proving-ground for the new critics' theory that the poem maintains a virtually independent existence from that of the poet. . . . But—for the good name of poetry—I suggest that in subsequent issues of this volume the New Directions editors get off their high Pegasuses and exclude the lament for "Ben [ito] and la Clara" and the more scatological sections of Cantos XIV and XV. (Or what's an editor for?)[35]

Although he was forced to price the book at $1.50, not his intended $1.00, Laughlin with this and similar volumes from the late 1940s and early 1950s finally began to reach his long-sought-after student market. As early as 1940 he had devised a plan of bringing modern poets in general and Pound in particular to the student market, writing to T. S. Eliot, regarding the short-lived Makers of Modern Literature series, that "[t]he idea back of the Series is that there are more colleges in this country than you could throw rocks at and they are full of earnest young people who dearly want to understand literature and read the right things. 50% of their professors are dead wood and either give them no encouragement or lead them to the wrong things. These books are for those kids—priced low enough so that they can buy them, written 'creatively,' so that they will be excited and stirred."[36] Although it appeared almost ten years later, *Selected Poems* was the book that finally achieved Laughlin's aim. It provided thousands of students with their first encounter with the poet, and as a result they knew Pound apart from his politics, if only briefly. *Selected Poems* was to become the most successful Pound book on the New Directions list, selling almost eight thousand copies even before a paperback edition appeared in 1957.

This episode demonstrates the difficulties Laughlin had in managing Pound's reputation, and the ultimate success of his approach. No one— not Laughlin, not Berryman, not Humphries, and not even Pound—got entirely what he wanted. Pound had conceded something even before the *Selected Poems* debate began, for the collection he wanted, and had wanted since the 1930s, would have combined poems and his political prose works—the *Selected Poems,* with its *Cantos* fragments, would give readers a distorted understanding of his opinions on politics and culture.[37] If the collection was not going to present his political ideas in full, then Pound wanted no mention of them. In the end, it was Laughlin's desires that came closest to being fulfilled, for when *Selected Poems* reached bookstores readers finally had a representative selection demonstrating the continuity of Pound's forty-year project to "make it new." The book presented a Pound who could be read solely through his poetry, poetry that could be read apolitically—Pound as a manifestation of the autonomy of the aesthetic.

Framing Pound's Works and Fostering a Critical School

Laughlin's desire to separate Pound's poetry from his personal activities constantly ran into obstacles in the 1940s and 1950s. Pound was notably uncooperative with one of the central pillars of the "counter-swing" effort—to produce several new, purely literary collections of his work. Eliot complained to Laughlin that the poet didn't understand the point of the proposed *Literary Essays* collection and kept wanting to include "one or two of his Italian pamphlets" (presumably, the pamphlets on economics that Pound wrote for use in the Italian public school system), and Laughlin responded with exasperation, as well: "I think that we are going to have a very difficult time getting Ezra's approval for a selection of essays which won't include any of the political material, but I feel that it is a fight which we have simply got to put through in his best interest. He pays no attention to me, of course, and, thinks I am an utter child who doesn't know what the world is about or what makes it tick, but I do believe he will take it from you. I urge you, therefore, to be strong and resolute in this good cause."[38] "I think the best way, to keep him from wanting to inject a lot of economics in the volume," he wrote Eliot the next year, as the *Literary Essays* project remained stalled, "would be simply to tell him that we are limiting it strictly to literary subjects, and that possibly there would be a later volume on more general themes."[39]

Although Laughlin wanted to improve Pound's reputation, he also wanted to make sure that his new prestige derived solely from his writings, not from any personal activities. As a result, the company showed little interest in publishing the poet's correspondence, even though Laughlin was aware that such a book would bolster his standing in literary history and even though many readers and critics who greatly admired him wanted to know more about his role as an exhorter, cajoler, editor, and promoter of the modernist movement. Pound, though, was more than willing for a collection of his correspondence to appear, so in 1950,

Harcourt, Brace and Company issued *The Letters of Ezra Pound*, edited by D. D. Paige and with an introduction by the well-known critic Mark Van Doren. Paige felt at first that Laughlin should undertake the project, but Pound urged him to do it himself. Paige's initial impetus was to "help him [Pound] clear his name," but Pound also told him that the project would be a help to his own career.[40] Paige was dubious: "you had to be careful to whom you told the fact that you had done this work on Pound. A lot of people considered that you were a traitor, too."[41] Readers clearly still associated any of Pound's writings—even three-decade-old letters—with his beliefs and wartime activities.

To try to counteract this tendency, New Directions published critical works on Pound that, like the firm's packaging of his works, proposed an apolitical way to read his poetry. While the Bollingen award and the support of T. S. Eliot seemed to grant the approval of established poets and critics to Pound's literary accomplishments, many other critics still disputed his value as a poet, and many more felt that his faults as a person damaged his poetry.[42] Writing in the first edition of the *Literary History of the United States* (1948), F. O. Matthiessen emphasized that Eliot was by far the most important poet of the age but pointed out Pound's "services to modern art"—specifically, his influence on Eliot. In his short description of his poetry, though, Matthiessen repeated the Eliot-Blackmur position that Pound was all style and no content, writing that "there is no denying the virtuosity of the sustained speaking voice [of the *Cantos*], even though it divagated into seemingly endless monologue, and often left the reader dazzled by the surface texture of the language, but with the sensation that it was hardly saying anything."[43] Matthiessen ended his piece by detailing Pound's "crackbrained ideas" and asserted that the poet "has become a catastrophic instance of what can happen when the artist loses all foothold in his society."[44] Immediately before the 1948 publication of *The Pisan Cantos*, Robert M. Adams wrote an essay for *Accent*, a journal of contemporary literature, lauding Pound's influence on the development of contemporary poetry but finally judging him a "traitor," an elitist, and a madman who has "discovered society's disease, but mistaken the growing and healthy tissue for the tumor."[45] R. P. Blackmur, in a 1952 *Kenyon Review* piece, barely revised his earlier assessment of Pound's value, arguing for his importance as a poetic influence but finally judging him to be a poet not "of the first position, but a position on one side" whose "expressive powers" were "deeply damaged" by his tendency to pronounce doctrines and form movements.[46] And in the British journal *English,* Robert A. Hume wrote that Pound's "name connotes treason and madness to many of his countrymen, but poetry to only a few."[47] John Crowe Ransom's 1951 retrospective "The Poetry of 1900–1950," as well, ranked Pound as a "Minor Poet," of lesser stature than "Major Poets" Edwin Arlington Robinson, Thomas Hardy, Eliot, Yeats, and Frost.[48]

New Directions' response was to recruit many of Pound's friends from the 1920s and 1930s, writers who had become established, to endorse the poet. In 1948 and 1949, Laughlin had used testimonials from such figures as Eliot and Allen Tate to promote *The Pisan Cantos;* the next year, he began to use other important writers to promote Pound's other literary works. In 1950, New Directions reissued in the United States *An Examination of Ezra Pound,* edited and originally published by Peter Russell in England earlier that year.[49] The *Examination* is a collection of short appreciations by eminent writers and brief critical assessments by his admirers, or, in the words of the advertisement, "an anthology of essays on many different aspects of Pound's career as poet, translator and stimulator of the arts by a distinguished group of international literary figures."[50] Contributors included Eliot, Edith Sitwell, Allen Tate, Ernest Hemingway, Ronald Duncan, G. S. Fraser, and Marshall McLuhan. When Russell proposed the book to Laughlin, the American publisher was enthusiastic.[51] The firm could sell "at least 1000 copies of such a book over here," Laughlin wrote to Russell, and he even proposed that he contribute an essay for the New Directions Makers of Modern Literature series.[52] Upon seeing the list of contributors, Laughlin did, though, suggest that Russell include "a few more American names to give it balance."[53]

When Russell's book came out in Britain, the *Spectator*'s Richard Murphy reviewed it, focusing especially on Eliot's article (which had appeared in *Poetry* four years previously) and responding directly to the idea that Pound's work could be separated from Pound the person. The emphasis given to Eliot is understandable, for he was not only historically linked with Pound but also had ascended to the place of preeminent authority in the British and American literary world. A previous article, his 1928 introduction to the Faber *Selected Poems,* had been "one of the most important critical foundations for the reputation of Pound's verse," and Murphy adds that in the *Poetry* article Eliot "has found nothing of importance to alter in his former view." In that 1928 piece, Eliot had deemed *Mauberley* a "great poem" and called the *Cantos,* then just begun, "by far [Pound's] most important achievement"; in this 1950 article, he argued for the necessity of looking at Pound's work apart from his political beliefs.[54] Did this mean, Murphy wondered, that Eliot had always advocated looking at Pound's work apolitically?

Russell's own contribution to the work, though, advanced a position different from the New Critical, Laughlinian position and argued that "to try to separate the poetic essence from the didactic substance of the poem would be valueless pedantry or, at best, adolescent romantic aestheticism."[55] Notwithstanding Russell's article, the book was an important statement by many literary figures advocating the separation of poetry from man. It also became the first manifestation of the final element of Laughlin's plan: nurturing a school of criticism that advocated his strategy.

A then-obscure contributor to the *Examination* was a young critic named Hugh Kenner. Within two years, Kenner became Pound's most important defender with his book *The Poetry of Ezra Pound,* the first full-length study of its subject. A native Canadian, from Peterborough, Ontario, Kenner had completed his Ph.D. at Yale in 1949 with a dissertation on Joyce and Ireland, working with New Critics W. K. Wimsatt and Cleanth Brooks.[56] While in graduate school, Kenner had visited Pound in St. Elizabeths many times, fascinated by the poet's method and subject matter. Unlike many of Pound's admirers and visitors at the time, though, Kenner was primarily interested in his literary accomplishments. He was convinced that Pound was the central poet of the age, and saw it as his mission to persuade readers and critics of this.

Laughlin had first become acquainted with Kenner in early 1949, after reading his evaluation of *The Pisan Cantos* in an early issue of the *Hudson Review*.[57] This review shows a casual expertise in all things literary, yet (as in many of Kenner's magazine pieces) its knowing sarcasm manages to convince readers that Kenner is no earnest ephebe. After reading it, Laughlin wrote to "David" Kenner that "I was very favorably impressed by the review which you wrote for the Pound Cantos, and I am wondering whether you have any writing plans that might conceivably fit into our publication schedule."[58] Laughlin was, at this time, interested in a good, uncontroversial book on Pound for his Makers of Modern Literature series—he had given up on asking Berryman to write one after the *Selected*

Poems episode. Kenner jumped at the opportunity. He informed Laughlin that he had a forty-page exegesis of Pound's poetry ready to go. This length, however, was inconvenient for Laughlin. "We are putting [these critical works] into hard covers," he wrote, "and things have to run to about twice the length which you mention."[59] When Laughlin saw Kenner's manuscript, though, he was impressed, and told Eliot that "A good deal of what Kenner writes is above my head, but I have to admit that he makes some very fascinating points. I have now met the young man personally, and it seems to me that he has one of the most powerful minds I have ever encountered. He seems to know the complete works of Ezra, yourself, and Joyce almost by heart. . . . It strikes me that the publication of this book on Ezra ought to be a trans-Atlantic cooperative affair."[60]

Kenner also submitted this long essay to T. S. Eliot at Faber and Faber in mid-1950. Eliot was impressed, but wondered about using Kenner to advance the counter-swing: "There is always something to be said," he wrote Laughlin, "for planting a book about one's own authors on some other Firm. It does good to show that an author is not merely being boosted by one's Firm, but is generally appreciated."[61] He later changed his mind, though, and accepted Kenner's work at Faber, with the suggestion that he eliminate the introduction to the book (a long poem written by John Reid), on the grounds that Reid's introduction brought up Pound's personality and political history—topics Faber, as well as New Directions, wanted buried. Regarding the Reid essay, Eliot told Kenner that talking about Pound's personal history would be a disservice to the poet. Instead, Kenner himself should provide an objective analysis of Pound's work. Eliot also asked Kenner to drop the reference to Pound's "biography" that Kenner had included in his own preface.[62] The disputed passage reads: "Because it is about Pound's poetry, this book eschews both his personality and the externals of his biography, which largely depend on his personality. This should not be taken to imply a schism in the subject, but a necessary limitation in the treatment. I have had to choose, and I have chosen rather to reveal the work than to present the man." Although the preface presents exactly the approach Eliot and Laughlin were themselves encouraging, it does so explicitly. Kenner was separating the poetry from the man, but he was telling readers he was doing so, thus reminding them of Pound the man. Notwithstanding Eliot's objections, however, the paragraph stayed in. The title also proved to be a problem: while Kenner wanted *The Rose in the Steel Dust*, an enigmatic phrase taken from the *Cantos*, Laughlin and Eliot needed one with immediate appeal to the mainstream, and Laughlin advised Kenner that "from a sales point of view, all other considerations aside, I think it is best to have a very plain and workmanlike title, such as The Poetry of Ezra Pound. The title you suggested, while dramatic, and poetic, would hurt sales, I am sure. It is too hard to remember, and does not have the definitive character that the more simple title has."[63] Eliot echoed this concern to Kenner, and the book, which appeared in 1951, was finally titled *The Poetry of Ezra Pound*.

Pound loved the book. After he saw the proofs, he wrote Kenner that

Undoubtedly a good job/ be
standard introd/ fer some time.
Glad yu putt in so much Confucio. Thanks for Appendices.
. . . Don't try to inflate grampaw beyond size of Landor, Browning and Hardy
. . . Don't eggzagerate re/ Muss/ BUT damn measure his human value against the filth of OOze, Church [Roosevelt and Churchill]. . . .[64]

Kenner's book received little advertising in America, but what publicity it did enjoy generally echoed Laughlin's, and his line on Pound. "Kenner demonstrates how Pound's poetry itself works out the critical positions set forth in his writings on literature and the art of verse," read the copy in the 1951 New Directions catalog; Laughlin clearly meant this book to complement the upcoming *Literary Essays* volume T. S. Eliot was preparing. Reviewers expressed both condemnation of Pound's politics and admiration for Kenner's insight. "It is always a serious matter for one's vanity to read an author whom one does not understand," Serge Hughes wrote in *Commonweal*. "Hugh Kenner tries to explain [what Pound means] . . . and praise be to Kenner, he does it well," he continues. "As a political thinker, Pound is of questionable value but as an unpedantic, unpretentious artist with a naturally cosmopolitan outlook, he can be superb." The *New Yorker* said that "Pound's fanatical side has attracted so much criticism, fanatical and otherwise, that it is a pleasure to read Professor Kenner's detached yet sympathetic analysis of the Poundian canon. . . . An indispensable text." Dudley Fitts—Laughlin's mentor from Choate and a New Directions author—disagreed with this, praising Kenner's exegetical talent but faulting his "indiscriminate adulation" in his review for the *New Republic*. The *New York Times Book Review* also criticized the book's tone as sounding like that of a disciple. In the Santa Barbara *News-Press* (in Kenner's adopted hometown, where he had taken a job at the new University of California campus), Ronald Scofield objected to the obscurity and difficulty of Pound's poetry, and asserted that no matter how clearly Kenner argued, it would never become mainstream fare.[65] The reception in the press shows how long a way to go Laughlin's strategy for rehabilitating Pound still had; almost every review mentions Pound's beliefs and activities, even though Kenner's book announced itself as being solely about the poetry.

Kenner's insight and the accessibility of his writing—and his willingness to look at Pound apolitically—delighted Laughlin. Writing soon after the book came out, Laughlin mentioned a recent conversation with Kenner's old teacher: "I saw Cleanth Brooks up at Yale the other evening . . . and we talked about you, and how you are going to set the world on fire, if you don't blow a fuse first."[66] For the rest of the 1950s, Kenner worked furiously from his position in Santa Barbara, which for the East Coast academic establishment might as well have been Patagonia. He wrote primarily on the modernists and on the Irish renaissance, but concerned himself with any subject even tangentially involved with literature. His relative fame as a critic and his resolute determination not to become a "commahunter," as he called strictly academic literary critics, made him influential outside the academy; as a result, his endorsement of the separation of Pound's poetry and politics made the concept seem less a cynical desire of academics and an interested publishing house, and more an acceptable general principle.[67]

Even if he wanted to keep the politics and poetry separate, though, Kenner was still a devoted Pound booster, and before reviewing his work, he would ask the poet what he wanted emphasized: before writing about *Literary Essays* for *Modern Philology*, Kenner wrote Pound, "bearing in mind an irreclaimably scholarly audience of commahunters, is there any partic. point Ez wd. wish stressed?"[68] In 1953, Kenner was hired at Pound's old magazine, *Poetry*, as a "consulting editor" in charge of book reviews. He saw the position as a chance to serve Pound's interests from an influential position in the literary establishment, and triumphantly wrote that "I've taken over POETRY's monthly rubric. Starting Jan. with a massacre of Mr. Blackmur. . . . I pick the books, & nominations welcome; i.e. nominations from D.C. . . . A piece on Ez which excuses its existence by containing the defn. of usura . . . will appear in October issue."[69] Pound was quite pleased, and immediately began to give more than "nomina-tions"; in fact, he seemed to think that he was back with Harriet Monroe, and gave Kenner lists of political topics to pursue. He also urged Kenner to undertake the project of reprinting his 1937–39 works from *Action*, the British Union of Fascists magazine, but Kenner ignored these requests. Much as Laughlin had fourteen years before with the "News from Eu-rope" proposal, Kenner told Pound that as much as he wanted to spread his influence, he just could not do it with this publication: "Arrangement is that I'm supposed to be reviewing books, not giving pep-talks re Kulch."[70]

Although they pursued very different courses in the world of literature, and although their interests occasionally conflicted, Kenner's role was fun-damental in Laughlin's strategy. Both worked to publicize, explain, and popularize Pound's poetry, and did so while downplaying the importance of Pound's politics and urging readers to do the same. In the 1950s, Ken-ner produced many books, articles, reviews, and lectures either about Pound or advancing an interpretation of modernist literature that placed him at the center of the movement. The attention he gave Pound both in literary journals and in general-interest publications such as the *National Review* during the early 1950s helped pave the way for the poet's public rehabilitation: in Laughlin's words, Kenner helped Pound "over a hump."[71] In the 1985 reissue of *The Poetry of Ezra Pound*, Laughlin acknowledged the importance of Kenner's role in "open[ing] up" the way for Pound's rehabilitation in the literary world, writing that with *"The Poetry of Ezra Pound* . . . things began to change, to open up. It wasn't an overnight miracle by any means. But it was the beginning, and the cata-lyst, for a change in attitude towards Pound on the American literary and educational scenes. Kenner's book was reviewed and got people talking. Most important, it was widely read in Academe. . . . Kenner got Pound listed on the academic stock exchange."[72] With Kenner as critic and New Directions as purveyor of the product, the message was coherent: Pound is a leading figure in twentieth-century literature, and if his poetry at times seems difficult or his criticism anachronistic, one needs only a ca-pable interpreter to make it all clear and perpetually rewarding. Kenner in the universities and the academic (*Hudson Review*) and mainstream (*National Review, Harper's*) press and Laughlin in publishing kept Pound's name in front of readers and critics, and they worked together to reassure readers that Pound's political beliefs were irrelevant next to his artistic accomplishments.

Soon after publishing Kenner's *Poetry of Ezra Pound*, Laughlin temporarily left New Directions to found and direct a Ford Foundation–funded, State Department–sponsored undertaking called Intercultural Publications. (This was, interestingly, not Laughlin's first joint venture with the State Department; the 1942 New Directions *Anthology of Contemporary Latin American Poetry*, edited by Dudley Fitts, had been produced and distributed with the cooperation of the coordinator of Inter-American Affairs at the Department of State, as part of wartime efforts to foster goodwill between the United States and Latin America.) Intercultural's primary product was the journal *Perspectives USA*, a quarterly digest of American literature and criticism aimed at European intellectuals. This journal, like its better-known counterpart *Encounter* (which was published by the Congress for Cultural Freedom, another State Department offshoot, but one that was also sponsored by the CIA) exemplified the collaboration among private enterprise, foundations, the government, and American cultural figures in the early years of the Cold War, and was explicitly intended to woo left-leaning Europeans away from the Soviet side in what Frances Stonor Saunders calls "the cultural Cold War."[73] *Perspectives USA* was intended to "expose highbrow American culture to Europe (and points East) thanks to the farseeing generosity of the Ford Foundation," Laughlin explained to Eliot.[74] In the first issue, he provided a publisher's introduction, explaining the purposes of the journal: "This magazine will present literary texts from and about the United States and examples of American art and music. Its editors will try to set materials before their readers that may enable them to view the culture of the United States in accurate *perspective*."[75] The article goes on to explain that *Perspectives USA* is intended to counteract both "the shortcomings of some of our own phenomena (such as Hollywood movies or the comic book) [and] antagonistic political propaganda." Laughlin's old antipathy to popular culture—expressed earlier in terms of distaste for commerce, but here as a desire to promote homegrown high culture—reappears in this introduction. Many of the leading intellectuals of the period appeared in the magazine, including New Critics John Crowe Ransom, R. P. Black-mur, and Allen Tate; New York Intellectuals Lionel Trilling, Philip Rahv, William Barrett, Sidney Hook, and Mary McCarthy; and many others. Members of the board of directors included Laughlin, Alfred Knopf, and William J. Casey (later to become director of the CIA under Ronald Reagan). In this journal, Laughlin's aesthetic formalist approach is used to a blatantly political end: bolstering U.S. cultural status among hostile Cold War–era European intellectuals—an aim to be accomplished, like Pound's rehabilitation, by the separation of politics and art.[76]

Perspectives USA's combination of aesthetic formalism and political objectives later played out directly on Pound's behalf, as well. The journal's 1956 final issue included a selection of his poems and an essay on "The Poetry of Ezra Pound" by Hayden Carruth.[77] Carruth—like Laughlin—drew a distinction between Pound's role as an intellectual and his role as a poet, arguing that those who saw him as an intellectual held him responsible for the social function of his poetry. Instead, Carruth proposed, we should see Pound as an artist, an artist whose work must be understood "autonomistically."[78]

From the publication of the collected *Cantos* to the time that he left New Directions to work with Intercultural Publications, Laughlin saw his "counter-swing," his "propaganda campaign," begin to succeed. The Bollingen Prize and students' fading memories of Pound's role in the war contributed to increasing acceptance, and Laughlin wrote him in 1948 (during the controversy about the introduction to the *Selected Poems*) that "I am feeling generally cheerful and hopeful about the public response to your poetry. The stores seem to be getting over their repulsion, and the kids are getting interested again, and are not afraid that some old prof is going to beat their ears down if he catches them with a volume of your verse."[79] Pound's work was making its way into college courses; both Archibald MacLeish at Harvard and Cleanth Brooks at Yale were teaching it in their poetry classes.[80] Pound was not, though, fully back in the good graces of "old profs," as Laughlin learned when he suggested that Harvard might have an Ezra Pound Room in one of the university's libraries, and was told by librarian William Jackson that "I . . . am not too certain that the authorities here would welcome any great amount of publicity concerning a Pound connection."[81]

With the momentum provided by its various successes, New Directions started filling in the gaps in its series of Pound's published works. Now that the company offered a volume of collected short poems (*Personae*), the collected *Cantos*, an award-winning volume of new poems (*The Pisan Cantos*), and a student-priced anthology (*Selected Poems*), it began to republish the poet's voluminous earlier nonpolitical writing—literary criticism, essays on education, and translations. Laughlin's aim was to reconstruct Pound as defined entirely by his literary writing; but he also had personal motives: he wanted to cheer up his depressed, institutionalized friend. According to Griselda Ohanessian, one-time New Directions managing director, the company's flurry of Pound books was meant to convince people "that this was a man with a lot of talent, despite things that one might not like about Pound. . . . It was a double thing: to make him happier in his situation and to let the world know that there was something worth looking at there."[82] Finally, bringing a number of new books to the market would supplement the impoverished Pounds' income, in addition to providing material for editors to include in anthologies (the modest permission fees Laughlin charged increased steadily during the 1950s).[83]

The first volume in the republication campaign—*Culture*, originally released by New Directions in 1938, and now restored to its original title, *Guide to Kulchur,* with an "Addenda" appended to the text—could have been the most controversial, but in a mixed blessing the 1952 reissue went almost unnoticed by reviewers. Pound's 1910 study *The Spirit of Romance* was reissued in 1953. These books started slowly (each sold under eight hundred copies in its first year of release), and did not even sustain their early sales momentum (sales of each dwindled to just over one hundred copies in 1956), and neither was widely advertised. In 1953, Hugh Kenner helped Laughlin select a volume of *The Translations of Ezra Pound*. These were overwhelmingly of European literary texts or criticism, as Laughlin was still hesitant to publish Pound's political writing. New Directions had a difficult time getting reviewers to pay attention to the book; managing editor Robert MacGregor wrote to Pound in 1953 that "We have had a singular lack of notice of the TRANSLATIONS volume. . . . The only explanation I can see is one that has been given me verbally by such people as Charles Rolo, of the ATLANTIC MONTHLY, that they want to wait until the LITERARY ESSAYS comes along and do the two of them together. That was the great danger as I saw it in having the two books on the same publishing schedule."[84] Not only was there little critical interest in the book, but sales were slow (794 copies) in the first year and sank quickly (147 in 1955, 91 in 1957). The $6.00 price—more even than the complete *Cantos,* and certainly more than the student-aimed books that were becoming the most successful New Directions offerings—may have contributed to weak sales.

The following year, New Directions published an American issue of the Faber anthology *Literary Essays of Ezra Pound* (1954), edited and with an introduction by T. S. Eliot, who did his part for Laughlin's "counter-swing," attempting to create a book that would "stand as a permanency" and refusing Pound's desire for a "cheeky title" like "Essays Polite and More or Less Literate."[85] Laughlin approved of Eliot's work, calling it "just what the doctor ordered."[86] The volume collects Pound's statements on literature, with hardly a controversial pronouncement in the lot: isolated from their original context, its once outrageous attacks on other literary figures seemed quaint and almost silly, as if Pound were as irrelevant an artifact as the writers he had attacked. New Directions advertising attempted to counteract the sense, created by the historical specificity of some of the essays, that Pound's day had passed: "The choices strikingly emphasize the objective of Pound's criticism, which Mr. Eliot calls in his introduction 'the refreshment, revitalization, and "making new" of literature in our own time.' "[87]

Eliot's preface to this book, his fourth major statement on Pound, argues the need to separate work and artist.[88] He takes to an extreme Laughlin's position that "artistic form can be considered apart from its content and moral meaning"[89] In fact, Eliot goes so far as to accuse the poet of being short-sighted in his attention to questions immediately at hand: "Mr. Pound has never valued his literary criticism except in terms of its immediate impact; the editor, on the other hand wished to regard the material in historical perspective, to put a new generation of readers, into whose hand the earlier collections and scattered essays did not come when they were new, into a position to appreciate the central importance of Pound's critical writing in the development of poetry during the first half of the twentieth century."[90] Eliot's preface blunts the effect of D. D. Paige's collection of letters. Both Eliot and Paige felt that their collections demonstrated Pound's central role in early-twentieth-century poetry's development. But for Paige, Pound's crucial role was personal: his relationships with other writers and with the patrons of the modernist movement, the *Letters* tells us, were his primary contribution. Eliot's preface, however, insists that it is "critical writing" that was so important; again it is the writing, not the man, that is the agent of change.[91] Read after the rediscovery of the original manuscript of "The Waste Land," Eliot's insistence that Pound's writing, not his personal involvement with poets, is of primary importance is ironic—and telling.

Although Kenner's work, Eliot's endorsement, and such projects as Russell's *Examination* were helping to steadily improve his reputation, a strong anti-Pound sentiment among many critics and writers persisted well into the 1950s. Louise Bogan's 1951 book on *Achievement in American Poetry* expressed the idea that the *Cantos* had been "sources of one kind of originality . . . up to the late thirties, when they became thoroughly warped in idea and overvehement in expression." Bogan compared the *Cantos* to Eliot's *Four Quartets*—unfavorably. The *Pisan Cantos* "lend the work a certain human pathos," but the "future must judge whether [Pound's] crude mistakes in theory and conduct entirely negate his frequent triumphs as a writer."[92] In 1953, Robert Graves ridiculed Pound in a short *Times Literary Supplement* entitled "Dr Syntax and Mr Pound," a mock dialogue in which Pound closes the discussion by calling his interlocutor a "pedant, Jew, pluto-democratic usurer!"[93] Although clearly intended to be humorous, the piece draws attention to the obscurity of much of Pound's poetry and to the controversy surrounding his political views. In his survey of *The Literature of the United States* (1954), Marcus Cunliffe judged the philosophy underlying Pound's works to be "ultimately incoherent," and also asserted Eliot's superiority.[94] New Directions was disappointed but not discouraged; Robert MacGregor wrote to Faber and Faber managing editor Peter du Sautoy that the lack of reviews for *Literary Essays* and *Translations,* and the hostility of the reviews that did appear, resulted from "bias due to Pound's wartime activities. Our sales have been disappointing, but I am convinced that in the long run both volumes because they are of solid importance will sell."[95]

After Kenner's book and the *Examination* appeared, New Directions stopped publishing criticism on Pound, and eliminated almost all critical works from its list.[96] Fortunately for poet and publisher, other critics took the opportunity to write on Pound even without direct New Directions support. Few other articles appear before 1955, but after that, such critics

as Carruth, Donald Davie, Robert Fitzgerald, Forrest Read, and Achilles
Fang (all of whom became important and well-known "Poundians" when
such a designation became imaginable) published work on Pound, which
falls into two groups: essays (like Blackmur's) arguing for his importance
in the modernist tradition, and exegetical articles explaining some facet of
the *Cantos*.

One of the latter, Louis B. Salomon's "The Pound-Ruskin Axis," appearing in 1955 in *College English,* exemplifies the separation of politics
and poetry. Like Laughlin's marketing, it holds that an unarguable and
(presumably) unchanging standard of aesthetic value necessitates Pound's
public rehabilitation. Always arguing for the aesthetic importance of
Pound's work, and against the idea that his "totalitarian" view of culture
makes politics an essential in his work, the critics who took this approach
adopted a calming and reasoned tone, as if they themselves were the voice
of these aesthetic standards: "Perhaps . . . comparison with a man [Rus-
kin] safely removed from the arena of current controversy may enable us
to see Pound in somewhat clearer perspective than was possible in the
more heated atmosphere of a few years ago, and thus help us to "place"
him where he belongs: in the company of those misunderstood reformers
who have a natural affinity for hot water. In tranquil times they are often
merely rebuffed or ignored like wayward children, but when the temper
of their fellow-countrymen runs high they inevitably get scalded."[97]

A few critics, like Kenner, did not even bother to address Pound's controversiality directly. Alfred Alvarez, writing in a 1958 study of twentieth-
century poetry, allotted Pound's politics only an aside: "His Americanism,
of course, involves much that is beyond the scope of this essay. In recent
years he has, for instance, become its victim: his obstinate insistence that
he is free to hold whatever political opinions he pleases has led to his ten-
year confinement in a mental hospital. And Pound's importance as a figure
on the American scene does owe something to the fact that he is, so far as
I know, the first major artist to be held as a political prisoner since the
Nazis took Alban Berg. I will have nothing to say here of Pound as a
person. . . ."[98] Notwithstanding this insistence, Alvarez's implicit comparison of the American government to the Nazis turned Pound's own politics
on their head. After this, though, Alvarez was as good as his word; his
attention was focused solely on the poetry, and he provided probably the
most lucid and concise explanation of Pound's strengths and weaknesses

seen to that time, explaining that the essence of Pound's talent is his ability to "work directly through [a] foreign language," to use "words as if he had just coined them. His language has no literary encrustations." Unfortunately, this also limits Pound's capabilities: he must be working with a translation in order to be at his finest: "His achievement depends directly on his ability as a translator, or, more accurately, on his growing intimacy with the poetry of other languages and the skill with which he adapted their techniques to English."[99]

Inspired by Kenner and other critics, by new professors in the universities who taught modernist literature, and by the sense that scholarship on Pound's poetry was indeed worthy, a younger generation of scholars and critics started writing on Pound—and they, too, adopted the aesthetic formalist stance. In 1954, a group of graduate students and faculty at the University of California at Berkeley started producing *The Pound Newsletter*, a typed, mimeographed thirty-page publication intended, in the words of the editors, to be "an effective and continuing means by which those interested in the achievement of Ezra Pound may meet to inform and to keep informed." The quarterly, which lasted for ten issues (until April 1956), published a wide variety of work: graduate-student papers, reminiscences by Pound's friends, translations, "state-of-the-field" reports, dissertation abstracts, and, most valuable, a continuing bibliography of works by and about Pound. John Edwards and William Vasse, who put the *Newsletter* together, saw their publication as a sort of meeting place for people interested in Pound, and printed a list of all subscribers in many of the issues, in hopes that they—professors, college librarians, students, poets, Italian and American friends of Pound, and many others— might correspond with each other. The *Pound Newsletter* is significant for the New Directions campaign because it wholly adopted the aesthetic formalist approach: in its pages there is absolutely no discussion of controversiality, politics, or anti-Semitism. In the "Notes and Queries" section, there are no requests for information about these topics, and in one article ("Suggestions for 'Work in Progress': A Symposium"), discussing possible future scholarly work, there is no suggestion that a scholar examine any of the issues that so obsessed Pound. Not all the work is strictly formalist—there is a great deal of writing about Pound's influences, about the Japanese, Italian, or Chinese themes in the *Cantos*, about discrepancies in the texts of the poems—but given Pound's deep and abiding concern with the effects of politics and economics on artistic production, the absence of any examination of these themes is remarkable. At times, this conspicuous silence seems unintentional: In an Australian article from that year, Pound's admirer G. Giovannini of the Catholic University of America observes that "at a [1955] meeting of the Modern Language Association at which the *Cantos* were being discussed, only one scholar knew of Pound's whereabouts, and then mistakenly assumed the poet was enjoying himself in a well-furnished apartment at St. Elizabeth's and did not want to be released."[100] Completely separate from Laughlin, the *Pound Newsletter* and the new Pound scholars went about doing exactly the same thing New Directions was doing: focusing attention on the formal aspects of the poetry. While New Directions worked among students and book buyers, the newsletter made its appeal to the professors who taught those students. Together, they presented a united front.

By the time the *Pound Newsletter* started publishing, the poet had begun to produce new work for his admirers to discuss. The several books published by New Directions between 1948 (*The Pisan Cantos*) and 1954 were reissues or collections of previously published work, but in 1954 a volume of entirely new work finally appeared—*The Classic Anthology Defined by Confucius,* published by Harvard University Press. Pound's translation of Enrico Pea's novella *Moscardino* appeared in *New Directions* 15 (1955), and later (1956) the poet published a translation of Sophocles' *Women of Trachis* with New Directions. In addition, in 1955 the small Italian literary publishing firm Vanni Scheiwiller issued an edition of brand-new cantos, titled *Section: Rock-Drill 85–95 de los cantares.* While Laughlin was familiar with Scheiwiller—an established Milan publisher and old friend of Pound's who specialized in limited editions and fine printings—it was a complete surprise to him that Pound had chosen that firm, and not New Directions or Faber, to introduce such an important work. The decision also caused copyright problems: Scheiwiller wanted to send a few of the books to America to sell in a rare limited edition, and Pound was eager for the extra income, but Laughlin found this unacceptable as a "violation of the copyright laws of this country which require that books by U.S. nationals be manufactured here to have copyright protection. Such introduction and sale here would seriously jeopardize copyright protection for these Cantos."[101] Laughlin wrote Pound in January 1956 that "any crooked anthologist who wants to can lift the stuff without paying a bean, and there's nothing we can do to stop him. I know you don't care about such things, but think, dear Sir, of your offsprings, who has got to eat for the next 52 years, and kindly in future to consult with Jas before taking steps which may lead to these sort of difficulties."[102] Laughlin was also apprehensive about allowing another publisher to serve as the vehicle for Pound's most important work—afraid that publisher might somehow hamper his long-term remaking of Pound. In the end, he convinced Scheiwiller not to export any books to America, and in exchange paid Scheiwiller for the U.S. copyright and produced, by offset printing, a trade edition of *Rock-Drill* for publication in the United States.

Critical reaction to *Rock-Drill* reflected the success of Laughlin's campaign. Reviewers praised Pound as a master of the lyric while dismissing objections to his politics. "Pound has no equal in his ability to fix a tone of voice or the 'tonality' of a person," Pound's admirer Noel Stock wrote in *Meanjin*. Alfred Alvarez stated that "Pound is writing personal verse better than anything he has done since the early twenties. That work of such subtle control and lucidity should come from a poet over seventy is extraordinary enough; that it should come from one who has been locked away longer than most of the Nazi war criminals is hardly credible. One may not admire Pound's politics—I certainly don't—but his integrity and courage as an artist is unequalled."[103] There were, of course, dissenting voices. For Philip Larkin, the "ultimate value" of the *Cantos* was "very small." Randall Jarrell felt that the poet was wasting an extraordinary creative talent in deep opacity: "what is worst in Pound and what is worst in the age have conspired to ruin the Cantos, and have not quite succeeded." Donald Davie, also, reserved judgment: "The great gamble continues. The method is being pressed to its logical conclusion. Either this is the waste of a prodigious talent, or else it is the poetry of the future."[104] But the detractors among the critics did not make their cases based on Pound's objectionability as a person or a thinker; they criticized his work.

In the late 1950s, New Directions felt confident enough to cautiously reintroduce Pound the person into its promotional materials. For his seventieth birthday, in 1956, MacGregor composed a pamphlet to be distributed to retailers, who could request any number of them to give away. His letter to the booksellers reads as follows:

Dear Bookseller:
    To celebrate Ezra Pound's 70th year, New Directions has asked a

number of eminent persons to give short statements on him, and has had replies from such people as Ernest Hemingway, W. H. Auden, Dame Edith Sitwell, T. S. Eliot, Archibald MacLeish, and Marianne Moore.

We are planning to publish these statements in a small eight-page pamphlet, roughly 3 1/2 by 4 3/4 inches, which will have on its front cover a new portrait of Ezra Pound by Sheri Martinelli and will end up with a list of the Pound books in print by all publishers. This list will not contain prices, since we do not want there to be the suspicion of any direct bookselling promotion connected with the pamphlet, but we will be able to imprint the names of bookshops on the back cover in the same way that our name will appear on the inside front cover. The booklet should sell many copies of these books for you.

We will be happy to supply these pamphlets imprinted for you if you give us an order and the proper imprint by May 18.
Robert M. MacGregor
Managing Director

MacGregor sent a copy of this letter to Dorothy Pound, and appended a P.S.: "The only statement, by the way, which even leans toward the controversial is Hemingway's, and he says, 'I believe he (Pound) made bad mistakes in the war in continuing to broadcast for that sod Mussolini after we were fighting him. But I also believe he has paid for them in full and his continued confinement is a cruel and unusual punishment.' "[105]

The pamphlet demonstrates the dignified New Directions promotional strategy, emphasizing literary accomplishment, linking Pound with the most important writers of the day, and downplaying his political works. (MacGregor's shunning of "direct bookselling promotion" also recalls the opposition to the intertwining of literature and commerce Laughlin had expressed in early New Directions documents.) In aiming to bring Pound back into the consciousness of the serious reading public; at least, it was successful. In a letter of 9 August 1956, MacGregor told Pound that *The Hudson Review* is sending out 1000 to their subscribers. Bookshops like Gotham in NY and others across the country have received 1000 each. It's also going out with our catalog, as you perhaps know."[106] Although most of the blurbs were complimentary, some only remarked on Pound's importance, carefully declining to pass judgments on his poetry. Eliot's paragraph is probably the most guilty of this faint praise: "His 70th birthday is not a moment for qualifying one's praise, but merely for recognition of those services to literature for which he will deserve the gratitude of posterity, and for appreciation of those achievements which even his severest critics must acknowledge."[107] A few books—*Guide to Kulchur, The Cantos,* and *Personae*—enjoyed a small jump in sales after the 1956 commemoration, but sales of most (apart from *Selected Poems*) continued to decline gradually throughout the decade.

Securing Pound's Freedom

The fact that the commemorative pamphlet did not seem to affect sales did not dampen New Directions' enthusiasm for this kind of publicity. In 1957, MacGregor put together another eight-page pamphlet "distributed to the friends of New Directions," this time with each page devoted to one of the six poets published that year by the company; excerpts from Pound's Canto 90 were included. This pamphlet had another aim apart from continued promotion. By 1956 Laughlin had begun in earnest to seek Pound's release from St. Elizabeths; the pamphlet—and especially Ernest Hemingway's contribution—was meant to contribute to this push.[108] (Hemingway wanted the steel heir Laughlin simply to buy Pound out of trouble, but Laughlin protested that he could find no "hand to grease" and wrote Eliot that he had told Hemingway to "call on Ike personally the next time he comes up to this country, reminding him that two old soldiers could surely see eye to eye."[109]) This pamphlet did not have the impact New Directions envisioned, though some outlets published reminiscences and other articles, most of which expressed the same view: Pound's actions were regrettable, but ten years of imprisonment were more than enough.[110]

More important than New Directions promotional material, of course, was the prevailing political climate—and in late 1956, Laughlin thought that he felt an auspicious wind blowing in the right direction. He wrote to Eliot that

> [i]t is my hunch that now is the time to really put on a drive to try to get Ezra out. I think it would have been impossible to swing it before the [1956 presidential] election, but it is a long time till another one, and the big majority should give the regime a considerable sense of security.
>
> We are fortunate in having turned up a new and very hopeful chan-

nel of approach. The man in question had a good deal to do with setting up C.A.S.E. (Committee of the Arts and Sciences for Eisenhower). . . . It is hoped that the group will have some sort of cultural exchange function and Mr. [William] Faulkner, who appears to have enjoyed his foreign visits, has been busily soliciting suggestions from other writers. Bill Williams had the good sense to tell him that the best thing that American writers could do to make themselves 'liked' abroad would be to get Uncle Ez out of the coop.

It is along this line that I hope we can proceed. I want to take counsel with MacLeish before going further, but I envisage a rather simple appeal, to be signed by perhaps a dozen really top literary figures, which would not be contentious about Ezra's beliefs, but would simply suggest that ten years' confinement is enough, and that his continued confinement only serves to create misunderstanding abroad, contributing to the propaganda myth that America has no regard for cultural values.

I feel certain that you would wish to sign such a letter, and am wondering whether you would be able to get the support of a few other very distinguished European writers. It seems to me that it would be very effective to have five or six countries represented, and a couple of other Nobel prize winners, if possible. Do you know Jimenez or Hesse? . . .

I am advised that all of this should be done very quietly. The less publicity for the present, the better.[111]

Pound did not always cooperate with this campaign to depoliticize him and to hide him from public attention. Granted more lenient visiting privileges by the administrators at St. Elizabeths, he began to lead a sort of salon, gathering around him poets like Charles Olson and critics like Hugh Kenner, as well as fervent admirers like Marcella Spann (with whom Pound compiled an anthology, *Confucius to Cummings*). Pound's energy and generosity showed itself in any number of little magazines of this time, as well as in other poets' work. He loved being considered an elder statesman—he called himself "Grampaw" to his young admirers—and encouraged visits. Often, his visitors' love, admiration, and respect were complemented by self-interest, a desire for the great poet's imprimatur on their own activities or perhaps even a quote from the mouth of Pound himself for their own publications. As eager as these admirers were to associate his prestige with their own publications, though, Pound was often just as eager to use their projects as vehicles for his own ideas. And although much of value resulted from Pound's inspiration and collaboration (including Marcella Spann's work, Sheri Martinelli's paintings, many of Charles Olson's poems, and much of Kenner's literary criticism), sometimes the visitors came for political advice and assistance, in an effort to gain some of Pound's cultural prestige for their ideas. John Kasper and T. David Horton were among these followers, and in 1950 they formed a publishing house expressly to carry out Pound's desire to publish works, unsuitable for New Directions, that would clarify certain aspects of the *Cantos* and educate students about what he saw as the nefarious elements controlling the world economy. Under his direction, Kasper and Horton produced six books in a student-aimed "Square Dollar Series" and four other books, all of which bore the unmistakable, though unacknowledged, stamp of his involvement. Pound wrote all of the publicity materials for the firm, chose their books, and directed their marketing, aiming both political and artistic works at the American academy; but because he needed to preserve his status as officially "insane," he was unable to take credit for any of his labor.

In 1956, Kasper became deeply involved in the anti-integration movement in Virginia and Tennessee, eventually serving time in a federal prison; late that year Pound's involvement with Kasper was publicized on television and in newspapers. This was a direct threat to the effort of Laughlin and Eliot to reintroduce a depoliticized Pound into the modernist canon; they, as well as Williams, MacLeish, and Hemingway, urged Pound to distance himself from Kasper. Pound refused, though, arguing that Kasper's dedication to the ideas of cultural totality (as evidenced in the Square Dollar Series) outweighed any purportedly bigoted sentiments he might have. This refusal delayed his own release from St. Elizabeths for at least one year.

Where Pound had previously been associated only with fascism and anti-Semitism, Kasper's friendship and his own comments brought America's legacy of racism into the mix. It was fortunate for Pound—and for Laughlin—that he did not have a public forum at the time, for his statements on the Kasper affair were as ugly as any he ever made. Comments from letters to Olivia Rossetti Agresti are typical:

Kasper acquitted of sedition/ public cheers/ still got another net spread re/ some technicality, but they cant soak him more than a year for it. His lawyer sd/ he had never heard of anyone accused of doing so many things by remote control. None of the kikecution witnesses stood up under cross Xam. At least god a little publicity for the NAACP being run by kikes not by coons.

Kasper's REAL ideology is far above ANY U.S. audience/ and am not sure it is useful to spread it among those who will NOT understand why Lincoln was shot.[112]

Pound's willingness to associate himself with any crackpot who would listen to his theories on usury and finance served him very poorly. The Square Dollar incident demonstrates many of his best qualities: his generosity, his boundless energy, his willingness to work on other people's behalf. But it also demonstrates many of the worst, not least his inability, in later life, to find fault with anyone who subscribed to his anti-Semitic conspiracy theories. His refusal to condemn Kasper's beliefs, or even to criticize his actions, also greatly complicated the effort to rebuild his image and to usher him into the realm of literary elder statesmen and into the academic canon.[113]

CHAPTER FIVE

❖ ❖ ❖ ❖

The Pound Era

I don't need to tell you what a phenomenon the "quality paperbacks" have been in publishing recently, and you may have noted we have been experimenting with some of them at New Directions, and I would like to try a few more.
                                    —James Laughlin to Dudley Fitts, 21 Feb. 1956

POUND was released from St. Elizabeths in 1958 and immediately returned to Italy, where he remained largely silent until his death in 1972. If the New Directions project to depoliticize him had been hindered during the 1950s by his continuing refusal to curb his potentially offensive political statements and activities, it benefited for most of the next decade from his silence and his absence from the United States. This allowed Laughlin to consolidate the advances he had made in the late 1940s and 1950s. Just before his release, in fact, the poet even began to show some awareness of the problems he had caused during the Kasper episode, and worried about the damage that might be precipitated by William Carlos Williams's including in *Paterson* V an attack on Franklin Roosevelt from one of his letters.[1] From the time of the poet's return to Italy in 1958, Laughlin was so successful that even though Pound continued to produce new poetry until 1968, it was generally ignored, in large part because New Directions had convinced readers and students to focus on his older work.

If Pound's mellowing and his fading from public consciousness aided Laughlin's efforts to depoliticize and rehabilitate him, other, larger changes in the publishing industry—specifically, the explosion in the student market in the postwar period and the development of the trade paperback format largely to serve that market—were also significant factors. In the 1950s, enjoying Pound's growing recognition as one of America's most important living poets, New Directions redirected its efforts from depoliticizing him to ensuring his presence in the American literary curriculum. At this time, New Directions had almost entirely ceased publishing the critical works that had previously been one of its main tools in re-creating Pound (these critics, and and many others, were publishing work with other houses). Instead of reaching students and professors directly through critics, New Directions now looked to reach them through the campus bookstore—through the trade paperback.

The Trade Paperback Format and the Student Market

New Directions was by no means alone in its use of the trade paperback during the mid- to late 1950s, and Pound was certainly not the only author whose reputation and place in the literary world changed as a result of the development of the format. The trade paperback's success and popularity transformed the literary marketplace almost immediately upon its introduction in 1953. The trade literary publishers Laughlin had known in his youth—Knopf, the Literary Guild, the Modern Library, and others—had encouraged consumers to find satisfaction not only in the text, but in the material qualities of their (always hardcover) books.[2] Many readers preferred the solidity and permanence of hardcover volumes, and the large established publishers, wary of the smaller profit margins and downmarket reputation of paperbacks, did little to counter this preference. The result was that literature, in the public mind, had become linked with hardcover books aimed at the middle class. Even though these objects were not necessarily costly (Modern Library books, for example, were quite inexpensive), they had a solidity and permanence that paperbacks lacked.

World War II changed all this. The British publisher Penguin Books, founded by Allen Lane in 1935, opened an American branch in 1939, and soon entered into an arrangement with the U.S. Army's Military Service Publishing Company to produce a series (Superior Reprints) for use by American troops. The popularity of these books suggested to a number of American publishers that a great potential market for paperback literature existed, especially after the GI Bill caused an enormous jump in college enrollments. In 1940, total undergraduate enrollment in U.S. colleges and universities had been 1.38 million; by 1948 the number had almost doubled, to 2.44 million.[3] This jump greatly broadened the student market, which was naturally responsive to inexpensive books. Soon, many large

American firms and American subsidiaries of British companies opened paperback publishing branches. Of these, the most important were Bantam, Dell, Pocket Books, and Penguin and its newly created American branch New American Library (whose imprints included Signet and Mentor).[4] These paperbacks were generally reprints of classic literature or new books by potentially popular authors; they were inexpensive and widely sold in such venues as train stations, drugstores, and newsstands.

Doubleday's 1953 introduction of the trade paperback—which Tebbell defines as "quality reprints . . . sold through trade book wholesalers and stores, rather than employing the multiple outlets of the mass marketers"[5]—changed the market for softcover books by using the paperback format for limited-appeal contemporary literary authors and selling these books in bookstores.[6] Where Signets, Bantams, Pocket Books, and other mass-market paperbacks were flimsy, almost throwaway products whose main purpose was to provide low-priced literature outside of bookstores, the trade paperback aimed to carry some of the permanence of the literary hardback at a price still much lower than the hardcover—85 cents to $1.25. Jason Epstein, the Doubleday editor generally credited as the first postwar publisher to extensively use trade paperbacks, explained that "the mass market houses were publishing mainly books that could be sold through magazine distributors, while Anchor and Vintage and the other trade paperback lines that came later found that they could distribute profitably through direct accounts. We were trying to reach a much smaller and more specific audience [than the mass market houses were], mainly academic, literary, highbrow."[7] Doubleday's imprint Anchor Books produced these books, which also differed from literary paperbacks of the 1930s and 1940s in the greater sophistication of their physical appearance. Soon afterward Knopf joined the market with its Vintage imprint, which reprinted the firm's hardcover titles. Anchor Books, in the words of Frank Schick, were "intended for the permanent collection of the serious reader," who recognized and accepted the special status of literary writing.[8] In *Paperback Parnassus*, Roger Smith writes that "the first Anchors . . . were unabashedly highbrow. Highbrow paperback lines had failed in the past, but the large postwar college population made it unlikely that this time history would repeat itself."[9] In addition, the trade paperback carried with it none of the sense of ephemerality or the lurid connotations of the mass-market paperback.

Soon after Anchor began to sell these books, other firms (notably Athenaeum and the Grove Press imprint Evergreen Books) began to profit from them, and in March 1954 Alfred A. Knopf, the most prestigious name in American literary publishing, announced the launch of its own trade paperback imprint, Vintage Books. New Directions, whose hardcover reprints were losing popularity to the trade paperbacks, joined the movement at the same time. Hugh Kenner informed Pound as early as 1953 that New Directions' hardcover " 'New Classics' series [is] badly undercut by Doubleday's Anchor Books, which are cheaper and benefit by a massive distribution; [Laughlin] isn't adding any more titles unless he can find ways of doing it real cheap."[10] As the books were sold exclusively in bookstores, the trade paperback was an especially promising format for New Directions, for the company had never used such jobbers as the American News Company to distribute to drugstores, supermarkets, train stations, and other nontraditional outlets.[11]

New Directions took advantage of the more dignified appearance of the trade paperback to create a distinctive identity for the company's paperbacks. Alvin Lustig, who had been responsible for the design of the New Classics dust jackets, helped create this "look." At first, the covers were all in black and white, a definite departure from the traditional paperback cover (the use of luridly colored cover illustrations was a mass-market paperback tradition that the early trade paperbacks imitated to some degree). "When we started doing paperbacks," explained former New Directions managing director Griselda Ohanessian, "the reason we did black-and-white was to make them look different from the other paperbacks that were starting to come out, all of which were copying the drugstore paperbacks. . . . The literary paperbacks were trying not to be garish but trying to be colorful, and some people thought we were doing black-and-white to save money, and it actually did save money. But at that time it was neither here nor there, we deliberately did black-and-white to stand out from the other trade paperbacks."[12] Trade paperbacks were also especially appropriate for New Directions because the firm relied heavily on its backlist. Few of the firm's titles sold in great numbers in their first year, but many of them had an enduring popularity, especially in the academic market. Because of their higher price and lower print runs in comparison with mass-market paperbacks, trade paperbacks could be kept on a backlist for years without substantial risk. Although New Directions continued to emphasize hardcover books on its list until well into the 1970s, the firm capitalized on the growing markets for trade paperbacks from the early 1950s, and began shifting many of its books into the paperback format as soon as initial hardcover stocks were exhausted.

"I don't need to tell you," Laughlin wrote Dudley Fitts in 1956, "what a phenomenon the 'quality paperbacks' have been in publishing recently, and you may have noted we have been experimenting with some of them at New Directions, and I would like to try a few more."[13] Pound and Laughlin had corresponded about which of Pound's books would work best in the format. The trade paperback was especially important to the campaign to rehabilitate Pound, for it was the perfect format in which to publish his earlier writings. Nonetheless, Laughlin feared that New Directions would not succeed as a publisher for the student market. "For that racket," he told Pound in 1955, after the poet had again insisted that New Directions work harder to get his books included in college courses, "you have to have a large staff of traveling salesmen who go about sugaring the professors, and almost nothing can be accomplished unless you go at it on a big scale with a vast list of titles."[14] But Laughlin was convinced that the trade paperback would benefit Pound even if he could not, at first, crack the student market. "We ought to get one of your books into the new paperback format at a low price," Laughlin wrote in late 1955. "But which one? Thought must be given to this problem."[15] "I think there is no doubt," he speculated in his next letter, "that 'Personae' would do well—Harcourt Brace has recently put out a selection of the Parson [Eliot] at a dollar—but I don't know that it is advisable to cut down on the sale of something which is standard and goes all right at the higher price." At $3.50, the hardcover *Personae* was selling between 300 and 400 copies a year, and as much as Laughlin wanted to broaden Pound's influence by using his uncontroversial earlier poems, decreasing *Personae*'s profit margin in exchange for what would probably be only marginally higher sales seemed a mistake. "Personally," Laughlin continued, "I lean to the idea of a kind of literary commonplace book with examples. . . . [It] would go like wildfire in paper form. . . . We would take various paragraphs and pages out of different books, all dealing with literary matters, and then add to them examples of the things you are talking about, in the original language and with translation. Thus, in effect, we would have Ez's short course in comparative literature, and I think it would be a knockout. . . . This would

give it to them in a nutshell, and would, I think, be something terrific
which would really crack the paperback text book market, as well as the
drug stores."[16]

In 1957, Laughlin brought out the first Pound trade paperback, a reissue of *Selected Poems* at $1.15, with a slightly different text than the
hardcover edition.[17] The cover, too, was different; the hardcover's dust
jacket featured a colorful abstract design and had no photograph of the
poet, while the paperback was stark, black and white, and was dominated
by a profile likeness of Pound that distinctly resembled a mug shot. (This
cover marked one of the first times since the 1930s that New Directions
had spotlighted, rather than submerging, Pound himself in any publicity
or marketing efforts for his books.) "We are hoping big things for the
$1.15 Selected [Poems]," Laughlin told Pound in 1957. "You can't go to a
Broadway moompitcher for that now, and nobody can complain you are
being priced out of circulation. Hope we can soon get more things down
to that level. It depends on the volume."[18] The trade paperback *Selected
Poems* was a distinct success, selling out its print run in less than a year.
Two years later, MacGregor informed Pound that "I have just run up the
total sales on your SELECTED POEMS in paperback form. I find that already this year close to three thousand copies have been sold, making a
total, since we published this paperbound volume less than two years ago,
of almost thirteen thousand copies sold."[19] By the poet's death in 1972
there were 125,000 copies in print. That paperback edition of the *Selected
Poems of Ezra Pound* became one of New Directions' most reliable titles
of the period, selling at least 10,000 copies a year throughout the 1960s.

The success of the trade paperbacks contrasted with the relatively low
sales for Pound's new hardcover titles. To take one important example,
the complete *Cantos* (available only in hardcover) took three years to sell
out its initial 1948 printing of 3,000 copies. Sales picked up significantly
in the mid-1960s—the revised and augmented *Cantos* 1–95 sold 2,000
copies when it was released in 1965, and New Directions ordered another
5,000 copies in December 1966—but the title never sold briskly. The new
installments of the *Cantos* had initial print runs of 1,525 (*The Pisan Cantos*, 1948), 2,081 (*Section: Rock-Drill*, 1955), and 3,000 (for both *Thrones*,
1959, and *Drafts and Fragments*, 1968). Although Laughlin had certainly
achieved his goal of outstripping Farrar and Rinehart's paltry press runs
of the 1930s (which averaged 1,000 copies), each New Directions hard-

cover edition took many years to sell out its relatively small print run, and there was no demand for a second printing. Pound's other, minor titles of the 1950s all experienced the same type of sales history. Each book was published initially in hardcover with a modest print run ranging from 5,000, in the case of *The Spirit of Romance* (1951), to 500, for *Gaudier-Brzeska* (1961); each took years to exhaust its first printing; and, unless it was an installment of the *Cantos,* each was bound as a paperback and priced usually at a third of the original cover price as soon as the first hardcover printing sold out. Beginning in the 1960s, books such as *Selected Cantos* that had a clear student audience, or *Love Poems of Ancient Egypt* that might appeal to an audience broader than poetry lovers and academics, were published as original paperbacks.[20] The paperbacks were vastly more successful than the hardcovers: they sold more copies, earned more for both writer and publisher, and brought Pound to the student market.

Even though paperback publication benefited Pound financially and fulfilled his long-term desire that his books be available in student-priced editions, he was unhappy with the smaller royalties he earned on paperback sales. In 1957, for instance, New Directions sold 4,623 copies of the paperback *Selected Poems*, but only 349 copies of the hardcover *ABC of Reading* (a New Classics title). After *ABC of Reading* sold out its entire hardback print run, MacGregor—with an eye to the sales potential of the trade paperback—wrote Pound asking for permission to bring the book out in the new format: "I would like to do ABC OF READING paperbound with a new cover sometime early in the spring. For this we would need your agreement to the 6% royalty which the paperbound editions all carry, as you know. Although the royalty is percentagewise lower (the royalty on ABC OF READING in the 'New Classics' series is 10%, as you know) in order to help make the lower cost, the increased sales make for a far better income. Also the distribution is much wider, and it seems that our paperbacks really are getting in the hands of students and others who are your real readers."[21] Pound grumbled about the 6 percent royalty (at $1.35, the book would earn him just over eight cents a copy), but agreed. *ABC of Reading* sold 10,000 copies in three years, 4,000 in its first year of paperback publication. Even at the lower royalty rate, Pound made six times as much money on the paperback over equivalent time periods (about $50 from the hardcover *ABC* in 1957, for instance, and a little over $300 from the paperback in 1961). The hardcover *Thrones* gave Pound about $315 in its first year, while *Selected Poems,* then in its third year, earned the poet just over $400. By 1973, *ABC of Reading* was in its tenth printing, and 73,000 copies of the paperback edition were in print.

Pound's misgivings about decreased income from paperback publication proved shortsighted. In fact, both because of the larger paperback sales and because of his more solid position in the American literary pantheon, the poet's earnings rose significantly in the 1960s, and for the first time he was able to support himself entirely on royalties. In 1962, for instance, his royalty check from New Directions totaled $2,853.95. On that year's itemized list, the book that provided Pound with the greatest royalties was the paperback *Selected Poems* with $115.85 on the third printing and $431.83 on the fourth (5,944 copies in all); second was the paperback *ABC of Reading* with $199.58 (2,464 copies).[22] Only one copy of the complete *Cantos* (available only in hardcover) sold that year. Pound's rendition of the *Love Poems of Ancient Egypt* (1962), issued only in paperback, was also a big seller. New Directions' royalty check for 1964 totaled $4,828.37. "Sales seem to keep building," Laughlin told Pound in 1967, "in a healthy way, all the time, particularly in college course adoptions. By the way, the hardbound edition of the 'Literary Essays' has now sold out, so we will be putting that into paperback next year, and I think we will get a very good college use on that one at the lower price."[23] At the end of the sixties, Pound was finally making a good amount of money from his New Directions royalties—the 1967 check was for over $8,500, 1968's topped $12,000, and in 1973, Pound's royalties were $13,718.84. Even the gross sales numbers were becoming considerable: in 1970, New Directions sold over 35,500 copies of Pound titles.

New Directions, as well, saw its sales rise dramatically as the firm adopted the trade paperback. Monthly gross trade sales ranged from $4,000 to $10,000 through the early 1950s, but by the end of the decade rose to between $15,000 and $19,000. In the early 1960s, as the trade paperback truly took hold and New Directions began to get its authors into syllabuses and its books into university classrooms, sales spiked again: in January 1960 gross trade sales were $23,000, and in August 1961 the gross reached $38,000. These figures do not, of course, indicate profits, but even taking into consideration the smaller margin on paperbacks, which accounted for so much of the company's gross, the rising cost of producing books and resultant increasing cover price, and added staffing, it is clear that the company was seeing significant growth.

Although they were both hopeful for increased sales that would benefit New Directions authors in the long term, in the 1950s neither Laughlin nor MacGregor was particularly fond of paperbacks. Both were convinced that consumers should want to own books that were finely made as well as finely written. The firm had always attempted to price its works in series such as the New Classics much lower than new literary hardbacks, in order to have them compete with the budget-priced Modern Library hardbacks. But at the same time, Laughlin (much like Knopf) had taken pride in working with well-respected printers and using high-quality materials.[24] Confident in the great value of its books and protective of its authors' incomes, New Directions initially was wary about the shift to paperbacks, feeling that the nominally lower price of the trade paperback did not make up for its significantly lower value. "It seems absurd but it is true," MacGregor wrote Pound in 1959, "that a hardbound book at $1.75, like ABC OF READING in the 'New Classics,' with a jacket, seems to be outstripped several times by the same book published at 50 cents less paperbound. It's absurd but there it is."[25]

The format's success, though, changed MacGregor's and Laughlin's minds, and by the early 1960s, New Directions had completely embraced the trade paperback, so much so that even promising new projects often were published simultaneously in hardcover and paperback. One such book was the anthology *Confucius to Cummings*, compiled by Pound with the assistance of Marcella Spann. *Confucius to Cummings* was intended to present Pound's final evaluation of intellectual and artistic history, and Laughlin hoped that this work would be "Ez's short course in comparative literature" that he had requested back in 1955.[26] He knew that Pound's most remunerative and culturally influential efforts would be his student-aimed projects, and consequently when Pound suggested *Confucius to Cummings* (which the poet called the "Spannthology"), he was "enthusiastic." He wanted more Pound in it than Pound did himself—"the more of yourself you can get into it—that is, translations, comments on what is good or bad about something, comparisons and correlations—the better it will go. People are interested in *you*," he reminded Pound.[27] Immediately after Pound's release, Laughlin had reiterated his eagerness to publish this work and even arranged for the photographer Richard Avedon to take portraits of Pound, presumably for the book's cover.[28] After Pound returned to Italy, Laughlin continued to cajole the poet to "beef the book up a bit by including an appendix which would reprint some of your important remarks from other books about the poets included. As I have said before, the more of EP that is in this book, the better it will sell, and while some industrious ones will be led to look back to earlier volumes, others, especially in the provinces, won't have the cash, or know how to find them."[29] Laughlin clearly wanted this book to be a sort of companion volume to *Selected Poems*. In addition, he knew that bookstores "in the provinces" were more likely to carry trade paperbacks than slow-selling hardcover editions of Pound's earlier volumes. As with *Selected Poems* and *ABC of Reading*, he saw the "Spannthology" as an opportunity to achieve greater penetration into the undergraduate market. When *Confucius to Cummings* finally appeared in 1964, it was published simultaneously in hardcover (at a relatively pricey $6.75) and in paperback ($2.75). Although sales figures on the book are not easily available, information on the print runs suggests that the paperback handily outsold the hardcover.[30] The first paperback printing was 6,000 copies, and a second of 3,500 was ordered in 1967, while the first hardcover printing of 2,400 copies lasted well into 1971.

Soon after the "Spannthology" appeared, Faber and New Directions began to urge Pound to help in compiling a paperback *Selected Cantos* for the student market. "We are constantly getting requests," Laughlin informed him in 1965, "for such a selection from the professors who teach the modern courses in literature in colleges here. They want to teach the 'Cantos' but find the big book too bulky and expensive for their students. Now I know there will be a big demand for the 'Selected Cantos,' so I hope you will be able to work on it soon."[31] Pound, by this time frail and old, could contribute little but a basic selection, with textual corrections made by Kenner and Laughlin, and the book appeared in 1967 in England and 1970 in the United States (the later publication allowed New Directions to include two pieces of *Drafts and Fragments*). Again, this paperback sold very well, exhausting three printings and fifteen thousand copies in America by late 1973.

The transition into paperback publishing was a fundamental change for New Directions, but it also greatly affected Pound's reputation. Probably no other nontextual factor enhanced his place in the American literary pantheon as much. By repositioning him for the student and academic market, New Directions emphasized the poet's status as a historical figure and reinforced the idea that he was now in the twentieth-century canon. Press releases and jacket copy on Pound's new books restated these ideas, as the defiant argument for the patriotism and aesthetic value of his work that was used in the publicity for *Cantos LII–LXXI* or *The Pisan Cantos* disappeared, replaced by the respectful sparseness of the copy for *Rock-Drill, Thrones,* and *Drafts and Fragments.* As the 1950s ended, New Directions encouraged readers and consumers to conclude that critical debate was over, since academic and critical authorities had given Pound their approval; in the 1960s, the house would succeed. Trade paperback publishing ensured that professors (who read the pro-Pound criticism published and publicized by New Directions) could assign Pound's books to their students, and that those students could afford those books.

The changes that trade paperbacks brought to publishing affected Pound as they affected other writers. Trade paperbacks broadened the audience for contemporary literature, their low prices enabling a larger segment of the public to buy books. Students, especially, benefited because professors were now able to assign recent texts without complaints about price. Smaller publishers, whose sales volume simply could not justify producing cheap mass-market paperbacks, could publish lower-priced books that did not require huge sales in order to turn a profit. Publishers could finally take the chance to produce low-priced collections by authors who had yet to attain the status of acknowledged classics. Finally, the trade paperback embodied both accessibility and material quality, because it was much more attractive and well-made than the mass-market paperback. Many students who bought New Directions (or other trade paperback) books because they were inexpensive became adults who bought New Directions books because they were worth keeping—and, presumably, worth reading.

Declawing and Canonizing Pound

Even as Laughlin was reprinting his older books in the trade paperback format, Pound was producing new poetry after his release from St. Elizabeths, including two more volumes of cantos. Critical reaction to the final two installments of cantos reflects the change in Pound's prestige during the last fifteen years of his life—specifically, his transformation into a

canonical author. When the first, *Thrones*, appeared in 1959, most American critics reasserted their bafflement at the direction the *Cantos* had
taken, and more than a few used the opacity of *Thrones* to argue that the
Cantos as a whole were a failed project, one whose politico-economic
agenda doomed any chance at artistic profundity. The widely circulated
photograph of Pound giving the Fascist salute as he arrived in Naples in
1958 mirrored the book's defiant difficulty; both images underscored
Pound's steadfast refusal to compromise (in the eyes of his admirers) or his
obstinate refusal to disavow past mistakes (according to his detractors).[32]

In 1959, even as Pound was quickly becoming canonical by virtue of
his older works, many critics remained convinced that the *Cantos* were a
failure. *Thrones 96–109 de los cantares* received reviews that were, if
anything, worse than those given to the volume that preceded it by twenty
years, *Cantos LII–LXXI*. While the critics had found the same faults in
each volume since 1940, the fact that *Thrones* seemed to display no development, improvement, or evolution beyond its predecessor—the impression that the *Pisan Cantos* were an aberration, not the "real" Pound—
caused many to conclude that Pound had simply reached a dead end, and
that it was truly only the earlier, now-available-in-paperback work that was
worth reading.[33] Delmore Schwartz, who had retained a complicated attitude made up of admiration and disgust toward Pound since the mid-
1930s, wrote in the *New Republic* that "little change or genuine development . . . have occurred throughout the entire [*Cantos*]. Through the
years Pound has remembered a great deal, but he has learned nothing—
nothing that could be called a new insight into the attitudes with which he
began to write."[34] Schwartz continues, stating a judgment that he shares
with the New Critics on the essentially flawed nature of Pound's technique
and execution, that "what is bad and self-indulgent in [Pound's work] is in-
separable from Pound's poetic genius at its best." In other words, Pound's
work is incapable of true brilliance because its great innovations—broad
historical scope juxtaposed with minute details of politics and economics,
suddenness of transition, and "the sense that all history is relevant to any
moment of history"—are also the sources of its tragic shortcomings.[35]

Even unenthusiastic reviews, though, acknowledged Pound's growing
status as an American classic. M. L. Rosenthal used the occasion to write
"The Pleasures of Pound," a tribute to the poet's career as a whole. His

review addressed *Thrones*, Clark Emery's study of the *Cantos*, and William Van O'Connor and Edward Stone's *Casebook on Ezra Pound*, a collection of materials, "intended to be used as Controlled Source Material for the Freshman English Course" in the words of the jacket copy, relating to Pound's treason indictment and the Bollingen controversy. Quoting approvingly from four-decade-old poems such as *Hugh Selwyn Mauberley* and "The Return," though, Rosenthal's piece barely mentions *Thrones*, while praising Pound's fifty-year career. Already Pound is subtly being turned into a figure from the past, fit for retrospectives. The scope of Rosenthal's review modeled the process of canonization started and encouraged by New Directions: the poetry, a critical survey, and "Controlled Source Material for the Freshman English Course" are packaged together in a way that removes Pound from the realm of contemporary writing and prepares him for the academy. Writing about *Thrones* in the *Yale Review*, poet Thom Gunn noted explicitly that Pound's partisans had gained this foothold in American higher education. "*Thrones* is probably selling pretty well . . . partly because [Pound] is a fashionable name in the universities. But I suspect," Gunn continued, "that the only people who will take real interest in this volume are those who intend to work it up into some kind of thesis." Gunn expressed a criticism of Pound's poetry shared by most of his detractors among practicing poets and academic literary critics: that he had once been very promising but had let his technique take over the poem and his didacticism overwhelm his aesthetic drive: "*Thrones* is the culmination of a method based on the assumption that, so long as there is a general topic to the poetry, it is legitimate for the author to introduce any information written in any manner and in any order. In other cantos, particularly the very early ones, Pound frequently used the method with moderation and success. . . . But here it is reduced to absurdity."[36] Gunn's feeling that Pound's work was destined for the academy and was quickly receding from the realm of contemporary poetry was soon proved correct.

New Directions' late-1950s and early-1960s advertisements for Pound's books reflect this new acceptance by the academy. Although many readers were disappointed by his newest poetry, New Directions knew that Pound's back catalog was now more important than his new books, and used the new books to sell the older ones. In the 1940s, announcements of new Pound publications would be buried in advertisements for the house's fall list, and only the works of such authors as Tennessee Williams or Henry Miller enjoyed separate advertising. The 1950s saw Pound become more prominent; by 1959; the publication of *Thrones* provided the occasion for a full-page advertisement devoted to all the Pound titles New Directions had in print. Appearing in the summer of 1959 in such academic journals as the *Kenyon Review* and the *Hudson Review*, the advertisement featured *Thrones* and two recent paperback titles, *The Confucian Odes* and *The Classic Noh Theatre of Japan*. Thirteen other Pound books are listed, including one other paperback (*Selected Poems*) and an expensive ($30) signed limited edition of *Diptych, Rome-London*. Also testifying to New Directions' confidence in Pound's newfound respectability is the absence in these advertisements of any of the blurbs or testimonials on his behalf that had characterized almost all Pound advertisements from the 1940s or earlier 1950s: Laughlin and MacGregor now felt that the works had enough prestige to speak for themselves.

This is not to say, however, that Laughlin was so confident that he did not fear reminding the public of the poet's inflammatory statements. Pound was convinced that he was no longer controversial, telling Laughlin in 1959 that "N.Directions Position shd/ be [that] . . . E.P. [is] no longer a Political figure, has forgotten what or which politics he ever had," but Laughlin was very aware that many in the literary community and in the broader public still had very strong feelings against him.[37] Five years later, Laughlin foresaw the threat to Pound's reputation that would be posed by an academic book collecting materials from his treason trial—a book, he was convinced, some scholar would soon compile. He sought the poet's approval for a project that would be a sort of preemptive strike:

> Here is another matter on which your thoughts are needed. It has to do with the court records and related material of the Washington period. These records are in the "public domain" and the danger exists that some busybody will cotton to this fact and publish them in an unfriendly way. To head this off, [Pound's lawyer Julien] Cornell has prepared a text of them, with related letters and notes, which is extremely accurate and very sympathetic. He wants to bring this out in a limited edition of about 200 copies, for the present, just to set the record straight, and I think this is a good idea, if you approve. There would be no publicity, review copies or advertising. Copies would just

go to certain key libraries, a few reliable authors, and be available for such friends as you might wish to have them. In effect, this should head off publication by unauthorized persons of an unpleasant nature.[38]

The book was published by the John Day Company in 1966 under the title *The Trial of Ezra Pound*. It is unclear whether Laughlin declined to publish it in an attempt to minimize attention (New Directions' list had a much higher profile than that of the John Day Company) or whether Cornell simply decided to publish it elsewhere; given the close association between Cornell and Laughlin dating from Pound's trial in 1946–47, however the former is more likely.

If attention to Pound's past personal activities was still taboo, by the mid-1960s Laughlin and MacGregor had decided that some attention to him as a figure in literary history was appropriate, and in 1965 they planned a publicity push for the poet's eightieth birthday. Where the previous (1956) birthday campaign had relied on testimonials, this one would capitalize on Pound's growing status in academia. Laughlin still wanted to control this celebration, though. Ten years before, New Directions had had to solicit comments from Pound's friends and admirers in the literary world to compile a commemorative pamphlet. In 1965 the growing community of Pound scholars was planning its own celebrations. "There will be, we hear," Laughlin told Pound, "a number of important articles in various American journals in celebration of your octagenariety come October."[39] Robert MacGregor wrote requests to Henry Rago of *Poetry*, Barbara Epstein of the *New York Review of Books*, Norman Cousins of the *Saturday Review of Literature*, and other important figures, urging them to prepare special issues for the articles Pound's friends and readers were writing. A few literary periodicals did just that, but perhaps as a result of Pound's perceived irrelevance or his transformation into a figure of interest primarily to academics, almost none of the mainstream magazines that had written extensively on him during the 1950s (the *Saturday Review of Literature*, the *Nation*, and the *New Republic*, for instance) included a notice of Pound's "octagenariety."

Pound Scholarship in the Academy, 1951–1972

By the 1960s, New Directions had made Pound's early essays on Provençal poetry and his translations of Noh plays easily available, but readers who wanted to examine his *ABC of Economics, Jefferson and/or Musso-*

lini, or radio broadcasts had to search them out; in the case of the radio broadcasts, they would have had to borrow the recordings from the FBI. The firm had successfully repackaged Pound as a nonpolitical author who was both one of America's premier poets and a founding father of modern literature. But the repackaging would remain only that—packaging—unless critics and readers accepted this new, apolitical, elder statesman Pound. As already detailed, the critical climate had changed in the 1940s, giving the aesthetic formalist approach ascendancy. At this time, though, most of the best-known formalist critics were lukewarm about or even dismissive of Pound's work. What was needed, Laughlin had quickly seen, were critics who would take this formalist approach to reading Pound, but who would come to the opposite conclusions about him. Laughlin published some of this work and nurtured at least one important critic (Hugh Kenner), but he knew that it would backfire, and appear to be just marketing, if New Directions were the sole sponsor of the critical "counterswing." Fortunately, in the 1950s not one but a group of formalist critics had engaged themselves in just such a project. In the 1960s, they succeeded, to the extent that, by 1969, more critical articles and books were being written and published about Pound than about any other twentieth-century poet.

The change in literary opinion that brought Pound to the fore in college classrooms, academic journals, and anthologies of contemporary verse was not solely a result of a few new critics arriving at different conclusions, however. Larger, structural changes in American academia and literary journalism had caused much serious criticism to migrate from the mainstream magazines and review outlets to the academy. Poetry was less and less a matter for book-review magazines. Modernist poetry, especially, was well respected but its admirers were intellectuals and professors, not journalists and reviewers. Now, in the late 1950s and early 1960s, the critics who were to work this transformation in Pound's reputation were in the universities, not at the *Saturday Review*. The professor and literary historian Jay Hubbell, writing at the end of the decade, noted that "the situation in the 1960s is vastly different from what it was a half a century ago. The reputations of our older American writers and of nearly all our twentieth-century poets are now in the keeping not of the poet-critics but of the professors of English, who are far more numerous than they were in the 1920s. It is the professors who select the authors whose books are to be studied; they prepare the handbooks; they write the literary histories; and they edit most of the anthologies."[40] The last fifteen years of Pound's life saw a dramatic improvement in his reputation as a poet, one advanced largely by young professors who were saying the same things Laughlin had been saying since 1948. After Pound's release, he became the focus of a group of scholars and critics—Kenner, of course, but also Noel Stock, Donald Gallup, Guy Davenport, Eva Hesse, Donald Davie, and others—who had already produced a preliminary body of critical work on him. New Directions had set the process of canonization in motion by issuing the first serious works (most notably Kenner's 1951 *The Poetry of Ezra Pound,* and the American edition of Peter Russell's *An Examination of Ezra Pound* that same year), but after Pound's 1958 release, dozens of scholars, employing the New Critical method but rejecting the original New Critics' opinion of his works, began to produce articles and books that built on this small but quickly growing body of scholarship. Formalist in approach, this criticism almost entirely avoided the controversial aspects of Pound's career; its only ventures *hors du texte* were to track down Pound's allusions.

When Kenner published his *Poetry of Ezra Pound* he was a pioneer. Laughlin, for one, felt that the book had been the "injection into our bloodstream" that made Pound's rehabilitation possible, writing in 1985 that "I can't *prove* that it was *The Poetry of Ezra Pound* that turned the tide for Pound, but I think it was. . . . Of course, Pound was always talking about the 'time lag,' the time it takes, as he had adduced from his studies, for an original work or tone or style to be accepted by the general public. Was that what happened in the 1950s? Doubtless so, but would it have happened that soon without the influence of Kenner's book?"[41] Kenner downplayed the importance of his book, yet acknowledged that it had played some role in changing the focus of criticism on Pound. After *The Poetry of Ezra Pound,* he wrote, "Pound before long was a stock on the academic exchange: a safe 'subject.' What that means is not that I'd 'discovered' him, or been magnetically persuasive concerning his virtues. What I'd done, unwittingly, at the threshold of two decades' academic expansion—people peering under every cabbage-leaf for 'topics'—was show how this new man with his large and complex oeuvre might plausibly be written about."[42] Following this book, Pound criticism began to appear, some by established critics but most produced by young scholars who did not accept the New Critics' predominantly negative attitude. Kenner continued to write on Pound, and while the poet was still held in St. Elizabeths many other young critics—Herbert Bergman, Noel Stock, Donald Davie, Edwin Honig, Forrest Read, John Espey, Lewis Leary, and others—produced articles on him, and Cal-Berkeley's *Pound Newsletter* printed many of those articles. Lewis Leary's collection *Motive and Method in* The Cantos *of Ezra Pound* (1954) was the first full-length critical work on the often impenetrable *Cantos,* and provided a number of critical frameworks that would allow other writers a starting point for their own studies of the poem. (Although it appeared before Leary's anthology, H. H. Watts's 1952 *Ezra Pound and the Cantos,* published by the trade firm Henry Regnery, had had little impact.) Later, Clark Emery's *Ideas into Action: A Study of Pound's* Cantos (1958) and George Dekker's *Sailing after Knowledge: The* Cantos *of Ezra Pound* (1963) supplemented the critical commentary. Two short books intended for undergraduate or non-academic audiences, M. L. Rosenthal's *A Primer of Ezra Pound* (1960) and G. S. Fraser's *Ezra Pound* (1960), served as brief introductions to the poet's life and work, neither emphasizing his politics. Other notable studies from this period include John Espey's *Ezra Pound's* Mauberley: A *Study in Composition* (1955), Walter Sutton's *Ezra Pound: A Collection of Critical Essays* (1963), Donald Davie's *Ezra Pound: Poet as Sculptor* (1964), K. L. Goodwin's *The Influence of Ezra Pound* (1966), and Walter Baumann's *The Rose in the Steel Dust: An Examination of the Cantos of Ezra Pound* (1967).

The characteristics of the new Pound criticism included an aesthetic formalist approach, acknowledgment of the central importance of tracing allusions, and the goal of interpreting the poet's work and arriving at a consistent answer as to what these fifty years of poetry meant. Few of these works employ Pound's literary-critical works (apart from the very earliest, such as "A Few 'Don'ts' by an Imagiste") as a means to interpret his poetry; even fewer attempt to examine his political or economic beliefs or to see how those contribute to the structure and meaning of the *Cantos.* As a result, they are at once aestheticist and incomplete. The ideology of strict formalism, applied to a text whose formal attributes were remarkable but by no means the primary feature of the poem, prevented any full examination of what Pound was doing. To readers today, these close readings are therefore marked by conspicuous absences and nagging lacunae.

The most important common feature of these critics is their shared contention, against the dominant stance of academic critics, that Pound, not Eliot, was the modern age's most important poet. Eliot might be more formally accomplished, and his works more hermetic, closed, and ambiguous, but Pound's very open-endedness made him the ideal prophet of his age.[43] Furthermore, Pound's personal activities in the 1910s and 1920s also made him more central to the development of modern poetry than Eliot. In an address at Durham University (reprinted in *The Tenth Muse*) just before Pound's release, Herbert Read asserted "so far as the English-speaking world is concerned, Pound is the animator if not founder of the modern movement in poetry." Read follows this assertion with a discussion of both Pound's poetic practice and his literary criticism, and ends by stating that the *Cantos* are "the greatest poetic achievement of our time."[44]

One work that provides a fascinating perspective on Pound's growing status in the academy is Jay Hubbell's 1972 *Who Are the Major American Writers?* Hubbell outlines what has come to be known as the marketplace of literary prestige, and traces the history of public esteem for authors who were considered major in the 1960s, as well as summarizing the judgments of twentieth-century critics or publications that had attempted to rank authors in terms of influence, popularity, or greatness. Although Hubbell's primary focus is on the nineteenth-century American Renaissance, he devotes the last quarter of his book to a discussion of twentieth-century authors, and concludes that the writers most often acknowledged as being great—Eliot, Pound, and the like—rarely even appeared in the rankings of critics or commentators during the first half of the century. "The 1920s and 1930s were a great period in American literary history," Hubbell writes, "but its poets, novelists, and playwrights are little read outside of college classes." (Until the 1960s, most college classes rarely covered the modernists, with the exception of Eliot.) Beginning just before World War II, however, the writers of the American Renaissance gained stature in the academy. The modernists benefited from this development because, Hubbell argues, they wrote about the same themes as the mid-nineteenth-century Americans. The twentieth century, Hubbell writes, "has singled out those writers who seem in some way alienated from the society in which they lived. This is especially the case with Poe, Melville, Thoreau, and Henry James . . . [but] none of them was so completely alienated as Ezra Pound or T.S. Eliot."[45]

Even though Pound's work (and Pound himself) embodied the "alienation" that critics praised in American literature, it was not until many years after the academic community embraced Eliot and Joyce that Pound began to share that status. A 1949 UNESCO poll asked twenty-six specialists in American literature—primarily professors, but including names known outside of the academy such as Van Wyck Brooks, Henry Seidel Canby, and Mark Van Doren—to list the most significant writers of the last half century. On this list there are no New Critics, Pound is nowhere to be found, and Eliot is only a runner-up. The poet Randall Jarrell, displaying New Critical–style judgment, remarks in *Fifty Years of American Poetry* (1962) that "it is surprising that a poet of Pound's extraordinary talents should have written so few good poems all his own."[46] He does, however, grant Pound a greater status that the New Critics do: "the generation of American poets that included Frost, Stevens, Eliot, Pound, Williams, Marianne Moore, Ransom," who were all "American classics," had established "once and for all the style and tone of American poetry."[47] Among those named as honorary fellows of the Modern Language Association by 1968—Eliot, MacLeish, Robert Lowell, Marianne Moore, Katherine Anne Porter, Ransom, Steinbeck, Wilder, Williams— notable writers such as Pound, Faulkner, and Hemingway are absent.

But by the end of the decade, Pound truly was accepted into the American canon. Hubbell argues that most professors in the late 1960s to the early 1970s were "still teaching students that the last word in critical standards is to be found in the essays of Henry James, T.S. Eliot, and John Crowe Ransom," but he also admits that in the *American Literary Scholarship* volumes for 1963–69, criticism on Pound dominated the work on the modernists, and soon after this Stevens and Williams joined Pound. In 1969, Professor Jackson Bryer of the University of Maryland conducted a poll in which American literature specialists were asked to name the ten most important twentieth-century authors; the results were (in descending order) Hemingway, Faulkner, Frost, Fitzgerald, Stevens, Dreiser, O'Neill, Pound, Robinson, and Eliot (who had less than half as many votes as Pound).[48] The 1960s saw a remarkable jump in the number of critical works published on Pound. The table below lists the number of books about Pound, articles on Pound listed in the *Social Science and Humanities Index,* and listings in the *MLA Bibliography* for articles on Pound, for the years 1951–69. Given the numbers, it is clear that interest

PUBLISHED ARTICLES AND BOOKS ON EZRA POUND, 1951–1969

	Books on Pound	Articles on Pound listed in *Social Science and Humanities Index*	*MLA Bibliography* listings
1951–4	4	19	19
1955–9	17	20	98
1960–4	22	15	110
1965–9	24	38	159

in Pound exploded in the 1960s, as did the academic acceptability of publishing on Pound and Pound-related topics.[49]

Pound and the "New American Poetry"

Literary criticism was not the only milieu in which the general opinion of Pound was being revised. As demonstrated by a group of widely known and well-respected anthologies of contemporary verse, the poets of such disparate groups of poets as the Beats, the Black Mountain School, and the northern California Buddhist school were recognizing Pound as a fundamental influence. As Eliot's preeminence was fading, Pound's importance was growing. These anthologies show that the generation of young poets that had come of age in the era of Eliot rejected Eliot's models, and looked instead to Pound and Williams, who they felt were more innovative in and had more control over line and rhythm. It is hardly coincidental that many of these young poets, like their elders, were published by New Directions, and that the same critics—Kenner especially—who championed Pound and Williams also wrote the first important critical appreciations of such poets as Louis Zukofsky, Charles Olson, Basil Bunting, and George Oppen (of the group who were active before World War II) and of postwar poets like Charles Tomlinson, Gary Snyder, Kenneth Koch, Jonathan Williams, Denise Levertov, Robert Creeley, and Robert Duncan. Laughlin and Kenner, as publisher and critic, assisted these writers and helped them to prominence; this in turn helped Pound, demonstrating his continuing relevance at a time when critics were establishing his literary-historical status and his worthiness as a figure for academic study.[50] By rejecting New Critical orthodoxy while still embracing aesthetic formalism, moreover, these anthologies argued for the reading strategies Laughlin had been endorsing since 1946.

Although Donald Allen's *The New American Poetry 1945–1960* (1960) was and continues to be the best-known anthology of this period, even spawning a companion volume of criticism and theory—*The Poetics of the New American Poetry* (1973)—at least four other influential anthologies of the time featured young writers accepting and even welcoming elements of modernism that had been devalued by the New Critics. Each of these anthologies—Donald Hall's *Contemporary American Poetry* (1962), Paris Leary and Robert Kelly's *A Controversy of Poets* (1965), Mark Strand's *The Contemporary American Poets* (1969), and Hayden Carruth's *The Voice That Is Great Within Us* (1970)—embraces the modernism of Williams and Pound, with its conversationally clipped lines, its exploration of Asian or ethnic American working-class themes, and its rejection of the epic voice the last, a characteristic that these poets take from Williams, of course, not Pound).

The anthologies were all boisterous statements of what they called a "revolution" in American poetry. A number allude to the 1950s rivalry between the Beat poets and the "academic" school but argue that the two had more in common than not, and that the true conflict was between the diverse voice of the young generation and the stifling dogmatism of the New Critics and their inspiration, Eliot. Hall's anthology defines the contest as well as any. "For thirty years," he writes in his introduction, "an orthodoxy ruled American poetry. It derived from the authority of T.S. Eliot and the new critics; it exerted itself through the literary quarterlies and the universities. It asked for a poetry of symmetry, intellect, irony, and wit. The last few years have broken the control of this orthodoxy." Modern American poetry "began in London shortly after the death of Queen Victoria" with the meeting of Eliot and Pound, Hall continues. "Pound was the link between London and Greenwich Village. . . . But he was unable to reconcile the slangy Williams and the polyglot Eliot. And it was the ideas of Eliot which proved attractive to the young men who took power. . . . People who learned from Williams, and from Pound's structure and metric, had a hard time of it until the fifties."[51] In the preface to his anthology, Allen agrees with Hall that it is the modernist tradition of Williams and Pound that inspired the poets of the 1950s and 1960s. "In the years since the war American poetry has entered upon a singularly rich period," he writes:

> It is a period that has seen published many of the finest achievements of the older generation: William Carlos Williams' *Paterson, The Desert Music and Other Poems*, and *Journey to Love*; Ezra Pound's *The Pisan Cantos, Section: Rock-Drill*, and *Thrones*; H.D.'s later work culminating in her long poem *Helen in Egypt*; and the recent verse of E.E. Cummings, Marianne Moore, and the late Wallace Stevens. . . .
>
> The new younger poets have written a large body of work [with] one common characteristic: a total rejection of all those qualities typical of academic verse. Following the practice and precepts of Ezra Pound and William Carlos Williams, it has built on their achievements and gone on to evolve new conceptions of the poem.[52]

For Robert Kelly, "the tradition of Blake, Whitman, Pound, Williams" was "the true tradition of craft and form in our time." Carruth dedicated his anthology "To E.P., from us all."[53] Young poets' interest in Pound's and Williams's innovations, and devotion to their legacy, as expressed in these anthologies, helped Pound and his contemporaries with the generation of readers who did not remember and had not been taught about his great accomplishments of the 1910s and 1920s, and who probably knew him only through the St. Elizabeths saga. Pound clearly exerted tremendous influence on the poets of the late 1950s and early 1960s. In 1972, Richard Kostelanetz identified not just these anthologies but also new periodicals such as *Stony Brook*, which had been "founded in the Poundian mold" in 1968, as indicators of Pound's centrality to the young writers of the 1960s. He also felt that the changing formal qualities of popular song lyrics (he specifically mentions Bob Dylan) reflected Pound's cultural impact just as much as "nearly every recent long poem in English."[54]

Almost as important as the anthologies for establishing the literary climate of the 1960s—and Pound's growing importance in that climate—were the periodicals put out by literary publishing firms. New Directions' annual anthology *New Directions in Prose and Poetry* and the *Evergreen Review* (published by Grove Press) attempted to construct and reinforce each house's identity by emphasizing its connection with the writers it published. The periodicals contributed greatly to the sense of community and shared enterprise among experimental writers in postwar America, and did much to replace the little magazines that had been the meeting place for so many of the first generation of modernist artists. Their spiritual links to those earlier little magazines were strengthened by publishing members of that first modernist generation (such as Pound) and European writers (such as Beckett and Camus) who were as much its Continental offspring as the San Francisco, New York, and Black Mountain schools were its American progeny. Each firm, through its journal, stressed the continuity of the modernist project, attempting to educate contemporary readers on the influence of the first generation and to convince academic critics and admirers of the older poets that the younger generation was indeed carrying the modernist torch.[55] Constructing a coherent narrative, the two publishers packaged modernism, changing the public understanding of American literature of the period in a manner friendly to each firm's writers. Needless to say, Pound frequently appeared in the *New Directions* anthologies.

The strong link that New Directions had with Pound, with the 1930s generation of poets (Olson and Oppen were New Directions authors), and with the poets of the 1950s and 1960s (Levertov, Tomlinson, Duncan, Creeley, Snyder, and many others published with New Directions) made the firm itself an important part of the relationship between readers and authors. It even became a metonym for the relationship, both positively— Donald Hall's 1962 introduction to his anthology recognized the important role the *New Directions* anthologies played in the transmission of this poetic tradition—and negatively—Dwight Macdonald had sneeringly referred to the "epigonism" of the New Directions list as far back as 1944.[56] By making Pound's work readily available and by providing readers with a nonpolitical version of the poet, Laughlin had made him more accessible and acceptable to young writers, who in turn, by describing Pound's influence on them, made him more accessible and acceptable to those who were reading their work. Pound's presence throughout the world of 1950s and 1960s poetry supported the argument that his entire contribution to that world, not just the success of his individual works, must be taken into consideration when evaluating his importance, and that this gave him an importance that other poets, such as Eliot, lacked.

Peering into the Dark Corners of Pound's Life

Poets and critics were not the only people writing about Pound. But where they examined his work and literary influence, journalists and biographers began in the 1960s to evaluate his life and personal activities through the lens of his fading notoriety and growing literary-historical importance. New Directions, as we have seen, had since the war pursued a strategy of rehabilitating Pound by constantly emphasizing the separation of man from work. But with a poet so controversial, this separation could never be fully attained, and a few incidents had set the New Directions campaign back temporarily. Press attention to the Bollingen affair had been a mixed blessing. Coverage of the Kasper incident, though, had been an unmitigated disaster. Near the end of Pound's incarceration, and spurred by the Kasper incident, many magazines and newspapers started paying attention to the imprisoned poet. A number of these, ironically, called for his release, holding that the punishment was now sufficient, and that the Kasper incident showed that he was probably more dangerous in St. Elizabeths than if he were to return to Italy. But even this coverage illustrates the effects of Laughlin's project. Implicit in these articles was the belief that Pound's literary accomplishments made him a special case.

Press interest in Pound began to grow in the months surrounding his release from St. Elizabeths. David Rattray's piece for the *Nation* in November 1957 emphasized the poet's continuing involvement with bigots, fanatics, and crackpots (especially Kasper). A 1957 article by Richard H. Rovere in *Esquire*, though, attempted to weigh poetic accomplishments against less laudable qualities, and judge which had the most enduring importance.[57] Rovere gave equal attention to Pound's generous support of other artists and to his assertion, in his radio broadcast of 26 May 1942, that "every reform . . . is an act of homage towards Mussolini and Hitler. They are your leaders." "It is possible to take the psychiatrists' way out and say that by then Pound was a nut not to be held responsible. But the matter will not rest there," Rovere insisted: "Some sort of accommodation must be reached between Pound-the-glorious-American-poet and Pound-the-loony-ideologue. Various possibilities suggest themselves. It has often been argued that there is an affinity between American populism and brutal American reaction. But this will not do for Pound the sweet singer;

except for his hatred of bankers and his funny money, he was never fetched by the Populist fallacies. . . . A more promising hypothesis is that he was beguiled—eventually into insanity—by a predilection for conspiracy theories of life and history."[58] Rovere concluded by detailing the tenuousness of the government's position that Pound continued to be insane and thus should still be held. "Not long ago, the government which detains Pound . . . circulated abroad, as part of its effort to persuade the world that we Americans really care about the finer things, a flossy periodical [*Perspectives USA*] in which it was asserted that Ezra Pound 'has done more to serve the cause of English poetry than anyone else alive'. . . . Hayden Carruth wrote in *Perspectives USA* [that] 'it is hard to think of a good reason why Pound should not have his freedom immediately.' "[59] Rovere—apparently unaware that Laughlin himself was behind *Perspectives USA*—pointed out the contradiction between the government's use of Pound as an exemplar of American cultural achievement and its position that he had committed crimes that necessitated his continuing institutionalization.

The reaction to Rovere's article, compared to the reaction to the Bollingen award, underscored the change in cultural climate. Where the Bollingen affair had caused a huge public furor and much soul-searching among American intellectuals, Rovere's assertion that Pound's accomplishments did, in the end, outweigh his offenses was greeted largely with approval. Supportive letters poured in to *Esquire* for months afterward, and in the February 1958 issue appeared a short, admiring piece on the poet by one of Pound's guards from the Pisa detention camp. That this view was expressed in *Esquire*, a decidedly middlebrow, glossy, celebrity-and-lifestyle magazine, demonstrates that Pound's supporters were by no means found solely among poets, critics, and the far right.

Rovere's article ushered in a brief spate of biographical writing and reconsiderations of the poet's legacy. Pound's 1958 release from St. Elizabeths and the appearance the same year of *Thrones* provided an opportunity for mainstream news magazines and literary journals to turn their attention briefly to the unrepentant septuagenarian. Many magazines that had supported his incarceration thirteen years earlier now called for his release. The *Nation,* for instance, insisted that "it would be a triumph of democracy if we set Pound free."[60] Literary journals were beginning to pay particular tribute to Pound—the *Yale Literary Magazine*'s December

1958 issue was devoted to him, and Laughlin saw this as confirmation that his reputation was rising. "I find some of the editorial material a little bit distressing," he wrote the poet when he saw the journal, "but no doubt the total impact and effect will be beneficial."[61] The "editorial material" in question, naturally, drew attention to Pound's political activities and beliefs.

These magazine profiles provided important perspectives on Pound's life, but in order for the poet to become truly canonical, students needed some way to understand his life as a whole. Pound was a natural subject for a biography, for he was a dynamic, active man who had known most of the important figures of modernism and had influenced almost everyone he had known. But Laughlin knew that a biography would also draw attention to his most petty and sordid statements and actions. During the 1950s, while Pound was still in Washington and stubbornly refusing to distance himself from those embarrassments, Laughlin was more than happy that the only remotely biographical project was D. D. Paige's 1950 edition of Pound's letters, a selection that concentrated on literary matters and whose coverage ended in 1941. During the 1960, however, five full-length biographies appeared, along with numerous biographical sketches focusing on particular periods of Pound's life. Although each addressed his political activities, only one concentrated on the "dark side" of Pound's character, and in the end the spate of studies only helped Pound become a historical figure and convinced the public that his transgressions of the past had little contemporary relevance.

All of Laughlin's and Pound's fears played out around the first biography, Charles Norman's *Ezra Pound* (1960). Norman, once a journalist for the moderately leftist New York newspaper *PM*, had earlier compiled the volume *The Case of Ezra Pound* (1948), a selection of Pound's radio broadcasts "with opinions," the dust jacket boasted, "by Conrad Aiken, E.E. Cummings, F.O. Matthiessen, William Carlos Williams [and] Louis Zukofsky," and published by the Bodley Press. The earlier book did not take a position supporting Pound, and was noncommittal about the stance of his mainstream supporters that he was insane and unfit to stand trial. As a consequence, the poet was hostile when Norman wrote him in late 1957 regarding a biography of his friend E. E. Cummings: "aren't you the buzzard," he responded, "who collected an enormous amount of cat-shit, shat by the ignorant and incurious, some years ago?"[62] A year later, when

Norman began to ask Pound about the possibility of writing his biography, he received a great deal of invective. Norman's correspondence was admiring, complimentary, even fawning at times, but Pound refused to accept the praise, writing him that "ENEMIES OF MANKIND unwittingly, but more dangerous than out and out perverters and open liars like the columnists are the Chas. Normans who, thoroughly brainwashed, print 80 and more % of the truth, and perhaps as much of it as they know, to the end, willing or unwilling, that they hide the great lies and the great betrayals."[63]

Laughlin, too, was leery about Norman's motivations, because he remembered that he had "attack[ed] Ezra rather vigorously at the time of the Bollingen award." He told Norman that "you will, I am sure, understand my reluctance to talk about Ezra with anyone who is in any way hostile to him."[64] He also feared, certainly, that a biography would refocus public attention on Pound's politics—since the Kasper incident and the release from St. Elizabeths, the poet's beliefs had disappeared from public attention—and he sought advice on what kind of information might be appropriate to discuss with Norman: "I didn't care at all for the little book he got out about you some years ago, and I thought it best to inquire of him, frankly, what his attitude might now be, since he had written to me, requesting an interview, to talk about you. . . . Whatever his basic attitude might be, I wouldn't want to discuss anything personal with him, but if he really does mean to do an honest job, and since he will have the backing of a large publisher in his publication, would it be advisable to talk to him about literary matters?"[65] Pound advised Laughlin to "get CUMMING's personal view of Norman before you slide on the greased pole."[66] The fact that Norman had "the backing of a large publisher" [Macmillan] was important to Laughlin, because this would ensure the book a chance to have a significant impact on public opinion. Macmillan had the publicity budget and distribution network that would bring the book to the attention of both reviewers and consumers in a way that New Directions could never match. Thus Laughlin was cautious about what type of book it would be. Norman, of course, reassured both Pound and Laughlin that it would be a fair treatment of the poet, and asserted that "I have no attention of attacking at any point in his story; in dealing with certain documents, I shall do so without comment."[67]

Over the next year, Laughlin continued to tell Pound about his reservations regarding Norman, writing in early 1960, "Charles Norman is causing me considerable worry. He has been in here several times, and we have had lengthy discussions, in which he exudes friendliness and great admiration for your works of beneficence and the merit of your poetry, but it seems quite clear, from little things that drop out of his mouth when he is cornered a bit, that he has included in the book a good deal of material which may not present all of your ideas in the most favorable light."[68] Especially disturbing was the possibility that Pound's anti-Semitic statements would appear in Norman's text—even if they were used in passing, to illustrate other, positive things about Pound: "I am troubled by the fact that Norman wants to quote so many passages from letters to Zukofsky where there are remarks which are bound to be misinterpreted by people who go out of their way to prove that you are anti-Semitic. . . . I certainly don't want to censor Norman, but neither do I want to be a party to fanning the flames of controversy."[69] Even the granting of permissions and the calculation of permissions fees were held up by suspicions about Norman's motivations: "[MacGregor] tells me that [Norman] wants to use about ten poems, complete, and one of the Cantos, complete. He is monkeying around trying to get these for nothing, but neither Bob nor I feel that he ought to have them without a decent fee. The amount . . . would depend on the tone of the book, whether it is a book that is going to help the sale of your works, or hurt them. So far, he has absolutely refused to let me see what he has been writing."[70] Pound opposed the reprinting of has poems in Norman's biography—"anyone buying a biog shd/have enough interest in the subject to OWN the text anyhow,"[71] he wrote Laughlin—and also requested that Laughlin not give Norman permission to reprint potentially offensive passages from their correspondence: "considering that E.P. now objects to violent language, there seems no reason to dig up examples that were never intended for the public eye, and which there is no use diffusing. The sense of communication made to an individual in circumstances of familiarity is simply not the sense that the general reader will see in it 20 or 30 years later."[72]

Norman's book appeared in 1960, and, much to Langhlin's relief, it was largely harmless: "I am happy to report, having finally seen it in toto, that Norman's book is not as unfortunate as we had feared. To be sure, there are things in it that you probably aren't going to like, but I think he has been very fair in several respects."[73] In his introduction, Norman humbly suggests, "It is unlikely that I have done more than characterize [Pound], recount some of his exploits, and credit him, anew, with teaching and influencing several generations of poets."[74] The biography is a chatty, unprepossessing, informal history of Pound's activities; its main contribution to Pound studies is that it was the first collection of the previously widely scattered body of the poet's opinions. For the first time, readers had access to quotes from his early literary writings, from his correspondence, from his poetry, and even from his radio broadcasts, all in one place.

The reviews of Norman's biography in mass-market publications testify to mainstream America's enduring revulsion, even fifteen years after World War II. In addition, they illustrate the time lag between the academy's acceptance of the separation of politics and poetry (at least in the case of Pound) and mainstream society's acceptance. *Time* portrayed Pound as a sadly misled figure, calling him "increasingly unstable" and explaining his shift from poetic to economic concerns in the 1930s as "the good Samaritan [becoming] the silly Samaritan." The radio broadcasts were "tawdry" and Pound an "economic crank." More importantly, the poetry was uneven. The review concludes by reinforcing the generally held opinion that Pound's beliefs would always stain his legacy: "Once an Italian journalist asked him about his tragically flawed character. 'How is it that you, who merited fame as a seer, did not see?' Ezra Pound could not answer."[75]

The *Herald Tribune Book Review* took much the same stance, stating that Norman's biography was "excellent" and showed how the past was in many ways a charlatan and a dissembler. His autobiography (the writer seems to be referring to *Indiscretions*) was simply a pose, and even Pound's public activities do not reveal the real man.[76] Although Laughlin's campaign to rehabilitate Pound's reputation had had great success in the academy, the reception of Norman's biography in mass-market periodicals showed how much Laughlin had left to accomplish among outlets that served a larger public. Dorothy, too, seems to have noticed this; she urged Laughlin to ask Norman to drop his discussion of the "Kasper incident" for the 1962 paperback reprint of the book.[77]

The next two biographies were written by devoted admirers, members of Pound's St. Elizabeths entourage. Eustace Mullins quickly followed Norman with *This Difficult Individual, Ezra Pound*—a short and loose discussion of Pound's life that, in a later biographer, J. J. Wilhelm's, comment, "portray[ed] a Pound acting as a guru for a group of debased disciples, some of whom he was feeding from hospital food."[78] Mullins had been one of the most vehemently anti-Semitic of the St. Elizabeths circle, and published a number of works of Poundian economics during the 1950s, one (*Mullins on the Federal Reserve*) with the firm of Kasper and Horton.[79] Pound did put more faith in Mullins than in Norman, though, telling Laughlin that "I plug fer the Mulligator" and assuring MacGregor that Mullins was "qualified, one of the 3 or 4 men I wd/trust with my personal papers."[80] Mullins cajoled Pound for approval of his proposed biography, and wrote to Laughlin for some time before he actually got started on his project, to emphasize that Pound wanted *him* to write his biography—and that New Directions should provide him with a grant to go to Italy and do just that.[81] Mullins can be most charitably described as a "character"—his stationery, much like Pound's in the prewar Italian years, featured regularly changing odd slogans, and at different times identified his business as "M&N Associates, Political Engineering/Creative Propaganda" and "Institute for Biopolitics." All of the reviews of his book prominently mention his close affiliation with Pound, but criticize Mullins for not using this closeness to offer unique insights. The *New York Times Book Review* expressed a typical judgment: "Luckily I knew that Ezra Pound was a fine poet before I took up this inept work about him. The purpose of the book—a brew of fact, half-truth, innuendo, evasion, distortion, carelessness, insult and sophomoric sermonizing—is stated at once: 'the case *for* Ezra Pound.' "[82]

Michael Reck, another disciple, published *Ezra Pound: A Close-Up* with the large firm McGraw-Hill in 1967. Reck's biography was a less developed version of Mullins's project. Because of Reck's personal involvement during the St. Elizabeths years, his biography gives 75 of its 193 pages to the postwar period of Pound's life: by contrast, only a ninth of Norman's biography (48 pages out of 466) is concerned with the trial and after, while Mullins's book gives Pound's thirteen years of incarceration approximately 100 of its 360 pages. Like Mullins's work, Reck's book is unapologetically supportive of Pound; unlike Mullins, though, Reck is considerably more circumspect about Pound's opinions.

Reck's book received a more favorable critical reception than did *This Difficult Individual*. Kenner, in the *New York Times Book Review*, wrote that it provided "tantalizing glimpses" into Pound's character, and was therefore "worth having for its authenticities." Still, he felt that Reck did not draw a complete enough portrait. Daniel Hoffman agreed, saying that the book was "more a snapshot than a portrait." Taking the middle ground between Pound's defenders and his detractors, Hoffman also argued that the "crank" ideas Reck quickly mentioned deserved a fuller explanation, for they served both as invective in epistolary harangues and as structuring principles allowing the *Cantos* to succeed. "These ideas," Hoffman wrote, "help shore up the wobbling pivot from which Pound surveys our crumbling culture and affirms what he can of its values."[83]

The 1970 publication of Noel Stock's *Life of Ezra Pound* provided an opportunity for critics to have their final word on Pound during his life, for the poet was frail, ailing, and clearly near death. Stock was Pound's primary disciple and emissary in Australia, and had edited a Pound-oriented literary magazine, *Edge,* in Melbourne for several years during Pound's incarceration. He was a great admirer at first, but over the years slowly came to the conclusion that, notwithstanding their isolated successes, the *Cantos* as a whole were a failure.[84] Ironically, this was also the impression many reviewers had of Stock's biography. Kenner saw the book as "a heavy box of oddments, many of them verifiable and most of them useless. . . . [T]he *Life* is . . . written with a radical inattention that infects the very structure of the sentences." Again the obligatory, and almost identical, judgments on Pound end the reviews. For Alfred Alvarez, the poet's life is "the tragedy of a major talent frittered away by some inner perversity." "Are we to forgive Pound's anti-Semitism," Geoffrey Wolff asked in *Newsweek,* "because he wrote 'Hugh Selwyn Mauberley?' "[85]

These four biographies offer similar answers to Wolff's question. But where Mullins and Reck felt no need to explain or apologize for Pound's political activities, Norman and Stock, admirers of the poetry, addressed the question gingerly, aware that the question of the ultimate value of Pound's work was still open and still much influenced by public sentiment about his anti-Semitism and pro-Fascism. Norman and Stock minimized the author's political involvement, acknowledging his faults but downplaying their importance.[86] Forgiving Pound's anti-Semitism was not a question for these biographers; recognizing the relative importance of such statements when compared to his body of work was the issue. For all their differences, they agreed in contending that his importance in determining the course of modern poetry had been under-appreciated and unacknowledged by the critical establishment.[87]

Clearly, what Laughlin had set into motion now had its own momentum. The aesthetic formalist approach to understanding Pound had made such strides in solidifying his improved literary reputation that by the end of the 1960s Pound's personal history could be reintroduced even into New Directions' promotional materials. His literary reputation, in short, was now helping his public image, whereas in the 1940s and 1950s his public image had damaged his literary reputation. Biographies that detailed his wartime activities and often anti-Semitic feelings had no apparent harmful effect on steadily increasing sales or his consecration by the academy, and they, too, finally endorsed the idea that poetic accomplishments outweighed repugnant beliefs. Many of the leading young poets of the day recognized Pound as their closest and most important ancestor. In the academy, more critics were writing about him than about any other twentieth-century poet. Pound had finally attained the status once enjoyed by his own protégé, Eliot. And a publishing house had initiated, nurtured, and perhaps ensured the success of this great shift.

Drafts and Fragments and the End of Ezra Pound

Even though Pound's prestige had become secure by the late 1960s, Laughlin still had a deep concern for managing the poet's public image and for maintaining control of his publications. Control over the image was put to the test with the composition, unauthorized publication, and official publication of the final work, *Drafts and Fragments of Cantos CX–CXVII* (1968). Although Laughlin wanted Pound to bring his epic to a strong close, to "write Paradise," the book was fragmentary and provisional, and its authorized publication was motivated by an illegal publication of the same "drafts and fragments." In the words of Peter Stoicheff, the leading interpreter of this book, *Drafts and Fragments* "is a volume whose title was not the author's creation, whose material was not wholly the author's choice, whose arrangement was partially imposed without the author's approval, and whose authorized publication was primarily a response to its premature pirated appearance."[88] Yet critics responded to the work as if it were Pound's summation of his sixty years as a poet, and in interpretating it they completed the rehabilitation of Pound's public image that had been initiated in the 1940s and 1950s.

The few cantos that Pound wrote after his return to Italy appeared sporadically, in a wide variety of periodicals. Most of these works were submitted not by the poet but by Laughlin, who wanted to maintain

Pound's identity as a practicing poet while at the same time attempting to solidify his status as a figure of historical importance.[89] He also sought to find the most remunerative magazines in which to place Pound's works, for the poet had had little income during his time in St. Elizabeths and now had to support a sizable group of relatives and friends. As far back as 1958, for instance, Laughlin had been suggesting that Pound look at journals that were willing to spend money freely. "Have you had any contact," he asked that year, "with this new and extremely opulent quarterly from the University of Texas? It is a very mixed bag of fish, but I could query them, if you'd like me to. There is apparently quite a lot of money there. They were the ones, I think, who paid the Parson [Eliot] $10,000 to come to Texas for two readings."[90] Appearing between 1962 and 1966, these cantos were published in forums ranging from small literary journals such as *Threshold* and the *Niagara Frontier Review* to wide-circulation magazines such as the *National Review*. Laughlin even attempted to place one of Pound's poems in the pages of his old nemesis, the *Saturday Review of Literature*: "I have been having some converse with John Ciardi, who is now the Poetry Editor at 'Saturday Review.' He is very well disposed toward you and would like to see a Canto, if any are ready. He apologizes most profusely for the bad behavior of the magazine in past days, but it was then under different management, and he had nothing to do with it. This would certainly be a good place to appear, since they have a very large circulation now."[91]

For most of the 1960s, Laughlin and Pound's other close friends in America wondered how the *Cantos* would end, for the poet clearly was running out of the energy and will to finish the work with a proper "Paradise," as he had asserted for years was his intention. "I need 20 hours sleep a day to make one coherent sentence," he told Laughlin in 1960.[92] The issue did not seem urgent, however, and New Directions felt no need to press him to finish or to provide them with the materials to issue a final collection. "Do you want to do anything at this point," Laughlin inquired in early 1967, "about the Canto fragments, or just let them sit until you have more written? No pressure on this, we have the "Selected [*Cantos*]" upcoming, but I just wanted to ask."[93]

But in that same year, a volume entitled *Cantos 110–116* appeared in a few New York bookstores, and this underground publication necessitated quick action by Pound's official representatives. Published under the imprint of the Fuck You Press, a small Lower East Side outfit run by the longtime underground figure Ed Sanders, the twenty-eight-page book contained versions of the few cantos that had been printed in magazines during the 1960s.[94] Laughlin was furious at this piracy, and "asked Sanders to the Russian Tea Room, where he treated his guest to a piece of his mind and some lunch," in Stoicheff's words.[95] The Sanders book prompted more than Laughlin's anger, though. Realizing that it imperiled New Directions' claim to U.S. copyright on the last cantos, and fearing that other pirate publishers could print the canto fragments that had been appearing in magazines, Laughlin stopped Sanders from printing any more of his books and worked quickly to compile an official version of these cantos. "One reason for putting this New Directions *Drafts & Fragments* out fast," Laughlin wrote to an associate at the time, "is to try to stop some more piracies of the Ed Sanders kind, his disgusting mimeographed version. . . . Pound's lawyers have gotten after Sanders, and he says he won't do it again, but with an anarchist like that you never know. It was on the basis of this piracy that I was able to persuade Ezra to do some work in putting these Drafts and Fragments into shape and let us bring them out now."[96] Laughlin contacted Pound in an effort to secure the poet's authorization, but Pound's health was failing and his will to continue working was weak. Laughlin persisted, though, telling him that

> that no-good bum, Ed Sanders, whose bookshop in the lower Village was closed by the police some months ago for his obscene publications, has now gone and mimeographed all of the Canto fragments and is selling them clandestinely through various booksellers who are willing to cooperate in this dirty deal. . . .
>
> This being the case, do you think you ought to change your mind about a proper book of the Canto fragments at this point, even though you haven't finished working on them? We could do some sort of limited edition of them for you, making it clear that these are just "drafts," and this might stop some of the piracy. . . .
>
> I have not sent you a copy of the pirate's stuff, because it is so obscene. Not only full of errors, but a hideous, semi-obscene cover, and words which I cannot dictate to the nice young lady who types my letters on the title page. This all comes out of the dope culture of the

Lower East Side. They are all high on one drug or another and don't care what they do.[97]

Pound was convinced, and upon receiving the proofs Laughlin responded, "O Venerable, you are still the Best with the words in the langwidge."[98] The first edition of 310 copies (a handprinted limited edition produced for New Directions by Iowa City's Stone Wall Press and priced at $100) was finished by late December 1968. Believing that the limited edition would sell by word of mouth, Laughlin did not bother advertising it, saving his efforts for the $3.75 version, which came out early in 1969.

The appearance of *Drafts and Fragments* was notably not an occasion for critics to have at Pound for excessive difficulty or past offenses, as had been the case with *Section: Rock-Drill* and *Thrones*. Instead, the book was greeted by reviews that commented approvingly on its more personal tone and on the gentleness of some of its passages. Perhaps swayed by Pound's nearly ten-year public silence and by his occasional mention of "errors" and "that stupid suburban prejudice, anti-Semitism," critics were willing to forgive the old transgressions.[99] This was partly a result of the different nature of the book. *Drafts and Fragments* is a highly tentative, wrenching, personal book of poetry, drastically different from the strident political rhetoric and historical arcana of the previous two volumes. Certainly it has its share of barely decipherable details and invective against usurers; but it also expresses Pound's regrets, his worries, and the terse meditations of his old age. The reviews for this final volume, then, are almost all summations of Pound's career, attempts to predict his ultimate importance, and praise for what is great in the *Cantos* rather than condemnation of what is didactic, bigoted, or obscure. In this, the reviews both lead and follow the change of opinion in the academy and in poetry circles. In the ten years between *Thrones* and *Drafts and Fragments*, the meaning of Pound himself had changed.

American reviewers were kind to Pound, or at least generous in assigning his place in literary history, even when they were critical of the poetry in this volume. Herbert Leibowitz's paragraph on *Drafts and Fragments* in the *Hudson Review* concentrated on poetry and not career, but Leibowitz did make it clear that he felt the *Cantos* a failed project. "Like some visionary architect still perfecting the grand plan of his life, Pound cannot let go of this petted child," he wrote, but added that the parts of

Drafts and Fragments that "constitute an act of public contrition, a poetic last will and testament . . . [are] very moving." The *Virginia Quarterly Review* was also very impressed by the tender tone, insisting that the book contained "some of the best" of Pound's work.[100] The *Yale Review*'s Louis Martz emphasized Pound's vast influence and his central role in American literary history. Placing his evaluation of Pound in the middle of a "New Books in Review" column, Martz stated that Pound "has made possible the existence of volumes such as those that we have just discussed" (by Robert Creeley and Robert Lowell). Implicitly supporting the growing notion of a "Pound era," Martz remarked that "these books . . . all appearing at once, give one the sense of a vital era ending." Pound, though, transcends his era—"Pound's career," Martz began, "enfolds the entire development of modern poetry, beginning with his shimmery vestiges of the Pre-Raphaelite world, then moving out into the vast universe of the Cantos." Martz did review the volume at hand, but his focus was on Pound's place in literary history, and the place of the *Cantos* with "Wordsworth's *Prelude* and Whitman's *Leaves of Grass*."[101] The comparison makes a great deal of sense for a critic who was attempting to solidify Pound's reputation at a time (the close of the 1960s) when the allusive, historical, difficult poetry of the modernist period was slowly losing favor, and when more attention was being given to Romantic and Victorian poetry, denigrated by the modernists for fifty years.

Scholars such as Stoicheff and Ronald Bush, in their discussions of *Drafts and Fragments*, emphasized the provisional quality of the volume and the way its open-endedness demonstrated that the book was a product of the convergence of numerous forces: the "readings" of its readers and editors and the business necessities of its publisher, in addition to the actual will of the author. Bush noted the "tentativeness" and "noncoercive" feeling of these poems, so different from the "authoritarian politics, natural order, and mystical perception" of *Section: Rock-Drill* and *Thrones,* and concluded that "Pound's reluctance to publish *Drafts & Fragments* . . . indicated how little [he] had come to terms with the submerged implications of his experimental style."[102] Pound's reluctance to publish these fragments, though, did not contribute to public understanding of the volume, which was that it was the last gasp of a poet who was returning to the style of his earlier, most successful works. To readers of the late 1960s, *Drafts and Fragments* was an opportunity to come to know again one of the poets from decades before and was the final proof of Pound's worthiness for inclusion in the ranks of the great. In both tone and subject matter, *Drafts and Fragments* brought Pound back to where he had been in the early 1920s, before politics dominated his understanding of what he was trying to do, and gave an apt sense of finality to New Directions' project to remake him.

It was clear, then, that Laughlin's "counter-swing" had been a triumph. Pound had joined the ranks of America's great poets, his wartime broadcast, treason indictment, and institutionalization notwithstanding. If critical reaction to his final work illustrates this long-awaited accession, though, we must also ascribe some responsibility to Laughlin's adoption of the trade paperback. With this format, Laughlin brought out all of Pound's early nonpolitical work and aimed his marketing directly at students. (*Drafts and Fragments* itself appeared in hardcover.) Confronted by a shelf of Pound's books, none of which give any evidence that the poet had ever been controversial, students could read him in the aesthetic formalist fashion Laughlin had been encouraging for years. Critics, too, seeing the controversies of the 1930s and 1940s fade in importance, grew willing to forgive and to come to conclusions about the force of Pound's contribution to literature. Laughlin used all of these circumstances as a wise marketer would: he attempted to direct public taste, to take advantage of the shifts in it that he had helped put into motion, and to appeal both to tastemakers and to the youth market that would determine taste in the decades to come. In advancing Pound's cause, he had in many ways become the kind of shrewd businessman that, in the 1930s and early 1940s, he had so passionately attacked.

Conclusion

❖ ❖ ❖ ❖

> It has been The Pound Era, right enough; and it was The Pound Era during a crucial period. Civilization is memory, and insofar as humane letters maintain the process of active remembering, you and those with whom you worked (and *on* whom you worked) have made it a little less likely that our children will grow up highly intelligent barbarians.
>
> —Hugh Kenner to Ezra Pound, 2 Dec. 1962

EZRA Pound's death in 1972 ends this story. Laughlin was named executor of the Ezra Pound Literary Trust, and for many subsequent years had to deal with the treacherous and often poisonous relationships among Pound's heirs: Dorothy Pound (Pound's wife), Olga Rudge (Pound's long-time lover), Mary de Rachewiltz (Pound's daughter with Olga), and Omar Pound. Laughlin, Mary de Rachewiltz, and Hugh Kenner, especially, continued to help produce new volumes of Pound's work and to correct errors in prior editions; only in 1986 did the "complete" *Cantos,* including the pro-Fascist Italian Cantos 72 and 73 and several fragments intended to follow the *Drafts and Fragments,* appear. Pound has not lost his central place in the modernist canon, even twenty years after his death marked the end of Laughlin's "counter-swing." But Laughlin's pendulum image was an appropriate one, for soon after the poet's death momentum began to swing the other way, against him. By the mid-1970s few critics still felt that he was the greatest or most important American poet of the twentieth century, and many poets rejected his allusiveness and stridency. Wallace Stevens came into ascendancy, and later Williams, as well.

Ironically, one of the most important forces in the ebbing of scholarship on and enthusiasm for Pound was Hugh Kenner. Although by the mid-1960s dozens of critics had become well-known for writing on Pound, Kenner remained the emblematic Poundian figure. His *The Poetry of Ezra Pound* had consolidated the formalist approach, giving college professors and nonacademic readers alike a way to read and understand

{ 197 }

Pound that did not require them also to be familiar with all of his source materials. Although many of Kenner's individual readings were idiosyncratic, and although he never fit into the conventional model of an academic critic, he did quickly become known as Pound's most important interpreter. Kenner was not driven solely by a desire that the academy acknowledge Pound's greatness; he was devoted to widening appreciation of an entire school of poetry that had sprung from Pound's (and Williams's) strains of modernism. Kenner was distinct from many of his colleagues in that although an academic, he did not confine himself within that identity. Throughout the 1960s, he became increasingly visible in mainstream publications. He had written and served as the poetry editor for the *National Review* from the early 1950s, but in the 1960s he became a frequent contributor to the *New York Times Book Review* and to *Harper's*. Like Pound, Kenner attempted to transcend the limitations of his vocation: Pound wanted to be a poet but also an economist, teacher, publisher, and huckster; Kenner wanted to break out of the role of college professor and to contribute to mainstream cultural discourse.

To accomplish this, Kenner wanted to write the definitive work on the modernist movement in literature, or what he had determined was "The Pound Era." In 1962, he wrote the poet that "I plan a book, partly on the assumption that if I don't do it with good will, someone else will later do it, likely with ill will. Title, THE POUND ERA. Scope, 1910–1960 approx. Theme, the life of the mind in that half-century. Cast, as many of 'em as I can compass."[1] Continuing, he explained that Pound's literary achievements and personal activities had been the most important factor in the birth and survival of the modernist movement.

> On the eve of 40, I find that my mind was principally formed on a few visits to St. Liz, and amid the ensuing correspondence. By analogy, I can dimly grasp what you have done for people of more talent. It has been The Pound Era, right enough; and it was The Pound Era during a crucial period. Civilization is memory, and insofar as humane letters maintain the process of active remembering, you and those with whom you worked (and *on* whom you worked) have made it a little less likely that our children will grow up highly intelligent barbarians. What the next generation knows of the past is what this generation tells it, plus what they find out for themselves by chance; and chance is too random

to trust. You and Eliot, Joyce, Yeats, the rest, kept attention focussed on the past during a time when the past was in danger of being not merely forgotten but actively discarded. One should not for instance underrate the effect of *Ulysses* in getting people to read the Odyssey, if only for clues; this at a time when the Odyssey was being chucked out of curricula.[2]

The very concept of Pound being the central poet of the age would have been laughable less than a decade previously, when he languished in his room at "St. Liz," but the diligent work of the critics of the 1950s and 1960s made such an idea progressively more plausible. Kenner first proposed this book to the Beacon Press in the United States and to Faber and Faber in England. Faber's managing editor, Peter du Sautoy, agreed that it sounded promising but notified Kenner that Eliot's approval would be necessary in order to publish it.[3] By April 1962, the contract was signed; Kenner was to deliver a manuscript by January 1963, a date that was later amended to January 1964. But the book did not appear until almost ten years after the first proposal. Kenner never proposed it to New Directions, because of what he called Laughlin's "penny-pinching" ("he would not have financed any photos," Kenner insisted, and the photographs were an essential part of the book's argument).[4] Instead, his American publisher was to be Beacon Press, and Faber would publish the British edition. After seeing a short excerpt from the book, however, the University of California Press's August Frugé, "scent[ing] an impending classic . . . moved to buy out existing contracts." Kenner explained that "My big incentive in shifting to U. Cal was not so much the money they offered (incrementally higher than in existing contracts) as the fact that they would do things like (1) obtaining both an editor and a compositor who could read, not just copy, Greek, [and] (2) printing the entire book on paper that would permit the photos appearing right next to the pertinent text, instead of in a slick-paper 'photo section.' "[5]

The Pound Era appeared from the University of California Press in 1971, and immediately and fundamentally challenged the entire Pound industry. Kenner used Pound's own ideogrammatic method to argue that the method had determined the entire trajectory of modernist literature. The chapter topics are not arranged chronologically or even thematically; Kenner discusses biography in one chapter, then moves to a close reading of some of Pound's poetry, then analyzes in detail one of Pound's source texts like Ernest Fenollosa's *Chinese Written Character as a Medium for Poetry*. As Pound had worked with the ideograms and "luminous details" he so admired, Kenner makes lateral intellectual moves as well as progressing forward and backward in time. More importantly, Kenner became the first critic to incorporate a discussion of Pound's ancillary—political and economic—writings into an analysis of the poetic oeuvre Until *The Pound Era*, no critic had acknowledged the centrality of social and economic thought to Pound's art; by doing so Kenner incontrovertibly demonstrated that a purely formalist approach to the poetry was irredeemably limited. After *The Pound Era*, writing on Pound that was predicated on the autonomy of the aesthetic became irrelevant—a development that both deepened understanding of Pound's accomplishments and made it impossible ever to accept the aestheticist view of him. Almost as soon as aesthetic formalism had come to be the structuring principle of literary criticism, Kenner's hugely influential book demonstrated that a formalist approach needed to be combined with careful research into a poet's biography, beliefs, and source texts. But the years of aesthetic formalism had made Pound canonical, and *The Pound Era* only solidified this status, for the book demonstrated a richness in Pound's work that had been previously ignored.

The Pound Era found a surprisingly broad audience, and was reviewed enthusiastically in a large number of publications, both literary and general-interest. Many used their reviews to advance Kenner's main contention, that Pound was the central poetic figure of the twentieth century. The *New Yorker* called the book "stunning," and Harriet Zinnes, in the *New Leader*, felt that it was "brilliant." Zinnes, moreover, was convinced by Kenner's argument: "The dethronement of T. S. Eliot is complete," she wrote, "and Pound—whose anti-Semitism and pro-fascism in that month (July 1972) provoked one more controversy when it became known that the governing council of the American Academy of Arts and Sciences had refused him the society's annual Emerson-Thoreau medal—is now proclaimed the King of literary Kings." The *Economist* agreed: "Will the 'Pound era' seem an appropriate designation, 50 or 100 years hence, for the epoch we think of as 'modern?' Mr. Kenner's brilliantly written book establishes an excellent case for supposing the answer to be 'yes.' "[6] Other mainstream publications—*Time*, the *Times Literary Supplement*, and numerous small newspapers—also received Kenner's book as the definitive summation of the modern era in art and literature. (The "dethronement" of Eliot and the ascension of Pound was also assisted by the discovery, in 1968, and facsimile publication, in 1971, of the manuscript of *The Waste Land*, which dramatically altered many readers' and critics' perceptions of the relative achievements of the poets.)

Many critics in what had become known as the Pound industry weighed in with their opinions. C. David Heymann, who would publish his biography four years later, wrote in the *Saturday Review* that Kenner's book was unnecessarily confusing, but a valuable contribution to Pound studies. Guy Davenport, a longtime friend of Kenner's and a fervent admirer of Pound, published his gushingly approving review of *The Pound Era* in the mainstream magazine (*National Review*) for which Kenner was poetry editor. For Davenport, Kenner writes with "compression and robust grace" and his scholarship is characterized by such a "peculiar genius" that Davenport can only marvel, "Has anyone since De Quincey written English with such verve and color? Has any scholar ever been so thorough?" Timothy Materer, in *Commonweal*, added his voice to Davenport's.[7] Not all of the Pound scholars were so friendly, though. In the *New York Times Book Review*, M. L. Rosenthal (author of two books on Pound) was more skeptical, feeling that the designation of the century as Pound's era gave the poet "an artificially inflated status." Denis Donoghue, in *The Listener*, was even more critical, stating that "it is a highly oblique mind which can call the twentieth century the Pound era." Finally, Frank Kermode wrote in the *Guardian* that Kenner's book suffered from unnecessary obscurity, but that "no other critic has made Pound seem so beautiful or so important."

By making purely aestheticist reading of Pound impossible, Kenner also finally invalidated the approach that New Directions had been using for a quarter-century. But New Directions no longer needed to rely on a tentative, provisional view of Pound. As a result of Laughlin's efforts and the secondary work of reviewers, critics, biographers, and other poets, Pound had become, in the eyes of a significant number of critics and anthologists, the most important American poet of the century. Kenner's image of the academic exchange is accurate, though, for Pound's stock has fallen in the almost three decades since the publication of *The Pound Era*, while the prestige of William Carlos Williams and Wallace Stevens has increased. But the New Criticism–inspired, aestheticist stance Laughlin had relentlessly promoted in the 1940s had made Pound's rehabilitation possible. The hard-won consecration that Pound had undeniably received by the time of his death in 1972 guaranteed that, for the foreseeable future, he did not risk being forgotten or relegated to the footnotes of literary history, even if readers and students learned about his political faults and personal bigotries as they read *Hugh Selwyn Mauberley* or the *Cantos*.

New Directions is still closely associated with Pound. The death of James Laughlin in 1997 proved that his desire to shape his firm's image alongside of that poet had a lasting effect, for no story about Laughlin neglected to feature Pound prominently. His role in building Pound's reputation and image are paralleled by Pound's own role in constructing the identity of New Directions Press. And while some may feel that this only demonstrates New Directions' irrelevance to the world of contemporary writing—a complaint as old as Dwight Macdonald's 1944 remark about the house's "epigonism"—I cannot help feel that the firm's enduring identification with Pound indicates something of deeper significance: the success of a campaign to transform literature by using the tools of the world of commerce.

The interdependence of Pound and New Directions provides us insight into some of the most enduring questions about the relationship of art and society in the mid-twentieth century, but it demonstrates especially how aesthetic formalism was used as a provisional tool. Pound both benefited from and was harmed by reliance on aesthetic formalism to market his works, for although this campaign undeniably made him canonical it also handicapped any reading of his work and made unlikely any social action he might have hoped his writing would spur. The reliance on aesthetic autonomy to market Pound also profoundly changed New Directions, causing the house to stand for a radically different notion of literature than Laughlin had first envisioned. He had wanted New Directions to be an activist force, undermining the market-based organization of the publishing industry and providing an outlet to writers who decried the unjust economic systems of the United States and the Western world. But Laughlin began to pull back from that position by 1946, and throughout the next quarter century New Directions came to be known as a firm whose writers were avant-garde but not political forces. Finally, by using aesthetic formalism to put Pound firmly in the mainstream of modern literary history, Laughlin—and Kenner—eventually and ironically struck a blow against aesthetic formalism. Pound's work in general, and the *Cantos* in particular, profoundly resist a simple aestheticist reading; aesthetic formalism, at least as it was used to rehabilitate Pound, is a self-consuming artifact whose short-term benefits ensured that it would be superseded.

All of these interactions, compromises, and unforeseen developments demonstrate the impossibility of ever fully separating any of the supposedly opposed realms of commerce and art, of market value and literary value, of aesthetic formalism and contextual criticism, or of a publisher's contribution to an artist's reputation and that artist's own seemingly solitary accomplishment. Modernism is a particularly powerful area in which to study these interactions, for the same debates about commerce and art and about aesthetic autonomy surface again and again, within the Bollingen committee, in the *Saturday Review,* or among academics. In fact, these debates seem less a context for the modernist moment than they seem to be the actual creators of modernism, equal in importance to the particular innovations, stylistic features, and philosophical preoccupations of modernist writing.

Notes

Abbreviations Used in the Notes

AL	autograph letter without signature
ALS	autograph letter signed
APCS	autograph postcard signed
EP	Ezra Pound
EPP, Yale	Ezra Pound Papers, Yale Collection of American Literature, Beinecke Rare Book and Manuscript Library
HLHU	Houghton Library, Harvard University
HRHRC	Harry Ransom Humanities Research Center, University of Texas at Austin
JL	James Laughlin
TL	typescript letter without signature
TLS	typescript letter signed
TPCS	typed postcard signed
WCW	William Carlos Williams

INTRODUCTION

1. In Parkinson, ed., *Casebook*, 24–27.
2. On Laughlin's early work with the Social Credit movement, see "Some Irreverent Literary History" in Laughlin, *Random Essays*.
3. In addition to the evidence I provide here regarding Laughlin's publicity work for Pound's books, Daniel Morris's discussion of Laughlin's marketing of Williams (in Dettmar and Watt, *Marketing Modernisms*, and in his own *Writings of William Carlos Williams*) is enlightening.
4. Laughlin did take to the road early on in his career, attempting to sell his books to stores in all parts of the country, but his efforts were largely unsuccessful. See Laughlin, *Random Essays*.
5. Adams, "Hawk," 208.
6. Ruskin, quoted in Raymond Williams, *Culture and Society*, 136. Brodhead points out that Arnold, fittingly, felt that Hawthorne fit his prescriptions for literature perfectly, and held him to be one of the greatest American writers (Brodhead, *School of Hawthorne*, 52).
7. Williams writes about the increasing sense in the nineteenth century that culture

was good for citizens, focusing on Cardinal Newman and Matthew Arnold, and pointing out that both drew on Coleridge's idea of "cultivation," or the process through which a person goes in order to be able to recognize and attain moral excellence (Williams, *Culture and Society*, 63).

8. Quoted in Brodhead, *School of Hawthorne*, 208.
9. Williams, *Autobiography*, 158.
10. Williams, *Culture and Society*, 63.
11. From "Essay, Supplementary to the Preface to the Edition of 1815," in *The Prose Works of William Wordsworth* v. 3, 80. Later, the realist William Dean Howells wrote in 1867 of Henry James that he would have to "in a very great degree create his audience" (quoted in Anesko, *"Friction with the Market,"* 37).
12. Quoted in Williams, *Culture and Society*, 33.
13. Williams, *Culture and Society*, 36.
14. Williams, *Culture and Society*, 40.
15. From "Preface of 1800" to *Lyrical Ballads*.
16. Clement Greenberg, in "Avant-Garde and Kitsch," writes of the same development: "the avant-garde poet or artist sought to maintain the high level of his art by both narrowing and raising it to the expression of an absolute in which all relativities and contradictions would be either resolved or beside the point: 'Art for art's sake' and 'pure poetry' appear, and subject matter or content become something to be avoided" (Greenberg, *Art and Culture*, 23).

One of the central figures in the development of modernist mistrust of the mass audience was Henry James, but James also points the way to the more complicated, compromised attitude toward audiences that Pound would later adopt. James was explicitly cognizant of the effects of mass culture on literature in such essays as "The Question of the Opportunities." James argues here that in aiming at a mass audience, writers must compromise the quality of their work. But he also foresees the fragmentation of the mass audience that the modernists often saw as deplorably uniform, and indicates that soon the public will break into "individual publics positively more sifted and evolved than anywhere else, shoals of fish rising to more delicate bait." Some of these "individual publics" would turn out to be the collectors and patrons who supported Pound in his early years. Later, others were such readers of the avant-garde as the Choate teacher, poet, and translator Dudley Fitts and Fitts's young student James Laughlin.

In addition, James initiated a conceptual shift in American literature in the late nineteenth and early twentieth centuries, one that began to confer cultural capital on expatriation to Europe, on living and working abroad. James's fiction often works out these anxieties about the superiority of European culture to American, and by the time the next generation arrived in Europe, Americans recognized the value of being European. Of American writers, Pound, Eliot, Stein, and Hemingway are only the most obvious examples of those who expatriated themselves—there were many other, lesser-known figures who combined artistic creation with such activities as publishing, criticism, and patronage.

Ironically, many modernist artists and writers were unquestionably fascinated by mass culture: Evidence would have to include the accoutrements of Leopold Bloom's daily life in Joyce's *Ulysses,* the newspaper clippings and advertisements in Picasso's collages and paintings, and the industrial noise featured in George Antheil's *Ballet Mécanique.* Even Pound allowed mass culture to intrude into his work, approvingly mentioning Walt Disney and quoting the 1950s pop song "Sixteen Tons" in a draft for Canto 116 ("to the poets of my time/ Disney/ & quasi-anonimo/ 'Ah sold mah soul/ to de company/ stoh'/ honour them.") T. S. Eliot's "Marie Lloyd" essay, if perhaps condescending, recognizes the accomplishment of this music-hall star and her contribution to culture. This fascination, however, generally coexisted with condemnation of mass culture and a devotion to some form of the autonomy of the aesthetic.

17. Brodhead, *School of Hawthorne,* 109–10. Brodhead points out how the critics of the modernist era—Van Wyck Brooks, Mencken, Mumford, and others—quickly revised the previous era's evaluation of Hawthorne to bring him in line with modernist principles. No longer a spokesman for New England values, Hawthorne becomes a typical modernist rebel, in Mencken's words "remain[ing] outside the tradition that pedants try so vainly to impose upon a literature in active being today" (quoted in Brodhead, 209). An interesting exception is the arch-modernist T. S. Eliot himself, who in *Notes towards the Definition of Culture* and *The Idea of a Christian Society* proposes an intellectual class that will, instead of commenting on and criticizing society, actually lead it. Eliot's idea, though, depended on a homogeneity of population and ambition (a "Christian society") that even he seems to realize would be impossible to achieve.

18. I have not attempted to give an exhaustive definition of the term *aesthetic autonomy* here; a good overview and starting point for an examination of that kind would be Terry Eagleton's *The Ideology of the Aesthetic* or Raymond Williams's *Culture and Society*.

CHAPTER 1

1. Redman, *Ezra Pound,* 280.

2. In the words of Robert L. Allen, a member of the DTC's medical staff. Allen's reminiscences were originally published as a letter in the Feb. 1958 issue of *Esquire* and reprinted in O'Connor and Stone, eds., *A Casebook on Ezra Pound* (quot. 38).

3. JL, TLS to EP, 4 Sept. 1945. EPP, Yale.

4. "Summary" (1917), in Anderson, *Anthology,* 145; letter to William Bird (17 Apr. 1924), quoted in Paige, ed., *Letters,* 188.

5. In Dana, ed., *Grain,* 17–8.

6. Pound's relationship to the little magazines has been dealt with extensively in Marek, *Women Editing Modernism* and Alpert, *The Unexamined Art,* and I will not recapitulate their arguments in detail here. In addition, a number of volumes

collecting Pound's correspondence with *Poetry*, the *Little Review*, and the *Dial* are available. For an account of his involvement with small-press publishers, see Ford, *Published in Paris*.

There are a number of excellent studies of the little magazines and of Pound's place in them, but the standard reference work is *The Little Magazine: A History and a Bibliography* by Frederick J. Hoffman, Charles Allen, and Carolyn F. Ulrich. On the topic of how the little magazines contributed to the public image and acceptance of modernism in general, Shari and Bernard Benstock's article "The Role of Little Magazines in the Emergence of Modernism" is a good survey, focusing on the holdings of the Harry Ransom Humanities Research Center at the University of Texas, Austin.

7. See Carpenter, *Serious Character*, and Wilhelm, *Tragic Years*, for a more detailed discussion of Pound's personal finances.

8. They also looked back enviously to the period of artistic patronage. Pound cultivated a number of patrons during his years in London; Margaret Cravens and the New York lawyer John Quinn were among the most important. He was never able, however, to support himself fully through patronage, and his efforts to establish patronage funds for both Joyce and Eliot were only partially successful. See esp. *The Selected Letters of Ezra Pound to John Quinn* (ed. Materer) for Pound's strategies to found a "Bel Esprit" stipend for Eliot.

9. Quoted in Ford, *Published in Paris*, 215.

10. Manifesto ("The Inquest into the State of Contemporary English Prose") reproduced in Matthew Bruccoli and Robert Trogdon, eds., *Dictionary of Literary Biography* Documentary Series v. 15 (*American Expatriate Writers: Paris in the Twenties*), 122. In another move that protected the writers of the series from the uncertainties of the marketplace, Pound made sure that these books were sold only by subscription.

11. Quoted in Katherine Rood's article on William Bird in the *Dictionary of Literary Biography*. v. 4 (*American Writers in Paris, 1920–1939*); 42. Also see Benton's *Beauty and the Book* and Rainey's "The Cultural Economy of Modernism" for a longer discussion of the role of private presses in creating a "cultural economy" of modernism.

12. I have not dealt with Pound's relationships to or involvements with the little magazines in any detail here. His attitudes toward and knowledge of publishing practices were certainly informed by his work with and for little magazines such as *Poetry*, the *Egoist*, the *New Freewoman*, and the *Little Review*—in fact, from the 1930s to the 1950s he continued to urge his publishers to found similar magazines.

13. See Rainey's "F. T. Marinetti and Ezra Pound," as well as his "Consuming Investments: Joyce's *Ulysses*" and "The Real Scandal of *Ulysses*." In addition, Hickman's "Pamphlets and Blue China" is also useful as a specific examination of how Pound moved beyond this.

14. Quoted in Paige, ed., *Letters*, 183. Pound's correspondence is characterized by

his extremely idiosyncratic language, spelling, punctuation, and typing. Most of the editors who have collected his letters transcribe them exactly, not standardizing his writing; when I use their transcriptions, I have copied them precisely as they are in their books. In the instances where I have transcribed Pound's letters myself, I have attempted to follow their practice and to reproduce the letters exactly as they appear in the originals.

15. EP, TLS to William Bird, 7 May 1924, quoted in Rainey, "Marinetti," 211.

16. Rainey, "Marinetti," 211.

17. Although the appeal to the "performance record of investments within a commodity economy" acknowledges the importance of the market system, the sale of such objects as rare editions or manuscripts also draws on the idea of patronage, and the production of limited editions intended for collectors was a way for Pound to enjoy the benefits of patronage. Apart from the writer's immediate circle of acquaintances, it was largely wealthy collectors who purchased these objects, and implicit in these purchases was the understanding that the purchasers (Quinn is an example of a patron for modernist writers, Peggy Guggenheim of a patron for modernist artists) had a lasting interest in the works produced by particular artists, and would continue to purchase them—in effect becoming patrons. In fact, because of this Pound held a long resentment against Random House (or, in his terms, "Random Louse") publisher Bennett Cerf, who he felt "organized a sort of de luxe book monopoly" in the 1920s, "and excluded everything alive [i.e., anything experimental]." Pound's ire appears to have been raised by the fact that John Rodker and the Three Mountains Press were unable to export their fine-press editions of the first two installments of the *Cantos* to the United States, thus depriving him of sorely needed purchasers. EP, TL to Peter Russell, 19 Sept. 195?. HRHRC.

18. Quoted in Alvarez, "Wretched Poet," 28. Pound was not successful, though, in seeing this work reprinted in the United States until 1965, when New Directions published it in hardcover as *A Lume Spento and Other Early Poems*.

19. From *Selected Letters of Ezra Pound to John Quinn*, ed. Materer. Quinn had commissioned this book from Eliot, and, through some subsidies given to the young publisher, convinced Knopf to publish it, as well as Pound's *"Noh"* and *Lustra*. Pound, Quinn, and Knopf all agreed that Eliot's book should remain anonymous so as not to diminish its authority by an appearance of logrolling: Pound wrote to Quinn in 1917 that "I agree fully with you and Knopf, that it should NOT be signed by Eliot, just now when I am booming his work" (TLS, 9 Sept. 1917).

20. EP, TLS to H. L. Mencken, 12 Mar. 1918 (Paige).

21. Materer, "Make It Sell!" in Dettmar and Watt, *Marketing Modernisms*. Ironically, Pound's talents at self-promotion were no match for Lowell's, and after the matronly Bostonian gained great public recognition for her place in Imagism, Pound left the movement, dismissing it as "Amygism." In an unpublished paper, "Ezra Pound, George Antheil, Mary Louise Bok, and the Politics of Patronage," Erin

Templeton points out how Pound used similar tactics to promote Antheil's opera *Transatlantic, the People's Choice* in 1928–30, engaging in such quintessentially commercial ploys as designing striking advertisements and attempting to ensure a friendly opening-night audience that would convince Paris society to come hear the piece.

22. Ezra Pound, TLS to John Quinn, 27 July 1916 (Materer).

23. In a letter to Felix Schelling of 17 Nov. 1916 (quoted in Paige, ed., *Letters*, 99).

24. The fact that Bennett Cerf turned *Ulysses* into probably the least-read best-seller in history testifies to the publishers' ability to transform public tastes and to the modernists' generally unacknowledged willingness to enter the realm of commercial culture. The work of the new trade literary publishers, in turn, was supplemented by the larger cultural development, in the 1920s, of mainstream literary and book review magazines and of book clubs, which attempted to integrate literature into into middle-class daily life. Although Pound never had a book sold through one of the major book clubs, their low-key acceptance of modernism helped bring the literature to a wider audience.

25. On Stone and Kimball, see Sidney Kramer's *History of Stone & Kimball and Herbert S. Stone & Co., with a Bibliography of Their Publications, 1893–1905* (1940); on Copeland and Day, see Kraus, *Messrs. Copeland & Day,* and Lehmann-Haupt, *Book in America*, 323–25. A figure looming behind this whole discussion is William Morris, for both Stone and Kimball and Copeland and Day attempted to translate Morris's craft-oriented approach to publishing to a large market.

26. This series was similar in important ways to the New Classics series that New Directions would introduce in the 1940s.

27. Faber and Faber might be the exception to this rule; T. S. Eliot joined the London trade firm Faber and Gwyer in 1926, and Faber soon began publishing some modernist books.

28. Radway, *Reading the Romance,* 20.

29. Radway, *Feeling for Books,* 166. Radway is speaking here of literary books, for of course there had been many genres of books over the centuries—almanacs, for instance—that had no pretensions to permanence.

30. Quoted in Tebbell, *History* v. 2, 502.

31. In his *School of Hawthorne,* Richard Brodhead details how the mid-nineteenth-century publisher James T. Fields had injected this type of promotion into publishing. "One way to define Fields' place in American letters," Brodhead specifies, "is to say that he recreated literature as a *form* of merchandise: a commodity aimed at a market, a market the producer undertakes to create. . . . But in a sense Fields' real accomplishment is less that he saw how to market literature than that he established 'literature' as a market category" (55). His efforts were remarkably successful in using the uncommercial category of "literature" in order to ensure commercial success for his books: Emerson, for one, wrote Fields to tell him that "your brilliant advertising and arrangements have made me so popular" (55).

Fields prefigures the publishers of the early 1900s in the way he bracketed a particular portion of writing as literature, and in his marketing emphasis on all of the cultural attributes of the literary: elevation, premium cultural value, refinement. As Brodhead demonstrates, Fields was successful in constructing a market category of the "literary," and then "devising ways to identify and confirm the literary *as* a difference before the market." In addition, Brodhead's description of the ways that Ticknor and Fields's books announced themselves as different, refined, and literary underscores the similarity between that firm and Knopf: "conspicuously good paper and handsome brown boards, promising that what is inside is serious and well-made . . . [and] the Ticknor and Fields imprint itself, which came, through its association with 'quality' authors, to create the presumption of quality in the books it adorned." See Winship's *American Literary Publishing* for a detailed discussion of Ticknor and Fields's marketing, as well as Groves's "Judging Literary Books by Their Covers."

32. Canby, *American Memoir,* 189–90.

33. Anesko, "*Friction,*" 35.

34. The controversy has been carried on in remarkably consistent terms throughout history: James T. Farrell's essay on the commercialization of literature in *New Directions in Prose and Poetry* 9 (1946) echoes many of the same themes that Quinn's attack on Liveright sounds, and the flurry of mergers and acquisitions in the publishing world in the 1990s has been discussed using the same images. Yet in all of the debate, what has been lost is that the specificity and unique status of the category of "literature" itself is a product of market considerations.

35. Catherine Turner's *Marketing Modernism* is by far the most complete analysis of the differences among the group that I call the "new trade literary publishers," and my necessarily brief summary of Knopf, Liveright, and Huebsch's history lacks the depth and complexity of her description.

36. *Pound/Joyce,* 107. In the period immediately preceding the declaration of war in 1914, Pound had been trying his hand in numerous American magazines, "little" and others. One magazine where he came to exercise some editorial influence was *Smart Set,* a self-described "magazine of cleverness" popular on college campuses for its adventurous humor and original fiction. Through epistolary gladhanding and cajoling, Pound convinced *Smart Set*'s editor, H. L. Mencken, to publish two of Joyce's stories, "The Boarding House" and "A Little Cloud," in May 1915. On the strength of this, Joyce found it easier to interest publishers in his books. In 1916, urged by Pound and John Quinn, Huebsch picked up the American contracts for *Dubliners* and *A Portrait.* He also pursued *Ulysses,* but in 1920 decided against publishing the book because he was not willing to sink money in a doomed legal cause—the courts upheld the banning of serial publication of the book at the same time that Huebsch was considering publishing it.

37. Turner, *Marketing Modernism,* 67, 43.

38. Tanselle, "In Memoriam: B. W. Huebsch," 727.

39. *Dial* 65 (14 Dec. 1918): 518. Turner's *Marketing Modernism* treats the ways in which this development was used in book advertising.

40. *New Republic,* 18 Nov. 1916: 213.

41. *Publishers' Weekly,* 11 Mar. 1916: 865.

42. On Knopf, see Knopf, *Portrait of a Publisher,* and Cathy Henderson, *The Company They Kept.*

43. Houghton Mifflin, perhaps underwritten by Amy Lowell, began issuing her *Some Imagist Poets* annuals in 1915.

44. EP, TLS to John Quinn, 19 Aug. 1916 (Materer).

45. Advertisement in the *New Republic,* 27 Oct. 1917: xi.

46. EP, TLS to Harriet Monroe, 1 Jan. 1918 (Paige).

47. T. S. Eliot, TLS to Henry Eliot, 27 Feb. 1919. In Eliot, ed., *Letters,* 272. Knopf had also published, at Pound's insistence, Lewis's *Tarr.*

48. Kreymborg and Man Ray had begun plans for the *Glebe* in 1913; in 1914 the magazine began to be financed by the Boni brothers, and although Kreymborg wanted to publish the Imagists in the first issue, the Boni brothers changed the plans.

49. Dardis, *Firebrand,* 52. In 1925, Bennett Cerf, who was then a vice president at Boni and Liveright, and his college friend Donald Klopfer bought the Modern Library for $215,000. As Cerf gleefully details in *At Random,* his memoirs, they immediately changed a number of the series' most distinctive features. Gone were the imitation leather bindings (which smelled like castor oil in hot weather), replaced by "an attractive semi-flexible binding covered with balloon cloth"; the colophon and endpapers were redesigned, and the types of books that the Modern Library published also changed—the series began to publish more contemporary and more American works (61). With the Modern Library as a backbone, Cerf and Klopfer later founded Random House.

50. *New Republic* 16 Apr. 1918.

51. The Modern Library was by no means the first modern publishing venture to use its books' appearance on the shelf as a selling point; Jeffrey D. Groves's essay "Judging Literary Books by Their Covers: House Styles, Ticknor and Fields, and Literary Promotion" (in Moylan and Stiles, eds., *Reading Books*) details the prestige attached to Ticknor and Fields's books in the mid-1850s and the ways other publishers imitated one of the firm's characteristic bindings.

52. The Modern Library was not the only venture of its kind. Before joining forces with Liveright, the Boni brothers had produced and sold the Little Leather Library, ten-cent reprints of public-domain classics bound in simulated leather. This short-lived series prefigured many of the essential elements of the later Modern Library: literary reprints packaged not cheaply, but resembling an object that at least aspired to permanence. At the other extreme was Emanuel Haldeman-Julius's Little Blue Books series, started in 1919. This also contained primarily public-domain classics at first, but later began including works of politics, personal hygiene, sex education, advice, religion, self-improvement, and in fact almost every topic imaginable. The books made no pretense to permanence, and their main features were their poor typesetting, small (3 ½ × 5) size, and low price—Haldeman-Julius sold them in bulk, at twenty for one dollar. By 1925 Haldeman-Julius, from his headquarters in Girard, Kansas, had sold sixty million

copies of his nearly two thousand titles. Although he was a socialist, he was cheerfully commercialistic in his promotion for the books. For years, he announced spurious "Last Calls" for the nickel-a-book price, and later, in order to spur demand, he threatened to stop publishing the classics and begin publishing only popular works. Haldeman-Julius eventually sold three hundred million Little Blue Books, the series losing popularity when the twenty-five-cent paperback emerged and took over much of his market. On the Little Blue Books, see Tebbell, *History* v. 3, 203–9; Madison, *Book Publishing*, 396–98. On the Modern Library, see Neavill, "Modern Library"; Dardis, *Firebrand*.

53. Dardis, *Firebrand*, 87.

54. For an extended discussion of the circumstances surrounding the publication of *The Waste Land*, see Rainey, "The Price of Modernism: Publishing *The Waste Land*," in Bush, ed., *T. S. Eliot: The Modernist in History*.

55. Dardis, *Firebrand*, 95.

56. Dardis, *Firebrand*, 94.

57. Dardis, *Firebrand*, 95. Quinn's strong anti-Semitism exacerbated—perhaps even caused—his distaste for these new publishers, all of whom were Jewish. Pound's unwavering support for Liveright and Huebsch, and his largely friendly association with Knopf, in the face of Quinn's unceasing objections, makes his later anti-Semitism all the more senseless and difficult to understand.

58. Quinn's hostility to the new immigrants flooding New York, who were now entering into the institutions of culture, was also linked to his distaste for the mass market and modern society. In 1920, he wrote Pound that America had "no first rate man of letters . . . no pleasant coterie," because "today there are conglomerations of different nationalities . . . victims of telephones, votaries of automobiles, worshipers at moving pictures, purchasers of the banalities of Amy Lowell, Edgar Lee Masters and the damned Jew spewing-up of the Untermeyers, the Waldo Franks, the H. L. Menckens, the George Jean Nathans and the other parasites and pimps in poetry, literature generally, painting, the theater . . . and sculpture" (Quoted in Materer, ed., *Selected Letters*, 174–75).

59. EP, TLS to JL, 11 Jan. 1940. New Directions Archive bMS Am 2077 (1371). HLHU.

60. Horace Liveright, TLS to EP, 7 June 1928. EPP, Yale.

61. Horace Liveright, TLS to EP, 16 June 1928. EPP, Yale.

62. Horace Liveright, TLS to EP, 31 Oct. 1934. EPP, Yale. New Directions' mission, of course, would be to disprove this contention of Liveright's, and one of Laughlin's first projects was obtaining the rights to *Personae* in order to sell it in a "cheap edition."

63. *Jefferson and/or Mussolini* was published by the Liveright Publishing Company. After Boni and Liveright folded, Horace Liveright opened the short-lived "Horace Liveright, Inc." in 1928. After his death in 1933, the company continued as the "Liveright Publishing Company" until 1974, when W. W. Norton purchased it.

64. Rinehart, the older of the two, had been a publicity agent in the Doran organiza-

tion, while Farrar had first edited the Doran journal *The Bookman* before attaining the position of editor-in-chief in 1925.

65. On Farrar and Rinehart, see Tebbel, *History* v. 3, 563–66.

66. Pound, hoping to broaden his American sales beyond an audience solely of collectors and like-minded writers, complained to MacLeish of the difficulty of finding his work in America. MacLeish agreed, responding that it was silly that "the greatest work of the man who, more than any other, is responsible for the emancipation of modern poetry from the prose tradition of the XIX Cent. should be obtainable in America o[n]ly in expensive European editions" (TLS to Abernethy, June 1932, quoted in Stone, "Ezra Pound and *Contempo*," 127).

   For the full story of Pound's association with *Contempo*, see Stone, "Ezra Pound and *Contempo*." Stone criticizes Pound's biographer Humphrey Carpenter for his inability to see how Pound sought a broad audience for his work. "Although Humphrey Carpenter . . . asserts that Pound 'showed no urgent desire to secure a wide readership' for his Cantos," Stone points out, "the poet's letters to *Contempo*, which Carpenter never located, indicate a wish to make his work available to a broad American audience" (127).

67. Archibald MacLeish, TLS to EP, 20 May 1932 (in Winnick, ed., *Letters*).

68. Royalty statements, EPP, Yale. By 1939, Pound's sales, admittedly, were declining because of more than just publishers' choices.

69. Ogden Nash, TLS to EP, 19 Oct. 1932. EPP, Yale.

70. If Farrar and Rinehart were reluctant to publicize Pound, the firm had no qualms about publicizing other authors. Tebbel notes that in 1937, the company was in the second tier of firms that advertised the most: the first tier (firms that placed more than 100,000 lines of advertising in newspapers and magazines) only had three firms, and the second, which included Farrar and Rinehart, had only nine (Tebbel, *History* vol. 3, 452).

71. John Farrar, TLS to EP, 26 Mar. 1934. EPP, Yale.

72. John Farrar, TLS to EP, 27 Nov. 1934. EPP, Yale.

73. Ford, "Ezra," 1.

74. Rubin, *Making*, 62. For a much more detailed and full discussion of these and other similar publishing and journalistic entities, see Rubin's excellent book.

75. Rubin, *Making*, 56. As befit a man who emphasized literature's edifying qualities, Sherman began his as a devoted Arnoldian, and wrote a book entitled *Matthew Arnold: How to Know Him* (1917).

76. Rubin, *Making*, 67.

77. Ezra Pound, TLS to Irita Van Doren, 14 Dec. 1931. Quoted in Rubin, *Making*, 90–91.

78. Canby, *American Memoir*, 287.

79. Canby, *American Memoir*, 287.

CHAPTER 2

1. Much of this information about Laughlin's family history and his early life is available in Susan Howe's interview with Laughlin in Henderson, ed., *Art;* in Cynthia Zarin's "Jaz"; in Robert Dana's interview with Laughlin in *Grain;* and in many of Laughlin's own autobiographical writings. The information about Jones and Laughlin comes primarily from Wollman and Inman's history of the company and from Zarin's profile.

2. Dana, ed., *Grain,* 15.

3. Dana, ed., *Grain,* 10–11.

4. Zarin, "Jaz," 42.

5. Quoted in Howe, "New Directions: An Interview with James Laughlin," 13.

6. JL, TLS to EP, 15 June 1935. New Directions Archive, bMS Am 2077 (1371), HLHU.

7. Dana, ed., *Grain,* 5–6.

8. JL, TLS to EP, 21 Aug. 1933. EPP, Yale. Fitts, who later joined the Andover faculty, was a sometime poet and translator with a particular interest in Latin American poetry (Laughlin chose him to edit the 1942 New Directions *Anthology of Contemporary Latin-American Poetry*) and the classics. He knew many of the important figures in American modernism and for many years served as a mentor to Laughlin—their correspondence spans decades.

9. Henderson, *Art,* 19.

10. Henderson, *Art,* 19.

11. Henderson, *Art,* 21.

12. Laughlin, "Letters from Pound and Williams," 97. Laughlin didn't give up writing because of Pound's offhanded judgment; the next year he submitted a story to Lincoln Kirstein's *Hound and Horn* (it was rejected) and he continued to write poetry for the rest of his life.

13. EP, TLS to JL, 27 Nov. 1933. New Directions Archive, bMS Am 2077 (1371), HLHU. At this time, Pound was also trying to cultivate a similar relationship with the Englishman Stanley Nott, a book distributor who published his political works in England in the 1930s. Because of the limited appeal of such works as *Jefferson and/or Mussolini* and the "Money Pamphlets," though, and because of Nott's significantly smaller financial resources, he could never fulfill the role that Pound then assigned to Laughlin.

14. Laughlin did not give up poetry, however, and in the 1950s Pound finally admitted that he might have been wrong in his initial evaluation. From the 1930s until his death, Laughlin published many books of verse and gained the respect of critics for his innovative meter and use of classical and foreign references.

15. EP, TLS to JL, 2 Dec. 1934. New Directions Archive, bMS Am 2077 (1371), HLHU.

16. It was not until July 1935 that Stanley Nott published *Jefferson and/or Mussolini* in London.

17. Laughlin, *Random Essays*, 221.
18. EP, TLS to T. R. Smith, 1 Mar. 1935. EPP, Yale.
19. EP, TLS to T. R. Smith, 1 Mar. 1935. EPP, Yale.
20. Zarin, "Jaz," 44; EP, TLS to JL, 30 Jan. 1935. New Directions Archive, bMS Am 2077 (1371), HLHU.
21. JL, TLS to EP, 9 Dec. 1933. EPP, Yale.
22. JL, TLS to EP, 23 Jan. 1934. New Directions Archive, bMS Am 2077 (1372), HLHU.
23. JL, TLS to EP, 23 Feb. 1934. New Directions Archive, bMS Am 2077 (1372), HLHU.
24. *The Bookman,* a journal aimed at editors and other professionals and devoted to discussions of literature and publishing, was published by Doubleday Doran. John Farrar, later Pound's publisher at Farrar and Rinehart, edited the *Bookman* through most of the 1920s.
25. Barry, "Ezra Pound Period," 171. Also see Elizabeth Delahanty's short piece in the 13 Apr. 1940 *New Yorker,* which chattily describes her visit to Rapallo and the omnipresence there of the poet whose moment had passed.
26. JL, ALS to EP, 14 Nov. 1933. EPP, Yale.
27. JL, TLS to EP, 8 Oct. 1933. EPP, Yale. The *Active Anthology* included work by Williams, Zukofsky, Hemingway, Eliot, Moore, and others.
28. JL, ALS to EP, 6 Nov. 1933. EPP, Yale.
29. JL, TLS to EP, 9 Dec. 1933. New Directions Archive, bMS Am 2077 (1371), HLHU.
30. EP, TLS to JL, 31 Dec. 1933. New Directions Archive, bMS Am 2077 (1371), HLHU.
31. EP, TLS to JL, 1 Jan. 1934. New Directions Archive, bMS Am 2077 (1371), HLHU.
32. EP, TLS to JL, 31 Dec. 1933. New Directions Archive, bMS Am 2077 (1371), HLHU.
33. JL, TLS to Henry Laughlin, 27 June 1939. New Directions Archive, bMS Am 2077 (1179), HLHU.
34. EP, TLS to JL, 3 Feb. 1934. New Directions Archive, bMS Am 2077 (1371), HLHU.
35. EP, TLS to JL, 28 Nov. 1936 New Directions Archive, bMS Am 2077 (1371), HLHU.
36. JL, TLS to EP, 9 Oct. 1933. EPP, Yale.
37. JL, TLS to EP, n.d. 1933. New Directions Archive, bMS Am 2077 (1372), HLHU.
38. EP, TLS to JL, 27 Oct. 1933. New Directions Archive, bMS Am 2077 (1371), HLHU.
39. JL, TLS to EP, 29 Nov. 1933. EPP. Yale.
40. EP, TLS to JL, 2 Dec. 1933. New Directions Archive, bMS Am 2077 (1371), HLHU.
41. EP, TLS to JL, 31 Dec. 1933. New Directions Archive, bMS Am 2077 (1371), HLHU.

42. EP, TLS to JL, 10 Dec. 1935. New Directions Archive, bMS Am 2077 (1371), HLHU.

43. JL, TL to EP, 18 Sept. 1936. EPP, Yale. *Make It New,* a collection of critical essays, was published by Yale University Press in 1934.

44. JL, TLS to EP, 8 Oct. 1936. New Directions Archive, bMS Am 2077 (1372), HLHU.

45. EP, TLS to JL, 3 Aug. 1936. New Directions Archive, bMS Am 2077 (1371), HLHU.

46. JL, TLS to EP, 28 July 1936. New Directions Archive, bMS Am 2077 (1371), HLHU.

47. JL, TLS to *North American Review,* 11 Nov. 1937. New Directions Archive, bMS Am 2077 (1246), HLHU. Although Laughlin submitted his own companion piece to the *Review,* they chose not to run it, sparking a series of sarcastic letters between Laughlin and the *Review's* editors. He wanted a kill fee for his article; they denied him this but paid him $50 for editing Pound's article.

48. The article appeared in the Winter 1937–38 issue, and in many ways sums up the themes of Pound's next volume of poems, *Cantos LII–LXXI,* including the unity of art with all other spheres of human activity. Pound's heroes Jefferson and Adams "stand for a life not split into bits. They tell of a kind of life that had wholeness and mental order. . . . Neither of those two men would have thought of literature as something having nothing to do with life, the nation, the organization of government" (Pound, "Jefferson-Adams," 320).

49. JL, TLS to EP, 8 Oct. 1936. New Directions Archive, bMS Am 2077 (1372), HLHU; JL, TLS to EP, 8 Oct. 1936. EPP, Yale. Pound's opposition to the New Deal was deep, and founded on (among other things) the inflationary effect of Roosevelt's monetary policies.

50. EP, TLS to JL, 3 Dec. 1935. New Directions Archive, bMS Am 2077 (1371), HLHU; JL, TLS to EP, n.d. 1935. EPP, Yale.

51. JL, TLS to EP, 22 Jan. 1936. New Directions Archive, bMS Am 2077 (1371), HLHU.

52. Quoted in Henderson, *Art,* 17–18. Laughlin did write reviews for *Hound and Horn* after Kirstein rejected one of his stories in 1933 (Lincoln Kirstein, TLS to JL, 16 Nov. 1933. New Directions Archive, bMS Am 2077 [922], HLHU).

53. Quoted in Zarin, "Jaz," 47.

54. Henderson, *Art,* 17–18.

55. Quoted in Zarin, "Jaz," 62. Laughlin's hostility to Cerf only grew when Cerf publicly called for Pound's conviction on treason charges after Pound was captured in 1945—in a typical statement from 1946, Laughlin calls Cerf "the symbol paramount of all that is swinish and foul and detestable in American publishing" (JL, TLS to T. S. Eliot, 22 May 1946, New Directions Archive, bMS Am 2077 [513], HLHU).

56. JL, TLS to Dwight Macdonald, 25 July 1938. New Directions Archive, bMS Am 2077 (1297), HLHU.

57. JL, TLS to Delmore Schwartz, 27 Apr. 1939. New Directions Archive, bMS Am

2077 (1514), HLHU. The aunt Laughlin mentions is Leila, his father's sister, who became a substitute mother to Laughlin after he began attending boarding school in New England (Eaglebrook and then Choate). In the 1940s, Leila built "Meadow House" for Laughlin on her Norfolk, Connecticut property; Laughlin moved there with his first wife (of three), Margaret Keyser, whom he married in 1942 and divorced in 1952, and lived there until the end of his life.

58. Laughlin, 1936 "Preface," vii.

59. Laughlin's criteria for judgment here are reminiscent of what Richard Brodhead identifies as one of the elements of the nineteenth-century definition of literature: that it be edifying or have a socially redeeming content, that "the dissemination of distinguished writing can improve the tone of a culture and rise the level of its intelligence." Brodhead, *School of Hawthorne*, 109–10.

60. JL, TLS to EP, n.d. 1936. EPP, Yale. Provided with a letter of introduction from Pound, Laughlin had contacted Williams soon after meeting Pound.

61. WCW, TLS to JL, 31 Mar. 1937 (Witemeyer).

62. EP, TLS to JL, 17 June 1937. New Directions Archive, bMS Am 2077 (1371), HLHU.

63. In Williams, *White Mule*, 292–93.

64. Laughlin, 1937 "Preface," xii–xiii.

65. Laughlin, 1937 "Preface," xvi.

66. JL, TLS to T. S. Eliot, 8 Mar. 1937. New Directions Archive, bMS Am 2077 (513), HLHU.

67. All quotes from JL, TLS to WCW, 29 Nov. 1937 (Witemeyer). Laughlin's strategy of enlisting critics to help him sell books was a consistent center of the New Directions approach: Williams, Pound, and even E. M. Forster benefited from it— "we were instrumental in the Forster revival," Laughlin wrote, "because I per- suaded Lionel Trilling to write a book about him, which was so brilliant it put him back into popularity" (Henderson, *Art*, 25).

68. Laughlin did include *In the American Grain* in the New Classics series, but was able to obtain the rights to the book for $100 only after an acrimonious negotia- tion with the Boni firm—during which Williams insisted that they broke their contract with him and referred to them as "shits." WCW, TLS to JL, 9 Aug. 1939; letters between Laughlin and the Bonis, 14, 18, 21, and 28 Aug. 1939. New Directions Archive, bMS Am 2077 (24), HLHU.

69. On the Laughlin-Williams split see Witemeyer, ed., *Selected Letters* (esp. 181) and Mariani, *New World*, 602–3.

70. Morris, *Writings of William Carlos Williams*, 112. In an unpublished paper on Williams, Laughlin, and the artist Charles Sheeler, Morris notes that when Wil- liams saw the profile of Sheeler in *Life* magazine, he indicated to Laughlin that the publisher should try to get such publicity for him, too.

71. Morris, *Writings*, 116. Morris also draws our attention to Laughlin's retrospective short story "A Visit," in which he recounts the visit of a young publisher to an eminent writer. The publisher, although he purports to be interested only in

advancing the writer's reputation, is actually driven by a hidden desire to use commercial techniques to popularize that writer and, in the process, to make money for himself. "A Visit" appears in Witemeyer, ed., *Selected Letters*, 255–73.

72. JL, TLS to WCW, 21 Jan. 1938 (Witemeyer). The war intervened before Laughlin could amass enough reprint rights to begin the "New Classics" series.

73. Laughlin, 1939 "Preface," xxi.

74. EP, TL to Peter Russell, 19 Nov. 195?. HRHRC.

75. EP, TLS to JL, 24 May 1940. New Directions Archive, bMS Am 2077 (1371), HLHU.

76. JL, TLS to EP, 26 Nov. 1939. New Directions Archive, bMS Am 2077 (1371), HLHU.

77. A typical example of Pound's anti-Semitic rhetoric of the times appears in a letter to Laughlin: "It is not for me to notice small rabbit shit. But it wd. be useful for you to take up and analyze the smear in Windsor Quarterly, fall 1936 re Jeff/Muss. Note that the little kike snot does NOT mention a single one of Jefferson's econ. principles; nor Confucius? NOR aduce ANY fact to disprove any of my directly observed facts. This is typical communist mentality in the U.S.A. it is also the kind of jew impertinence that creates antisemite nazism and pogroms" (EP, TLS to JL, 12 Jan. 1935. New Directions Archive, bMS Am 2077 [1371], HLHU).

78. See Stephen Spender, untitled review of *The Fifth Decad of Cantos;* Edwin Muir, untitled review of *The Fifth Decad of Cantos.*

79. EP, TLS to JL, 28 Feb. 1937. EPP, Yale.

80. JL, TLS to EP, 9 Mar. 1937. EPP, Yale.

81. JL, TLS to EP, 7 Jan. 1938. EPP, Yale.

82. JL, TLS to EP, 26 Nov. 1939. EPP, Yale. William Carlos Williams's *In the American Grain* was the first volume of the New Classics series.

83. EP, TLS to JL, 10 Jan. 1940. New Directions Archive, bMS Am 2077 (1371), HLHU.

84. Arthur Pell, TLS to JL, 26 Feb. 1940. New Directions Archive, bMS Am 2077 (1246), HLHU. For bibliographical information on *Personae,* see Gallup 62–65. Interestingly, in Pell's next letter to Laughlin (1 Mar. 1940) he offered the young publisher his "sizable stock of JEFFERSON AND MUSSOLINI" and Laughlin took him up on the offer, purchasing 550 bound copies for $100 on the understanding that Laughlin would pay royalties directly to Pound. One can only speculate whether Laughlin bought these copies with the intention to eventually sell them, with the intention to simply keep them off the market, or both.

85. "Among the Publishers," 1142.

86. Laughlin, "Ez as Wuz," 207.

87. JL, TPCS to EP, 21 Oct. 1938. EPP, Yale.

88. JL, TLS to EP, 7 Jan. 1939. New Directions Archive, bMS Am 2077 (1371), HLHU.

89. JL, TLS to T. S. Eliot, 8 Feb. 1938. New Directions Archive, bMS Am 2077 (513), HLHU.

90. Williams, "Penny Wise, Pound Foolish," 230.

91. *Publishers' Weekly,* 22 Nov. 1985: 26.

92. EP, TLS to JL, 22 Oct. 1938. EPP, Yale.

93. JL, TLS to EP, 10 Apr. 1939. EPP, Yale. Stone was a frequent contributor to, among other magazines, the avowedly "radical conservative" and fascist-sympathizing *American Review,* a St. Louis–based journal that published from 1931 to 1938. Pound admired Stone's views on Eliot, Wyndham Lewis, and modern literature in general.

94. EP, TLS to JL, 23 Mar. 1939. EPP, Yale. Another factor contributing to Laughlin's leeriness about Pound's potential to harm his company was the financial pressure put on him by his family, who still held his purse strings and were threatening to cut off the money. See Phillips, ed., *Selected Letters,* esp. letters from April 1939.

95. JL, TLS to Delmore Schwartz, 27 Apr. 1939 (Phillips). Delmore Schwartz was a good friend of Laughlin's; he and his wife, Laughlin attested, "ran the New Directions business during the later years of my period at Harvard" (Henderson, *Art,* 33). Laughlin was an early champion of Schwartz's writing, publishing his *In Dreams Begin Responsibilities* in 1938 and asking him to contribute to the "Makers of Modern Literature" series.

96. JL, TLS to Delmore Schwartz, 27 Apr. 1939 (Phillips). In one of his few forthright political stances, Laughlin—along with Williams, Schwartz, Kay Boyle, James Farrell, Kenneth Rexroth, Katherine Anne Porter, and Gorham Munson—signed a pronouncement written by Dwight Macdonald for the Fall 1939 *Partisan Review* calling for American neutrality in Europe.

97. Philip Rahv, TLS to JL, 15 Nov. 1937; JL, TLS to Philip Rahv, 22 Nov. 1937. New Directions Archive, bMS Am 2077 (1297), HLHU.

98. For as long as New Directions continued to publish literary criticism and student-aimed textbooks Laughlin maintained his association with Ransom in particular, who published the New Critical manifesto with the house. In 1940, for instance, Ransom proposed a volume on I. A. Richards and William Empson for the New Directions Makers of Modern Literature series; the book was never published. Laughlin proposed in 1949, after the Bollingen controversy blew over, that Ransom produce a textbook for New Directions. (John Crowe Ransom, TLS to JL, 22 Apr. 1940; JL, TLS to John Crowe Ransom, 1 Nov. 1949. New Directions Archive, bMS Am 2077 [1413], HLHU). See Chapter 3 for a more extended discussion of the New Critics and New York Intellectuals. Laughlin's letters with Ransom, Rahv, and Phillips can be found in the New Directions collection at the Houghton Library at Harvard.

99. JL, TLS to EP, n.d. 1939. EPP, Yale.

100. JL TLS to Delmore Schwartz, 27 Apr. 1939 (Phillips).

101. JL, TLS to EP, n.d. 1939. EPP, Yale. In many of his earlier letters to Pound, Laughlin uses such slurs as "kike" and "yid" frequently. One of Laughlin and Pound's earliest discussions of Jews took place in the mid-1930s, while Laughlin

was dating a Jewish woman. Pound consistently made slurs to Laughlin: "jews IZ temptin when 18, but about 26 they begins to THICKEN, and the older they gets the MORE RACE shows, more it oozes thru every pore" (EP, TLS to JL, 27 Feb. 1936. New Directions Archive, bMS Am 2077 [1371], HLHU)—but Laughlin refused to respond until he and his girlfriend broke their relationship off. In the letter following the breakup, Laughlin echoes many of Pound's comments for one of the few times in their correspondence.

102. Quoted in Wilhelm, *Tragic Years,* 146.

103. Quoted in Holmes, ed., *Correspondence.*

104. Angleton, then a student at Yale, was an admirer of Pound, a graduate of the Ezuversity, and in fact Pound and Laughlin visited him during Pound's 1939 U.S. trip. Later, he became famous as the CIA's obsessed mole-hunting chief of counterintelligence.

105. Heymann, *Last Rower,* 88.

106. "Dr. Ezra Pound," 22.

107. WCW, TLS to JL, 7 June 1939 (Witemeyer).

108. Laughlin, "Ez as Wuz," 20.

109. EP, TLS to JL, Oct. 1939. EPP, Yale. In Berkeley, "The Way It Was," 48.

110. Later, on his 1937 stationery, Pound added the following mottoes to the top left corner: "A tax is not a dividend" and "A nation need not pay, nor should it pay, interest on its own credit."

111. JL, TLS to EP, 26 Nov. 1939. EPP, Yale.

112. JL, TLS to EP, 5 Dec. 1939. EPP, Yale.

113. JL, personal interview with the author, 7 Jan. 1997.

114. EP, TLS to JL, 21 Oct. 1937. EPP, Yale.

115. JL, TLS to EP, 5 Dec. 1939. New Directions Archive, bMS Am 2077 (1372), HLHU.

116. EP, TLS to JL, 2 Jan. 1940. New Directions Archive, bMS Am 2077 (1371), HLHU. Pound appears to have parted ways with Watkins, as well, at this time, writing Laughlin that she "done left me cause I said England wd/ lose the war or something." After this point, Laughlin acted as Pound's agent *and* publisher, with the poet's blessing: "Anyhow I never did see why a agent was necessary between us, ONCE you git the habit of payin me on time. . . . You thought we ought to have Ann or a naygent, cause other wise YOU wd:nt feel like a businesslike publisher." (EP, TLS to JL, 24 July 1940. New Directions Archive, bMS Am 2077 (1371), HLHU.

117. EP, TLS to JL, 22 Nov. 1940. New Directions Archive, bMS Am 2077 (1371), HLHU.

118. JL, TLS to EP, 5 Dec. 1939. EPP, Yale.

119. JL, TLS to EP, 5 Dec. 1939. EPP, Yale.

120. JL, TLS to EP, 5 Dec. 1939. EPP, Yale.

121. EP, letter to JL, 10 Jan. 1940. EPP, Yale. The use of boldface here and in subse-

quent transcriptions of Pound's letters generally indicates his use of the red ribbon on his typewriter; in a few occasions, however, I have used boldface to indicate a handwritten word or two inserted by Pound.

122. EP, TLS to JL, 10 Jan. 1940. EPP, Yale.

123. EP, TLS to JL, 10 Jan. 1940. EPP, Yale.

124. EP, TLS to JL, 24 Feb. 1940. EPP, Yale.

125. JL, TLS to EP, 5 Feb. 1940. EPP, Yale.

126. JL, TLS to EP, 25 Apr. 1940. EPP, Yale.

127. The difference between the typeface of the 1940 original and the 1986 insertion is noticeable in the editions that restore Pound's words.

128. EP, TLS to JL, 10 Jan. 1940. EPP, Yale.

129. JL, TLS to EP, 5 Feb. 1940. EPP, Yale.

130. JL, TLS to EP, 5 Feb. 1940. EPP, Yale. Pound also wanted maps of China, drawn by his wife Dorothy, and diagrams of Chinese dynastic history to be used on the inside front and back covers, but Laughlin refused this.

131. JL, TLS to T. S. Eliot, 1 Apr. 1940. New Directions Archive, bMS Am 2077 (513), HLHU.

132. T. S. Eliot, TLS to JL, 19 Apr. 1940. New Directions Archive, bMS Am 2077 (513), HLHU.

133. JL, TLS to EP, 25 Apr. 1940. EPP, Yale.

134. EP, TLS to JL, 24 May 1940. EPP, Yale. EP, TLS to JL 9 June 1940. EPP, Yale.

135. The cover photograph was taken by James Jesus Angleton.

136. See Carpenter, *Serious Character*, 565.

137. Delmore Schwartz, TLS to EP, 5 Mar. 1939. EPP, Yale.

138. Delmore Schwartz, TLS to JL, 2 Apr. 1940 (Phillips).

139. Delmore Schwartz, TLS to JL, 2 Apr. 1940 (Phillips). The disputed lines are "Remarked Ben: better keep out the jews/ or yr/ children will curse you."

140. *Publishers' Weekly* 21 Sept. 1940: 1051; *Saturday Review of Literature* 19 Oct. 1940: 22.

141. Denying Williams's request to put one of his books out in the spring, separate from the customary New Directions fall list, Laughlin wrote, "We don't get very far with books done separately. It is for this reason that I plan to do almost nothing except in the fall. Here's the reason: what sells books is catalogue, mailing list, salesman's visits, advertising. Now all those things cost so damn much that we can only afford them by bunching the books together and splitting the expense. . . . Fall is the time for books; people are serious then. In Spring they're too happy." JL, letter to WCW, 17 Mar. 1939 (Witemeyer).

142. EP, AL to JL, 6 Apr. 1946. New Directions Archive, bMS Am 2077 (1371), HLHU. His comment about "Harrold Hairbrain," as well, refers to H. H.'s essay in the pamphlet and is a knowing dig at Laughlin. Pound wrote this letter from St. Elizabeth's, where he was incarcerated; he had not seen the book when originally published because of the cutoff of trade between Italy and the United States. Laughlin did insert an erratum slip at one point, although when is unclear.

143. Bogan, review of *Cantos LII–LXXI*, n.p.; Untermeyer, review of *Cantos LII–LXXI*, 381; untitled review of *Cantos LII–LXXI* in the *Nation*, 637; untitled review of *Cantos LII–LXXI* in *Accent*, 122; Tate, "Last Omnibus," 242.

144. JL, TPCS to EP, Feb. 1941. EPP. Yale. In 1940 he had, though, purchased 550 bound copies of the book from Liveright for $100. Arthur Pell, TLS to JL, 1 Mar. 1940. New Directions Archive, bMS Am 2077 (810), HLHU.

145. JL, TLS to EP, 2 Aug. 1941. EPP, Yale.

CHAPTER 3

1. Henderson, *Art*, 27.

2. JL, TLS to EP, 23 Aug. 1941. EPP, Yale. Pound, who began broadcasting in January 1941, was paid approximately $17 a month for his broadcasts, which formed part of EIAR's "American Hour."

3. Tietjens, "End of Ezra Pound," 39–40.

4. Benét, "Poetry's Last Twenty Years," 102.

5. Plimpton, ed., *Writers at Work*, 53–54.

6. Carpenter, *Serious Character*, 626.

7. JL, TLS to EP, 24 Sept. 1945. EPP, Yale. Laughlin is here already separating "the values of literature" and the content of Pound's statements.

8. Canby, "Ezra Pound," 10.

9. Pound had, ironically, written for the *New Masses* in the late 1920s, and in 1928 the editors appended a preface to one of his articles in which they asserted that "Pound is the leader of the most vital wing of the younger American writers" (Redman, *Fascism*, 73).

10. FBI Office Memo, to D. M. Ladd from J. C. Strickland, 2 Mar. 1946, quoted in Spoo, ed., *Letters in Captivity*, 285.

11. Henderson, *Art*, 26.

12. Laughlin, 1946 "Preface," xv. Laughlin's 4-F classification is somewhat mysterious; he wrote Eliot on 22 April 1942 lamenting that he had to go in the Army "next week," but says nothing about it to Pound or to Eliot afterward. Laughlin's father Henry had suffered from severe manic-depression, and Laughlin himself took Prozac in the last years of his life, so it is possible that his depressive tendencies were the reason for his 4-F. Cynthia Zarin notes in her excellent *New Yorker* profile that the doctor who classified Laughlin 4-F had also treated his father and grandfather for psychiatric problems.

13. Laughlin, "Preface," xviii.

14. JL, TLS to EP, 5 Dec. 1939. EPP, Yale.

15. In the same issue of *New Directions*, the novelist James T. Farrell published an essay on the same topic entitled "Some Observations on the Future of Books." Laughlin's and Farrell's protests for the special nature of publishing, and against treating books as commodities, repeat John Quinn's attacks on Knopf's and Liveright's vulgarizing of the literary trade in the 1910s, and were themselves echoed

in the controversy over the consolidation of publishing under larger corporate control in the 1990s.

16. Promotional pamphlet. New Directions Archive, bMS Am 2077, HLHU. Laughlin originally based the New Classics on a Faber and Faber series of inexpensive reprints of contemporary poets (JL, TLS to T. S. Eliot, 24 Feb. 1940. New Directions Archive, bMS Am 2077 [513], HLHU). While the Poet of the Month series did not last long—according to Laughlin, booksellers refused to stock and sell the thirty-two-page pamphlets because of the low profit margin and because "they object to the fragile format"—the Makers of Modern Literature and New Classics series thrived well into the 1960s. (JL, TLS to Hugh Kenner, 20 Apr. 1949. HRHRC).

17. *Publishers' Weekly* 26 Sept. 1942.

18. JL, TLS to Dudley Fitts, 11 Aug. 1946. New Directions Archive, bMS Am 2077 (576), HLHU.

19. Stephen Vincent Benét, TL to JL, n.d. New Directions Archive, bMS Am 2077 (161), HLHU. The thirty-two page Poet of the Month series was not intended only to support young poets, either; Laughlin used hand printers to print the pamphlets (which he still sold for fifty cents apiece). In the end, he issued forty-two numbers of the series.

20. Book-of-the-Month Club, TLS to JL, 23 Nov. 1942; JL, TLS to Book-of-the-Month Club, 24 Nov. 1942; Book-of-the-Month Club, TLS to JL, 27 Nov. 1942 (New Directions archive, HLHU 2077, item 216).

21. JL, TCC to Dorothy Pound, 4 Nov. 1945. New Directions Archive, bMS Am 2077 (1370), HLHU.

22. JL, TLS to T. S. Eliot, 3 Oct. and 11 Oct. 1934. New Directions Archive, bMS Am 2077 (513), HLHU.

23. JL, TLS to T. S. Eliot, 9 Sept. 1936 and 8 Feb. 1939. New Directions Archive, bMS Am 2077 (513), HLHU.

24. JL, TLS to T. S. Eliot, 22 Apr. 1942. New Directions Archive, bMS Am 2077 (513), HLHU.

25. T. S. Eliot, TLS to JL, 11 Oct. 1945. New Directions Archive, bMS Am 2077 (513), HLHU.

26. JL, TLS to T. S. Eliot, 23 Oct. 1945. New Directions Archive, bMS Am 2077 (513), HLHU.

27. JL, TLS to T. S. Eliot, 14 Dec. 1945. New Directions Archive, bMS Am 2077 (513), HLHU.

28. JL, TLS to T. S. Eliot, 23 Oct. 1945. New Directions Archive, bMS Am 2077 (513), HLHU. Ironically, the complete *Cantos* that Laughlin wanted to get to "in due time" appeared in 1948, nineteen years before the first *Selected Cantos*.

29. JL, TLS to T. S. Eliot, 22 May 1946. New Directions Archive, bMS Am 2077 (513), HLHU.

30. JL, TLS to T. S. Eliot, 23 Dec. 1945. New Directions Archive, bMS 2077 (513), HLHU.

31. JL, TLS to T. S. Eliot, 4 Jan. 1946. New Directions Archive, bMS Am 2077 (513), HLHU.

32. JL, TCC to T. S. Eliot, 15 Feb. 1946. HRHRC.

33. Malcolm Cowley, TLS to JL, 28 May 1946. New Directions Archive, bMS Am 2077 (403), HLHU.

34. "New Directions," 804.

35. "New Directions," 804.

36. These authors themselves helped create New Directions' new aesthetic formalist identity. Melville, James, and Baudelaire were all, at this time, most often read as writers whose works embodied the notion that art was best understood as exclusively an aesthetic, not a social, matter; Matthiessen's 1941 *American Renaissance* was an important early statement urging readers to understand Melville's works as products of a social nexus.

37. T. S. Eliot, TLS to JL, 5 July 1946. New Directions Archive, bMS Am 2077 (513), HLHU.

38. Schwartz, *Creating Faulkner's Reputation*, 73 ff.

39. Radway, *Feeling for Books*, 258.

40. Cerf, *At Random*, 172, 92. Cerf does not mention here, as he detailed in his *Saturday Review* column for 16 March 1946, that he had received 142 letters opposing the exclusion of Pound and 140 supporting it (Carpenter, *Serious Character*, 791). He inadvertently shows himself to have taken precisely the same attitude earlier in the same book, calling Pound a "great man of the times" when telling the story of using the poet's endorsement of *Ulysses* as a marketing tool.

41. *Perspectives USA* was a short-lived journal (1952–54) published under the auspices of Intercultural Publications, a nonprofit funded by the Ford Foundation, on which Laughlin served as publisher. See Chapter 4 for a more extended discussion of this journal.

42. Wilford, *New York Intellectuals*, 34.

43. See Brooks and Warren, *Understanding Poetry*, xiii; Teres, "Remaking Marxist Criticism," in DiBattista and McDiarmid, eds., *High and Low Moderns*, 69. Each, however, saw very different things in Eliot. The New Critics admired Eliot's method of criticism, his very self-conscious place in the literary tradition, and his essential conservatism; the *Partisan Review* writers supported Eliot's view on the special nature of art, its particular "way of living and seeing" (70). Teres's article, moreover, concentrates on the period when *PR* was at its most sympathetic to the ideas of Communism; later, Rahv's and Phillips's ideas came much closer to those of the New Critics.

44. Good sources on the New Critics include Ransom, *New Criticism;* Leitch, *American Literary Criticism;* Jancovitch, *Cultural Politics of the New Criticism;* Winchell, *Cleanth Brooks;* and Fekete, *The Critical Twilight*.

45. "New Criticism," *New Princeton Encyclopedia of Poetry and Poetics* (1993), 883.

46. Leitch, *American Literary Criticism*, 29–30.

47. Quoted in Hubbell, *Who Are?*, 329.

48. Although the New Critics were obviously very diverse in their outlooks, a model of their conception of the ideal society can probably best be found in *I'll Take My Stand* and in two important works of Eliot's, *The Idea of a Christian Society* and *Notes towards the Definition of Culture*.

    The typical image of the New Critics as pure formalists is not accurate. Although their theoretical writings stress the primary importance of formal analysis, a brief look at their critical writings will show that they did not hesitate to bring in elements of an author's biography or of the historical background to deepen this analysis. Moreover, this school greatly admired such intertextual works as Eliot's *The Waste Land,* a poem that cannot be fully understood without reference to other writers' works alluded to or incorporated in it. The image of the New Critics as pure aestheticists, though, derives largely from the immense influence they have had over pedagogy. Their textbooks—especially *Understanding Poetry*—taught secondary-school and college teachers to approach literature in a strictly formalist way, and they passed this approach on to their own students.

49. In von Hallberg, *Canons,* 359. Also see I. A. Richards's appendix on Eliot in his 1925 *Principles of Literary Criticism,* an important early touchstone for New Critical thought.

50. Von Hallberg, *Canons,* 365. Another advocate for Eliot in the academy, though not a New Critic, was F. O. Matthiessen.

51. The New Critics' conception of the work of art as having a unique type of existence brought them close to Pound in some ways, for in his articulation of the idea the "luminous detail" or the "vortex" also resisted being split apart; in the end, however, the New Critics found him to be an important figure, with many virtues, if not a poet of the first rank.

    The New Critic who remained one of Pound's strongest defenders was Allen Tate. Although he did not write a great deal on Pound during the 1930s or 1940s, Tate was a Fellow of the Library of Congress and was instrumental in the process that awarded Pound the Bollingen Prize in 1948. Laughlin used Tate's statements respecting the award in New Directions advertising for years after that.

52. "Further Remarks on the Pound Award," 666.

53. Blackmur, "Masks."

54. EP, TLS to JL, 23 Jan. 1934 EPP, Yale. *Hound and Horn* has a special place in the history of the burgeoning influence of the New Criticism on the American academy, for it was one of the first journals located geographically and intellectually in the mainstream of American intellectual life to embrace the New Critical ideology. "The rejection by the *Hound & Horn* of social commitment," says Leonard Greenbaum in his history of the journal, "led quite naturally to early manifestations of what came to be known as 'the new criticism'—the concentration on explication, on technical analysis, as the first approach necessary to the understanding of literature" (Greenbaum, *Hound and Horn,* 14). Greenbaum devotes a chapter to the contentious relationship between Pound and *Hound and Horn* editor Lincoln Kirstein, emphasizing Pound's customary strategies of urging the

magazine to aim itself at certain influential people (Bernard Berenson and Wyndham Lewis, for example) and to bolster, rather than to exclude, the edifying content of the journal by including such pieces as Pound's own Fenollosa essay and his *How to Read*.

55. JL, TLS to EP, 18 Jan. 1934. EPP, Yale.

56. Hubbell, *Who Are?*, 322. Hubbell's book is a work of amazing breadth, written by a professor whose career spanned sixty years, encompassing the birth, heyday, and academicization of modernism, as well as the professionalization of literary study.

57. Shumway, *Creating American Civilization*, 235.

58. Ransom, *World's Body*, 328–29.

59. Such a proposition could not have been more horrifying to Pound, whose experiences in American universities left him despairing that academics could ever appreciate, much less set the standards for, good literature. Fired from Indiana's Wabash College for his bohemian dress and habits, and denied a Ph.D. from the University of Pennsylvania for his unsystematic thesis, Pound launched invective at American higher education throughout his life. The idea that academics were determining literary value must have been very disheartening for him. In yet another of the ironies of his public position in the 1930s and 1940s, though, it was largely as a result of the decontextualized approach to art possible only in the universities that Pound was able to join the ranks of academically endorsed poets. He later accepted this, urging Laughlin to make an effort to market to the professors; but Laughlin had taken that approach from the very beginnings of his firm.

60. Interestingly, the New Critical methodology also had the effect of deprofessionalizing literary criticism, for once a person had mastered the technique of close reading, no further training—only the aesthetic sensibility—was necessary in order to fully appreciate a work of art. Unlike the philological, historical, and biographical schools of criticism that had held sway previously, the New Criticism was in many ways profoundly democratic. Ransom's call for "Criticism, Inc.," and for a specialized course of training for literary critics, should not be equated with the current requirement that professors of literature have Ph.D.s—few of the early New Critics had doctorates.

61. Although the New Critics did not feel that literature was in no way good for readers, they differed from that Arnoldian position in that, for them, the edification brought about by literature, if it did not make better citizens, made more complete and enlightened people.

62. There are a number of excellent studies of the New York Intellectuals. Early works, written while many members of the group were still quite active, include Daniel Aaron's *Writers on the Left* (1960), James Burkhart Gilbert's *Writers and Partisans* (1968), and John Diggins's *Up from Communism* (1975). In the 1980s, after the immediate impact of these thinkers had faded, appeared Terry Cooney's chronological study *The Rise of the New York Intellectuals* (1986), Alexander Bloom's *Prodigal Sons,* a study of the group's Jewish heritage (1986), and Alan M.

Wald's exhaustive *The New York Intellectuals* (1987). Lawrence Schwartz's book on *Creating Faulkner's Reputation* (1988) relies heavily on a discussion of their links with the New Critics, and David Shumway's *Creating American Civilization* (1994) argues that the Intellectuals' project to "move beyond a criticism of vulgar Marxism to a sophisticated theory of [the] relations" between culture and society failed. Finally, Neil Jumonville's *Critical Crossings* (1991) and Hugh Wilford's *The New York Intellectuals* (1995) examine their activities and the impact in the postwar period.

63. The New York Intellectuals' most immediate ancestor was Van Wyck Brooks, whose sociological approach to literature melded Emerson's urging for a native American strain of art with a Ruskinian drive for social reform. Brooks sought to wrest American literary history away from the English tradition and to establish a tradition indigenous to the United States. Although one of the most important American critics of the 1910s through the 1930s, Brooks had little interest in Pound. The eclectic tradition, as embodied in Pound's Italo-Renaissance Confucian Americanism and Eliot's "ideal order," was very definitely not nativist. For Brooks, the movement spearheaded by Eliot and Pound "was largely the creation of displaced persons . . . all of whom had left behind the countries of their origin and for whom human beings were more or less abstractions." Brooks's vision of cultural totality, though, was in a direct line from Ruskin's, and was quite similar to Pound's in that each writer saw literature as an expression of social and economic conditions, and felt that literary criticism had to take these into account but not let them entirely determine aesthetic evaluation.

64. The most important of the New York Intellectuals' adversaries on questions about literature were Mike Gold, editor-in-chief of the *New Masses* and the U.S. Communist Party's point man on cultural issues, and Granville Hicks, the Marxist critic who served as that magazine's literary editor after 1934. Hicks and Gold held the strict Communist position that all "bourgeois" art was without merit, and they focused *New Masses'* attention on proletarian literature. In their view modernism, although nominally opposed to bourgeois society, in actuality expressed the values of bourgeois society, and was incapable of truly revolutionary or radical sentiment.

65. On this, see Clement Greenberg's *Art and Culture* and Serge Guilbaut's *How New York Stole the Idea of Modern Art*.

66. Wald, *New York Intellectuals*, 226; Wilford, *New York Intellectuals*, 4.

67. John Guillory points out that in England, F. R. Leavis had by 1930 formulated a theory of "majority culture" and "minority culture" that bore a great resemblance to the Intellectuals' later high- and lowbrow groupings (Guillory, *Cultural Capital*, 134–140).

68. The alimentary imagery is the Intellectuals' own.

69. Barrett, "Pilgrim," 128.

70. Howe, *Critical Point*, 113. The Intellectuals were essentially unable to conceive of sophistication or critical intelligence existing in America's great hinterlands

(outside of Boston, New York, or parts of Chicago); "provincial" was shorthand for most kinds of non–New York intellectual thought.

71. Although critics and historians have since drawn important distinctions between the "mass" and the "popular," distinctions that generally define the "mass" as something mass-produced by an elite for a large market, and the "popular" as an organic product of the popular culture intended for its own consumption, for the New York Intellectuals they were one and the same.

72. Quoted in Hubbell, *Who Are?*, 322.

73. Howe, in "Our Country and Our Culture," *Partisan Review* 29.5 (Oct. 1952): 75–81.

74. On the institutionalization of literary criticism, see also Webster, *Republic of Letters*.

75. Laughlin bought the remaining stock of this volume from Liveright in the late 1930s.

76. JL, TLS to E. E. Cummings, 2 May 1946. New Directions Archive, bMS Am 2077 (490), HLHU.

77. JL, TLS to EP, 6 Aug. 1946. New Directions Archive, bMS Am 2077 (1371), HLHU. Donald Gallup notes that many copies of this book were destroyed by Allied forces because its title led them to believe it was Axis propaganda (Gallup, 74).

78. Fitzgerald, "What Thou," 22.

79. Martz, "Recent Poetry," 144–48.

80. Williams, review of *Pisan Cantos*, 11.

81. O'Connor, "What Does," 15–16.

82. JL, TLS to T. S. Eliot, 24 June 1948. New Directions Archive, bMS 2077 (513), HLHU. The Faber edition was published one year after the New Directions edition.

83. *Quarterly Review of Literature* 4.3, inside front cover.

84. Seelye, *Charles Olson*, 76. This criticism was most likely a result of Pound discovering the John Adams–John Quincy Adams mix-up on the jacket of *Cantos LII–LXXI*.

85. Seelye, *Charles Olson*, 84.

86. Carpenter, *Serious Character*, 788.

87. Library of Congress Press Release no. 542 (20 Feb. 1949).

88. Quoted in McGuire, *Bollingen*, 210. Evans's worries about relations with Italy are particularly far-fetched, considering that at this time U.S. ambassador Clare Booth Luce had just been warning Italy in no uncertain terms about the possible consequences of a Communist vote in the 1948 elections. It is difficult to believe that a prize given to Ezra Pound would outweigh Luce's and Harry Truman's strong-arm political tactics in Italian minds.

89. JL, TLS to T. S. Eliot, 24 Mar. 1949. New Directions Archive, bMS Am 2077 (513), HLHU.

90. Barrett, "Prize," 344.
91. Barrett, "Prize," 347. Wilford explains that the public reaction to Barrett's editorial was confusion; no one was sure whether he supported or opposed the Bollingen decision.
92. *PR* May 1949: 518.
93. *PR* May 1949: 520.
94. *PR* July 1949: 667.
95. Hillyer, "Treason's Strange Fruit," 10.
96. JL, TLS to T. S. Eliot, 6 June 1949. New Directions Archive, bMS Am 2077 (513), HLHU.
97. JL, TLS to T. S. Eliot, 10 Aug. 1949. New Directions Archive, bMS Am 2077 (513), HLHU.
98. MacLeish, *Letters,* 344. This letter was submitted for publication but never made it into the magazine.
99. Harrison Smith, TLS to JL, 14 Sept. 1949. New Directions Archive, bMS Am 2077 (1371), HLHU. Ironically, Smith later (in 1956) offered his help with obtaining Pound's release from St. Elizabeths.
100. MacLeish, *Poetry and Opinion,* n.p. (preface).
101. Schwartz, *Creating Faulkner's Reputation,* 154.
102. Winchell, *New York Intellectuals,* 279. Gerald Graff also sees the Bollingen moment as a defining one for the cultural impact of the New Criticism, writing that "the Bollingen judges were able to dismiss the poem's fascist and anti-Semitic doctrines as poetically irrelevant by applying the New Critical principle that poetry is impervious to assertion." (Graff, *Professing Literature,* 229. Also see Casillo, *Genealogy of Demons,* on the New Critics and the Bollingen controversy.)
103. Leitch, *American Literary Criticism,* 90.

CHAPTER 4

1. JL, TLS to EP, 5 Dec. 1939. EPP, Yale.
2. *Personae* had been in print continuously since 1926, and was in its sixth printing when Laughlin took it over from the Liveright Corporation in 1946. At that time, he bought 465 bound copies and 525 sets of sheets from Liveright. The new edition of 1949 was produced by offset printing from the Liveright book, with a number of previously uncollected poems—all pre- 1920—added at the end.
3. Laughlin could have used the 1928 Faber *Selected Poems,* edited and with an introduction by T. S. Eliot, but in his introduction to that volume—and in his more recent critical essay, from *Poetry* of April 1946—Eliot had argued that Pound's poetic accomplishments, while significant, were ultimately flawed.
4. Quoted in Witemeyer, "Making of Pound's *Selected Poems*," 74.
5. EP, TL to JL, n.d. 1947. EPP, Yale.
6. JL, TLS to Dorothy Pound, 14 May 1947. New Directions Archive, bMS 2077 (1370), HLHU.

7. Paige was at the time compiling a collection of Pound's letters for Harcourt, Brace. Dorothy Pound, ALS to JL, 20 May 1947. New Directions Archive, bMS 2077 (1370), HLHU.

8. See EP, TL to JL, n.d. 1949. EPP, Yale.

9. EP, TL to JL, n.d. 1949. EPP, Yale.

10. EP, TL to JL, n.d. 1949. EPP, Yale.

11. Quoted in Witemeyer, "Making of Pound's *Selected Poems*," 76.

12. EP, TL to JL, n.d. 1949. EPP, Yale. One critic at least—Hugh Witemeyer—sees Pound's reluctance to include large sections of *Pisan Cantos* as an effort to play down the later, controversial aspects of his poetry. Witemeyer argues that "the Pounds wished to marginalize *The Pisan Cantos* and to define the [Selected] as an edition primarily of 'the Early Poems,' out of a desire to alter the current public image of the poet. In their view, neither the contents nor the introduction of the *Selected Poems* should call special attention to the poet's activities during the most recent decade of his career" (Witemeyer, "Making of Pound's *Selected Poems*," 78–79). The Bollingen controversy of February 1949 was still fresh, Witemeyer adds, and the Pounds had no desire to fan the flames of public opinion. But Witemeyer has little compelling evidence that this was, in fact, the Pounds' objective, and ignores Pound's willingness to be controversial even from St. Elizabeths (illustrated by his continued public statements on politics and economics and culminating in his involvement with John Kasper and other conspiracy theorists during the 1950s). Moreover, when Eliot, at Faber, had contacted Pound in 1940 about a revised and updated edition of his *Selected Poems* (1928), Pound had been more than eager to emphasize his most political works: "if [readers] aint had sense enough to get canters 52/71 why the hell shd/ I kindergarten . . . Better use . . . Usury Canto [XLV]" (quoted in Taylor, "Textual Biography," 244). Of course, this letter was written before the war, before the treason indictment, before Pisa and St. Elizabeths, but judging from his correspondence, I see no essential change in Pound's attitude toward his own writings in the intervening nine years. On the contrary, if anyone would have wanted to downplay Pound's politics and omit the *Pisan* sections it would have been Laughlin; but Laughlin knew the value of *The Pisan Cantos* both as poetry and as publicity, and therefore insisted on their inclusion. In the end, long excerpts from six of the eleven *Pisan Cantos* were included.

13. Quoted in Witemeyer, "Making of Pound's *Selected Poems*," 76.

14. JL, TLS to EP, 6 Dec. 1948. New Directions Archive, bMS Am 2077 (1371), HLHU.

15. EP, TL to JL, 20(?) Jan. 1949. EPP, Yale.

16. Berryman finally published the essay as "The Poetry of Ezra Pound" in the April 1949 issue of *Partisan Review*.

17. T. S. Eliot, TLS to JL, 4 Jan. 1949. New Directions Archive, bMS Am 2077 (513), HLHU.

18. Humphries, "Jeffers and Pound," 349. His statement in that review that "I would

rather see [Pound] saved from death by drowning, or the firing squad, than Bennett Cerf" must have especially appealed to Pound.

19. Rolfe Humphries, TLS to JL, 1 Jan. 1949. EPP, Yale.

20. JL, TLS to EP, 8 Feb. 1949. EPP, Yale.

21. Quoted in Witemeyer, "Making of Pound's *Selected Poems*," 78.

22. EP, TL to JL, 7 Feb. 1949. New Directions Archive, bMS 2077 (1371), HLHU.

23. Dorothy Pound, ALS to Rolfe Humphries, 9 Mar. 1949. Quoted in Witemeyer, "Making of Pound's *Selected Poems*," 78.

24. Rolfe Humphries, TLS to JL, 8 Feb. 1949. New Directions Archive, bMS Am 2077 (829), HLHU.

25. Rolfe Humphries, TLS to JL, 9 Feb. 1949. New Directions Archive, bMS Am 2077 (829), HLHU.

26. Dorothy Pound, ALS to JL 21, Mar. 1949. EPP, Yale.

27. JL, ALS to Rolfe Humphries, Feb. (?) 1949. New Directions Archive, bMS Am 2077 (829), HLHU.

28. Quoted in Witemeyer, "Making of Pound's *Selected Poems*," 80.

29. Quoted in JL, TLS to EP, 28 Mar. 1949. EPP, Yale.

30. EP, TL to JL, 29 Mar. 1949. New Directions Archive, bMS Am 2077 (1371), HLHU.

31. Rolfe Humphries, TLS to EP, 2 Apr. 1949. New Directions Archive, bMS Am 2077 (829), HLHU.

32. EP, TL to JL, 20 Apr. 1949. New Directions Archive, bMS 2077 (1371), HLHU.

33. JL, TLS to Rolfe Humphries, 31 Mar. 1949; JL, TLS to EP n.d. 1949. New Directions Archive, bMS 2077 (829 and 1371), HLHU.

34. List advertisement in *Publishers' Weekly* 3 Sept. 1949. This is ironic, given that Laughlin had reassured the Pounds that the *Selected* would not cut into the market for *Personae*.

35. Meyer, "A Sampling of Pound and Modern Man," 14.

36. JL, TLS to T. S. Eliot, 1 Apr. 1940. New Directions Archive, bMS Am 2077 (513), HLHU.

37. See Chapter 2 for an example of this—Pound's objections to the content of Faber's *Polite Essays*.

38. T. S. Eliot, TLS to JL, 29 Mar. 1949; JL, TLS to T. S. Eliot 20 Apr. 1949 New Directions Archive, bMS Am 2077 (513), HLHU.

39. JL, TLS to T. S. Eliot, 26 Oct. 1950 New Directions Archive, bMS Am 2077 (513), HLHU.

40. Carpenter, *Serious Character*, 786.

41. Norman, *Ezra Pound*, 434. In 1971, after Laughlin had succeeded in making Pound a canonical author, New Directions took over the *Letters* and reissued it as a paperback.

42. Eliot, "Ezra Pound."

43. Spiller et al., *Literary History of the United States* (1948), 1339.

44. Spiller et al., *Literary History of the United States* (1948), 1340. The 1953 second

edition of the same book briefly mentions the *Pisan Cantos*, the Bollingen controversy, and Hillyer's articles, and concludes by alluding to how "Eliot's definition
of poetry as an escape from emotion and personality, expressed in 1920, had
become by 1950 the cornerstone of the school of the 'new criticism' " (*Literary
History of the United States* [1953], 1397).

45. Adams, "Hawk," 214.

46. Blackmur, *Form and Value*, 379, 374.

47. Hume, "Contribution of Ezra Pound," 60.

48. Ransom, "Poetry," 445–54. Judging poets on their "prospects of surviving a few
half-centuries," Ransom ranked Pound a Minor Poet, along with Williams, Marianne Moore, E. E. Cummings, Allen Tate, Walter de la Mare, and Hart Crane;
poets ranked between Minors and Majors were A. E. Housman, Wallace Stevens,
W. H. Auden, and Dylan Thomas.

49. Like Stanley Nott, Russell had published some of Pound's economic and political
works during the 1930s and 1940s—*ABC of Economics* in 1933 and *America,
Roosevelt, and the Causes of the Present War* in 1944—and also reprinted his
"Money Pamphlets" and "Gold and Work" in 1950–51. Ever the self-promoter,
Pound wanted Russell to try to get Britain's most important reprint houses and
publishers of classic literature to issue his own works: "dont neglect getting
KULCH etc/ into Everyman or Penguin," Pound wrote him, "along with the 20
great classics/ which shd/ precede 'em. Suitable Penguin/Kulch/ ABC Reading/
Everyman: Cavalcanti"(EP, TL to Peter Russell, 29 Nov. 195?. HRHRC).

50. Inside back cover advertisement from the *Nation*, 16 Dec. 1950.

51. For years, Laughlin had recognized the value of testimonials by well-respected
artists and critics for the task of improving a writer's status in the literary community—in 1939, he had planned just such a volume on behalf of William Carlos
Williams, a volume that would, as in his later strategy for Pound, use the divergent
voices of the New Critics and the New York Intellectuals to urge respect for a
particular artist. Writing to Delmore Schwartz in 1939, Laughlin had planned "to
have all the guys like Blackmur and Ransom and the *PR's* [*Partisan Review* writ-
ers] to do essays on various aspects of Williams' genius, and put them in a book
along with various photographs and personalia. There seems to be no way to
establish Williams except to have all the writers make a racket about him" (JL,
TLS to Delmore Schwartz, 16 Jan. 1939 [Phillips]).

52. JL, TLS to Peter Russell, 20 Apr. 1949, HRHRC.

53. JL, TLS to Peter Russell, 7 June 1949, HRHRC.

54. The question of how much outside information a poem can require a reader to
know is one that greatly problematizes the New Critical approach. Eliot, in "Tradition and the Individual Talent," clearly feels that poets and readers must know
the tradition in order to fully understand great poetry; in *The Well-Wrought Urn*,
however, Cleanth Brooks emphasizes that a poem's greatness lies in its formal
excellence, and that no special training in the tradition is necessary for readers to
identify this. Even though their positions were sometimes contradictory, though,

both Eliot and Brooks agreed the *Cantos* were flawed because readers would need such specialized, nonliterary knowledge to understand them.

55. Russell, *Examination,* 17.

56. According to Lawrence Rainey, Brooks liked to tell the story of advising Kenner on his dissertation, and simply sitting silently while Kenner spoke: he had absolutely no advice to give the brilliant young scholar (personal conversation).

57. "In the Caged Panther's Eyes."

58. JL, TLS to Hugh Kenner, 28 Mar. 1949. HRHRC.

59. JL, TLS to Hugh Kenner, 20 Apr. 1949. HRHRC. Pamphlets, Laughlin was discovering, did not sell well, and bookstores did not like stocking them.

60. JL, TLS to T. S. Eliot, 6 Oct. 1949. New Directions Archive, bMS Am 2077 (513), HLHU. Houghton Library, Harvard University.

61. T. S. Eliot, TLS to JL, 24 Oct. 1949. New Directions Archive, bMS Am 2077 (513), HLHU.

62. T. S. Eliot, TLS to Hugh Kenner, 29 June 1950. HRHRC.

63. JL, TLS to Hugh Kenner, 10 Oct. 1950. HRHRC. The *Rose in the Steel Dust* title was used for a 1967 study of the *Cantos* by Walter Baumann.

64. EP, TL to Hugh Kenner, 25 July 1951. HRHRC. Later, he added some suggestions for Kenner's future endeavors—suggestions that Kenner did not take: "K's capacity for lucid summary/ indicate he cd/ do another vol/ size and general design of that on Ez/ Hist. of precious metals/ mon/ systems/ Divine Augustus Money in various countries" (EP, TL to Hugh Kenner, 31 July 1951. HRHRC).

65. Hughes, review of *The Poetry of Ezra Pound,* 42; untitled anonymous review of *The Poetry of Ezra Pound* in the *New Yorker*; Fitts, "Too-Good," 80; untitled review of *The Poetry of Ezra Pound* in the *New York Times,* 30 Sept. 1951; Scofield, review of *The Poetry of Ezra Pound.*

66. JL, TLS to Hugh Kenner, 19 Feb. 1951. HRHRC.

67. Kenner was also a proponent of the work of Wyndham Lewis, another politically problematic author. In the 1950s, Kenner urged Laughlin to reissue any of Lewis's works that he could acquire cheaply, and Pound encouraged him: "what about stimulatin the Erections [New Directions] to a vol of the part of Lewis his oldest ally enjoys reading??" (TL to Hugh Kenner, 22 Oct. 1950. HRHRC. In another letter, Pound offered to provide an introduction to Lewis's work. EP, TL to Hugh Kenner, n.d. 1950. HRHRC). Tellingly, though, Laughlin consistently demurred, and here the parallels between Pound and Lewis become significant. The two authors had similar political profiles, although Lewis's public taint was not an affiliation with Mussolini but with the infinitely more horrifying Hitler. Laughlin, however, seems to have felt that taking on the difficult task of depoliticizing a writer who had made far fewer contributions to serious literature than Pound would be fruitless. Laughlin could urge readers to ignore Pound's politics and read his *Polite Essays,* his *Cantos,* his *ABC of Reading;* in Lewis's case, though, the fact that New Directions was not an art-book publisher and could not provide readers with reproductions of Lewis's paintings gave the firm very little

with which to deflect reader's attentions from his politics. Laughlin realized that he could not have sold many copies of a Lewis book, and as he told Kenner, he simply did not feel strongly enough about Lewis's value as a writer to take a loss on him. Kenner complained about this to Pound. After informing the poet that he was composing a 45,000-word book on Lewis for Laughlin's Makers of Modern Literature series, he adds, "this Jas is of course the same Jas who won't print a book BY Lewis, specifically Vulgar Streak, which I've been urgin on him for some time. Sez he tried to read it 10 years ago, & was so bored he stopped at page 50. Encyclical from St. Liz might be of some use; it can't at this stage do any harm" (Hugh Kenner, TLS to EP, 20 June 1953. EPP, Yale).

68. Hugh Kenner, TLS to EP, 12 Mar. 1954. EPP, Yale.

69. Hugh Kenner, TLS to EP, 28 Sept. 1953. EPP, Yale.

70. Hugh Kenner, TLS to EP, 14 Oct. 1953. EPP, Yale.

71. Laughlin, personal interview, 10 Jan. 1997.

72. Laughlin, *Random Essays*, 224.

73. Saunders's book, *The Cultural Cold War: The CIA and the World of Arts and Letters*, is a valuable historical survey of the CIA's involvement in the Congress for Cultural Freedom and other cultural initiatives undertaken by the U.S. government in the early years of the Cold War.

74. JL, TLS to T. S. Eliot, 10 Feb. 1951. New Directions Archive, bMS Am 2077 (513), HLHU.

75. Laughlin, "The Publisher," 1.

76. Many of the European intellectuals at whom this propaganda was aimed, moreover, were perfectly aware of what this publication was intended to accomplish, and ridiculed it. "The magazine provoked widespread resentment in Europe, not only because it was 'so obviously an American package,' but also because of its 'inauthentic' institutional origins," Wilford remarks, quoting a letter from Stephen Spender to Allen Tate (Wilford, *New York Intellectuals*, 201). After Laughlin left *Perspectives USA*, he worked for Intercultural Publications in India.

77. *Perspectives USA* 16 (Summer 1956): 120–28. The poems included were "De Aegypto," "Alba," "Ité," "Taking Leave of a Friend," a selection from *Sextus Propertius*, a short piece from *Mauberley*, and Cantos III, XLV, and LXXXI.

78. Carruth, "Poetry," 158. Beginning with a biographical sketch, Carruth traced Pound's career to the present, and evaluated each of his successive phases of composition. Judging the *Cantos* to be a fine but ultimately flawed work, he explained that, paradoxically, in its failure to hold together as a whole, Pound's work demonstrated its formal virtuosity. Carruth prefaced his essay with a remarkable paragraph laying out what he saw as the two conflicting ways of seeing poetry—the "expressionistic," which holds that "a poem is an instrument which conveys or arouses the ideas and emotions that are current between the poet and his readers," and the "autonomistic," which "holds that a poem is a 'self-sufficient' or 'autonomous' structure which embodies inextricably the ideas and emotions that have been discovered in its unique inception" (129–30). This paragraph

makes it clear that the fading of expressionism's dominance is a welcome development, and that autonomism (which is similar to what I have been terming "aesthetic formalism") should replace it in critical practice. Although Carruth barely touches on this duality in the body of his essay, the implication is clear: Pound's poetry is of superior quality, but only an autonomistic approach can get beyond the ultimately irrelevant objections to his person and examine the work in isolation. It seems clear that Laughlin took advantage of his power as publisher of *Perspectives USA* to include an apology for Pound—an essay that argued not that he was innocent, but that recently enlightened critical practice demonstrated that his poetry must be evaluated without reference to his person.

79. JL, TLS to EP, 6 Dec. 1948. New Directions Archive, bMS 2077 (1371), HLHU.

80. JL, TLS to EP, 7 Nov. 1950 and 19 Feb. 1951. New Directions Archive, bMS 2077 (1371), HLHU.

81. William Jackson, TLS to JL, 26 Sept. 1949. New Directions Archive, bMS 2077 (1371), HLHU.

82. Personal interview, 30 July 1996.

83. In 1953, for instance, Pound's New Directions royalty statement lists $67.50 in permissions fees; in 1955, the total was $439.00; by 1958 Pound was earning almost $200 quarterly from permissions fees and royalties. (Royalty statements. EPP, Yale). Another indication of Pound's meager 1950s income comes from Eliot, who offhandedly remarked to Laughlin—who was asking for an advance to help pay Pound's legal expenses—that "in an off-year when there is no new Pound book issued, the royalties cannot be expected to be more than £150 a year" (T. S. Eliot, TLS to JL, 14 Nov. 1957. New Directions Archive, bMS Am 2077 (513), HLHU).

84. Robert MacGregor, TLS to EP, 14 Oct. 1953. EPP, Yale. For most of the 1950s, Robert MacGregor was the most important figure in the day-to-day operations of New Directions. Coming to the company from his own firm, Theatre Arts Books, in 1950, he was initially hired at $100 a week plus commissions to supervise the New Directions distribution agreement with Paragon and to be the head salesman for the New York City area. In 1952 and 1953, when Laughlin began spending most of his time abroad in behalf of Intercultural Publications and the Ford Foundation, MacGregor wrote Laughlin frequent, detailed letters updating him on the progess of all of the company's books. Those letters, housed at the Houghton Library at Harvard, provide the best overview of New Directions activities during the 1950s. MacGregor died in 1974.

85. T. S. Eliot, TLS to JL, 22 Aug. 1953. New Directions Archive, bMS Am 2077 (513), HLHU.

86. JL, TLS to T. S. Eliot, 3 May 1953. New Directions Archive, bMS Am 2077 (513), HLHU.

87. *Western Review,* Spring 1954.

88. The first was Eliot's anonymous *Ezra Pound His Metric and Poetry* for Knopf in

1917, the second his introduction to the Faber *Selected Poems* of Pound (1928), and the third a 1946 article in *Poetry*.

89. In the words of Peter Viereck, who wrote an article critical of this strategy (Viereck 1951, 342).

90. Pound, *Literary Essays*, x. This is quite a change from Eliot's 1928 article "Isolated Superiority," in which he questioned Pound's ability to convince readers that his subject matter is important: "I confess that I am seldom interested in what he is saying, but only in the way he says it. . . . As for the meaning of the *Cantos*, that never worries me, and I do not believe that I care. I know that Pound has a scheme and a kind of philosophy behind it; it is quite enough for me that he thinks he knows what he is doing; I am glad that the philosophy is there, but I am not interested in it" (Eliot, "Isolated Superiority," 4–7). (For a discussion of Eliot's introduction, see Coyle, "Determining Frontiers," 249.)

91. It should also be noted that Eliot's perhaps willful omission of the poet's personal activities in the early part of the century might also stem from his unwillingness to confront Pound's (then unknown) role in the editing of Eliot's *The Waste Land*.

92. Bogan, *Achievement in Modern Poetry*, 99, 106.

93. Graves, *Common Asphodel*, 218.

94. Cunliffe, *Literature of the United States*, 324.

95. Robert MacGregor, TLS to Peter du Sautoy, 30 Apr. 1954. New Directions Archive, bMS Am 2077 (513), HLHU.

96. Laughlin did cooperate with William Van O'Connor in his preparation of his 1959 *Casebook on Ezra Pound,* a student-aimed paperback compilation of source materials for term papers on Pound. A horrified Laughlin called this project "a shocking educational method—I used to say that the only thing I learned at Harvard was how to find information"—but he saw the book as an important way to get students to read Pound. JL, TLS to T. S. Eliot, 12 Dec. 1958. New Directions Archive, bMS Am 2077 (513), HLHU.

97. Solomon, "Pound-Ruskin Axis," 276.

98. Alvarez, *Shaping Spirit*, 48.

99. Alvarez, *Shaping Spirit*, 55.

100. Quoted in Meacham, *Caged Panther,* 61.

101. Dorothy Pound (for the Committee for Ezra Pound), TLS to Vanni Scheiwiller, 12 Dec. 1955. EPP, Yale.

102. JL, TLS to EP, Jan. 1956. EPP, Yale.

103. Stock, review of *Section: Rock-Drill*, 114; Alvarez, review of *Section: Rock-Drill*, 15.

104. Larkin, review of *Section: Rock-Drill*, 4; Jarrell, review of *Section: Rock-Drill*, 103–6; Davie, review of *Section: Rock-Drill*, 317.

105. Robert MacGregor, TLS to Dorothy Pound, 5 Mar. 1956. EPP, Yale.

106. Robert MacGregor, TLS to EP, 9 Aug. 1956. EPP, Yale.

107. "Ezra Pound at Seventy." Promotional pamphlet, 1956. Even this faint praise

from Eliot was difficult to Laughlin to obtain—when he asked for a contribution to the pamphlet, Eliot begged off because "I have already said . . . what I have to say in praise of Ezra Pound. . . . I am left with the alternative of repetition or critical qualification" (T. S. Eliot, TLS to JL, 9 Nov. 1955. New Directions Archive, bMS Am 2077 (513), HLHU).

108. Hemingway's first sentence was "Will gladly pay tribute to Ezra but what I would like to do is get him the hell out of St. Elizabeth's; have him given a passport and allow him to return to Italy where he is justly valued as a poet."

109. JL, TLS to T. S. Eliot, 9 Nov. 1955. New Directions Archive, bMS Am 2077 (513), HLHU.

110. Sam Hynes's 1955 article "The Case of Ezra Pound" in *Commonweal* is an example of this.

111. JL, TLS to T. S. Eliot, 13 Nov. 1956. New Directions Archive, bMS Am 2077 (513), HLHU.

112. Letters dated 24 Nov. 1956 and 20 May 1957. From Pound, *"I Cease Not to Yowl."*

113. For a more extensive discussion of the Kasper affair, see my " "Hitch Your Wagon to a Star': The Square $ Series and Ezra Pound" (*Papers of the Bibliographical Society of America* 92.3).

CHAPTER 5

1. EP, TLS to Robert MacGregor, 25 Feb. 1958. New Directions Archive, bMS Am 2077 (1051), HLHU. See also Mariani, *New World Naked,* 714.

2. The actual quality of the binding varied from company to company, certainly, and the pliable, fishy-smelling faux leather of the Modern Library had little in common with the Knopf books. All of the companies, though, stressed the material qualities of their books—their feel, their appearance, their endurance, and the status that they brought to consumers.

3. *Statistical History of the United States,* 210.

4. For more on the initial growth of paperbacks after World War II, see Smith, *Paperback Parnassus;* Tebbell's *History* v. 4; Davis, *Two-Bit Culture;* Bonn, *Heavy Traffic.*

5. Tebbell, *History* v. 4, 350.

6. Paperback publishers had already been bringing out contemporary, experimental writing in periodical form. In the 1950s, many started their own "little magazines" for experimental, modernist-influenced work. Pocket Books brought out *Discovery,* Avon Books started *New Voices,* the New American Library founded *New World Writing,* and Anchor Books began the *Anchor Review.* The publishers hoped that these would do for them what *New Directions in Prose and Poetry* had done (on a much smaller scale) for Laughlin: provide them with a means for discovering and capturing promising young writers and reaching a market of

student readers who would then buy the books of the company sponsoring the magazine.

7. Quoted in Tebell, *History* v. 4, 350. Also see Epstein, *Book Business,* 52–56.

8. Schick, *Paperbound Book,* 182.

9. Smith, *Paperback Parnassus,* 78.

10. Hugh Kenner, TLS to EP, 14 Oct. 1953. EPP, Yale.

11. The firm's distribution network was very limited in the 1940s, when bookstores could obtain its books only directly through the company itself; later, New Directions struck distribution deals with other publishers (first Lippincott and then W. W. Norton) who also lacked the great range of the magazine and mass-market distributors.

12. Griselda Ohanessian, personal interview, 30 July 1996.

13. JL, TLS to Dudley Fitts, 21 Feb. 1956. New Directions Archive, bMS 2077 (576), HLHU.

14. JL, TLS to Ezra Pound, 21 Nov. 1955. EPP, Yale. In the 1950s, New Directions did print a series of hardcover college textbooks under the direction of Laughlin's friend Dick Smyth, but because of distribution and sales problems the series was discontinued by the early 1960s.

15. JL, TLS to EP, 21 Nov. 1955. EPP, Yale.

16. JL, TLS to EP, 12 Dec. 1955. EPP, Yale. Such a book never appeared, although Laughlin and MacGregor would attempt to market *ABC of Reading* and *Confucius to Cummings* as one; moreover, New Directions never succeeded in selling its books in drugstores.

17. Hugh Kenner and Hayden Carruth had made some textual suggestions, the "Autobiography" chronology was retitled "Biography," and New Directions added sections from two Cantos and from Pound's translation of the *Women of Trachis.*

18. JL, TLS to EP, 26 Aug. 1957. EPP, Yale.

19. Robert MacGregor, TLS to EP, 3 Sept. 1959. EPP, Yale.

20. *The Classic Noh Theatre of Japan,* Pound's 1916 essay, was also published as a paperback reprint (New Directions Paperbook P79) in 1959 without appearing in hardcover.

21. Robert MacGregor, TLS to EP, 3 Sept. 1959. EPP, Yale.

22. Robert MacGregor, TLS to EP, 3 May 1963. EPP, Yale. Although $3,000 seems like little money, this only accounts for his American sales. Moreover, $3,000 was a great deal more than Pound had ever earned on book sales before the 1960s, and it enabled him to stop writing for periodicals. Before World War II, he had always had to support himself by magazine and journal contributions; during the war he lived off contributions and his wages for the Rome Radio broadcasts, and in 1946–58 he lived at St. Elizabeths. The royalty statements for 1967 and 1968 are from the James Laughlin Archive, HLHU.

23. JL, TLS to EP, 8 May 1967. EPP, Yale. Laughlin was correct; the first printing of 5,000 copies sold so quickly that a second printing (3,500 copies) had to be

ordered fourteen months later; by contrast, it took fifteen years to sell out the 5,000 hardcover copies of the same book.

24. In the 1930s, for instance, Laughlin had most New Directions books printed by small craft printers across the United States.

25. Robert MacGregor, TLS to EP, 3 Sept. 1959. EPP, Yale.

26. JL, TLS to EP, 12 Dec. 1955. EPP, Yale.

27. JL, TLS to EP, 18 Oct. 1957. EPP, Yale.

28. JL, TLS to EP, 16 June 1958. EPP, Yale.

29. JL, TLS to EP, 11 Aug. 1958. EPP, Yale.

30. The New Directions office was unable to locate the sales figures for a number of the early years of the firm, as well as for a number of years in the early 1960s.

31. JL, TLS to EP, 4 May 1965. EPP, Yale.

32. In his article "Ez as Wuz," Laughlin asserts that Pound's biographer Humphrey Carpenter had examined this famous picture closely and concluded that Pound was somehow making a joke about his past Fascist affiliation; however, in Carpenter's published description of the incident (*Serious Character*, 848), he expresses no doubt about the sincerity of the gesture.

33. Notwithstanding the reviews, *Thrones* sold quite well; Pound received royalties on 893 copies for the book's first year.

34. Schwartz, "Ezra Pound and History," 19; Rosenthal, "The Pleasures of Pound," 370; Robie, review of *Thrones*, 285.

35. Schwartz, "Pound and History," 18.

36. "Voices of their Own," review of *Thrones* et al.; *Yale Review* Summer 1960: 589–91.

37. EP, TLS to JL, 24 Nov. 1959. EPP, Yale.

38. JL, TLS to EP, 21 Apr. 1964. EPP, Yale.

39. JL, TLS to EP, 5 Aug. 1965. EPP, Yale.

40. Hubbell, *Who Are?* 322.

41. Laughlin, "Foreword" to Kenner, *Poetry of Ezra Pound* (rpt. 1985), xiii.

42. Kenner, "Making of the Modernist Canon," 372.

43. By arguing that Pound's accomplishments transcended the formal but at the same time refusing to read the poems in any but formalist ways, this group of critics undermined their own arguments.

44. Read, *Tenth Muse*, 272.

45. In the late 1940s, Pound rarely appeared in lists of the best or most influential authors of the century. In Asa Don Dickinson's three-volume *The Best Books of Our Time* (three volumes, the first published in 1928 and covering 1901–25, the second published in 1937 and covering 1926–35, and the third published in 1948 and covering 1936–45), Pound is absent. In 1925 Pound had only four endorsements, and in 1935 none of his books appear on the list; this however, could result from the fact that books, not reputation in general, were listed, and in 1935 Pound had only two books with much circulation at all in the United States (*Lustra* and *Personae*). In 1945, he was not on Dickinson's "Fifteen Best Books about Litera-

ture" (but neither were Eliot or the New Critics), nor did he appear on the list of the sixteen most important books of American poetry of the period 1935–45 or of the six hundred runners-up. Hubbell, *Who Are?*, 292–99.

46. Quoted in Hubbell, *Who Are?*, 233.

47. Quoted in Hubbell, *Who Are?*, 234.

48. Hubbell, *Who Are?*, 323.

49. By the late 1960s a backlash against Pound, one with deep roots in the antimodernism of such writers as Van Wyck Brooks and Robert Hillyer, was beginning. "Since the ascendancy of Pound and Eliot," the poet James Dickey said in an address to the Library of Congress in 1967, "the poem has become a sort of high-cult *objet d'art*" and is unable to "speak to people deeply about matters of general concern." Quoted in Hubbell, *Who Are?*, 193.

50. Twentieth-century literary anthologies had often included Pound's work, and permissions fees for the inclusion of his poems in anthologies became a significant source of income for him in the 1950s. In 1953, for example, six requests for the inclusion of his poems in anthologies were made, for a total of $67.50; for 1955, thirteen, for $439.00; for the first half of 1958, eleven, for $196.25; and for the first half of 1959, eleven, for $447.75 (EPP, Yale).

Although there has been no scholarship on Pound's appearance in literary anthologies and those anthologies' impact on the American poetry canon, Craig S. Abbott's "Untermeyer on Eliot" (1988) is a fine study of how one important anthologist—Louis Untermeyer, who also had a correspondence with Pound—solidified Eliot's place in the canon and his role as the preeminent English-language poet of his time. John Lowney's *The American Avant-Garde Tradition* (1997) touches on how anthologies, including many of the anthologies discussed below, have affected the canonization of another of Pound's contemporaries, Williams.

51. All quotes from Hall, ed., *Contemporary American Poetry*, 25–30.

52. Allen, ed., *New American Poetry*, xi.

53. Kelly, ed., *Controversy of Poets*, 566; Carruth, ed., *Voice That Is Great Within Us*, xvii.

54. Kostelanetz, review of *The Cantos*, 411.

55. New Directions also published an anthology, *A New Directions Reader* (1964), that had much the same effect, placing Pound and Williams among the new generation of experimental writers in such a way as to emphasize their almost parental relations with younger New Directions writers.

56. Hall, *Contemporary American Poetry*, 29; Macdonald, "Theory of 'Popular Culture,'" 21.

57. Pound had served as a contributing editor to *Esquire*, on Hemingway's recommendation, during part of the 1930s.

58. Rovere, "Question of Ezra Pound," 78.

59. Rovere, "Question of Ezra Pound," 70.

60. "What the Pound Case Means," 335.

61. JL, TLS to EP, 22 Dec. 1958. EPP, Yale.

62. EP, TLS to Charles Norman, 5 Dec. 1957. EPP, Yale.

63. EP, TL to Charles Norman, n.d. 1958. EPP, Yale.

64. JL, TLS to Charles Norman, 5 Feb. 1959. New Directions Archive, bMS 2077 (1242), HLHU.

65. JL, TLS to EP, 27 Feb. 1959 EPP, Yale.

66. EP, TLS to JL, 16 Mar. 1959. EPP, Yale.

67. Charles Norman, TLS to JL 16 Feb. 1959. New Directions Archive, bMS 2077 (1242), HLHU.

68. JL, TLS to EP, 31 Mar. 1960. EPP, Yale.

69. JL, TLS to EP, 31 Mar. 1960.

70. JL, TLS to EP, 18 Feb. 1960. EPP, Yale.

71. EP, TLS to JL, 24 Feb. 1960. EPP, Yale.

72. EP, TL to JL, n.d. 1960. EPP, Yale.

73. JL, TLS to EP, 22 June 1960. EPP, Yale.

74. Norman, *Ezra Pound*, x.

75. All quotes from "The Sightless Seer," 111–12.

76. Untitled anonymous review of *Ezra Pound*, 4.

77. JL, TLS to Charles Norman, 29 Sept. 1962. New Directions Archive, bMS 2077 (1242), HLHU.

78. Wilhelm, *Tragic Years*, 308.

79. Later, this Virginian, a self-described "descendent of the Lees, Randolphs, and Oakes," became a fixture of the far right. His name today appears on numerous neo-Nazi Web sites, and he has been a frequent guest on far-right short-wave radio talk shows such as Tom Valentine's.

80. EP, TLS to JL, 6 Mar. 1959, and to Robert MacGregor, n.d. 1959. New Directions Archive, bMS Am 2077 (1371), HLHU.

81. Eustace Mullins, TLS to JL, 12 Oct. 1958. This is only one of many such letters. Laughlin handled Mullins's pestering professionally, writing on 9 March 1959 that "I have enjoyed very much the two drafts of the preface which you have sent along. . . . I do wish that it were possible for us to advance you something on a contract, but I am afraid that is quite out of the question now." New Directions Archive, bMS 2077 (1199), HLHU.

82. Creekmore, "Poet and Disciple," 32. Mullins's book has a remarkable number of factual errors, misspellings, and misattributions that even a person with only a casual knowledge of Pound's life could spot. He incorrectly identifies Alfred Kreymborg's magazine as *The Broom,* not *Broom* (p. 148), and adds a superfluous *The* to Henry Miller's two *Tropic Of . . .* titles (p. 152); refers to Pound's trip with Hemingway to the Italian cities of "Piombono and Ortobello," rather than the correct Piombino and Orbetello (p. 146); mentions Sylvia Beach's "Shakespeare Head Bookshop" (p. 136); and misspells a number of names of figures in Pound's life.

83. Kenner, "Focus on Pound," 6; Hoffman, "Old Ez and Uncle William," 62.

84. In his *Reading the* Cantos (1966), he asserts that the poem is largely composed of "unresolved implications," that it is "a disjointed series of short poems, passages, lines and fragments, often of exceptional beauty or interest, but unformed, poetically or otherwise, by larger purpose" (117). Stock's apparent reneging on the Pound faith infuriated at least one reader—in a copy of *Reading the Cantos* I found at a used book store, a scrawl on the inside front cover reads "A HATCHET JOB BY A BACKSTABBING POUND DISCIPLE!!"

85. Reviews of Stock's *Life of Ezra Pound* include Kenner, "Incurious Biographer," 31; Alvarez, "Wretched Poet," 27–29; "Accelerating Grimace," 122–23; and "The Puzzle of Pound," 72.

86. Later biographies of Pound—C. David Heymann's *Ezra Pound: The Last Rower* (1976), John Tytell's *Ezra Pound: The Solitary Volcano* (1987), Humphrey Carpenter's *A Serious Character: The Life of Ezra Pound* (1988), and James J. Wilhelm's *Ezra Pound: The Tragic Years, 1925–1972* (1994)—have all examined the poet's political beliefs and activities in detail, taking as one of their primary subjects how they color the poetry.

87. C. David Heymann's 1976 *Ezra Pound: The Last Rower* was the first biography to downplay Pound's importance.

88. Stoicheff, *Hall of Mirrors,* 78.

89. A detailed list and discussion of these publications is available in Stoicheff, *Hall of Mirrors,* 171–73.

90. JL, TLS to EP, 27 Oct. 1958. EPP, Yale. Laughlin is referring to *Arion.*

91. JL, TLS to EP, 12 Aug. 1960. EPP, Yale.

92. EP, AL to JL, n.d. 1960. EPP, Yale.

93. JL, TLS to EP, 23 Mar. 1967. EPP, Yale.

94. According to Stoicheff, Sanders obtained his copies of the poems from Tom Clark, a student of Donald Hall, who in turn had been entrusted with a typescript by Pound while he was interviewing the poet in Italy for the *Paris Review.* Sanders printed 300 copies of *Cantos 110–116,* most of which he sold at premium prices through New York's Phoenix Bookshop.

95. Stoicheff has published a number of articles on *Drafts and Fragments,* as well as a full-length book on the topic, *The Hall of Mirrors.* Other valuable sources include Ronald Bush's "Excavating the Ideological Faultlines of Modernism: Editing Ezra Pound's *Cantos*" in Bornstein, ed., *Representing Modernist Texts,* and Richard Taylor's "Towards a Textual Biography of the *Cantos*" in Willison, Gould, and Chernaik, eds., *Modernist Writers and the Marketplace.*

96. JL, TLS to Robert Gales, 9 Sept. 1968 (quoted in Stoicheff, "Composition and Publication History" 60).

97. JL, TLS to EP, 12 Jan. 1968. EPP, Yale.

98. JL, TLS to EP, 30 May 1968. EPP, Yale.

99. From the 1960 *Paris Review* interview.

100. Leibowitz, "The Muse," 501; untitled anonymous review of *Drafts and Fragments of Cantos CX-CXVII,* cxxxiii.

101. Louis Martz, review of *Drafts and Fragments of Cantos CX-CXVII*, 261–64.
102. Bush, "Excavating the Faultlines of Modernism," 88.

CONCLUSION

1. Hugh Kenner, TLS to EP, 2 Dec. 1962. HRHRC.
2. Hugh Kenner, TLS to EP, 2 Dec. 1962. HRHRC.
3. Peter du Sautoy, TLS to Hugh Kenner, 5 Jan. 1962. HRHRC. Here du Sautoy tells Kenner that Faber doesn't want to publish Kenner's study of Eliot, *The Invisible Poet*, because it doesn't do books on Eliot.
4. Hugh Kenner, personal e-mail correspondence, 23 July 1998. Laughlin did welcome the book as an important addition to the by now succeeding campaign to rehabilitate Pound, and granted free permission for all quotes from Pound's work.
5. Hugh Kenner, personal e-mail correspondence, 23 July 1998.
6. Zinnes, "Eponymous Poet"; untitled anonymous review of *The Pound Era*, 47.
7. Heymann, review of *Pound Era*. Davenport, "Vortex," 525–26; Materer, "Value of a Pound."

Bibliography
❖ ❖ ❖ ❖

Abbott, Craig S. "Modern American Poetry: Anthologies, Classrooms, and Canons." *College Literature* 17.2–3 (1990): 209–21.

"Accelerating Grimace." *Nation* 17 Aug. 1970: 122–23.

Adams, Robert M. "A Hawk and a Handsaw for Ezra Pound." *Accent,* Summer 1948: 205–14.

Allen, Donald and Warren Tallman, eds. *The Poetics of the New American Poetry.* New York: Grove, 1973.

Alpert, Barry Stephen. *The Unexamined Art: Ezra Pound and the Aesthetic Mode of the Little Magazine.* Thesis, Stanford University 1971. Ann Arbor: Xerox University Microfilms, 1974.

Altieri, Charles. *Canons and Consequences: Reflections on the Ethical Force of Imaginative Ideals.* Evanston, Ill.: Northwestern University Press, 1990.

Alvarez, A. Review of *Section: Rock-Drill,* by Ezra Pound. *Observer* 3 Mar. 1957: 15.

———. *The Shaping Spirit: Studies in Modern English and American Poets.* London: Chatto and Windus, 1958.

———. "The Wretched Poet Who Lived in the House of Bedlam." *Saturday Review,* 18 July 1970: 27–29.

"American Writers: Who's Up, Who's Down?" *Esquire,* Aug. 1977; 77–81.

"Among the Publishers." *Publishers' Weekly* 23 July 1938; 1142.

Anderson, Margaret, ed. *The* Little Review *Anthology.* New York: Hermitage House, 1953.

Anesko, Michael. *"Friction with the Market": Henry James and the Profession of Authorship.* New York: Oxford University Press, 1986.

Bacigalupo, Massimo. "Ezra Pound's Cantos 72 and 73: An Annotated Translation." *Paideuma* Spring-Fall 1991: 9–41.

———. *The Forméd Trace: The Later Poetry of Ezra Pound.* New York: Columbia University Press, 1980.

———. "La scrittura dei Cantos." *Lingua e Letteratura* 8.16 (Spring 1991): 56–77.

Bann, Stephen, and John E. Bowlt. *Russian Formalism.* New York: Barnes and Noble, 1973.

Barbour, Douglas. Review of *Drafts and Fragments of Cantos CX–CXVII,* by Ezra Pound. *Queen's Quarterly* 77.3 (Autumn 1970): 460–61.

Barker, George. Review of *A Draft of Cantos XXXI–XLI,* by Ezra Pound. *Criterion* 14 (1935): 649–51.

Barrett, William. "Pilgrim to Philistia." *Partisan Review* 13 (1946): 126–29.

———. "A Prize for Ezra Pound." *Partisan Review* 16.4 (Apr. 1949): 344–47.

Barry, Iris. "The Ezra Pound Period." *Bookman* Oct. 1931: 158–71.

Baumann, Walter. *The Rose in the Steel Dust: An Examination of the* Cantos *of Ezra Pound*. Bern, Switz.: Francke Verlag, 1967.

Benét, William Rose. "Poetry's Last Twenty Years." *Saturday Review of Literature* 5 Aug. 1944: 102.

Bennett, David. "Periodical Fragments and Organic Culture: Modernism, the Avant-Garde, and the Little Magazine." *Contemporary Literature* 30.4 (Winter 1989): 480–502.

Benstock, Shari, and Bernard Benstock. "The Role of Little Magazines in the Emergence of Modernism." *Library Chronicle of the University of Texas at Austin* 20.4 (1990): 69–88.

Benton, Megan. " 'Too Many Books': Book Ownership and Cultural Identity in the 1920s." *American Quarterly* 49.2 (June 1997): 268–97.

Berkley, Miriam. "The Way It Was: James Laughlin and New Directions." *Publishers Weekly* 22 Nov. 1985: 45–49.

Berryman, John. "The Poetry of Ezra Pound." *Partisan Review* Apr. 1949: 377–95.

Bishop, John Peale. "The Talk of Ezra Pound." Review of *Cantos LII-LXXI*, by Ezra Pound. *Nation* 21 Dec. 1940: 637–39.

Blackmur, R. P. *Form and Value in Modern Poetry*. New York: Anchor, 1957.

———. "Lord Tennyson's Scissors: 1912–1950." *Kenyon Review* 14.1 (Winter 1952): 1–20.

———. "Masks of Ezra Pound." *Hound and Horn* 7 (Jan.–Mar. 1934).

Blaine County (Idaho) Historical Museum. *Ezra Pound: Poetry and Politics*. Pamphlet.

Bloom, Alexander, *Prodigal Sons: The New York Intellectuals and Their World*. New York: Oxford University Press, 1986.

Bloom, Harold, ed. *Modern Critical Views: Ezra Pound*. New York: Chelsea House, 1987.

Bogan, Louise. *Achievement in Modern Poetry*. Chicago: Regnery, 1951.

———. Review of *Cantos LII–LXXI,* by Ezra Pound. *New Yorker* 9 Nov. 1940.

Bonn, Thomas L. *Heavy Traffic and High Culture: The New American Library as Literary Gatekeeper in the Paperback Revolution*. Carbondale: Southern Illinois University Press, 1989.

Bornstein, George, ed. *Ezra Pound Among the Poets*. Chicago: University of Chicago Press, 1985.

———. *Representing Modernist Texts: Editing as Interpretation*. Ann Arbor: University of Michigan Press, 1991.

Bourdieu, Pierre. *The Field of Cultural Production: Essays on Art and Literature*. Ed. Randal Johnson. New York: Columbia University Press, 1993.

———. *Outline of a Theory of Practice*. New York: Cambridge University Press, 1977.

———. *The Rules of Art*. Trans. Susan Emanuel. Stanford: Stanford University Press, 1996.

Brodhead, Richard. *The School of Hawthorne*. New York: Oxford University Press, 1986.

Brooke-Rose, Christine. *A ZBC of Ezra Pound*. Berkeley: University of California Press, 1971.

Brooks, Cleanth. *Modern Poetry and the Tradition*. Chapel Hill: University of North Carolina Press, 1939.

Brooks Cleanth, and Robert Penn Warren. *Understanding Poetry*. 3rd ed. New York: Holt, Rinehart and Winston, 1960.

Bürger, Peter. *Theory of the Avant-Garde*. Trans. Michael Shaw. Minneapolis: University of Minnesota Press, 1984.

Bürger, Peter, and Christa Bürger. *The Institutions of Art*. Trans. Loren Kruger. Lincoln: University of Nebraska Press, 1992.

Burke, Kenneth. *The Philosophy of Literary Form: Studies in Symbolic Action*. New York: Vintage, 1957.

Burns, Gerald. "Our Common Reader Attacks the Greats." Review of *Drafts and Fragments of Cantos CX–CXVII*, by Ezra Pound. *Southwest Review* 54.3 (Summer 1969): 333–34.

Bush, Ronald. "Excavating the Ideological Faultlines of History: Editing Ezra Pound's *Cantos*." In Bornstein, *Representing Modernist Texts*. 67–98.

———. *The Genesis of Ezra Pound's Cantos*. Princeton: Princeton University Press, 1976.

———. *T. S. Eliot: The Modernist in History*. Cambridge: Cambridge University Press, 1991.

Calkins, Ernest. *Business the Civilizer*. Boston: Little, Brown, 1928.

Canby, Henry Seidel. *American Memoir*. Boston: Houghton Mifflin, 1947.

———. "Ezra Pound." *Saturday Review of Literature* 15 Dec. 1945: 10.

Carpenter, Humphrey. *A Serious Character: The Life of Ezra Pound*. New York: Delta, 1988.

Carruth, Hayden. "The Poetry of Ezra Pound." *Perspectives USA* 16 (Summer 1956): 129–59.

Carruth, Hayden, and James Laughlin, eds. *A New Directions Reader*. Norfolk, Conn.: New Directions, 1964.

Casillo, Robert. *The Genealogy of Demons*. Evanston, Ill.: Northwestern University Press, 1988.

Cerf, Bennett. *At Random*. New York: Random House, 1977.

Charvat, William. *The Profession of Authorship in America, 1800–1870*. Ed. Matthew Bruccoli. Columbus: Ohio State University Press, 1968.

Cooney, Terry A. *The Rise of the New York Intellectuals: Partisan Review and Its Circle*. Madison: University of Wisconsin Press, 1986.

Corrigan, Robert A. "What's My Line? Bennett Cerf, Ezra Pound, and the American Poet." *American Quarterly* 24.1 (Mar. 1972): 101–17.

Coser, Lewis A., Charles Kadushin, and Walter W. Powell. *Books: The Culture and Commerce of Publishing*. New York: Basic Books, 1982.

Cowley, Malcolm. *After the Genteel Tradition: American Writers 1910–1930*. Carbondale, Ill.: Southern Illinois University Press, 1964.

———. "The Battle over Ezra Pound." *New Republic* 3 Oct. 1949: 17–20.

Coyle, Michael. "Determining Frontiers: T. S. Eliot's Framing of the *Literary Essays of Ezra Pound.*" *MLQ* 50.3 (Sept. 1989): 248–72.

———. *Ezra Pound, Popular Genres, and the Discourse of Culture.* University Park: Pennsylvania State University Press, 1995.

Creekmore, Hubert. "Poet and Disciple." Review of *This Difficult Individual, Ezra Pound,* by Eustace Mullins. *New York Times Book Review* 15 Oct. 1961: 32.

Crider, Allen Billy, ed. *Mass Market Publishing in America.* Boston: G. K. Hall, 1982.

Cunliffe, Marcus. *The Literature of the United States.* London: Penguin, 1955.

Dana, Robert, ed. *Against the Grain: Interviews with Maverick American Publishers.* Iowa City: University of Iowa Press, 1986.

Dardis, Thomas A. *Firebrand: The Life of Horace Liveright.* New York: Random House, 1995.

Dasenbrock, Reed Way. *The Literary Vorticism of Ezra Pound and Wyndham Lewis.* Baltimore: Johns Hopkins University Press, 1985.

Davenport, Guy. "The Pound Vortex." Review of *The Pound Era,* by Hugh Kenner. *National Review* 12 May 1972: 525–26.

Davidson, Cathy N. *Reading in America: Literature and Social History.* Baltimore: Johns Hopkins University Press, 1989.

Davie, Donald. *Ezra Pound: Poet as Sculptor.* New York: Oxford University Press, 1964.

———. Review of *Section: Rock-Drill,* by Ezra Pound. *New Statesman and Nation* 9 Mar. 1957: 317.

Davis, Kenneth C. *Two-Bit Culture: The Paperbacking of America.* Boston: Houghton Mifflin, 1984.

Davison, Peter, Rolf Meyersohn, and Edward Shils, eds. *Literary Taste, Culture, and Mass Communication.* 14 vols. Cambridge: Chadwyck-Healey, 1978.

D'Epiro, Peter. *A Touch of Rhetoric: Ezra Pound's Malatesta Cantos.* Ann Arbor: UMI Research Press, 1983.

de Rachewiltz, Mary. *Discretions.* Boston: Little, Brown, 1971.

———. "Family Lore and Letters." *Journal of Modern Literature* 15.1 (Summer 1988): 7–15.

———. "Fragments of an Atmosphere." *Agenda* Spring 1979: 157–70.

———. "Pound as Son: Letters Home." *Yale Review* Spring 1986: 321–30.

Delehanty, Elizabeth. "A Day With Ezra Pound." *New Yorker* 13 Apr. 1940: 76–77.

Dettmar, Kevin J. H., and Stephen Watt, eds. *Marketing Modernisms: Self-Promotion, Canonization, Rereading.* Ann Arbor: University of Michigan Press, 1996.

DiBattista, Maria, and Lucy McDiarmid, eds. *High and Low Moderns: Literature and Culture, 1889–1939.* New York: Oxford University Press, 1996.

Dieterich, H. R. Untitled review of *Impact,* by Ezra Pound. *Western Political Quarterly* 13 (1961): 1098.

Dobrée, Bonamy. "Make it New." Review of *The Poetry of Ezra Pound,* by Hugh Kenner. *Spectator* (London) 16 Nov. 1951: 662–63.

"Dr. Ezra Pound." Editorial. *New York Times* 13 June 1939: 22.

Domville, Eric. *Editing British and American Literature, 1880–1920*. Toronto: University of Toronto Press, 1976.

Donoghue, Denis. "A Novel about Pound." Review of *The Pound Era*, by Hugh Kenner. *Listener* 23 Nov. 1972: 718–20.

Eagleton, Terry. *The Ideology of the Aesthetic*. Cambridge, Mass.: Basil Blackwell, 1991.

Edwards, John, ed. *The Pound Newsletter* 1–10 (Jan. 1954–Apr. 1956).

Eliot, T. S. "Ezra Pound." *Poetry* Sept. 1946: 326–43.

———. "Isolated Superiority." *Dial* Jan. 1928: 4–7.

———. *The Letters of T. S. Eliot: Volume One, 1898–1922*. Ed. Valerie Eliot. New York: Harcourt Brace Jovanovich, 1988.

———. *Notes towards the Definition of Culture*. London: Faber and Faber, 1949.

———. *Selected Prose of T. S. Eliot*. New York: Harcourt Brace Jovanovich, 1975.

Elliot, Charles. "Old Ez." Review of *The Pound Era*, by Hugh Kenner. *Time* 22 May 1972: 100.

Epstein, Jason. *Book Business: Publishing Past and Future*. New York: W. W. Norton, 2001.

Erlich, Victor. *Russian Formalism: History—Doctrine*. 2nd ed. The Hague: Mouton, 1965.

Escarpit, Robert. *The Book Revolution*. London: George C. Harrap/Paris: UNESCO, 1966

———. *Sociology of Literature*. London: Frank Cass, 1971.

Eysteinsson, Astradur. *The Concept of Modernism*. Ithaca: Cornell University Press, 1990.

"Ezra Pound, Silvershirt." *New Masses* 17 Mar. 1936: 15–16.

Farrell, James T. "Some Observations on the Future of Books." *New Directions* 9 (1946): 6–37.

Faulkner, D. W., John Harrison, and David Dzwonkoski. "New Directions Publishing Corporation." In *Dictionary of Literary Biography* v. 46, *American Literary Publishing Houses 1900–1980: Trade and Paperback*, ed. Peter Dzwonkowski. Detroit: Gale Research, 1986.

Fekete, John, *The Critical Twilight: Explorations in the Ideology of Anglo-American Literary Theory from Eliot to McLuhan*. London and Boston: Routledge and Kegan Paul, 1978.

Feuchtwanger, Lion, et al. "Should Ezra Pound Be Shot?" *New Masses* 25 Dec. 1945: 4–6.

Fiedler, Leslie. *What Was Literature? Class Culture and Mass Society*. New York: Simon and Schuster, 1982.

Fitts, Dudley. "Everything Was Made Simple, but Not Everyone Understood." Review of *Impact*, by Ezra Pound. *New York Times Book Review* 3 July 1960: 4.

———. "The Too-Good Friend." Review of *The Poetry of Ezra Pound*, by Hugh Kenner. *New Republic* 10 Dec. 1951: 80.

Fitzgerald, Robert. "Mr. Pound's Good Governors." Review of *Cantos LII–LXXI*, by Ezra Pound. *Accent* 1 (1940): 121–22.

———. "What Thou Lovest Well Remains." Review of *The Pisan Cantos*, by Ezra Pound *New Republic* 16 Aug. 1948: 21–23.

Fletcher, John Gould. Review of *A Draft of XVI Cantos of Ezra Pound for the Beginning of a Poem of Some Length* and *A Draft of the Cantos XVII to XXVII of Ezra Pound*, by Ezra Pound. *Criterion* 5.8 (1929): 514–24.

Flint, R. W. "Pound and the Lyric." Review of *An Examination of Ezra Pound*, ed. Peter Russell. *Hudson Review* 4.2 (Summer 1951): 293–304.

Ford, Ford Madox. "Ezra." *Books* 9 Jan. 1927: 1, 6.

Ford, Hugh. *Published in Paris: American and British Writers, Printers, and Publishers in Paris, 1920–1939*. New York: Macmillan, 1975.

Fox, Peggy. "Copyright for Scholars." *Paideuma* Sept. 1985: 129–35.

Gallup, Donald. *Ezra Pound: A Bibliography*. Charlottesville: University of Virginia Press, 1983.

Gelpi, Albert. *A Coherent Splendor: The American Poetic Renaissance*. New York: Cambridge University Press, 1987.

Gilman, Richard. "Ezra Pound: the Meritorious and the Meretricious." Review of *Impact*, by Ezra Pound, and *Ezra Pound*, by Charles Norman. *Commonweal* 23 (Dec. 1960): 342–43.

———. "Standing Up to Ezra Pound."*New York Times* 25 Aug. 1991: sec. 7, 1.

Gilmer, Walker. *Horace Liveright: Publisher of the Twenties*. New York: David Lewis, 1970.

Goldman, Eric F. *The Crucial Decade—And After: America 1945–1960*. New York: Vintage, 1960.

Gordon, Arthur. "Intruder in the South." *Look* 19 Feb. 1957: 27–31.

Gordon, James M., ed. *Ezra Pound and James Laughlin: Selected Letters*. New York: W. W. Norton, 1994.

Graves, Robert. *The Common Asphodel: Collected Essays on Poetry 1922–1949*. London: Hamish Hamilton, 1949.

———. *The Crowning Privilege: Collected Essays on Poetry*. Garden City, N.Y.: Doubleday, 1956.

Greenbaum, Leonard. *The* Hound and Horn: *The History of a Literary Quarterly*. The Hague: Mouton, 1966.

Greenberg, Clement. *Art and Culture: Critical Essays*. Boston: Beacon, 1961.

———. "State of American Writing." *Partisan Review* Aug. 1948: 876–79.

Gregory, Horace, and Marya Zaturensky. *A History of American Poetry 1900–1940*. New York: Harcourt, Brace 1946.

Groves, Jeffrey D. "Judging Literary Books by Their Covers: House Styles, Ticknor and Fields, and Literary Promotion." In Moylan and Stiles. 75–100.

Guilbaut, Serge. *How New York Stole the Idea of Modern Art: Abstract Expressionism, Freedom, and the Cold War*. Trans. Arthur Goldhammer. Chicago: University of Chicago Press, 1983.

Gunn, Thom. "Voices of Their Own." Review of *Thrones, 96–109 de los cantares* by Ezra Pound. *Yale Review* Summer 1960: 589–91.

Gussow, Mel. "James Laughlin, Publisher with Bold Taste, Dies at 83." *New York Times* 14 Nov. 1997: A22.

Hall, Donald. "Ezra Pound Said Be a Publisher." *New York Times Book Review* 23 Aug. 1981: 13, 22–23.

Halpenny, Francess, ed. *Editing Twentieth Century Texts*. Toronto: University of Toronto Press, 1972.

Hardy, Barbara. "Barbara Hardy on a New Monument for Pound." Review of *The Pound Era*, by Hugh Kenner. *Spectator* 26 Aug. 1972: 1–2.

Healy, J. V. "The Pound Problem." Review of *Cantos LII–LXXI, ABC of Economics, Polite Essays, and Culture*, by Ezra Pound. *Poetry* 57.3 (Dec. 1940): 200–214.

Henderson, Bill. *The Art of Literary Publishing: Editors on Their Craft*. Yonkers, N.Y.: Pushcart Press, 1980.

Henderson, Cathy. *The Company They Kept: Alfred A. and Blanche W. Knopf, Publishers*. Exhibition catalog. Austin: Harry Ransom Humanities Research Center, University of Texas, 1995.

Heymann, C. David. *Ezra Pound: The Last Rower*. New York: Seaver, 1976.

———. Review of *The Pound Era*, by Hugh Kenner. *Saturday Review* 13 May 1972: 71–74.

Hickman, Miranda B. "Pamphlets and Blue China (or 'cheap books of GOOD work'): Pound's Preference for Plainness in the 1950s." *Paideuma* 25.2–3 (Fall-Winter 1997): 165–79.

Hillyer, Robert. "Poetry's New Priesthood." *Saturday Review of Literature* 18 June 1949: 7–9, 38.

———. "Treason's Strange Fruit: The Case of Ezra Pound and the Bollingen Award." *Saturday Review of Literature* 11 June 1949: 9–11, 28.

Hoffman, Daniel. "Old Ez and Uncle William." Review of *Ezra Pound: A Close-Up* by Michael Reck. *Reporter* 2 Nov. 1967: 59–62.

Holbrook, David. "Groping . . ." Review of *Drafts and Fragments of Cantos CX–CXVII*, by Ezra Pound. *Twentieth Century* 178. 1045 (1971): 56–57.

Homberger, Eric, ed. *Ezra Pound: The Critical Heritage*. London: Routledge and Kegan Paul, 1972.

Howe, Irving. *The Critical Point*. New York: Horizon, 1973.

Hubbell, Jay. *Who Are the Major American Writers?* Durham: Duke University Press, 1972.

Hughes, Serge. Review of *The Poetry of Ezra Pound*, by Hugh Kenner. *Commonweal* 19 Oct. 1951: 42–43.

Hume, Robert A. "The Contribution of Ezra Pound." *English* 8.8 (Summer 1950): 60–65.

Humphries, Rolfe. "Jeffers and Pound." Review of *The Pisan Cantos*, by Ezra Pound. *Nation* 25 Sept. 1948. 349.

Huyssen, Andreas. *After the Great Divide*. Bloomington: Indiana University Press, 1986.

Hynes, Sam. "The Case of Ezra Pound." *Commonweal* 9 Dec. 1955: 251–54.

Jacobson, Marcia. *Henry James and the Mass Market*. Tuscaloosa: University of Alabama Press, 1983.

Jancovich, Mark. *The Cultural Politics of the New Criticism*. New York: Cambridge University Press, 1993.

Jarrell, Randall. Review of *Section: Rock-Drill*, by Ezra Pound. *Yale Review* Sept. 1956: 103–6.

Jensen, Robert. *Marketing Modernism in Fin-de-Siècle Europe*. Princeton: Princeton University Press, 1994.

Johnson, Samuel. "Preface to Shakespeare (1765)." *Yale Edition of the Works of Samuel Johnson* v. 7, *Johnson on Shakespeare*. New Haven: Yale University Press, 1968.

Jumonville, Neil. *Critical Crossings: The New York Intellectuals in Postwar America*. Berkeley and Los Angeles: University of California Press, 1991.

Kaufmann, Michael. *Textual Bodies: Modernism, Postmodernism, and Print*. Lewisburg, Pa.: Bucknell University Press (Associated University Presses), 1994.

Kearns, George. "Ad Astra." Review of *Thrones, 96–109 de los cantares,* by Ezra Pound. *Kenyon Review* 22.4 (Autumn 1960): 702–4.

Kenner, Hugh, "Focus on Pound." Review of *Ezra Pound: A Close-Up,* by Michael Reck. *New York Times Book Review* 7 Jan. 1968: 5–6.

———. "Incurious Biographer." Review of *The Life of Ezra Pound,* by Noel Stock. *New Republic* 17 Oct. 1970: 30–32.

———. "In the Caged Panther's Eyes." Review of *The Pisan Cantos,* by Ezra Pound. *Hudson Review* 1.4 (Winter 1949): 580–86.

———. "The Making of the Modernist Canon." In *Canons,* ed. Robert von Hallberg. Chicago: University of Chicago Press, 1984. 363–75.

———. "Praestantibusque Ingeniis." Review of *The Letters of Ezra Pound,* ed. D. D. Paige. *Kenyon Review* 13.2 (Spring 1951): 342–45.

———. *The Poetry of Ezra Pound*. Norfolk, Conn.: New Directions, 1951.

———. *The Pound Era*. Berkeley and Los Angeles: University of California Press, 1971.

Kermode, Frank. "Still Pounding Away." Review of *The Pound Era,* by Hugh Kenner. *Guardian* 28 July 1972.

Knopf, Alfred A., et al. *Portrait of a Publisher 1915/1965*. 2 vols. New York: Typophiles, 1965.

Koch, Vivienne. *William Carlos Williams*. Norfolk, Conn.: New Directions, 1950.

Kostelanetz, Richard. *The End of Intelligent Writing: Literary Politics in America*. New York: Sheed and Ward, 1973.

———. Review of *The Cantos,* by Ezra Pound. *Commonweal* 28 July 1972: 410–12.

Kraus, Joe W. *Messrs. Copeland & Day, 69 Cornhill, Boston 1893–1899*. Philadelphia: George S. MacManus, 1979.

Kreymborg, Alfred. *Our Singing Strength*. New York: Coward-McCann, 1929.

Krieger, Murray. *The New Apologists for Poetry*. Bloomington: Indiana University Press, 1963.

Larkin, Philip. Review of *Section: Rock-Drill*, by Ezra Pound. *Manchester Guardian* 26 Mar. 1957: 4.

Laughlin, James. "Editor's Notes." *New Directions* 9 (1946): xv–xxiii.

———. "Ez as Wuz." *San Jose Studies* 12:3 (Fall 1986): 6–35.

———. "Ezra Pound's Propertius." *Sewanee Review* 46.4 (Oct.–Dec. 1938): 280–91.

———. "Letters from Pound and Williams." *Helix* 13/14 (1983).

———. *The Master of Those Who Know: Ezra Pound*. San Francisco: City Lights, 1986.

———. *Pound as Wuz*. London: Peter Owen, 1989.

———. "Preface: New Directions." *New Directions in Prose and Poetry* 1 (1936): vii–xii.

———. "Preface: New Directions." *New Directions in Prose and Poetry* 2 (1937): xii–xiv.

———. "Preface: New Directions." *New Directions in Prose and Poetry* 3 (1938): n.p.

———. "Preface: New Directions." *New Directions in Prose and Poetry* 4 (1939): xiii–xxii.

———. "The Publisher: The Function of This Magazine." *Perspectives USA* 1 (Fall 1952): 1–2.

———. *Random Essays: Recollections of a Publisher*. Mt. Kisco, N.Y.: Moyer Bell Limited, 1989.

———. "What I Learned at Ezuversity." *New York Times Book Review* 12 June 1988.

Lauter, Paul. *Canons and Contexts*. New York: Oxford University Press, 1991.

Lears, T. J. Jackson. *No Place of Grace: Antimodernism and the Transformation of American Culture, 1880–1920*. New York: Pantheon, 1981.

Leavis, F. R. *New Bearings in English Poetry*. Ann Arbor: University of Michigan Press, 1960.

Lehmann-Haupt, Hellmut. *The Book in America*. New York: R. R. Bowker, 1952.

Leibowitz, Herbert. "The Muse and the News." Review of *Drafts and Fragments of Cantos CX–CXVII*, by Ezra Pound. *Hudson Review* 22.3 (Autumn 1969): 501–2.

Leitch, Vincent B. *American Literary Criticism from the Thirties to the Eighties*. New York: Columbia University Press, 1988.

Levenson, Michael H. *A Genealogy of Modernism: A Study of English Literary Doctrine, 1908–1922*. New York: Cambridge University Press, 1984.

Linden, Eugene. "Eulogy: James Laughlin." *Time* 24 Nov. 1997: 39.

Long, Elizabeth. "The Book as Mass Commodity: The Audience Perspective." *Book Research Quarterly* 3.1 (Spring 1987): 9–30.

Longenbach, James. *Modernist Poetics of History: Pound, Eliot, and the Sense of the Past*. Princeton: Princeton University Press, 1987.

Lowell, Amy. *Tendencies in American Poetry*. Boston: Houghton Mifflin, 1917.

Lowenthal, Leo. *Literature and Mass Culture*. New Brunswick, N.J.: Transaction Books, 1984.

———. *Literature, Popular Culture, and Society*. Englewood Cliffs, N.J.: Prentice-Hall, 1961.

Lowney, John. *The American Avant-Garde Tradition: William Carlos Williams, Postmodern Poetry, and the Politics of Cultural Memory*. Lewisburg, Pa.: Bucknell University Press, 1997.

Lynes, Russell. *The Tastemakers*. New York: Harper and Brothers, 1954.

Macdonald, Dwight. *Against the American Grain*. New York: Random House, 1962.

———. "Homage to Twelve Judges: An Editorial." *Politics* Winter 1949: 1–2.

———. "A Theory of 'Popular Culture.'" *Politics* 1.1 (Feb. 1944): 20–23.

Machor, James L. *Readers in History: Nineteenth-Century American Literature and the Contexts of Response*. Baltimore: Johns Hopkins University Press, 1993.

MacLeish, Archibald. *Letters of Archibald MacLeish*. Ed. R. H. Winnick. Boston: Houghton Mifflin, 1983.

Madison, Charles A. *Book Publishing in America*. New York: McGraw-Hill, 1966.

Marek, Jayne E. *Women Editing Modernism: "Little" Magazines and Literary History*. Lexington: University Press of Kentucky, 1995.

Mariani, Paul. *William Carlos Williams: A New World Naked*. New York: McGraw-Hill, 1981.

Martz, Louis. "Recent Poetry." Review of *The Pisan Cantos* and *The Cantos*, by Ezra Pound. *Yale Review* 38.4 (Autumn 1948): 144–49.

———. Review of *Drafts and Fragments of Cantos CX–CXVII*, by Ezra Pound. *Yale Review* 59.4 (Autumn 1969): 261–64.

Materer, Timothy. "Make it Sell! Ezra Pound Advertises Modernism." In Dettmar and Watt. 17–36.

———. "Value of a Pound." Review of *The Pound Era*, by Hugh Kenner. *Commonweal* 28 July 1972: 409–10.

———. ed. *Pound/Lewis: The Letters of Ezra Pound and Wyndham Lewis*. London: Faber and Faber, 1985.

May, Derwent. Review of *Drafts and Fragments of Cantos CX–CXVII*, by Ezra Pound. *Observer* 15 Mar. 1970: 38.

McDonald, Peter D. *British Literary Culture and Publishing Practice, 1880–1914*. Cambridge: Cambridge University Press, 1997.

McGann, Jerome. *The Textual Condition*. Princeton: Princeton University Press, 1991.

McGuire, William. *Bollingen: An Adventure in Collecting the Past*. Princeton: Princeton University Press, 1982.

McLaughlin, Robert L. "Oppositional Aesthetics/Oppositional Ideologies: A Brief Cultural History of Alternative Publishing in the United States." *Critique: Studies in Contemporary Fiction* 37.3 (Spring 1996) 171–86.

Meacham, Harry M. *The Caged Panther: Ezra Pound at Saint Elizabeths*. New York: Twayne, 1967.

Meyer, Gerard Previn. "A Sampling of Pound and Modern Man." Review of *Selected Poems,* by Ezra Pound. *Saturday Review of Literature* 24 Dec. 1949: 14.

Miller, Vincent. "Pound: Life and Work." Review of *Impact* and *Thrones,* by Ezra Pound (among others). *Southwest Review* 46.3 (Summer 1961): 262–66.

Moore, Marianne. Review of *A Draft of XXX Cantos,* by Ezra Pound. *Criterion* 13 (1934): 482–85.

Morgan, Frederick. "A Note on Ezra Pound." Review of *The Letters of Ezra Pound,* ed. D. D. Paige. *Hudson Review* 4.1 (Spring 1951): 156–60.

Morris, Daniel. *The Writings of William Carlos Williams: Publicity for the Self.* Columbia: University of Missouri Press, 1995.

Morrisson, Mark. "Selling Modernism." *Modernism/Modernity* 5.2 (Apr. 1998): 155–62.

Moylan, Michele, and Lane Stiles, eds. *Reading Books: Essays on the Material Text and Literature in America.* Amherst: University of Massachusetts Press, 1996.

Muir, Edwin. Review of *The Fifth Decad of Cantos,* by Ezra Pound. *Criterion* 17 (1937): 148–49.

Mullins, Eustace. *This Difficult Individual, Ezra Pound.* New York: Fleet, 1961.

Murphy, Richard. "Books and Writers." *Spectator* (London) 15 Nov. 1950: 516.

Nadel, Ira B., ed. *The Letters of Ezra Pound to Alice Corbin Henderson.* Austin: University of Texas Press, 1993.

Neavill, Gordon B. "The Modern Library Series and American Cultural Life." *Journal of Library History* 16.2 (Spring 1981): 241–52.

Nelson, James G. *Elkin Mathews: Publisher to Yeats, Joyce, Pound.* Madison: University of Wisconsin Press, 1989.

"New Directions Completes Its First Decade." *Publishers' Weekly* 24 Aug. 1946: 803–7.

"New Directions Offers Title Prize," *Publishers' Weekly* 18 May 1940: 1910.

Norman, Charles. *The Case of Ezra Pound.* New York: Bodley Press, 1948.

———. *Ezra Pound.* New York: Macmillan, 1960.

O'Connor, William Van. *Sense and Sensibility in Modern Poetry.* Chicago: University of Chicago Press, 1948.

———. " 'What Does Mr. Pound Believe?' " Review of *The Pisan Cantos* and *The Cantos of Ezra Pound,* by Ezra Pound. *Saturday Review of Literature* 4 Sept. 1948: 15–16.

O'Connor, William Van, and Edward Stone, eds. *A Casebook on Ezra Pound.* New York: Thomas W. Crowell, 1959.

Parkinson, Thomas. *A Casebook on the Beat.* New York: Thomas W. Crowell, 1970.

Pearson, Norman Holmes. "The Square Dollar Series." *Shenandoah* 8.1 (Autumn 1955): 81–84.

Perrino, Mark. "Marketing Insults: Wyndham Lewis and the Arthur Press." *Twentieth Century Literature* 41.1 (Spring 1995): 54–80.

Perry, Lewis. *Intellectual Life in America: A History.* Chicago: University of Chicago Press, 1989.

Phillips, Robert, ed. *Delmore Schwartz and James Laughlin: Selected Letters*. New York: W. W. Norton, 1993.

Popham, John N. "Kasper Convicted with Six Others in Clinton Riots." *New York Times* 24 July 1957: 1.

Pound, Ezra. *ABC of Reading*. New York: New Directions, 1960.

———. *The Cantos*. New York: New Directions, 1948.

———. *I Cantos*. Trans. Mary de Rachewiltz. Milan: Mondadori, 1986.

———. *Cantos LII–LXXI*. New York: New Directions, 1940.

———. *The Chinese Written Character as a Medium for Poetry*, by Ernest Fenollosa. Trans. Pound. San Francisco: City Lights, 1968.

———. *The Correspondence of Ezra Pound and Senator William Borah*. Ed. Sarah Holmes. Urbana: University of Illinois Press, 2001.

———. *Dk/Some Letters of Ezra Pound*. Ed. Louis Dudek. Montreal: DC Books, 1974.

———. *Drafts and Fragments of Cantos CX–CXVII*. New York: New Directions, 1968.

———. *Eleven New Cantos XXXI–XLI*. New York: Farrar and Rinehart, 1934.

———. *The Fifth Decad of Cantos*. New York: Farrar and Rinehart, 1937.

———. *Guide to Kulchur*. New York: New Directions, 1970.

———. *"I Cease Not to Yowl": Ezra Pound's Letters to Olivia Rossetti Agresti*. Ed. Demetres F. Tryphonopoulos and Leon Surette. Urbana: University of Illinois Press, 1998.

———. *Impact: Essays on Ignorance and the Decline of American Civilization*. Chicago: Regnery, 1960.

———. Interview with D. G. Bridson. *New Directions in Prose and Poetry* 17 (1961): 159–84.

———. Interview with Donald Hall. In George Plimpton. *Writers at Work: The Paris Review Interviews, Second Series*, ed. New York: Penguin, 1977. 37–59.

———. "The Jefferson-Adams Correspondence." *North American Review* Winter 1937–38: 314–24.

———. *The Letters of Ezra Pound 1907–1941*. Ed. D. D. Paige. New York: Harcourt, Brace, 1950.

———. *Literary Essays of Ezra Pound*. Ed. T. S. Eliot. New York: New Directions, 1954.

———. *Pavannes and Divagations*. New York: New Directions, 1958.

———. *Personae*. New York: New Directions, 1990.

———. *The Pisan Cantos*. New York: New Directions, 1948.

———. *Polite Essays*. London: Faber and Faber, 1937.

———. *Pound/The Little Review. The Letters of Ezra Pound to Margaret Anderson: The* Little Review *Correspondence*. New York: New Directions, 1988.

———. "Publishers, Pamphlets, and Other Things." *Contempo* 1.9 (15 Sept. 1931): 1–2.

———. *Section: Rock Drill 85–95 de los cantares*. New York: New Directions, 1956.

——. *The Selected Letters of Ezra Pound to John Quinn 1915–1924.* Ed. Timothy Materer. Durham: Duke University Press, 1991.

——. *Selected Prose 1909–1965.* Ed. William Cookson. New York: New Directions, 1973.

——. *The Spirit of Romance.* New York: New Directions, 1968.

——. *Thrones 96–109 de los cantares.* New York: New Directions, 1959.

Pound, Omar, and Robert Spoo, eds. *Ezra and Dorothy Pound: Letters in Captivity 1945–1946.* New York: Oxford University Press, 1999.

"Pound's Poems, Previously Barred by Cerf, to Go into a New Edition of Anthology." *New York Times* 14 Mar. 1946: 23.

"The Puzzle of Pound." *Newsweek* 27 July 1970: 72.

Radway, Janice. "The Book-of-the-Month Club and the General Reader." In *Reading in America: Literature and Social History,* ed. Cathy N. Davidson. Baltimore. Johns Hopkins University Press, 1989. 259–84.

——. *A Feeling for Books: The Book-of-the-Month Club, Literary Taste, and Middle Class Desire.* Chapel Hill: University of North Carolina Press, 1997.

——. "Mail-Order Culture and Its Critics." In *Cultural Studies,* ed. Lawrence Grossberg, Cary Nelson, and Paula Treichler. London: Routledge, 1992. 512–30.

——. "Reading Is Not Eating: Mass-Produced Literature and the Theoretical, Methodological, and Political Consequences of a Metaphor." *Book Research Quarterly* 2.3 (Fall 1986): 7–29.

——. *Reading the Romance: Women, Patriarchy, and Popular Literature.* Chapel Hill: University of North Carolina Press, 1984.

——. "The Scandal of the Middlebrow." *South Atlantic Quarterly* 89.4 (Fall 1990): 703–36.

Rahv, Philip. *Image and Idea.* New York: New Directions, 1949.

Rainey, Lawrence. "Consuming Investments: Joyce's *Ulysses.*" *James Joyce Quarterly* 33.4 (Summer 1996): 531–68.

——. "The Cultural Economy of Modernism." In *The Cambridge Companion to Modernism,* ed. Michael Levenson. Cambridge: Cambridge University Press, 1999. 33–69.

——. "F. T. Marinetti and Ezra Pound." *Modernism/Modernity* 1.3 (Sept. 1994): 197–219.

——. "The Real Scandal of *Ulysses.*" *Times Literary Supplement* 31 Jan. 1997: 11–13.

——. ed. *A Poem Containing History: Textual Studies in* The Cantos. Ann Arbor: University of Michigan Press, 1997.

Ransom, John Crowe. "Mr. Pound and the Broken Tradition." *Saturday Review of Literature* 19 Jan. 1935: 434–35.

——. *The New Criticism.* Norfolk, Conn.: New Directions, 1941.

——. "The Poetry of 1900–1950." *Kenyon Review* 13.3 (Summer 1951): 445–54.

——. *The World's Body.* Port Washington, N.Y.: Kennikat Press, 1938.

Rattray, David. "Weekend with Ezra Pound." *Nation* 16 Nov. 1957: 343–49.

Read, Herbert. *The Tenth Muse*. New York: Horizon Press, 1958.

Reck, Michael. *Ezra Pound: A Close-Up*. New York: McGraw-Hill, 1967.

Redman, Tim. *Ezra Pound and Italian Fascism*. New York: Cambridge University Press, 1991.

Regnery, Henry. *Memoirs of a Dissident Publisher*. New York: Harcourt Brace Jovanovich, 1979.

Riding, Laura, and Robert Graves. *A Survey of Modernist Poetry*. London: William Heinemann Ltd., 1927.

Robie, Burton A. Review of *Thrones, 96–109 de los cantares* by Ezra Pound. *Library Journal* 15 Jan. 1960:285.

Rodden, John. *The Politics of Literary Reputation: The Making and Claiming of "St. George" Orwell*. New York: Oxford University Press, 1989.

Rosenthal, Michael. Review of *The Pound Era*, by Hugh Kenner. *New York Times Book Review* 26 Mar. 1972: 7, 33–34.

Rosenthal, M. L. "The Pleasures of Pound." Review of *Thrones, 96–109 de los cantares* by Ezra Pound, *Ideas into Action: A Study of Pound's* Cantos by Clark Emery, and *A Casebook on Ezra Pound*, ed. William Van O'Connor and Edward Stone. *Nation* 23 Apr. 1960: 368–71.

———. *A Primer of Ezra Pound*. New York: Macmillan, 1960.

Rovere, Richard H. "The Question of Ezra Pound." *Esquire* Sept. 1957:67–80.

Rubin, Joan Shelley. *The Making of Middlebrow Culture*. Chapel Hill: University of North Carolina Press, 1992.

Saunders, Frances Stonor. *The Cultural Cold War*. New York: New Press, 2000.

Schick, Frank L. *The Paperbound Book in America*. New York: R. R. Bowker, 1958.

Schiffrin, André. *The Business of Books*. New York: Verso, 2000.

Schlauch, Margaret. "The Anti-Humanism of Ezra Pound." *Science and Society* 13.3 (Summer 1949): 258–69.

Schwartz, Delmore. "Ezra Pound and History." Review of *Thrones, 96–109 de los cantares,* by Ezra Pound. *New Republic* 8 Feb. 1960: 17–19.

Schwartz, Lawrence H. *Creating Faulkner's Reputation: The Politics of Modern Literary Criticism*. Knoxville: University of Tennessee Press, 1988.

Scofield, Ronald. Review of *The Poetry of Ezra Pound*, by Hugh Kenner. *News-Times* (Santa Barbara, Calif.) 25 Nov. 1951.

Seelye, Catherine, ed. *Charles Olson and Ezra Pound: An Encounter at St. Elizabeth's*. New York: Grossman, 1975.

Shumway, David. *Creating American Civilization: A Genealogy of American Literature as an Academic Discipline*. Minneapolis: University of Minnesota Press: 1994.

"The Sightless Seer," review of *Ezra Pound* by Charles Norman. *Time* 7 Nov. 1960: 111–12.

Smith, Roger H. *Paperback Parnassus*. Boulder, Colo.: Westview Press, 1976.

Solomon, Louis B. "The Pound-Ruskin Axis." *College English* 16.5 (Feb. 1955): 270–76.

Spender, Stephen. Untitled review of *The Fifth Decad of Cantos*, by Ezra Pound. *Left Review* July 1937: 361.

Spiller, Robert E., Willard Thorp, Thomas H. Johnson, and Henry Seidel Canby, eds. *Literary History of the United States*. New York: Macmillan, 1948 (2nd ed. 1953).

Statistical History of the United States from Colonial Times to the Present. Stamford, Conn: Fairfield Publishers, 1965.

Stillinger, Jack. *Multiple Authorship and the Myth of Solitary Genius*. New York: Oxford University Press, 1991.

Stock, Noel. *The Life of Ezra Pound*. New York: Pantheon, 1970.

———. *Reading the Cantos*. New York: Funk and Wagnalls, 1966.

———. Review of *Section: Rock-Drill*, by Ezra Pound. *Meanjin* Mar. 1956: 112–14.

Stoicheff, R. Peter. "The Composition and Publication History of Ezra Pound's *Drafts & Fragments*." *Twentieth Century Literature* Spring 1986: 78–94.

———. *The Hall of Mirrors*: Drafts & Fragments *and the End of Ezra Pound's* Cantos. Ann Arbor: University of Michigan Press, 1995.

Stone, Brian Edward. " 'Not to Damn But to Fructify': Ezra Pound and *Contempo*." *Library Chronicle of the University of Texas at Austin* 25.3 (1995): 111–31.

Strychacz, Thomas. *Modernism, Mass Culture, and Professionalism*. New York: Cambridge University Press, 1993.

Sutton, Walter, ed. *Pound, Thayer, Watson, and the* Dial: *A Story in Letters*. Gainesville: University of Florida Press, 1994.

Sutton, Walter, ed. *Twentieth Century Views: Ezra Pound*. Englewood Cliffs, N.J.: Prentice-Hall, 1963.

Tanselle, G. Thomas. "In Memoriam: B. W. Huebsch." *Antiquarian Bookman* 30 Aug. 1965: 727.

Tate, Allen. "Further Remarks on the Pound Award." *Partisan Review* 16.6 (June 1949): 666–68.

———. "The Last Omnibus." Review of *Cantos LII–LXXI*, by Ezra Pound. *Partisan Review* 8.3 (May–June 1941): 241–43.

Tate Gallery. *Pound's Artists: Ezra Pound and the Visual Arts in London, Paris, Italy*. London: Tate Gallery, 1985.

Taylor, Richard. "Towards a Textual Biography of *The Cantos*." In Willison, Gould, and Chernaik. 223–57.

Tebbel, John. *Between Covers: The Rise and Transformation of Book Publishing in America*. New York: Oxford University Press, 1987.

———. *A History of Book Publishing in the United States*. 4 vols. New York: R. R. Bowker Co., 1981.

Teres, Harvey. "Remaking Marxist Criticism: *Partisan Review's* Eliotic Leftism." In DiBattista and McDiarmid. 65–84.

Tietjens, Eunice. "The End of Ezra Pound." *Poetry* Apr. 1942: 38–40.

Torrey, E. Fuller. *The Roots of Treason: Ezra Pound and the Secret of St. Elizabeth's*. New York: Harcourt Brace Jovanovich, 1984.

Turner, Catherine. *Marketing Modernism Between the Two World Wars*. Amherst: University of Massachusetts Press, 2003.

Tytell, John. *Ezra Pound: The Solitary Volcano*. New York: Doubleday, 1987.

Untermeyer, Louis. Review of *Cantos LII–LXXI*, by Ezra Pound. *Yale Review* 30.2 (Winter 1940): 381–84.

Untitled anonymous review of *Cantos LII–LXXII*, by Ezra Pound. *Nation* 21 Dec. 1940: 637.

Untitled anonymous review of *Cantos LII–LXXII*, by Ezra Pound. *Accent* 1 (1940): 122.

Untitled anonymous review of *Drafts and Fragments of Cantos CX–CXVII*, by Ezra Pound. *Virginia Quarterly Review* 45.4 (Autumn 1969): cxxxiii.

Untitled anonymous review of *Ezra Pound*, by Charles Norman. *New York Herald Tribune Book Review* 13 Nov. 1960: 4.

Untitled anonymous review of *Impact*, by Ezra Pound. *New Yorker* 25 June 1960: 105–6.

Untitled anonymous review of *The Poetry of Ezra Pound*, by Hugh Kenner. *New Yorker* 29 Dec. 1951.

Untitled anonymous review of *The Pound Era*, by Hugh Kenner. *New Yorker* 13 Jan. 1973: 90–92.

Untitled anonymous review of *The Pound Era*, by Hugh Kenner. *Economist* 29 July 1972: 47.

Untitled anonymous review of *Thrones 96–109 de los cantares*, by Ezra Pound. *Library Journal* 15 Jan. 1960: 285.

Vanderbilt, Kermit. *American Literature and the Academy*. Philadelphia: University of Pennsylvania Press, 1986.

Viereck, Peter. "Pure Poetry, Impure Politics, and Ezra Pound." *Commentary* Apr. 1951: 340–46.

Wald, Alan M. *The New York Intellectuals: The Rise and Decline of the Anti-Stalinist Left from the 1930s to the 1980s*. Chapel Hill: University of North Carolina Press, 1987.

Walkiewicz, E. P., and Hugh Witemeyer, eds. *Ezra Pound and Senator Bronson Cutting: A Political Correspondence, 1930–1935*. Albuquerque: University of New Mexico Press, 1995.

Warner, Michael. "Professionalization and the Rewards of Literature: 1875–1900." *Criticism* 27.1 (Winter 1985): 1–28.

Webster, Grant. *The Republic of Letters: A History of Postwar American Literary Opinion*. Baltimore: Johns Hopkins University Press, 1979.

Wernick, Robert. "Ezra Pound, America's Perfidious Poet." *Smithsonian* 26.9 (Dec. 1995): 112–27.

West, James L. W. *American Authors and the Literary Marketplace since 1900*. Philadelphia: University of Pennsylvania Press, 1988.

Wexler, Joyce. *Who Paid for Modernism? Art, Money, and the Fiction of Conrad, Joyce, and Lawrence*. Fayetteville: University of Arkansas Press, 1997.

"What the Pound Case Means." *Nation* 19 Apr. 1958: 335.

Wilford, Hugh. *The New York Intellectuals: From Vanguard to Institution*. Manchester: Manchester University Press, 1995.

Wilhelm, James J. *Ezra Pound: The Tragic Years, 1925–1972*. University Park: Pennsylvania State University Press, 1994.

Williams, Raymond. *Culture and Society 1780–1950*. New York: Columbia University Press, 1983.

———. *The Long Revolution*. New York: Columbia University Press, 1961.

———. *The Politics of Modernism*. New York: Verso, 1996.

Williams, William Carlos. *The Autobiography of William Carlos Williams*. New York: Random House, 1951.

———. "Penny Wise, Pound Foolish." *New Republic* 28 June 1939: 229–30.

———. Review of *The Pisan Cantos,* by Ezra Pound. *Imagi* Spring 1949: 10–11.

———. *White Mule*. Norfolk, Conn.: New Directions, 1937.

Willison, Ian, Warwick Gould, and Ian Chernaik, eds. *Modernist Writers and the Marketplace*. New York: St. Martin's Press, 1996.

Wilson, T. C. "Rhythm and Phrase." Review of *A Draft of XXX Cantos,* by Ezra Pound. *Saturday Review of Literature* 1 July 1933: 77.

Winchell, Mark Royden. *Cleanth Brooks and the Rise of Modern Criticism*. Charlottesville: University of Virginia Press, 1996.

Winship, Michael. *American Literary Publishing in the Mid-19th Century: The Business of Ticknor and Fields*. New York: Cambridge University Press, 1995.

Witemeyer, Hugh. "The Making of Pound's *Selected Poems* (1949) and Rolfe Humphries' Unpublished Introduction." *Journal of Modern Literature* 15.1 (1988): 73–91.

———, ed. *William Carlos Williams and James Laughlin: Selected Letters*. New York: W. W. Norton, 1989.

Wollman, David H., and Donald R. Inman. *Portraits in Steel: An Illustrated History of Jones & Laughlin Steel Corporation*. Kent, Ohio: Kent State University Press, 1999.

Wordsworth, William. *The Prose Works of William Wordsworth,* vol. 3. Ed. W. J. B. Owen and Jane Worthington Smyser. Oxford: Clarendon Press, 1974.

Zabel, Morton Dauwen. *Literary Opinion in America*. 2nd ed. New York: Harper and Bros., 1951.

———. Review of *The Fifth Decad of Cantos,* by Ezra Pound. *Southern Review* vol. 3 (1938): 814–17.

Zarin, Cynthia. "Jaz." *New Yorker* 23 Mar. 1992: 41–64.

Zinnes, Harriet. "Eponymous Poet." Review of *The Pound Era,* by Hugh Kenner. *New Leader* 24 July 1972: 18–19.

Index

❖ ❖ ❖ ❖

Gregory Barnhisel was born in Portland, Oregon, and raised in nearby Corvallis. He received his B.A. in English from Reed College in 1992 and, while working at HarperCollins Publishers, earned his M.A. in English from New York University. In 1999 he received his Ph.D. in English from the University of Texas at Austin. A specialist both in rhetoric and in modernist cultural studies, he has taught at Southwestern University and Texas Lutheran University, worked as director of the Writing Center at the University of Southern California, and is currently assistant professor of English and director of First-Year Writing at Duquesne University. He was awarded the 2003–4 Stanley J. Kahrl Fellowship in Literary Manuscripts at the Houghton Library, Harvard University, for work on *James Laughlin, New Directions, and the Remaking of Ezra Pound*. In addition to this book, Barnhisel has also published a composition textbook, *Media and Messages: Strategies and Readings in Public Rhetoric*. He lives in Pittsburgh with his wife, Alison, and son, Jonathan Henry.